WET
Westbrook Elite Book 1

CAMBRIA HEBERT

art by Caravaggia

WET Copyright © 2022 CAMBRIA HEBERT

All rights reserved, including the right to reproduce this book, or portions thereof, in any form without written permission except for the use of brief quotations embodied in critical articles and reviews.

Published by Cambria Hebert
http://www.cambriahebert.com

Interior design and typesetting by Classic Interior Design
Art & Design by Tal Lewin / Caravaggia
Edited by Cassie McCown
Copyright 2022 by Cambria Hebert

This is a work of fiction. Names, characters, places, and incidents either are the product of the author's imagination or are used fictitiously, and any resemblance to actual persons, living or dead, business establishments, events, or locales is entirely coincidental.

Welcome to Westbrook University...

Where the only thing more elite than the Ivy League academics and exclusive enrollment for the monied is the swimmers.
Some colleges might revere football, baseball, or even hockey, but not Westbrook.
At Westbrook, it's all about the water.
Or rather, who's in it.
More than one Elite swimmer has gone on to become a
decorated Olympian and nationwide sensation,
so it's all eyes on the hot men who spend more time in Speedos than jeans.
Eventually, though, these guys have to get out of the pool.
And when they do...
Love, drama, and jealousy await.

Westbrook Elite is a college sports romance series of stand-alone novels
with sexy swimmers, suspense, and page-turning plots.
The only promise the author makes is that each book will have a happy ending...
But who knows what it will take to get there?

WET
CAMBRIA HEBERT

Making decisions I regret is basically a hobby.

So I guess it really wasn't that surprising when I went out on a date with an Elite.

And then he tried to assault me.

I might be small, but I'm strong. I fought him off… then went straight to the dean.

He didn't believe me. No one does.

And now my date from hell is in revenge mode, and I somehow end up in the campus pool.

Did I mention I can't swim?

Lucky for me, a knight in shining armor saves me from drowning.

Except he's not wearing shining armor. He's naked.

And he's also Elite.

Seriously, what is up with these Elite swimmers?

Of course, I have no intention of ever seeing his very good-looking, naked highness again.

Elite obviously can't be trusted.

Until he wraps me in his hoodie and promises to believe me.

Now I'm drowning again—but this time in his enigmatic cobalt eyes and addictive touch.

My only oxygen is him. I think I maybe could fall in love.

But will he keep his promise when I tell him the truth about his teammate?

Or will trusting Ryan with my heart and my life be just another decision to regret?

WET
Westbrook Elite Book 1

CAMBRIA HEBERT
art by Caravaggia

One

Rory

Sometimes I make dumb decisions. Like the time I texted my ex on his birthday.

Happy Birthday! <insert smiley face emoji>

You just cringed, didn't you? Don't worry. I'll feel that shame for the rest of my entire existence.

You'd think a girl would learn from the error of her ways, right? Well, apparently, I'm the type of girl who has to make horrible mistakes multiple times before I learn any type of lesson, something that was being sorely hammered home by the fact I was currently hiding in a bush.

A girl's gotta do what a girl's gotta do, and this was one mistake I refused to regret for the rest of my life. Even if that meant having a branch poke me in places it really should *not*.

Wrinkling my nose, I started to shift, but the sound of a muffled, familiar voice made me freeze. Forgetting the branch, I tipped my head to the side, peering between the green leaves offering concealment.

His laughter rumbled quietly, a charming sound that set my teeth on edge. I'd been fooled by that husky chuckle, big brown eyes, and athletic body attached to it all.

"I'm serious," the voice said, not quite as husky as his laugh but still not an unpleasant sound. How entirely deceiving. "You really are more beautiful than any star we saw tonight."

I had to bite down on my tongue to keep from groaning as my stomach twisted with disgust. What a freaking jerk! He used the exact same line on me!

A giggle. "You're so sweet."

The couple came into view, Jonas looking as he always did, teetering the line between preppy and casual wearing a pair of dark jeans and a white polo left unbuttoned at his throat. His light-brown hair was brushed back off his face as if he'd just run his hand through it, and all his attention was focused on the dark-haired girl walking alongside him. She was wearing a flirty skirt that floated out around her hips and a crop top that showed just a hint of her midsection. Her long, thick locks floated out around her as they strolled, fluttering like velvet ribbons in the night.

"You think so?" he cajoled, leaning in to bump his shoulder lightly against hers.

She giggled. "Yes. This is the first time anyone has taken me stargazing on a date."

I rolled my eyes. Still, I had to hand it to Jonas. Taking his conquests on a date to the campus planetarium was pretty genius. Hell, I'd been excited too.

Until afterward.

I lifted the Canon EOS camera, pointing it right at the couple, then glanced down to make sure they were in frame. I wasn't sure if the mic would pick up their voices from inside a bush, but if things went the way I was almost positive they would, the video wouldn't need sound.

"Well, you gazed at the stars, but all I could stare at was you," Jonas said smoothly, sliding in front of his date and stopping her on the sidewalk.

Even though it was night, the campus had many well-placed streetlamps to keep it from being too dark, which was also helpful in collecting evidence.

"You really are so beautiful," he murmured, brushing her hair back from her shoulder, letting his knuckles graze over her exposed collarbone.

A knot formed in my stomach as he leaned in and sealed their lips together. It was a gentle kiss at first, but then he deepened it, reaching around to cup the back of her head.

She made a soft sound, and he shifted closer. She pulled away first, ducking her head. "I have to get back now, but this was fun."

"Already?" He pouted.

I fell for that too.

"Curfew at the dorms is soon," his date explained.

"Just a few more minutes," he cajoled, curling his hand around her waist. She had a nice curvy frame, her side dipping in perfectly for his palm.

She smiled, and he kissed her again. The knot in my stomach coiled tighter, the fingers holding on to the camera turning white with the force of my hold. I knew what was coming, and my eyes automatically averted, but I forced them back up.

I had to see. I had to make sure I captured it all on camera. Jonas Hughes wouldn't get away with this.

A surprised sound zeroed in my focus. Jonas's hand disappeared beneath her skirt, totally feeling her up. His wandering touch jolted their lips apart, but Jonas just smiled. "Come back here."

"I have to go." The girl tried to wiggle away.

He pulled her more firmly against him. And though it was her he was holding, it sparked a memory for me.

How his possessive palm gripped my ass. The biting and clear warning delivered by the tips of his fingers digging into my crack.

Jonas's free hand went up to drag along the little strip of exposed skin at her waist. "You are so sexy."

"Let go, Jonas. I have to go."

"Oh, I'm not done with you yet," he said, swiping at her skin again.

"Well, I am!" she insisted, putting both palms on his shoulders and shoving.

He stumbled back, and she spun, her skirt floating out around her. Jonas caught her around the waist from behind, dragging her body into his. My hands started to tremble when he thrust his crotch into her ass.

"Jonas!" The alarm in her voice was something I knew well.

He grunted, putting one hand on the back of her head, forcing her to bend at the waist. "Yeah, that's it." He grunted, rutting against her. "Let's go back to my room."

"No."

"No?" He pulled her around so they were facing each other. "Here's good, then."

He tried to kiss her again, and she bit him.

He howled, jerking back. Anger bloomed around him, polluting the air. I wanted to jump out of the bush and yell, but I held back, wanting to get more on camera.

The sound of skin hitting skin when he slapped her across the face reverberated over the sidewalk. She cried out, putting a hand to her cheek to stare at him incredulously.

"Listen here," he intoned, taking an arrogant step toward her. "I took you out and showed you a good time, and now it's your turn to show me a good time," he insisted, reaching under her skirt with both hands.

"No!" she shrieked, and he lifted her off her feet.

"Please. You were giving me signals all night. I know you're into me."

"Stop!" she said, slapping him on the shoulder as he hauled her closer to where I hid in the bush.

Sick inside, I decided I'd had enough and pushed out of the branches and leaves. A few snapped and cracked as I practically fell out of the shrub, stumbling a bit as I went.

His footsteps stuttered, and the girl he was carrying gaped at me.

"What the fuck are you doing here?" he snarled the second I straightened and he saw my face.

I smirked. "Did you really think I'd let it go that easily?"

"You really should have." The dark declaration made the hair stand up on the back of my neck.

Lifting the camera, I hit a little button and snapped a photo. The flash was like a burst of lightning in a storm.

"You stupid bitch," he muttered darkly, practically dumping his date onto the pavement.

She scrambled up, staring at me with wide eyes.

"Go," I told her.

She hesitated, and I snapped, "Run!"

She took off, and Jonas didn't even watch her go. Instead, all his attention was focused on me. On the camera I was gripping.

"I'd like to see the dean ignore my *allegations* now that I have proof," I said with much more bravado than I felt. In truth, suddenly, I felt like I was back there in that moment with him when he made me feel so weak.

His face darkened, and he took a menacing step forward. My knees actually started to shake, matching the trembling in my hands. I hadn't really thought this through, had I?

I mean, sure, the plan was to get concrete evidence that Jonas was a rape-y bastard—which I did. But I never really thought about after. I should have stayed hidden. But how could I? That girl might not have been lucky like me and able to get away. There was no way I would hide in a bush while this douche raped her.

He took another step forward, eyes glittering and jaw locked. "Your proof is only as good as that camera."

He lunged, and I screamed. I threw myself back at the bush, cutting through it and coming out the other side. I didn't stop running even as I felt a stinging, burning pain in my cheek. Jonas gave a hoarse shout, and footsteps pounded the pavement behind me.

He can't catch me! If he got ahold of this camera, all of this would be for nothing, and God only knew what he would do to me.

Adrenaline surged through my limbs, jumbling my thoughts, making it hard to rationalize. All I could think was, *Get away!* A hard hand slapped down on my shoulder, and I gave a strangled yell. His fingertips dug into my bone as he spun me. I stumbled and fell onto my hip, crying out in pain.

He dove to tackle me into the dirt, but I rolled and lurched up. He caught my ankle with a grunt, and I shook my leg like it was on fire. He yanked, but instead of falling back, I went forward.

Glancing back, I noted his dumbfounded look as he sat there with my shoe in his hand.

Run!

I tore off again, running crooked and out of balance now that I only had one shoe. My lungs burned and my eyes watered in the night air, but I kept running, hyperconscious of his pounding behind me.

Up ahead, a light glowed, and I let out a strangled plea. *Please let someone be there. Please let the building be open.*

He lunged, catching the back of my shirt, and I screamed. The fabric ripped, and we both fell in a tangle of limbs. He rolled, pinning me to the pavement. A sick, triumphant look darkened the eyes I once thought looked puppyish. I don't know how I ever thought that because now he just appeared rabid with flared nostrils and wild hair.

He grinned maniacally and rolled his hips into mine with a grunt. "You really should have left well enough alone."

The camera was still clutched in my hand, and I swung wide, slamming it into the side of his head. He groaned, falling off me, and I was up and running again, tears streaming down my face.

The panic was so overwhelming I couldn't think. I just ran on wobbly legs, eyes latched on the well-lit building. *Please just let me get there.*

Two

Ryan

Late-night swims were the best kind of swims. No one else was around, hogging up the water, no one there to scrutinize your every stroke. It was just me and the silky waves caressing my skin as I cut through the water with precision.

My limbs were quivering when I finally hoisted myself out of the pool with a heavy sigh. I was probably going to feel that in the morning, but it would be worth it. Pulling off the goggles and swim cap, I grabbed my towel but didn't bother drying off.

In the locker room, I dumped everything on the bench and left it there to go toward the back where the walk-in showers were located. It was basically a giant communal shower, a huge square with many showerheads and ledges for soap and shampoo bottles. All the water ran into the center of the space where it was carried away by several drains. The walls leading inside were glass, and they separated the open shower from the rest of the locker room.

No one cared there was no privacy. Hell, we all walked around in tiny Speedos anyway, and it wasn't like we all lingered in here. It was get in, get out, and move on. Besides, why did I need to scope out another dude's junk? Mine was far superior.

I turned on the spray, then stepped back as it heated to peel off my Speedo. It was basically a glorified black banana hammock, and I hated wearing it, but it came with the job. It slapped against the tiles when I dropped it and then stepped under the warm spray.

An involuntary groan slipped between my lips as the heated water hit my shoulder muscles. I stood there, head bowed for long minutes, just letting the spray work some of the soreness out of my body. Just as I reached for the shampoo, a noise made me pause.

It was more of an echo really. Like the slamming of a door.

The muffled yell that followed had me turning toward the sound. Leaning forward, I gazed through the glass wall toward the locker room doors. Straining over the sound of rushing water, I listened for more, partially expecting someone to burst through the doors.

No one did.

Shaking my head, I grabbed up the shampoo and popped the lid.

A scream cut through everything.

Dropping the bottle, I raced through the locker room, snatching a towel as I went and looping it around my hips. My wet feet slapped the tiles as I rushed toward the pool.

Sharp striking sounds made my feet quicken and my muscles bunch. A gurgle and a gasp made my heart lurch.

The water wasn't still as it had been when I'd left the pool. Instead, it rippled with turbulence and sloshed as someone fought against it.

"Hey!" I shouted toward the body struggling so violently in the pool.

I couldn't make out who they were or what they looked like because they were splashing and gasping so much. I watched as they scrambled for purchase on the water, which was not solid and would never offer support.

"H-he—" the person called, but the words cut off on a wet gurgle as the water sucked them under.

My heart lurched when they didn't resurface.

With a shout I rushed forward, the towel around my waist falling to my feet. Instinct taking over, I dove into the water headfirst, arms cutting through the water with ease toward the sinking body.

It was a girl. She had orangish-red hair that practically glowed in the lighted pool. The strands were long and floated out around her like a halo.

My arm wrapped around her midsection as I angled up, propelling us toward the surface. The second our heads broke free, hers lolled to the side, and panic clutched my heart.

"Breathe!" I demanded, trying to keep us afloat with one arm while holding her with the other.

A loud mechanical sound cut through my labored breathing and the pounding of my heart. It took me a few moments to rip my eyes from the girl's face, but when I did, I swore and jerked us both back beneath the water.

Her auburn hair snaked toward me, reaching out like an embrace. Noting the small bubbles releasing from her nose and floating toward the surface, I did the only thing I could in the moment.

Pinching her nose together, I held it tight, crashing my lips against hers. My legs kicked furiously as I struggled to keep us upright as one hand pinched her nose and the other grabbed her jaw to squeeze. The second her lips parted just a little, I blew into her mouth, sharing all the breath I had to give.

As I did, a dark shadow moved over us like epic storm clouds slithering over a summer sky. Despite the lights within the pool, the water darkened a fraction, and a shiver of unease slithered down my spine.

Pulling back, I looked at the girl whose eyes were still shut, head lolled to the side. Muscles on fire, I kicked up, sucking in great breaths the second my face hit the surface.

Trying not to panic, I looked across the water, but it was too late. As I stared, the automatic cover reached the edge of the pool, clicking into place, locking mechanisms engaged.

I gazed up at the taut material stretched over our heads.

Inches. We had mere inches of air keeping us from drowning.

We were trapped.

Three

Rory

Awareness came in the sensation of something wet and heavy over my mouth. Anxiety jolted, and the urge to struggle overwhelmed my brain, but it seemed my body struggled to obey.

"Come on!" an angry voice growled.

Pain bit into my cheeks, followed by a heavy rush of air that burned my throat and made my lungs prick with discomfort.

A spasm rocked me, making my body arch, and then I was coughing, hacking as water spewed from my lips, trickling over my chin and jaw.

"*Thank God*," that same angry voice swore, but this time it was more like relief.

I coughed again, tears blurring my eyes as I tried to pry them open. They felt heavy and wet, my whole body weighed down as if it were being tugged underwater…

"Agh!" I gasped, eyes flying wide, body going rigid.

Flinging out an arm, I reached for something to anchor myself with, but there was nothing. Everything my fingers grabbed seemed to flow right between them.

Pool. Water. Drowning.

I gasped again.

"Whoa, it's okay. Calm down."

"I can't swim," I rasped, throat burning.

"Yeah, I figured that when you almost drowned." His voice was sardonic, and the tone gave me the anchor I'd been desperately seeking.

Lashes fluttering, I tried to focus on the face so close to mine. Dark hair… *Jonas!*

"No!" I lurched, trying to get away. "Leave me alone!"

"Whoa, whoa," the voice said again, the arm around my waist tightening, my body easily towed against his. I thought I would panic more, but I didn't. And it was for that reason that I squinted at him again.

"You aren't him."

His head tilted. "Who?"

"Hold still," I said. The way he was bobbing around made it hard to focus.

But he wouldn't hold still. He kept moving, almost like we were on a boat.

I started to cough more, my chest shuddering as I wheezed for breath. Dark hair leaned in and open lips pressed against mine, shocking me so much that my eyes flew wide. The cough in my throat died when he blew air into me, making my cheeks puff out.

Even though I was alarmed and confused, my body did what it needed and took in the air, my lungs settling into a mildly upset state.

Dark hair stopped blowing, pulling back just a little, but our lips still brushed together. His eyes were blue.

Definitely not Jonas.

I stared at him for a few heartbeats until I realized he was kissing me.

I yanked away, forcing myself out of his grasp. I started to sink, but his arm locked around me again.

"You're kissing me!" I insisted, voice hoarse. And why did it feel so... claustrophobic here?

"I am not."

"Really? Then what would you call it?" I sniped.

"CPR."

I jolted, and the way his arm tightened just a bit around me made me feel oddly protected. "What?"

"You fell into the pool. When I got to you, you were already unconscious. I was giving you air."

As I blinked intentionally, the fact we were still in the pool finally penetrated my brain. Everything but our heads was submerged.

"Well, if I was drowning, why are we still in the pool?"

He glanced up, and I followed his gaze.

I gasped. "What is that?" I panicked, my chin sliding under the water when I reached up to push at the covering above us. It was unyielding and strong.

Are we trapped?

"It's the pool cover. I didn't have enough time to get us out."

"We-we're trapped?" I whispered, panic clawing at my throat all over again.

"Yeah, but not for long."

"You can get us out?" I asked, hopeful.

He adjusted his hold, grunting a little. I noticed then that he was treading water, keeping us both above surface.

"You're swimming for me?"

"I was under the impression you didn't want to drown."

Tears rushed to my eyes, the emotion so thick and warm

they spilled over my cheeks without hesitation. "I'm sorry I can't swim."

His fingertips tightened at my waist. "It's okay."

"But we're trapped here. You can't swim for us forever!"

A small smile curved the corners of his wide mouth. "We aren't going to be in here forever."

Oh, that's right. "'Cause you can get us out?"

"No."

My face fell.

"But I know someone who can." He held up his arm, letting his wrist break the surface to show me his Apple Watch. The movement caused us both to slip farther into the water.

Scared, I wrapped myself around him, trying to climb up his long body. In my haste, my leg brushed against something. Something that should have been covered.

"Are you naked?" I gasped, letting go of him completely.

I dropped below the surface, panic opening my eyes wide. *Yep. Definitely naked.*

In case you've wondered, the male anatomy floats.

A strong hand fit beneath my arm and yanked me up. I gasped, water dripping down my cheeks and my hair plastered to the sides of my head and ears.

"Let go of me, you naked freak!"

He seemed completely amused. "So next time I should just stay in the shower and not come rescue you?"

I paused. "You were in the shower?"

"Well, why else would I be naked?"

"Maybe you're a pervert. Just like *him*."

"I am not a pervert," he said, irritated. Then curiosity took over. "Him who?"

I pressed my lips together.

"He the reason you're here?"

I gave a nod.

The hand under my arm moved, curling around my back, making me sputter. "Hey!"

"Look, I'm a good swimmer, but let's not see how much I can endure to keep us both afloat until help gets here," he said, his breath a little labored.

Guilt assailed me, but still, I gave him a doubtful look.

"I'm not going to do anything weird." He seemed sincere.

I relented because, really, he was the only thing keeping me from drowning. And he was the least of my worries right now. "Are we going to run out of air?" I stressed, looking at the dark cover overhead. There was so little space between it and the water.

"No," he promised, towing me back into his chest. He was broad and muscular, his arms long and defined.

He started swimming away from the side of the pool, and I gripped his shoulder, panicked. "What are you doing?"

"Kick your legs a little," he instructed.

I hesitated but then gave a couple small kicks, pushing the water around. We propelled a little farther in the direction he had us going.

"Good girl." He grunted. "Again."

I did it again, the praise oddly pleasing.

"Grab on to this," he said, placing my arm over a blue rope running down the pool. It was dim under the cover, but because the water was lit from beneath, I could see the other lines floating in the pool too.

"Other arm too," he said, practically draping my entire upper body over the rope. All of my weight went onto the float, the line dipping a little under my weight.

"It's sinking!" I panicked, reaching for him again.

"It's okay—" He began.

Then the lights I'd just been so thankful for went out.

Darkness like I'd never quite experienced dropped over everything like the heaviest of blankets. Suddenly, the cover overhead seemed much more ominous and the depth of the water endless. The bright-blue waves turned inky black, bottomless, and so opaque it made my stomach roil.

The rope I clutched seemed thin and tenuous, and it sank into the water, dragging me down with it as if it would offer me to the black water as a sacrifice. The only sound was the rippling waves, but it was not a restful sound. If anything, it was menacing and foreboding.

Abandoning the tenuous rope, I leaped onto my rescuer, suctioning myself against his midsection like an octopus. He felt much more dependable than the partially sinking rope. A surprised sound vibrated his throat as both arms locked around me, and we slipped beneath the surface of the water.

I opened my mouth, releasing a scream along with several bubbles, and though my eyes were open, I could make out nothing in the darkness.

Pale fingers came out of nowhere, sliding around my jaw, giving the side of my face a reassuring squeeze. My eyes found his in the darkness, and though I couldn't see his expression, I felt it.

Don't be afraid. I got you.

Our heads burst from the surface, both of us gasping for breath.

"What's going on?" I worried, curling a little closer to him, my chin nearly on his shoulder.

I felt him rumble with something that distinctly felt like silent laughter. "I think you suddenly don't care I'm naked."

I made a rude sound. "Don't be flattered. It's you or the pool of doom."

He snickered, the sound so close to my ear that goose bumps broke out across my arms. "Why did the lights go out?"

"They're on a timer."

"Is the pool cover on a timer too?"

"No." He paused. "Did you hit that button?"

"I can't swim, but you think I would know enough about pools to close the cover before hurling myself into the water to drown?"

His entire body went rigid, and then he shifted back. A tiny part of me mourned the loss of body contact. His eyes were somber, even in the dark, his gaze intent on mine.

"You didn't jump in here... right? You weren't..." His voice trailed away.

I scoffed. "Trying to kill myself? No." I paused. "I told you the reason I'm here is him."

"Someone pushed you into the pool?"

"Yeah."

"Hold on to the rope again," he said, treading water as I clung to him.

"It can't hold me." I worried.

"Yes, it can."

"It went underwater last time."

"But *you* didn't."

His confidence was reassuring, but it only made me want to cling to him more. My voice dropped as the pads of my fingers pressed a little harder into the bare, slick skin stretched over his defined shoulder.

"It's really dark."

"Look at me," he said, voice ringing with confident authority.

Even though it was every bit as dark as I claimed, I still turned to where he was, his face like a beacon in the blackness. Again, I couldn't make out his expression or even his features, but his presence seemed to make up for all of that times ten.

"Thank you for saving me," I whispered.

His face came closer, and my lashes swept down as his lips pecked a warm, lingering kiss on the tip of my nose. I didn't know what to say. How to react. Suddenly, my stomach bobbed and swayed just as the lane rope did before.

"Hold on to the rope, Carrot."

That snapped me out of whatever weird spell he'd put me under. "Carrot!"

"Your hair is orange." Was that laughter in his voice?

I gasped. "It is not! It's auburn!"

"You sure about that?" He needled. "When I dove into the pool, I thought you were being attacked by an orange octopus."

My chest puffed up. The freaking nerve of this guy! "If I didn't need you to get me out of here, I'd clobber you!"

He leaned forward, and I could almost taste the grin I knew stretched over his face. "Lucky for me, you need me."

Prickles of awareness climbed over my scalp, and I threw myself at the rope. Suddenly, the precarious float seemed safer than this stranger.

It just really wasn't my day, though. *Sigh.*

The rope wasn't where I anticipated, so I plunged below the surface with startling ease. My nose burned as water rushed inside, making me freak, arms and legs flailing.

A warm, muscled arm wrapped around my waist and pulled. For a suspended moment, I was caught in a tug-of-war between the waves trying to trap me in their depths and the man towing me to the surface.

I kicked my feet like he said before, and my head burst from the surface.

Chest heaving and nose burning, I blinked my stinging eyes and gasped for breath. Without thinking about it, I wrapped my legs around his waist, locking my ankles to keep me in place. My breathing was still labored when my chin hit his shoulder and one arm flung around his neck.

"I don't want that rope," I confessed breathless, tightening my thighs around him.

"I got you," he vowed. "It's okay."

I shivered a bit at his husky tone, pressing a little closer.

He shifted a bit, and I noticed he had the rope under his arm, using it to help keep us afloat. "I'm gonna text my friend on my watch and have him come get us out."

"Okay," I replied, not moving.

"We're gonna dip in the water a little when I lift my hand, but I won't let you go under, okay?"

I nodded once against his shoulder.

"What's your name?" he asked, his palm splaying across my back. His fingers nearly spanned the entire width.

"Aurora," I answered. "Rory for short."

"I'm Ryan."

I hummed a little at the info. "Rory and Ryan trapped in a pool…" I started to sing to the tune of that rhyme about kissing in a tree.

That big hand left my back, and nimble fingers sank into the heavy wetness of my hair. "Hey," he commanded, pulling me off his shoulder.

I clung to him, noting for the first time the way my arms and legs were trembling violently.

"Look at me."

I pulled back just enough that I could see his face.

"No going into shock. You're fine, okay? I got this. I will not let you drown. I won't let anything bad happen."

"Where were you before?" I mumbled.

"Before?" He wondered.

I didn't answer, too caught up in the storm raging inside me.

"Rory."

I turned slightly, lips colliding with the corner of his mouth. We both froze, shock rendering us motionless for the span of a single heartbeat. He moved first, drawing away, but it made the churning inside me worse. Whimpering, I followed, drawn to his warmth, comforted innately by the steadiness he seemed to provide.

We were so close I felt him swallow, felt the momentary debate inside him. When his lips brushed mine again, I sighed in relief, seeking more.

The shock overtaking me receded, the quivering of my limbs gentling under his strength. *Oh.* His lips were so warm, making me realize how cold I felt.

He nibbled at me lazily, giving more than he took. When the tip of his tongue slid across the seam of my lips, I parted on instinct, but he didn't enter, choosing to just kiss me softly as his warmth chased away the worst of my fear.

The tight grip tension had on me loosened a bit, making me sigh as my hand slid into his hair, the silky wet locks clinging to my digits as I dug into his scalp and kissed him back with surprising need.

He drew back slowly, letting me go just a little at a time until our mouths no longer touched, and the sound of uneven breathing floated in the tiny space above our heads.

"I was about to have a panic attack," I whispered, brain still muddled.

"And now?"

Taking stock of myself, I noted how I didn't shake any longer. I just felt unsteady. The polarizing panic wasn't so polarizing anymore, and I felt I could breathe just a bit easier.

"I think it's better."

"Glad I could help," he murmured, fingertips tightening a bit at my side.

He did help. I realized. There was something about him that just made me feel safe.

"Hold on to me," he said after a moment, his body shifting when he lifted both arms. "I'm texting Jamie."

We did sink into the water a little, but true to his word, I did not go beneath the surface.

After a few minutes, he lowered his arms, one wrapping back around my waist. "He'll be here in a few."

"How long?" I worried.

"Not long. He lives in the dorms close by."

"Do you live in the dorms?" I asked.

"Yeah."

"Me too," I echoed.

Silence descended, the only sound being the water lapping against the sides of the pool. Most people probably thought it was a peaceful sound, but to me, it sounded like danger.

"Hey, Rory?" Ryan asked after a few silent minutes.

"Yeah?"

"How the hell did you end up in the pool?"

"He was chasing me. I saw the lights, so I came in without really thinking..."

"And then he just shoved you in the pool?" There was a hard edge to his voice that hadn't been there before.

"Something like that."

"Why?"

Muffled sounds from overhead burst into the room. "Ryan!" someone yelled. "Ryan!"

"Jamie!" Ryan yelled, his voice much louder than I was used to.

The arm around my waist left, and Ryan started beating on the cover over our heads. "Here, Jamie!"

Following his lead, I started banging on the cover too. "Help us!"

The sound of footsteps echoing was followed by a curse. Seconds later, a loud buzzing cut through the dark, and then the turning gears took over.

I made a sound of relief, craning my neck to try and see if

the cover was moving. The underwater lights burst on, and I blinked wildly against the brightness.

"Hold on," Ryan instructed and started swimming.

He definitely was a good swimmer because he cut through the water while keeping hold of me. The cover was sliding back, light from above filtering in.

Ryan headed right for it, not stopping until we burst from beneath the cover out into the open.

"Holy shit, man!" his friend called, squatting at the edge of the pool. One of his arms reached out, waiting for us to get there.

The quivering in Ryan's muscles accompanied by his heavy breathing made me feel bad he was doing all the work. I tried to kick my legs like before, but I was suddenly exhausted and weak.

"Grab her." Ryan panted.

Hands slid under my arms, towing me away from my safety net, and all the energy I'd been devoid of shot through me like a surge. "No!" I whimpered, fighting against the hands, trying to reach for Ryan.

My attempts were in vain because I was lifted out of the water as if I didn't weigh a thing, even with my saturated, heavy clothes. A voice over me grunted a bit, and Jamie fell back onto his ass, two jean-clad legs on each side of me.

I started to scramble up, wanting out of his lap, but my legs were so wobbly and I started coughing again. "R-Ry-an." I hacked, looking toward the edge of the pool.

Almost as if I conjured him up, those large hands slapped onto the edge, and the heavy sucking sound of water accompanied by splashes filled my ears as he pulled himself up. A dark head, water cascading down the angular face, gave way to bulging wide shoulders that seemed to have no problem hoisting the rest of his lean body out of the pool.

His feet slapped the tile, and he unfolded, straightening in all his dripping-wet glory… completely naked.

"Duuude," the guy behind me drawled. "Skinny-dipping!"

Ryan's laugh was husky and warm, making my eyes drag upward to the sound. And maybe my gaze snagged on the center of his body and the way his muscles cut into a sharp V, which practically pointed to a cock that was surprisingly attractive without even being hard… *Probably why he isn't even embarrassed.*

I choked on the thought.

A hand slapped between my shoulder blades, making me jolt. "Hey, you okay?"

I stiffened, remembering I was sitting between the legs of some guy I didn't know. I surged away, body clearly still in flight mode from before.

Ryan scooped me up, pulling me away from his friend and sitting down with me between his legs instead. One of his knees was up, and he pressed my back against it, peering into my face.

"You still with me, Carrot?"

"Do not call me that!"

"You need some more CPR?" he asked, leaning in and wagging his eyebrows.

I tried to smack him, but my arm fell weakly between us.

He frowned and looked toward his friend. "Maybe we should call 9-1-1."

Jamie pulled out a cell phone.

"No." I gasped, pulling away from my backrest. "I'm fine."

"You look the opposite of fine," Jamie retorted. His shirt was soaking wet, his jeans were splattered, and dirty-blond hair fell into his light-colored eyes.

"Don't call anyone," I insisted.

Jamie looked away from me to his friend. "Ryan?"

"I don't need his permission!" I yelled, then coughed some more.

Ryan's fingers curled around my shoulder, gently tugging me back so I could lean against his bent knee. A wash of relief overcame me when I didn't have to hold up my own weight, but I did my best to not let it show.

"So, uh, what the hell happened?" Jamie asked.

Two sets of eyes turned to me.

I gasped. "My camera!" Straightening, I scrambled toward the side of the pool. Hands on my knees, I bent at the waist, staring into the water, eyes searching out and finding the black camera parked at the bottom.

"The plot thickens," Jamie quipped from behind.

I had a feeling this guy had a one-liner for everything.

Ryan sighed, the sound quickly followed by a blur of movement and a splash. I watched as his long, lithe frame glided toward the bottom of the pool, his arms propelling him with ease.

"He's a really good swimmer," I murmured, unable to keep my eyes away from the graceful way he slid through the water. Back slightly bowed, leg muscles flexed, and arms outstretched… he radiated power.

No wonder I feel safe with him.

"The best." Jamie agreed.

Ryan snatched the camera off the pool floor and then pushed off the bottom, his body a streak of peach as it fired up to the surface. At the side of the pool, he placed the completely ruined, very expensive piece of equipment beside my foot.

"You mind getting me some clothes, bro?" Ryan asked his friend, wiping the water from his eyes with his fingers.

"Bro, sure." Jamie made it a couple steps toward the locker room when he called out, "Bro, you need anything?"

When I said nothing, Ryan patted my foot. My eyes fired

to where he bobbed in the water, finding him grinning and pointing to his friend.

I spun, pointing to myself. "Me?"

Jamie lifted his arms. "Who else?"

"You called me bro."

He made a face. "So? It's gender-neutral."

Maybe my brain was waterlogged. "Uh, a towel," I said.

"Bro, sure." Jamie agreed and jogged the rest of the way to the locker room.

I gazed down at Ryan, who was still in the water. Probably because he was naked.

"He must like you," Ryan said, smiling wide.

I blinked. "Why do you say that?"

"He doesn't just call everyone bro."

"It's gender-neutral," I mocked. "Apparently, he calls *everyone* bro."

Ryan laughed, then hauled his dripping-wet, hard body out of the pool. When he straightened, I swallowed thickly and tried to avoid looking at him. It was rather difficult. He towered over me. I barely came to his shoulder.

"Why didn't you stay in there?" I demanded, pointing back to the rippling water.

"Why bother, Carrot?" he asked, a glimmer of mischief in his blue gaze as he leaned down to whisper, "You've already seen it."

Four

Ryan

I studied her as I tugged the blue T-shirt over my towel-dried hair. The wet clothes plastered against her frame left little to the imagination. She was small. Borderline tiny. I mean, I wouldn't say it out loud, but she looked kinda like a drowned chihuahua standing there drying off the ends of her orange hair.

Excuse me. Her *auburn* hair.

She was loud and vicious like a chihuahua, too, and lacked the size to back up her bark. I mean, it would be cute… if someone hadn't just tried to drown her.

"Are you sure you don't want us to call someone? Take you to the med clinic?" I offered, tugging the hem down against my hips.

She glanced up from the towel in her hands. "No. There's no point."

"I'm pretty sure attempted murder is the point," I said, irritation making my lip curl.

"Are there cameras in here?" she asked, hope lighting her tone as she gazed up toward the ceilings.

"I don't think so," I replied.

Her shoulders drooped. "Then, yeah, there's no point. No one will believe me anyway."

I glanced at Jamie, and we shared a look.

Carrot cleared her throat and dropped the towel at her feet. Leaning down, she picked up the ruined camera, hugging it to her chest. "Well, ah, thank you for keeping me from drowning." She shifted from foot to foot.

"Where is your shoe?"

Her head snapped up. "What?"

I pointed to her foot. "Your shoe is missing. Did it fall off in the pool?" I turned, reaching for the hem of my shirt to prepare to dive back in.

"No!" She spoke quickly. "It's not in the pool."

I swung back to her, raising a brow. "Then where is it?"

She shrugged. "I lost it."

"This girl is a mess," Jamie mused. "Bro, you sure can pick 'em."

Rory's slim shoulders stiffened. "He didn't pick me!"

Jamie held up his hands in surrender.

"What happened tonight?" I asked point-blank.

"It doesn't matter. I need to go." She started forward.

Jamie and I moved to form a wall in front of her, folding our arms and blocking her path. Her steps faltered as she glanced between us. "Move."

"We will," Jamie said good-naturedly.

I nodded, adding, "After you tell us why I had to interrupt my shower to fish you out of the pool."

"I'm not telling you!" she insisted and started around us.

Freaking stubborn. "Fine," I declared. "I'll call the dean, and you can tell him instead."

She stopped.

Turned.

The withering look on her face was impressive. For a shrimp. "Don't bother. He didn't believe me last time."

Something heavy and hot settled in my gut like a rock. My eyes narrowed until the only thing in the sliver of vision was her. "Excuse me?"

With a little huff, she tried a step, but Jamie blocked her again.

Striding forward, I grabbed her by the waist, carrying her toward the bleachers like a ball tucked under my arm.

"Ryan!" she bellowed, smacking my forearm. "Put me down!"

I did. I planted her feisty ass right on the first row of bleachers.

Jamie and I took up our positions in front of her again, this time glaring. "Start talking, Carrot. You aren't leaving until you do."

She folded her arms over her chest, mirroring our positions. It was ridiculous and not threatening at all. *Kinda cute, though.*

"And why should I?" she demanded. "Why should I trust you? You're probably friends with him."

Offended, I dropped my arms to my sides. "Look, I know you don't know me, but I'm pretty sure I just proved I'm not a murdering bastard."

"Aren't you guys like loyal to a fault?" she pressed.

I frowned. She really didn't trust me. It bothered me a hell of a lot more than it probably should have. Usually, I'd just walk. Her loss. But I couldn't just then. It seemed like that would make me no better than whoever made her like this.

She shivered, and I zeroed in on the goose bumps over her arms. Her T-shirt was still wet and plastered against her, as were her jeans. The toes on her one exposed foot were colorless and so were the tips of her fingers.

Without a word, I backtracked to the pile of clothes Jamie brought from my locker. Snatching up the zip-up hoodie, I went back and draped it around her shoulders. Sinking into a squat in front of her, I tugged the open edges around, tucking them together under her chin.

Her eyes were gray, something I hadn't noticed until now. I liked them. They spoke of her tumultuous personality. A gray sky could go one of two ways:

1. Give way to an epic storm
or
2. Clear to make room for the sun

Aside from their unusual color, they were very catlike. Watchful and still. Like every ounce of her wide yet elongated stare measured me with some sort of wisdom I would never have.

"I'll believe you." I spoke quietly, not really a whisper but a vow.

Her pupils flared a bit with the words, and my fingers tightened in the edges of the hoodie.

"What?" she whispered, almost as if she'd heard wrong.

Pulling my hands from the fabric of the hoodie, which frankly swallowed her whole, I gave a little tug on one of the strings. "I'll believe you. Whatever you say."

Our gazes collided for one electric second, and with it came a zap of awareness. Those gray eyes searched mine, and I let them, allowing her to see I meant what I said. Quickly, her stare slipped away as if she were unnerved.

I straightened, putting some space between us as Jamie said, "Me too."

Suspicion filled her face. "Why?"

How could anyone not believe you? I shrugged one shoulder. "Why wouldn't we?"

She turned her eyes to Jamie, making me feel disgruntled. "You're on the swim team too, right?"

"Got the best butterfly stroke on the team."

"Thought so," she murmured to herself.

My attention sharpened. "You familiar with the team?"

"A little." She hedged, tucking the camera into the folds of my hoodie.

An inkling of recognition presented in my head. "I've seen you around at competitions," I murmured, thinking… "You work for the school paper?"

"I take photos for them."

I didn't feel bad about not putting it together before now. I mean, we'd hardly been in a normal situation for me to really look at her. And usually, at competitions, I tried to stay focused and kept my eyes out of the crowd. But at our last meet, I noticed a photographer and had been amused that the camera she used basically concealed her entire face.

I bet she didn't have an angry scratch across her cheek that day. Fingers curling into my palm, I felt a burst of irrational, hot anger consume me. Whoever did this to her was an asshole who deserved my fist in his face.

"Tell me," I said more impatiently than I meant, but I was tired of the conversation. I wanted answers. Now.

Her lips rolled in on themselves.

Jamie made a sound. "Better start talking, camera girl. When he gets like this, he always gets his way."

"My camera is ruined," she bemoaned, still wasting time and pissing me off.

"Rory!" I barked.

Her eyes shot up.

I felt the side-eye Jamie leveled my way but chose to ignore it.

"I went out on a date with an asshole. An asshole who… ah, tried to force me…"

My teeth ground together, and my nostrils flared. "You were raped?" I demanded.

Fuck my fist in his face. I'd just kill him. Maybe drown him like he tried to do to her.

"No!" she was quick to say, but not willing to meet my eyes. Her cheeks were pink like this was embarrassing to talk about.

Too damn bad.

"I said he tried. I fought him off," she explained.

Jamie made a sound. "How?"

"What?" she asked, brows knitting together.

"How did you fight him off?"

"What does it matter?" she mused.

Jamie made a gruff sound. I knew he was pissed off too. Men who assaulted women were scum. "Considering you probably are barely a hundred pounds sitting there soaking wet, I'm assuming this clump nugget was larger, so how did you fight him off?"

"I weigh a hundred and five," she muttered, clearly offended.

For some reason, having her confirm just how small she was made me unreasonably angry. "You should probably eat more protein."

Her mouth dropped, but her stormy eyes rolled. "Yes, because eating an extra chicken breast is going to make me as big as you are and so much more capable. Get real."

Jamie suppressed a snicker. I mean fine, she had a point. It was a stupid thing to say, but her vulnerability scared me. So much, so fast that it was unsettling.

When I said nothing, she turned exasperated. "I do eat. I eat a lot! I just don't gain weight."

I grunted. Her idea of a lot was probably pathetic.

She snarled at me, then turned back to Jamie while I fought the urge to smile.

"I sprayed him with pepper spray," she said. "My dad gave it to me, told me to put it in my bag. I managed to get it and spray him in the face. While he was screaming like a little bitch, I ran away."

Jamie chuckled. "Bro. Nice move."

"Campus security happened to come by, and I asked him for a ride back to my dorm." She elaborated.

Silence fell. The only sound was the light rippling of the pool. The quiet seemed heavy somehow, and when I finally glanced up, I realized it was because they were both staring at me.

Jamie gave me a WTF look and gestured toward her with his blue eyes. When I followed his direction, I saw her glance away like she didn't want to be caught staring… waiting for my response.

I didn't know what to say. I mean, I didn't feel as good-natured as Jamie that she sprayed this asshole with pepper spray and then hitched a ride with some campus goon in uniform.

But it seemed she was waiting for something…

Her eyes came back to me, looking up from beneath wet lashes.

"You did good," I told her, gruff.

That's when I saw it. The sun breaking through the gray clouds in her eyes.

It nearly blinded me.

Shit.

"He was waiting outside one of my classes the next day." She went on as if she had indeed been waiting on my praise.

Again. *Shit.*

Shit that she wanted my praise. Shit that I wanted to give it.

"He asked me not to say anything. Said he was sorry."

I stiffened, the tired muscles in my back and shoulders practically screaming with the movement.

"Yeah, and I'm the next president." Jamie scoffed.

"When I didn't seem convinced, he offered me money."

My upper lip curled in disgust.

She sniffed, clearly insulted by his offer. "So I went to the dean and reported him."

A small sound left my throat, and I smiled. "Good girl."

"He didn't believe me. Apparently, *he* had gotten to him first and told him we had a bad date and he was worried the girl might 'cause trouble' for him because he wasn't interested."

"Brooo," Jamie drawled.

My hands curled into tight fists at my hips. "Are you fucking shitting me?" Then I asked, "When was this?"

"About two weeks ago. And yes, it was my word against his, and his carries more money and connections. So I decided to get proof, something no one could deny."

"And that's how you ended up in the pool." Jamie surmised.

She nodded, subconsciously tugging the hoodie closer around her. She looked swallowed up in that thing. Swallowed up by me.

I liked it.

"I got some footage of him assaulting another girl tonight, but, ah, my plan was derailed when I had to jump out of the bush to keep him from, you know… raping her."

"Tell me his name," I ground out. "Right now. I'll make sure he's off this campus by tomorrow."

She shook her head. "He has everyone fooled." Before I could reply, she went on. "He chased me across campus, and I came in here because I saw the light. He threw my camera into the pool to get rid of the evidence."

"Then he tossed you in too?" Jamie asked.

"To be fair, he probably didn't know I couldn't swim. He probably thought he would just scare me some more."

To be fair? Uh, fuck no. There was no to-be-fair to a well-connected, rich, douchey rapist. Even if she could swim, anything could have happened. She could have hit her head. She could have panicked because the cover was closing. She could be trapped. What he did was dangerous.

"Don't say it again," I nearly growled.

Her back stiffened. "Say what?"

"To be fair," I spat. "If I hadn't been here, you would be dead."

Color leached from her face as she pushed up, the jacket falling off her body behind her. "I told you, and now I'm leaving."

She was so cold you could see the hard pebbles of her nipples through her T-shirt. Probably tasted hella good. I shot Jamie a look, making sure he wasn't looking where he wasn't supposed to.

He was a good bro. He kept his eyes averted.

Swiping up the hoodie once more, I draped it over her. "Arms in," I said.

She started to protest, but I bent at the waist to pin her with a stare. "Arms in."

Making a face, she shoved her arms in one at a time and then hung the ruined camera around her neck. Reaching behind her head, I tugged the hood up, draping it over her wet locks.

"Come on. We'll walk you to your dorm."

"Oh, you don't need—"

"You must really like the sound of your own voice," Jamie said, falling into step on her other side.

"Excuse me?"

"'Cause you sure do say a lot of unnecessary shit."

She gasped.

"Let's go," I said, putting a hand to the small of her back. My palm spanned her entire waist easily.

I put up with her crooked, uneven steps until we made it out on the sidewalk. Letting out a frustrated sound, I dropped in front of her, offering my back.

"What are you doing?" she asked suspiciously, stopping so close I felt the whisper of a touch from her knees at my back.

"You can't walk home with one shoe."

"No—"

I didn't even bother letting her finish. "Jamie," I called.

He grunted, and she gasped, but her body draped over my back.

"Was that so hard?" Jamie asked as I hooked my hands behind her knees and stood.

"My camera."

"Is ruined," Jamie said, holding it up.

"Maybe I can have it fixed."

"You think?" he asked, looking at it with renewed interest.

"No," she muttered darkly, her arms sliding around my neck. Awareness zinged right down into my shorts, stirring my dick, which frankly had been so well-behaved tonight.

Guess he'd had enough of that.

I stopped midstride and lifted her a little higher onto my back. Her arms tightened around my neck, and I made a sound. "Need to breathe."

"Oops," she said quietly, looping her hands more loosely around my shoulders.

"Which dorm?" I asked, trying not to think how light she was even for my exhausted upper body.

"Spade Hall."

"I'm in Peregrine."

"We are," Jamie corrected.

"You two are roommates?"

"Who else is gonna put up with him?" Jamie cracked.

"Says the man who is the worst morning person in the history of morning people ever," I retorted.

"Ugh, mornings suck," she said, her words tickling the back of my ear.

"My people," Jamie declared, holding his fist out.

Rory gave a low laugh, one of her arms pulling away from me so she could pound it out with my bro.

I turned just slightly, giving him the same side-eye he gave me earlier. He saw, holding his hands up in surrender.

"Go back to the dean. We'll go with you. He can't ignore three of us," I told her, the stone façade of Spade Hall coming closer more quickly than I wanted.

She made a rude sound. "Wanna bet?"

"I won't let him."

There was a slight movement, and then her chin hit my shoulder. "I don't want to talk about it anymore." Her voice was quiet, holding a note of weariness.

We walked the rest of the way to the front of Spade Hall. The dorms here were not co-ed, and girls hung out around the old but well-kept stone building, talking and lingering before they had to be inside for the strict curfew campus imposed.

The building was large, probably the biggest dormitory on campus with tall trees surrounding it and green ivy growing up one side of the structure. It was four stories high, and all the windows had black windowpanes. The stone itself was light, and the doors were sizable warm-colored wood that arched on top.

There were streetlamps all around and several long sidewalks leading up to the building that all converged into one wide walkway that led to the massive front entrance.

Some windows were lit up, some dark. I'd been out with a few girls from this dorm, so I'd been here before, and I also knew there were several side entrances and a couple at the back.

"Well, thanks for the, uh, ride," she said, patting my shoulder when I made no move to put her down.

"Anytime, Carrot," I replied, lowering so she could stand.

She made a rude sound, turning to Jamie. "Would you please tell him that my hair is *not* orange?" As she spoke, she plucked out a wet clump to hold out for Jamie to study.

He laughed under his breath but shook his head. "Uh-uh, no can do, camera girl. If my bro here says it's orange, then I'm gonna have to go with him."

"But it's not orange!" she insisted, shaking the strand again.

Jamie shrugged.

She dropped her hair. "See? Loyalty among bros," she muttered and started off.

My fingers curled around her wrist, whirling her around. She gasped, the sound drawing some stares from a few girls sitting on the steps near the entrance.

I waved at them. "Ladies."

"Hey, Ryan," one of them called, and a few others giggled.

"I'm hurt," Jamie lamented.

More giggling. "Hey, Jamie."

"Ladies," he drawled.

"Give me a name," I said, forgetting everyone else to pin her with my stare.

"Why? This isn't your problem. This doesn't have anything to do with you."

My eyes narrowed. "I pulled you out of that pool."

Twisting her wrist, she tugged it out of my grasp and lifted her chin. "And I am grateful for that. Thank you. But beyond that, there's no need for you to get involved."

She walked away.

This time, I wasn't as gentle when I tugged her back around, my fingers cutting into her small elbow.

"Go home, Ryan. Loyalty among bros." She said it without malice, but the words lodged in my throat, making me feel oddly uncomfortable.

I let her go, and she spun, hurrying inside behind that massive wooden door.

"Bro, you didn't take your hoodie back," Jamie said, stepping up beside me as I stared.

"I know," I told him.

"We have to wear that to practice."

I slapped his shoulder and grinned. "Yeah. But now I have a reason to see her again."

"Bro," he intoned, pride dripping from the word.

I felt my eyes sparkle. "*Bro.*"

Our laughter drew more stares from the ladies as we headed toward our own dorm.

"You aren't gonna let this go, though, right?" he questioned.

A rude sound cut through the night. "Fuck no."

"Count me in." He agreed.

I nodded. I definitely wasn't going to let this go. I had a bad feeling Carrot hadn't seen the last of her abuser/would-be murderer.

Five

RORY

PING. PING. PING.

The light sounds roused me from deep sleep. Irritable, I rolled away, tugging the blankets farther up around me.

Ping. Ping.

"What is that?" my roommate Kimberly's lethargic voice cut further into my already disturbed mood.

I moaned, burrowing deeper into my pillow. If I ignored it, it would go away.

Clack!

My eyes shot open, the sound no longer just an inconvenience but alarming. Both Kimberly and I jolted up, staring through the dark at each other with wide eyes.

"The window," she whispered.

The ominous memory of plunging into the depths of a crystal-clear pool, the burning sensation of water rushing up my nose, and my lungs squeezing from lack of oxygen assaulted me. *What if it's Jonas?* What if he really had meant for me to drown, and when he realized I didn't, he was coming back to finish the job?

"Go look." I urged, hands trembling.

"Me? Why do I have to be the one to go?"

"Together?" I asked.

She nodded, and we both climbed out of our beds and crept to the window, which was covered with flimsy, sheer white curtains. I never really considered opaque ones until now.

Until someone tried to kill me.

Dim light filtered in from the window, and I realized it wasn't pitch black out, but it wasn't quite day yet either. Craning around, I glanced at the clock near the bed. 4:55 a.m.

I gasped. *What an ungodly hour! The least that murdering perv could do is wait to kill me at a decent time!*

"What do you see?" Kimberly whispered, panicked, her long, straight black hair like a sleek waterfall over her shoulders, framing her Asian features, which were filled with alarm.

"It's the middle of the night," I said, jabbing a finger at my clock.

"Bad things happen in the middle of the night," she lamented.

I was scared, but now I was also pissed off. Pissed and scared was not a good combo. Pissed off, scared, *and* forced awake at this unholy hour?

The only person getting murdered right now was whoever the hell was out there.

Clack!

Both of us jumped. The window shuddered even after what knocked into it bounced back.

Using my pounding heart as motivation, I stormed forward, ripping aside the curtain to glare through one of the windowpanes and down into the grass.

A tall figure stood below, dressed in sweatpants and a T-shirt, a rock clutched in his raised fist. Our eyes collided almost instantly, and my mouth dropped open.

He lowered his hand, letting the rock fall next to his foot, and signaled for me to open the window. I hesitated for a brief moment before unlatching the lock and shoving up the heavy wood frame.

"What are you doing?" Kimberly worried from behind. "Who's out there?"

"An idiot," I intoned, leaning out into the cold air. Goose bumps prickled my skin almost instantly. "Ryan. What do you want?" I hissed.

We were on the second floor of the building, but it didn't seem as far down as usual, probably because the man standing beneath the window was so tall.

"What kind of greeting is that?" he called up.

Kimberly was suddenly more curious than afraid. "Ryan?" she repeated, then came forward, her shoulder brushing against mine as she stuck her head out the window.

A light sound escaped her, and she glanced at me. "Is that Ryan Walsh?"

"The one and only," he replied.

"I didn't know you knew him."

"I don't. Which makes this middle-of-the-night visit very stalkerish."

Kimberly's eyes widened as she looked between us. "If you don't know him, how did he know where we live?"

A trickle of unease slid up my spine. Wrapping my arms around myself, I glared down at him. "Good question."

"It's not the middle of the night. The sun is coming up," he argued.

More accurately, avoided the question.

"The sun isn't up yet. It's the middle of the night," I retorted.

"I need my hoodie."

Kimberly made another sound, rotating to look at me completely. "You have his hoodie?"

"He's the one that helped me at the pool."

Kimberly gasped. "*Him!* Rory, you told me it was just some random guy."

"Save a girl from drowning, and she calls you random," he muttered, clearly listening to our entire conversation.

"You almost drowned! You left that part out too." Kimberly accused me.

Geez, she was suddenly acting like we were besties and I had to tell her everything. I mean, sure, we were friendly and got along, but I wouldn't go as far as to call us friends. We didn't spend time together outside this room. And when I tried telling her about Jonas a couple weeks ago, she seemed surprised I hadn't just gone with his advances. So no, I didn't go into detail about nearly drowning. Why bother?

Huffing, I left the window, stomping to my small desk to snatch up the sweatshirt I'd worn inside last night. Carrying it to the window, I dangled it out, waving it around like a flag. "You want me to believe you came here in the middle of the night because you need this right now?"

"I have to wear it to practice. If I don't, I'll get docked points."

I squinted at him, trying to decide whether he was telling the truth.

"Swim practice starts at five thirty," he explained.

Kimberly yawned dramatically. "Well, this was anticlimactic. Now that we know we aren't about to be murdered in our sleep, I'm going back to bed."

She sent Ryan a little finger wave, then tucked herself back in bed, disappearing beneath her pile of blankets.

I glanced back down to Ryan. He was frowning. "I scared you."

I opened my mouth to tell him to forget it, but he didn't let me speak.

"I'm coming up," he announced, already backing up like he was going to take a running leap at the window.

"You can't," I said. "I'll just toss this down—"

He sprinted through the grass, the messenger bag flung over his chest smacking against his hip.

There is no way he will make—

The negative thought was interrupted by the slap of a hand large enough to span my entire waist on the windowsill.

I stared as he grappled for footing, finding it on the window below ours. "Move back." He grunted, and I did as he hoisted himself up, throwing a long leg over the window so he was half inside, half out.

"Are you insane?" I gaped as his lean waist twisted so he was angled toward me, his broad shoulders filling the entire window, blocking out anything beyond them.

"You look like an octopus head again," he mused, eyes alight with mischief.

I slapped a hand against my head, a strangled sound filling the space between us. I didn't have the gorgeous, sleek Asian hair Kimberly was blessed with. No, I'd been cursed with wild, wavy hair that did what it wanted and never behaved. So yeah, my bedhead was next level.

"I do not," I demanded, though I knew I probably looked like I'd just stuck my finger in a light socket.

His warm, low chuckle made my lower belly turn wobbly and the goose bumps on my arms prickle anew.

"Come here, Carrot."

My feet obeyed before my brain realized what I was doing. I halted midstride.

He laughed again, the sound more of a vibration that hummed in the air around us.

I was close enough for him to reach, and his hand curled around my upper arm, towing me the rest of the way until my waist brushed against the outside of his thigh.

A slight catch in my throat made it hard to swallow as my heart fluttered erratically.

Grasping the end of the braid falling over my shoulder, he gave it a tug. I usually slept with it in pigtails in an attempt to at least tame it. It never worked, but I kept on trying.

"I'm sorry I scared you." He spoke quietly as he had when we'd been trapped in the pool.

How reassuring his voice had been. His presence.

"You didn't," I argued, but my voice was quiet too.

The fingers tugging my braid, curled around the back of my neck, cupping it easily. Ripples of pleasure made their way down my spine, making my stomach buzz. "I tried to come inside downstairs, but the old badger guarding the door wouldn't let me in," he explained, eyes twinkling and making me completely forget I'd been mad at him. "But I managed to sweet-talk her into telling me what room you're in."

I started to talk, but the pads of his fingers traced a lazy circle on the side of my neck, making my voice falter.

"I'm sorry," he whispered again, everything about him like a magnet drawing me in. His presence made me dizzy, his sincerity and soft voice. Something about him made me want to surrender, which was not a feeling I was used to but one I could almost not deny.

The space between us reduced to mere inches when a tingle of awareness nudged my brain. I jolted back, completely breathless and muddled, warmth flooding my cheeks. *He was about to kiss me.*

"Here," I said, thrusting the hoodie into his lap. "This is what you want, right?"

"It's what I came for, but it's not what I want."

My eyes flew to his. What could only be described as obvious want glittered in his blue stare as it held mine. The bottom fell out of my stomach, and my fingers started to shake. I was not inexperienced. I was no virgin or a stranger to dating.

But *this*? This was something else entirely.

"Give me your phone,"

I blinked. "What?"

The corner of his mouth lifted. "Let me see your phone, Carrot."

I squinted. "Why?"

He turned all kinds of exasperated. "Are you always so suspicious of everyone?"

"I learned the hard way that I need to be," I deadpanned.

A dark look passed behind his eyes, and his jaw turned to granite. "Give me a name."

Oh, the ominous promise in the way he practically growled those words. It was so delicious I wanted to stick out my tongue to try and taste it in the air. "No."

The muscle in his jaw ticked again.

Crossing to my desk where my phone was docked, I plucked it up, carrying it over and holding it out.

He gazed at it, then lifted his cobalt stare. "Unlock it for me, sweetheart."

My stomach turned inside out. How did he manage to make everything he said into a caress?

I unlocked it, and he took it, fingers flying over the screen.

"What are you doing?"

"Putting my number in," he said without glancing up. "I

want you to call me if he hassles you again. Or if you get scared."

"Why?" I burst out, stomach still fluttery and mind still muddled.

He paused in his task, looking up. "Because I want you to."

I scoffed. Like I'd just give in to what he wanted.

Feeling his stare, I glanced up, immediately drawn into his ocean eyes and the sincerity occupying their depths. "And because I want to prove there are good guys out there too. Because I want to be there when you need someone."

You already did when you kept me from drowning.

Ryan lifted my phone, holding it out, and snapped a selfie.

"Hey!" I gasped, lunging for the device.

He laughed and held it out of my reach. "Shrimp."

"I will push you out the window," I growled.

"You're cute," he mused, finishing whatever he was doing and clicking the phone dark before handing it over. "Now you have my number." He leaned in close, so close I felt his breath fan over my cheek when he spoke. "You gonna give me yours?"

It wasn't lost on me that he was literally holding my phone. That he could just send himself a text and have my number instantly.

He didn't do that, though. Instead of taking advantage, he'd asked.

"No," I said anyway, curious what he would do.

Immediately, he pulled back. "That's okay. It'll be that much sweeter when you finally do."

He didn't get mad. He didn't try and force me. Holding out my hand, I said, "Let me see your phone."

A wide smile transformed his face as he unlocked and handed it over.

"Your head is so big you're going to topple out the window," I muttered as I typed in my number.

Laughing under his breath, he tugged on the hoodie. "Gotta go before I'm late to practice."

My stomach tightened a little thinking about him going to the pool. Thinking about who would be there with him.

It evaporated some of the spell he'd managed to cast me under.

"Hey," he intoned almost as if he felt me pulling away. His hand roped around my waist, tugging me in. I told myself I went because if I fought him, he might actually fall out the window.

We all know what I told myself was a big, fat lie.

The pads of his fingers pressed harder against me, grip tightening. His head started to lower, and my breath caught.

I watched him warily, stomach bouncing all over the place until my eyes slid closed, anticipating the brush of his mouth on mine.

It never came.

Cracking one eye open, I was startled to find him watching me.

Wariness crept in… but before it could take hold, he whispered. "You gonna let me kiss you?"

He was asking for permission.

My lips curled in on themselves. Disappointment flashed in his eyes, and he started to pull back.

Panicked, I grabbed the hand holding my waist. "Yes."

A gruff sound echoed deep in his throat, and then the full weight of his mouth settled against mine. The hand not holding my waist came up to cup the side of my face, his fingers rubbing subtly against my earlobe, eliciting a quiet moan. He led, and I followed, lips meeting over and over as just the very tip of his tongue flirted with my lower lip.

It wasn't a long kiss, but when he lifted his head, I was

drunk and felt slightly seduced. It was almost unfair the power he had over me, and I might have panicked if I didn't see the softness reflecting in those blue orbs.

He had such beautiful eyes. Deep blue, rimmed with thick dark lashes.

"Call me anytime, Carrot. I'll answer." His voice was hoarse, slightly rough, and it brushed over my exposed nerves like sandpaper.

Before I could answer, he was gone, racing across the lawn, the open edges of the hoodie flapping around him.

Pressing my fingers against my tingling lips, I watched him go, completely entranced until I noticed the logo for the swim team across the back of the hoodie.

It was a hard smack of reality reminding me that falling for Ryan would be a *very* bad idea.

Six

Ryan

First, she refused to give me a name.

Now she's not answering my calls.

If she hadn't let me kiss her the other morning, I might really think I was being blown off.

I had no experience with this, with a girl not wanting my attention. I didn't like it. It was putting me in a foul mood.

"Bro," Jamie said, rolling up beside me in the locker room. The whole place was permeated with the scent of chlorine, but I barely noticed it anymore. I was so used to the odor I was practically nose blind to it. "After the meet, we'll go out. You can forget her name by learning someone else's." He held out his fist as though it were some epic idea.

I glanced between him and his fist before shoving it away.

His low whistle reverberated between us. "You got it that bad?"

"She kissed me back."

Jamie leaned a shoulder into the locker and regarded me. "Don't deck me, but maybe she didn't like the sample."

I whipped my head around, incredulous.

Jamie laughed. "Your face right now."

"Fuck you."

Straightening, Jamie slapped me on the back. "Some girls just don't have taste, bro."

A rude noise broke free from my throat as I peeled my windbreaker off and shoved it into the locker. "That's what I don't get," I told him, frustrated. "She liked the sample."

"Bro, you sure?"

I gave him another fierce look, and he held up his hands in surrender. "I know when a girl is into me, asshole."

"Then why isn't she calling you back?"

Pushing a hand through my hair, I turned, leaning against the cold metal. "That's what I don't get," I muttered.

Despite the way we met, there was chemistry between us. So much that it could be felt even in that pool, even when she was terrified of drowning. Sure, maybe I could believe she'd been desperate and scared out of her mind and it made her cling to me, but she hadn't been in danger in her room when I crawled through her window.

When she told me I could kiss her.

The air was electrified around us, her body practically overruling her mind, giving itself up to my hands. That's why I asked for permission.

Actually, there were two reasons for that:

1. I literally watched her body obey me, and while it turned me the hell on, I wanted to give her mind a chance to catch up. I wanted her to be *all* in.
and…
2. That douche who attacked her, then tossed her in the pool

tried to take from her. I didn't want to be anything like that bastard.

Her whispered *yes* sang through my bloodstream, heating my veins and hyping me up before our lips even touched. But then they did. And oh, the hype I thought I achieved before? It paled in comparison.

Her lips were sweet, her mouth small but eager. She let me lead, holding out her trust as if she knew I'd do her right. I could have fallen into her mouth and kissed until our lips were numb, but I held back, not only because I was due to practice but because I didn't want to scare her off.

That didn't work out too well for me.

Maybe she felt the way I held back. Maybe she thought *I* didn't like the sample.

I groaned.

"Maybe what happened with that jackass made her wary of men," Jamie offered.

I glanced at him, considering the idea. "Yeah." I agreed, thinking back to how I'd seen fear in her eyes in the window that morning. How she'd definitely been afraid the night we met. "Yeah, I think you're right."

The worst of my foul mood evaporated, leaving behind a bad taste in my mouth courtesy of the no-name asshole who did this to her.

I *really* wanted that name.

I was a pretty peaceful guy, but I had no chill when it came to this.

"Let's get wet, assholes!" Coach Resch roared, coming into the locker room with a tablet in hand, his Westbrook Elite windbreaker over his pants, and a silver whistle hanging around his neck.

Beside me, Jamie snickered, and I grinned. Dude had a dirty mind.

Coach chose to ignore the muffled laughter to bellow, "Leave whatever else you got going on in here because, out there, it's nothing but water and team."

When no one said much, he blew the whistle obnoxiously hard. "What was that?" he yelled.

We all roared.

"That's more like it! When you're in that pool, everything else—including oxygen—is overrated. Now let's go!"

"Dude would not care if we drowned as long as we got top time before we died," Jamie muttered.

I laughed. He was totally right.

"Hey," he said, grabbing my shoulder as we all made our way out of the locker room toward the pool, toward our third meet of the season.

"Yeah?"

"Don't worry about camera girl, okay? We'll hunt her down after the meet."

"You'd do that?"

Jamie wasn't the kind to chase after any girl. He let the ladies come to him. Hell, up until I met Rory, I'd been the same.

"Bro, sure."

I grinned. "Thanks, bro."

"All right. Now go show everyone who freestyles the best."

Without even thinking, our hands slapped together in perfect rhythm, executing the epic handshake we'd created freshman year, and we headed to the pool.

Seven

Rory

I didn't want to be here.

Yet here I was.

Yay for me.

No one could or would cover the swim meet today. Not that I blamed them for the lack of enthusiasm. Being here basically sacrificed an entire Friday night. The meet started at three but wouldn't end until eight. And I was supposed to stay for all of it.

Again, yay for me.

I didn't usually mind. Photography was my passion, and photographing sports was a good challenge because it was constantly moving and made it hard to get a great shot. Even though I couldn't swim, water made a beautiful subject.

But not here. Not today.

For two reasons. Both of them men, both of them entirely different yet perversely the same.

One of them made me nauseous to even look at and, if I

was honest, afraid. The other? I actually *wanted* to see him, so much so, again, I was actually afraid.

And so my automatic reaction was to avoid them both.

Ryan called me three times this week. Texted too. Oh, I practically itched to answer, and my eyes hungrily roamed the texts he sent as I lay in bed at night in the dark. My lips still tingled with the echo of our window kiss, and I recalled more than once what it felt like to be wrapped around his hard body.

I shouldn't recall that particular memory with heat. I'd been drowning. He'd been naked. Yet here I was forgetting that part—okay, I couldn't forget he was naked—and only focusing on how it felt to be in his arms. I wondered if it would feel the same when I wasn't scared out of my mind.

I wondered if it would feel better.

Yes. It will.

The thoughts were making my cheeks warm and my heart patter quickly, so I forced them aside, dragging in a heavy breath. I was here to work. The pungent, unmistakable burn of chlorine filled my senses, but instead of recoiling, it made my lower belly clench anew because it reminded me of Ryan.

I would see him today. He was probably pissed I'd blown him off, and instead of one angry swimmer glaring at me across the pool, I'd now have two.

Work, Rory. You're here to work.

I should have feigned sick and forced someone else to come today.

Yet here I was, making another decision I would likely regret. It was becoming a horrible pattern. Maybe this school should offer a class on decision-making. I'd probably fail.

A swim meet was a busy place, which was something that surprised me the first time I came to photograph one for the school news. Honestly, I hadn't much thought about swimming as a sport or its popularity until I got to Westbrook. Football and baseball always seemed to be the big crowd draw, but here at WU, it was swimming. Our university swim team was elite and a mega flex for this school. More than one swimmer from this campus made it to the Olympics, which I guess, considering the exclusivity of Westbrook U to begin with, shouldn't at all be a surprise.

Even after I'd seen the crowd these meets drew, I didn't quite get just how powerful this team was... until I went against one. Until I was drawn in by the hum of excitement in the air and a charming smile.

Until I became its victim.

Not even the accusation of attempted rape and physical assault was enough to have the dean go against one of the school's elite swimmers. It was almost a sacrilege I would even dare suggest something that could tarnish this school's biggest pride.

Sniffing, I went toward the team tents set up outside the swim building, not quite ready to go inside where I'd almost drowned. Smiling at one of the students behind one of the tables, I grabbed a program with all the information for today's meet and stuck it in the crossbody bag I had over my chest. It would be helpful for whoever wrote up the article to accompany the photos later, which, to be honest, would likely be me. They'd all say I would do it best because I was here.

Which was stupid. How was I supposed to pay attention to the details and competition when I was trying to get a good shot?

I snagged another pamphlet I saw and stuck that in my bag too. Maybe the more material I handed over, the less likely they would pin the entire article on me.

I went to the other university tables and grabbed similar information, jamming it all into my bag. A lot of the tents were handing out otter pops—you know, those freezer pops in the clear plastic everyone ate as kids. Otter pops seemed to be a tradition at swim meets, so when someone thrust one at me, I took it and smiled. I ate the cold treat, ignoring the way my fingers tingled, and wandered around the tents a little longer. Since I was totally procrastinating, I took a few shots of said tents to make me feel like I was doing more than just dodging going inside.

One of the tents had some temporary tattoos and buttons with the team logo on it. Staring down at it, I flashed back to seeing the logo across Ryan's back as he rushed across the yard after kissing me.

Fingers numb from the otter pop and the chilly outdoor temps, I ruffled through the bucket of buttons, the pop nearly falling from my lips when my gaze caught the edge of one.

Walsh - Freestyle

It was plastered across the deep ivy-green button in bold white font. A small wave was centered beneath the writing.

He had his own button. I mean, I guess I knew he was pretty well-known around campus. Most of the swimmers were. Elite, remember? But seeing it like this seemed to make it more real.

My fingers shifted, and the one under Ryan's slid free toward the side of the bucket. It was for Jonas.

My lips curled as the fruity, sweet flavor of the ice pop turned sour. Automatically, my hand jerked away. The buttons I'd had my fingers buried in started to slide around, moving to cover up Ryan's. Without overthinking, I shout out my hand, snapping up his button before it could be hidden.

My fingers curled around it as I tugged my fist into my chest.

That's when I noticed the girl behind the table watching me. I was embarrassed, but she just smiled. "They're free."

"Thanks," I said, still holding the button against my chest, refusing to let it go.

Stepping away, I bypassed the T-shirts and all the other stuff with the team logo plastered all over it—seriously, why did people need giant foam fingers for this?—and tossed what was left of the pop in a nearby trash bin.

I thought longingly of grabbing some coffee but decided against it because my hands would be busy with the camera. Opening my fingers, I gazed down at the button lying in my palm. I couldn't just leave it back there next to *his*.

Unclasping the pin at the back, I stabbed it through the strap on my bag, fastening it in place, and headed inside.

It wasn't much warmer inside with the pool because it wasn't heated. Something I had firsthand knowledge of since my little plunge into the icy depths. Apparently, swimming in cold water was easier.

The bleachers were full all the way to the railing that separated the spectator section from the row of seats on the pool level for the teams. The other two competing universities were already there and seated, but the section for Westbrook was empty.

Just as I realized this, the school's fight song blared through some massive overhead speakers, making my heart skip in my chest. The crowd in the bleachers was deafening as people stood and stomped their feet, adding to the already audacious noise.

The double doors leading into the locker room burst open, and the team rushed out, smiling and waving up at their fans. Since this was a home meet, we clearly had the most supporters on deck today.

They were all dressed in tiny black Speedos, most of them carrying the team windbreaker, swim cap, and a pair of goggles.

Coach Resch was in a pair of pants and a team windbreaker and was carrying a tablet. He was also the only one wearing shoes.

I tried not to seek out Ryan. My eyes did it anyway, going to him almost immediately like they knew exactly where he'd be.

The second he filled my line of sight, my stomach fluttered excitedly, and I bit the inside of my lip. His body was lean and well-defined, the Speedo leaving little to the imagination—which I didn't need anyway because I'd already seen him naked.

His shoulders were broad and strong, chest smooth, and his hands were just as big as I remembered.

Almost as if he could feel my stare, he turned, our gazes colliding instantly. The loud, raucous cheering echoing through the huge space fell away, and all I heard was the pounding of my own heart as my stomach fizzled with nerves.

There was an instant flash of awareness in his gaze before those intoxicating blue eyes narrowed.

Yep. He's pissed.

I started to avert my gaze. I mean, really, I didn't care if he was pissed. But I guess I did because even from way across this crowded, busy space, he somehow managed to refuse to let me look away, beckoning my full stare and forcing me to hold his until he let go.

Jerk.

He was smirking when he took a seat on the bench, probably feeling gigantic-headed because I listened. A hand clapped onto his bare shoulder, and it broke whatever silent little game we played. I looked away, dragging in a wobbly breath.

Jamie sat beside him, face turned toward Ryan as he spoke. When I met him the other night, he had on clothes. I mean, yeah, I guess I noticed he was built, but damn. Boy had some shoulders. Wide, round… strong.

Feeling a prickle of something, I snapped my eyes off Jamie's upper body and back to Ryan who was glowering at me.

Oops.

I spun away, busying myself with my camera and getting everything ready.

I didn't look back again until a prickle of unease tickled the back of my neck like cold, bony fingers tapping against my flesh.

Following the eerie feeling, I glanced toward the end of the bleacher where Jonas was sitting, the team windbreaker covering his upper body.

Our stares clashed, his nearly attacking me with animosity and smug arrogance.

The shrill sound of a whistle cut through the air, silencing everyone and signaling the beginning of the meet.

Blowing out an unsteady breath, I resolved to focus on the photos and nothing else.

Eight

Ryan

Was she checking out my best friend?

Bro, no.

I might have been hella pissed off at this turn of events, but her eyes had been on me first. I felt them the second I stepped out of the locker room. Her stare was different than the other hundred around the pool. I knew it was her before I even looked.

Something inside me eased just knowing she was here. The second I found her watching me from across the pool, the prickly way I'd been feeling drowned in the water between us.

It was still there. That vibe between us. The undeniable chemistry. She was trying to deny it. Deny me. I didn't like it.

Oh, hell no.

She recoiled from my intensity. So I doubled it, pulling her right back in. I wasn't going to let her get away that easily.

But then the meet started, and I had to be all in. No distractions in the pool. I wanted to be the top freestyle swimmer at WU, and to do that, I had to hardcore focus.

I was swimming in four events today. The hundred- and two-hundred-meter freestyle, the medley relay, and the four-hundred freestyle. My events were spaced out a bit to give the body time to relax a bit before going hard again, but it was still going to be exhausting.

Throughout the entire meet, I still managed to keep track of her. She looked cute hiding behind that big camera. I wondered if she realized she stuck her tongue out when she was concentrating.

"Two hundred freestyle, get ready!" Coach Resch bellowed to the team, and I stood, pulling the swim cap down over my hair and rotating my shoulders.

"You got this, bro," Jamie said nearby.

I nodded.

"Walsh!" Coach bellowed, making me turn. "Lane four."

"For real?" I asked, adrenaline already pumping through my limbs. Lane four was the most coveted spot. It was usually reserved for those with the fastest times.

"Yeah, don't make me regret it."

My whoop cut through the air, and I grinned wide.

Jamie followed up my whoop with one of his own. "That's my boy," he called.

"What the hell, Coach?" my teammate snapped, coming up to stand beside me.

I glanced over at Hughes, one of our best swimmers who happened to swim freestyle like me. He was one of the reasons I was hitting the pool at night for some extra practice time. He was a damn good swimmer, but I knew I was better. He had a year on me, though, and was good at kissing Coach's ass. And yeah, sometimes his time was better than mine. But I was working on it. And I happened to be just a little faster in the hundred-meter event.

"Don't give me that," Coach snapped. "If you want lane four, swim faster."

Hughes gave me a look.

I slapped him on the back and smiled. Swimming was sort of an individual sport, but we were all still on the same team, and the university was big on fostering sportsmanship. "No hard feelings, bro. Let's leave these other teams in our wake out there."

Something flickered in his eyes, but then he banked it to smile. "Let's do it."

I offered him my fist, and we bumped it out. Then, as all the swimmers did, we flattened our hands out and smacked the backs together like flippers.

As I was pulling my goggles over my cap, I felt something shift in the air and glanced up, catching Rory staring, a haunted look in her stormy eyes.

I felt my brows draw down, but she averted her gaze almost immediately, spinning away from where we stood and lifting the camera to cover her face.

Beside me, Hughes grunted low. "Don't waste your time on that one, man. Definitely more trouble than she's worth."

I stiffened, turning to stare at my teammate. "What?"

"Positions!" Coach bellowed.

Hughes moved off first, but I followed almost immediately, trying to shake off his words.

Does he know Rory? How?

I was still having trouble shaking it off, which led to a prickle of panic because now wasn't the time for distractions. I shook my head. *Lane four, bro. Focus.*

As I stepped up, I found myself looking for Rory again, finding her instantly. I expected her to brush me off again, but this time she didn't. It was almost like she knew.

The corner of her mouth ticked up, offering me a small smile. As she did, she gave me a thumbs-up, then pushed her camera aside to show me the round button fastened to the front of her bag.

The only button she had on.

Mine.

Energy buzzed through me, revving me up so I was rearing to go.

Bro, yeah.

I grinned wide, feeling all kinds of confident, and turned back to the pool to position my goggles.

I was about to own this pool.

Nine

Rory

The cheers were deafening, and yeah, maybe I threw out a couple of my own. Looking up and seeing Ryan and Jonas all buddy-buddy like was a kick right to my midsection. A stark reminder of why I was avoiding Ryan to begin with.

Loyalty among bros.

Loyalty among teammates. Ryan's whispered *I'll believe you* echoed menacingly in the back of my head as I watched those two interact. Jonas had everyone fooled, his own teammates at the top of that list. So why would Ryan be any different?

Ryan would believe me until he had to go against one of his own.

You shouldn't be here right now, Rory.

I knew it. I also knew it was a monster of a bad idea that I smiled at Ryan the way I did right before he swam.

But how could I not?

After his little exchange with Jonas, a dark cloud seemed

to roll in over his head. I could almost feel him slipping. I didn't want that. Ryan was a good swimmer. I had firsthand knowledge of it. The last thing I wanted was for something to creep into his headspace and ruin all the work I knew he did.

And yeah, I couldn't help but wonder if something Jonas said to him made him that way. The guy was poison. He corrupted everything he touched.

So when Ryan looked at me, I encouraged him.

Considering the way he cut through the water, coming in first place, I'd like to think maybe it helped.

And yeah, maybe most of the photos I took during this event were of him.

The roar of the crowd was thunderous. Their stomping on the bleachers made it sound like this whole place would collapse. The fastest swimmers celebrated when the times flashed up on the screen, and my heart was pounding erratically when Ryan hauled himself up out of the pool.

His smile was infectious.

I clapped, unable not to, forgetting the camera for a moment, just letting it hang around my neck.

Jamie leaped on him for a hug, and the two screamed in each other's faces like they were five. It was kinda charming.

Everyone moved off toward their seats, making way for the next heat. That's basically another round of the event, which happens when there are more swimmers than there are lanes.

I fitted the camera back against my face. The second I swung it around, focusing the lens, a scowling face filled the viewfinder. Gasping, I jolted backward, the lens slipping a little in my grasp.

Swallowing thickly, I stared, feeling like a gnat caught in a spider's web as Jonas dripped pool water and glared hotly at me.

Lowering the camera completely, I cleared my throat, ignoring the sick feeling worming around in my middle. *I've been at this a while. A break would be good. Maybe I'll get that coffee now.*

Feeling Jonas's malicious attention, I turned my back, a knot of tension coiling between my shoulder blades as I left as quickly as possible without trying to look like I was fleeing from a crime scene.

I mean, technically, the pool kinda was. Attempted murder was *definitely* a crime.

What was I thinking coming here?

A small concession cart parked down the sidewalk on the opposite side from all the team tents filled the cool autumn air with the scent of coffee and drew me forward.

Because it was the middle of the meet, there was no line, so I stepped right up to order a hazelnut latte. My cheeks stung a bit with the cold as I waited for them to make up the drink and then scan my phone for payment.

My muscles relaxed a bit when both my hands wrapped around the warm paper cup, and I sighed. Instead of heading back inside, I walked past the cart alongside the building, stopping at the corner. It was quieter here away from the noise of the meet. I didn't notice until now, but the sun had already gone down, the sky darkening with every passing moment. A quick glance at my phone, and I realized it was already after six.

Thank God it's almost over.

I sipped the sweet drink, leaning my head back into the stone building, letting the warmth coat my throat as I stared up at the dark sky.

A low creak like the opening of a door filled the calm night, making me stiffen. A disturbance in the air rippled close, but before I could do anything at all, something launched forward, slapping the coffee right out of my hold.

"Hey!" I gasped as my cup hit the ground, the black plastic lid popping off.

A hard, cold hand slapped over my mouth and nose, making all-too-familiar panic flare inside me.

I struggled and kicked out as I was dragged behind the side of the building and through an open door.

The rough hands forcing me shoved, making me stumble into the room and onto my knees. As I flinched against the pain, my hands went to the camera I wore first. It was the department's equipment because mine was beyond repair.

Only after making sure it was in one piece did I glance up to make out my surroundings. The lights were dim. The ones overhead were off, but farther into the room, some were on.

It was the team locker room. The scent of chlorine was thick and unmistakable even in here. The tile floor beneath my knees was hard and cold, the door at my back some kind of alternate entrance for the team. Or maybe it was an emergency exit.

This was *definitely* an emergency. Gasping, I shot up off the floor, ignoring the ache in my knees, and spun toward the door I'd just been forced through.

A tall, broad body slid in front of me, blocking my path.

"Jonas." I gaped, not really surprised but still entirely alarmed. "What are you doing?" I demanded, hands curling around the camera protectively.

"Oh, suddenly, you want to take my picture now?" He snarled, crossing his arms over his chest. He was wearing the team windbreaker, the dark green of it blending in with the darkness.

"What?" My voice was breathless as I tried to speak over the pounding of my heart.

He made a rude noise. "You think I didn't notice?"

"Notice what?"

"The way you've been taking photos of everyone and

everything but me during this meet. You trying to keep me out of the school news? Trying to make me look bad in front of the scouts?"

My nose wrinkled even as my stomach plummeted. My first reaction was to deny and apologize. Eff that.

"Well, maybe I'd feel more like taking your picture if you hadn't tried to rape me then drown me."

He sucked in a breath, eyes flying around the room as though he was afraid someone had heard. It gave me immense pleasure to see him frightened, if only for a second.

I'm not powerless, you twit.

He took an ominous step forward, and that thought shriveled up and died inside my brain. "You better watch what you say around here, bitch. You keep opening up that mouth of yours and spreading lies and you're going to really piss me off."

"You mean you weren't really pissed off when you tried to drown me?"

He scoffed. "It's your word against mine." When he leaned in, I felt his stagnant breath brush over my cheek. "And we both know whose word is gold around here." I practically heard him smirk. "Don't believe me? Ask the dean."

Anger lit me up inside. Anger and indignation. How dare this asshole assault me repeatedly and then laugh in my face when no one believed me? He was the worst kind of attacker, and he was also the reason so many victims stayed silent.

Rearing back, I shoved both my hands into his shoulders and pushed. The anger I had behind me knocked him a little unsteady, and I kept going, barreling past him toward the door. If my legs were shaking, well, I would ignore them.

"Stay away from me, Jonas, or you're going to wish you had," I intoned, reaching for the door.

His hand fisted in my hair, knotting his fingers in and twisting. I cried out, knees practically buckling under the eye-watering pain. Reaching up behind me, I slapped at his arms, and he laughed.

A second later, he spun and tossed me into the wall, my teeth gnashing together. I shoved off the tile, ready to run, but he caged me in, using his size to force me in place.

Funny how Ryan's big frame never once scared me, but Jonas? I would likely have nightmares about this.

"Get off!" I wailed, shoving him back.

He laughed at the attempt and grabbed my chin with his hand, squeezing until more tears rushed to the backs of my eyes.

"Listen here, bitch. Stop tattling. Stop trying to make trouble for me."

I thought to spit in his face, but my mouth had gone dry.

I tried to turn away, but he squeezed harder, forcing my head against the wall. "If you don't—"

Suddenly, the fingers crushing my chin were no longer there, the hulking weight keeping me hostage gone.

I slumped forward a bit, shuddering in relief.

A low scuffle reminded me I wasn't safe yet, and I straightened off the wall, ready to run.

Hands caught my shoulders, and I started to fight. "No!" I wailed. "Let me go!" I raised my fist, but the voice stopped me in my tracks.

"It's me, Carrot. It's me."

Only one person ever called me that ridiculous name. Only one person's voice had ever inspired such instant calm inside me.

"Ryan," I whispered.

He bent, his dark head lowering until we were eye to eye, his blue gaze filled with worry. "You okay?"

That reminded me. Eyes flaring, I strained up on tiptoes to look over his shoulder at Jonas.

"I told you to stay away from her, man." Jonas glowered, a mean streak glinting in his stare when ours collided.

I ducked back behind Ryan's frame.

His hands, which were covering my shoulders, gave a gentle squeeze before he let go, spinning around to face his teammate.

His friend.

"What the fuck, Hughes?"

"She's trouble. And she's a shitty photographer. I've been watching her. She hasn't got one good shot of me this entire meet!"

"So you, what, dragged her in here to attack her?" Ryan's voice was low and somehow menacing.

"We were just talking," Jonas refuted. "I had a minute between events. Was hoping she could get some good shots in my next one."

I snorted.

"Shut your mouth," Jonas intoned, lunging toward me.

Ryan stiffened, shoving him back. "Stay back." He warned him. Then over his shoulder, he glanced at me. "What happened?"

Jonas scoffed. "Go ahead. Tell him. See who he believes."

I slumped into the wall. I was tired.

A change came over Ryan with Jonas's words, and I took a chance, trying to flee.

Ryan caught me easily, wrapping an arm around my waist and towing me into him. "This him?" he demanded.

"Him who?" Jonas asked, a hint of wariness overtaking his cocky stare.

"This the guy who tried to rape you then shoved you in the pool to drown?"

I made a small sound, and Jonas shot up. "What? Is that what she's been saying? Man, this chick is off her rocker. We had one date. *One*. I tried to let her down easy—"

"If I were you, I'd shut up," Ryan said quietly, the room practically covered in ice.

Jonas shut up, eyes wide.

"Rory, this the guy?" His voice was incredulous but so very hard to read.

I nodded, miserable.

His arm tensed around me. A few beats of heavy silence filled the dim room.

And then he let go.

He doesn't believe you.

I nearly stumbled away from him, my legs taking a second to pick up their own slack. The camera smacked against my stomach, making it ache.

"Thanks, man. I knew I could count on you," Jonas said. I felt him look at me, but I couldn't get my stare up off the floor. "Shame on you for telling lies. My bro here knows I'd never do the shit you said."

All the fight and anger I'd felt before drained away, leaving behind just a girl—a victim—on trembling legs.

Was I even really a victim?

Innocent until proven guilty. How could I prove Jonas was in fact guilty if no one would listen?

Tears flooded my eyes to the point I was blind. A sob fought its way up my throat, but I absolutely refused to let it out. Instead, I rushed away, throwing my entire body into the exit and falling out into the dark.

I heard my name shouted behind me, but I pushed up and started to run.

I never should have come here. He doesn't believe me.

No one does.

Ten

Ryan

I said before that this university and Coach Resch fostered team sportsmanship. Swimming is sort of an individual sport because it's up to the swimmer to do the work. But the team is there, making the individual feel not so alone. They're in your corner. We cheer for each other. When there is a rough set, we make it a point to yell and scream and throw encouragement like confetti. When someone needs a lap counter, we man up. When someone is down, we build them up. That's what teams do.

But yeah, we're essentially competitors, especially those of us who swim the same stroke. But we all work together. We show up at ungodly hours to jump into frigid water to basically shred our muscles to earn just a fraction of a second. There's comradery among us, a bond that is built in struggle because swimming the way we do is mentally and physically challenging. So no, these guys aren't my competitors. They're my friends.

At least, they're supposed to be.

So imagine my surprise when Jonas drops some snarky comment about my girl.

Yeah, *my* girl. She can avoid it all she wants, but she's *mine*.

I can blow it off—I did blow it off because I had to swim. Because he's on my team.

But then imagine the way I caught him staring at her after the event. The way his eyes followed her when she fled desperately. I started getting this feeling.

A feeling I did not like.

Suddenly, my bro had to take a piss in the middle of the meet. All right, okay, it happens. Maybe the reason he was swimming slower than usual was that his bladder was full.

I watched the door. Sure took him a long time to piss.

Except he wasn't pissing.

He was attacking my girl.

And apparently… it wasn't the first time.

So I say… What in the twisted fuck?

It all made perfect sense to me now. Clear as a freshly shocked pool. The reason Rory didn't want to tell me who assaulted her was that he was my teammate. She thought he was my friend.

And yeah, maybe he was.

Not any-fucking-more.

Loyalty among bros. Jesus, how that must have sounded to her. It coated my tongue with the worst kind of flavor and made me feel like the worst kind of man.

Of all the people she could have named, I never expected any of us. This team was supposed to be elite. We were supposed to be better than this.

Shock rendered me speechless for a brief moment.

And then he was saying, *"Thanks, man. I knew I could count on you. Shame on you for telling lies. My bro here knows I'd never do the shit you said."*

The fuck? Before I could even tell him what a raging case of hemorrhoids he was, Rory was tearing out of the place like it was on fire. Like *I* was the fire.

"Rory!" I yelled, lunging after her. "Rory!" I yelled again when she just kept going. I was partway out the door when Jonas pulled me back.

"Let her go, man. We have to finish the meet."

I swung, knocking his arm off me so aggressively he fell back on his ass.

My chest heaved as I stepped over his sitting body. Planting my feet on either side of his legs, I bent at the waist and shoved my face into his. I practically smelled his alarm when my nostrils flared.

"You son of a bitch," I growled. "You are goddamn lucky we have a meet right now and the entire team would be punished if I kicked your ass the way you deserve."

His eyes flared. "You believe her."

"Yes. Yes, the hell I do, and let me make it clear right the hell now that everyone else will too." I stepped away, my hands curling into tight fists. The urge to punch him was so intense. I glanced back at the door, the urge to chase after Rory the most intense of all.

Jonas pummeled me from the side, ramming me against the wall. "You better keep your damn mouth shut, or I'll take you both down. If you think I'll let you take my spot on this team and my reputation, you're a lot stupider than you look."

With a growl, I spun, dislodging the pathetic hold he had on me, and smashed him into the wall, pinning him there with my hand wrapped around his throat.

Genuine fear cracked through his expression before he banked it to stare at me fiercely. Dude thought he was scary.

Maybe he was to a girl a quarter of his size. But to me? To me, he was a joke.

I leaned in, letting my angry breath smother his face. "Enjoy this meet, Hughes. It's gonna be the last one you ever swim in."

I gave his throat a tight squeeze, and just when panic flared in his expression, I let go, watching him hunch over gasping for breath.

Damn pansy.

I gave one last glance at the exit, thinking about Rory and what she must be going through.

She thinks you don't believe her.

Cursing, I stepped toward the door.

Out in the main part of the locker room, another door was shoved open. "Bro!" Jamie yelled. "The medley's coming up."

Shoving a hand through my hair, I gave Jonas one last withering glare before jogging out to catch up with Jamie. I had to finish this meet.

Then after, I would find Rory.

Eleven

Rory

All my life, I'd been a loner. Maybe because growing up as an only child, I learned early on how to be content with my own company. Sure, I had friends but no one really that close to me.

But there was a difference.

A difference between being a loner and being alone.

One felt like a choice, and the other—it felt like a sentence. Like some kind of punishment for something I didn't even do.

I'd hoped he was different.

Hope was dangerous. And kind of a bitch. It had a way of making you forget to be cautious; it had a way of making your fears and worries seem less than they were. Hope masqueraded as something gold and shiny, sort of like the sun eclipsing a dark day.

But hope was nothing but a lie.

He's just like the rest of them.

I let those beguiling blue eyes, charming smile, and the fact that he'd saved me overrule caution, and what did it get me?

Teardrops staining my pillow.

My scalp still stung where Jonas pulled my hair, and my knee ached from when I fell. My sight was blurred from all the tears I cried, and my throat was raw from holding in the sobs.

But you know what hurt worse than all of it?

My heart.

Ryan taking Jonas's side was worse than any physical pain I could endure.

Jamie was right that night in the pool. I was a mess. A big one.

The thought made more tears slip free. Sniffling, I curled even tighter into a ball in the center of my bed, beyond thankful it was Friday night and Kimberly was out. I just wanted to wallow in misery for a while before I had to pull myself back together. I didn't want to explain that I let my heart get broken.

Your heart's not broken, R. It's way too soon for your heart to even be involved.

My hollow sob rang around the quiet room, and I pushed my hand against my lips. The material of my long-sleeved pale-yellow sweater was soft against my dry lips.

I appreciated the way my mind tried to protect me, but I wouldn't be lying here sobbing if my heart wasn't involved. I'd had actual relationships end and didn't even cry like this.

But my heart didn't operate on a clock when it came to Ryan.

Groaning, I wiped my cheek on the pillow and then wiped the other with my sleeve. My skin prickled with cold, but I didn't bother to tug a blanket over me. I just lay there and replayed the scene in the locker room over and over again.

Ryan was definitely shocked I would name Jonas as my attacker. Shocked I would make something up about his teammate.

Maybe I should just let it go. Drop it all and stay the hell away from the entire swim team. Nothing good was going to come of it. How many more times was I going to get hurt?

What if he rapes someone because you kept quiet?

The thought was tormenting, basically forcing me to choose a faceless woman over my own mental and physical wellbeing. No one else had chosen me. Should I also turn my back on myself?

Squeezing my eyes shut, I prayed for sleep to pull me under. I didn't want to think anymore. I didn't want to feel. I just wanted some peace.

Ping. Ping. Ping.

My eyes opened at the familiar clinking sound against the window.

Ping. Ping. Ping.

My lower lip wobbled as I recalled the last time I heard that sound.

Ping. Ping.

Pushing up onto one arm, I blinked owlishly at the window. *Ryan?*

There it was again. That damn hope.

"Not today, Satan," I muttered, tumbling back into my pillow. Whoever it was could get bent.

The sound this time was different. Not a light *ping*. Not even a *clack* from a bigger stone.

Knock. Knock. Knock-knock-knock.

I sat up again, peering at the window, gasping when I saw the shadow of a man beyond the sheer curtains.

Yeah, totally time to get blackouts.

"Open up, Carrot." Ryan's voice was muffled but definitely audible when he spoke.

I couldn't help but gape. How was he in the window? Was he hanging on to the ledge? *What is he even doing here?*

A muffled curse accompanied by his slipping figure had me rushing across the room to anxiously peer through the windowpanes.

He grunted, then pushed up, clearly finding his footing on the windowsill below. "Open up before I fall." His voice was strained.

I crossed my arms over my chest and glared. "No."

I thought he might yell or even just leap back onto the ground and take his leave.

Instead, that big hand of his that my eyes always seemed to stray to flattened against the glass, all five of his fingers spread wide. "Open the window, baby."

He spoke low and rumbly, but I heard. Dear God, every nerve in my body heard, and they crackled with the sweet demand.

I opened the window.

It wasn't because he called me baby.

It wasn't because the sight of his wide palm made me shiver.

It wasn't because of hope.

It was because I couldn't forget the way he made me feel.

"I think that dragon lady you have guarding the door down there might be soulless. She is impervious to charm." He grunted, hoisting himself into the window, swinging one long leg over the ledge, and following it with the other.

He was still in the windbreaker he wore to the meet with a matching pair of pants.

"Why are you here?"

He paused in the middle of peeling the duffle bag off his

shoulder, cocking his head to the side. "Because you ran out before I could catch you."

I turned away. "I don't want to see you."

The sound of his duffle hitting the ground was simultaneous with his hand curling around my hip to tug me back. I stiffened as I was drawn between his legs, his arms looping around me and my back coming flush with his broad chest.

"Do you want me to let go?" The whispered question made my stomach flip.

I should want that, but I didn't.

So I said nothing.

His shoulder hit my chin, arms hugging me just a little tighter. "I'm sorry I'm late."

I turned my face away from his, looking across the room. I hoped he couldn't feel the way my pulse literally hammered inside me.

"I wanted to chase you so damn bad, but I couldn't screw over the team like that. They work so fucking hard." His soft, near whisper accompanied by his warm, comforting body would be my undoing.

No. It already was.

It was exactly the reason my heart felt so raw.

"I'm sorry." He tried again, nuzzling the side of my neck with his nose.

Goose bumps broke out over my entire body, rippling across my skin like they were doing their own version of the wave. The tip of my tongue pressed against the roof of my mouth as I willed myself not to cave. As I willed myself to be stronger than whatever it was his presence did to me.

No one has ever made me feel like this before.
No one has ever made you cry this way either.

The thought was like a bucket of ice water tossed over my warming insides.

I stiffened instantly, but he held firm, tucking himself even farther around me.

"I believe you, Carrot."

My sharp intake of breath made an audible sound. My face whipped in his direction as I stared out of the corner of my eye. "What?" I rasped, hoping he thought it was because I was angry and not because I'd cried too many tears.

"I know you think I sided with him back there. That's exactly what he wanted you to believe. I called out to you, but you ran off." He squeezed me tighter, but I didn't feel afraid. I knew he'd let go if I told him to. "Stop running away from me, Carrot."

I ignored the way my heart fluttered with his words. "He's your teammate. Your friend."

"*No.*" The denial was quick and sharp, much more aggressive than anything else he'd said since climbing through my window. Since he'd wrapped me in his arms.

I really like his arms.

"That fucking scumbag is not my friend. He never was. We got along for the team because it was expected. As much as I tried, there's always been a bit of a competitive streak between us. I always thought he was an arrogant prick, but I never thought he was an arrogant prick rapist."

"He didn't rape me," I said miserably, not wanting to sound like I was taking up for Jonas but also wanting to tell the truth.

"He put his hands on you, and I will never forgive him for that." The fierceness in his tone made me turn farther over my shoulder. The glittering blue in his eyes reminded me of the hottest part of the flame when we lit our Bunsen burners in chemistry.

"He hurt you. He tried to drown you. And if you weren't so strong, he probably would have raped you." His eyes grew colder as he spoke, and despite the frostiness in their depths, his anger was scorching hot.

A few moments of thick silence passed between us as I felt the heavy rise and fall of his chest against my back. I could feel his ire, his frustration.

That's why the soft kiss he pressed gently against the corner of my mouth caught me by surprise.

It was a direct contrast to everything he was vibing.

"Ry," I whispered, my heart starting to cave.

"Oh, I'm pissed," he rumbled against my ear. "It took everything in me not to beat the living crap out of him right there in the locker room. But it's him I'm pissed at. Not you, sweetheart. Never you."

I swallowed, my throat incredibly tight.

His hands nudged me gently. "Turn around here," he cajoled, and my body obeyed without any hesitation at all.

Both his palms settled against my hips, his fingers playing gently with the hem of my sweater while his thumbs lazily dragged over my jeans. "I won't ever take my anger out on you."

My chin dipped, eyes staring down between our bodies, noting just how little space remained between us. The curtains rested against his spread knees, and as the cool autumn air wafted in, the sheer fabric floated around us. Outside, the sky was dark, and the only light in the room came from the small lamp near my bed.

"I came here as soon as the meet was over. As soon as we rang the victory bell on the quad. I didn't even change. All I could think about was getting to you."

My fingers curled into my palms, my fists hidden inside the long sleeves of my sweater. His thumbs were still dragging over my hips, and my skin was starting to buzz. One of his hands pulled back, pushing up my chin so I would have to meet his eyes.

"I believe *you*."

A sob tried to rip free, but I forced my lips to remain closed. He heard, though, his eyes darkening with a tender expression. It was that look that was going to shred what was left of my resolve.

I was a strong girl, but I was powerless when it came to him.

"You've been crying," he observed, lightly caressing my cheek with his finger. "I don't like it when you cry."

I glanced up then, letting myself look my fill. His dark hair was messy from the swim cap he'd been wearing, fluffy and uncombed. It fell by his ears and over his forehead. His dark lashes still seemed a little damp like he really did run here right from the pool. Chlorine swirled around us, mixing with the crisp scent of fall. The collar of the windbreaker was against his neck on one side but falling over on the other. And his cheekbones were slightly red as though maybe he was cold.

"You really believe me?" I whispered, ignoring all of that to stare right into the blue of his eyes. The pressure in my chest was so intense it actually hurt, and I pulled in a deep breath, trying to ease the tightness. I'd never wanted someone to believe me as much as right now. Not even the dean.

I didn't want to be alone. I wanted someone to choose me.

Nudging me closer, his strong thighs practically trapped me. His hands cradled my face, swallowing it completely, making me feel like I was wholly at his mercy.

And maybe, just maybe, being at Ryan's mercy would be the best place I'd ever been.

"Oh yes, sweetheart. I believe you. You can tell me anything at all, and I will never doubt a word."

"But…" I paused to search his eyes. I found nothing but the truth. "Why?"

"Because you're *mine*."

I started to shake my head, but his grip on my face tightened. I was indeed at his mercy because the second the weight of his stare locked on mine, I was shackled in place.

"Yes. You are. You were mine from the minute my naked ass dove into that pool to save you. Mine the second I gave you the breath right out of my lungs. I didn't just forget to take my hoodie that night. I left it here so I would have to come back. You can ignore my calls, stare longingly at my unanswered texts—"

I jolted in his hold, eyes going wide like a deer caught in headlights.

He chuckled, and the sound made my toes curl against the floor. "Oh yes," he murmured knowingly. "Avoiding me won't change it. Nothing will. You can tell me anything," he repeated.

He leaned forward, barely perched on the window ledge until our faces were mere centimeters apart. His eyes were half-mast when he finished speaking, the words nothing but a murmur but a deafening sound right into the chambers of my heart.

"Fuck loyalty among bros. Loyalty to my girl rules all."

I let out a shuddering breath because it was literally all I could manage.

Ryan pressed a gentle kiss to the center of my forehead, and another wobbly breath whooshed out of me.

A peck on the corner of my eye.

A peck on the tip of my nose.

My lips quivered. My whole body was unsteady. The short, blunt edges of my nails dug into the palms of my hands as I fought for any kind of awareness.

But all I felt was him.

"If you don't want me to kiss you right now, you better shove me out the window," he murmured, mouth hovering over mine.

I felt his quick smile when I did nothing at all, and then his lips were on mine, hiding them from the rest of the world, keeping them all for his own.

Opening my fists, I reached up, grabbing his ears and pulling him a little closer. He made a sound as our mouths parted, pressing together fervently, tongues swirling, breath sharing, and bodies merging.

My arms wound around his neck as he kissed deeper, my breasts crushed against his wide, firm chest. Breath expelled over my top lip as he kissed, tongue stroking mine with unbridled passion. I gave in to it all, swept up in a delicious haze of desire and want, of being wrapped up and held by him. The sheers continued to waft around us, cold air swirling inside. Shivering, I made a desperate sound, wanting even closer.

Without breaking the kiss, he tugged so I was in his lap. The second my thighs straddled his, he pushed off the floor and stood, carrying me like I weighed nothing at all.

One hand fit against my ass, holding me firmly in place, while the other glided up my spine, coming up to grip the back of my neck as I squeezed his waist with my thighs. He sat on the edge of my bed, not letting me go as I felt him kick off his shoes.

Our lips made a light smacking sound when he pulled back, and I blinked at him through a heavy haze. "This okay?" he asked, dilated eyes drifting back to my lips.

I nodded, and he moved, tucking me under him, his long, large body stretching out over mine, pressing me into the bed and blocking out literally everything but him.

"I will stop the second you tell me to, Carrot. We won't do anything you don't want."

I nodded, my legs fell open, and he settled between them, sucking my lip between his before dragging over to nip at my ear, then kiss down the side of my neck. My hands found his waist, holding on while he basically ravaged my skin, biting lightly over the collarbone sticking out above the rounded neckline of my sweater.

He shifted, the pads of my fingers met skin, and a whole new zing of awareness shot through me. Gliding under the jacket, I explored the smooth, tight skin stretching over his side and lower back.

When I tried to go farther, the windbreaker got in my way, and I tugged at it, frustrated, wanting it gone.

Ryan pushed up and ripped it away, giving me a close-up view of the body he honed with all the swimming. He started back down, but I made a sound, flattening my palm against his pec and pushing.

He moved back immediately, still between my legs but offering me some space. I followed him as he went, leaning in to flick my tongue over his nipple.

His groan of satisfaction had me smiling, my tongue swirling around the puckered skin as his hand delved into my hair and pushed me closer. I took that as a sign and sucked deeper, drawing him into my mouth.

He moaned again, and I kept up the pressure while my hands slipped around his back to rub. After a moment, I moved to the other, definitely noticing the way his hips bucked toward me and the unmistakable bulge between his legs.

When I released his skin, I glanced up, and he tackled me back into the mattress, all his weight plastering me into the bed as our tongues danced again. His hips rocked into me, and I gasped at the sensation. He stilled, starting to pull back, a low curse falling between us.

"Ry," I beckoned, and he glanced at me immediately. "It's okay," I murmured, trying to tug him back down.

Unmistakable hunger flared in his gaze, the tip of his tongue darting out to swipe over his bottom lip. His hair was messy from my hands, and his lips were shiny from our kisses.

He started back in but then cursed and pushed away, climbing off the bed to stand beside it.

The air felt cold when it brushed my body, his absence startling and surprisingly foreign.

"I'm, ah, sorry. I didn't mean to go so fast."

"Pretty sure I was participating," I said, glancing down at his chest.

A growl rumbled there as he watched me stare. Shoving a hand through his hair, he paced away. "You test my patience, Carrot."

The fact that I'd let him get away with that ridiculous nickname was proof I wasn't asking him for patience.

God, what he does to me.

He paced away from the bed, expelling a breath, clearly trying to rein in the desire filling this room.

"Ry…"

He made a pained sound.

"Ryan?" I tried again.

"Ry's good," he managed. "I fucking like it."

"Come back over here, Ry," I beckoned. Look, I wasn't really all that wanton, but apparently, this guy tested my patience as well.

He spun, his expression part angry, part desperate. "I don't want to be like *him*. I'm *not* like him. I'll wait. I—"

"Ryan." I cut off his spiraling.

He looked up.

"I know you aren't like him. There's a big difference between you and him. Between you and every other guy on this campus."

He took a small step forward, the muscles in his stomach contracting with the movement. "Yeah?" he asked, half smiling, still half pained. His cock was still straining impressively against his pants. "What's that?"

"I'm yours."

A single heartbeat passed, and then possessiveness flared, transforming his features to something dark and delicious. He was on me again, and I was melting beneath him as he growled into my mouth. At some point, my sweater went missing, and the button on my jeans popped open.

Using his teeth, he dragged my bra strap away from my shoulder so he could kiss across it without any barrier at all. His lips lingered, moving down to the swell of my breast (push-up bras for the win!), his wide tongue licking over it entirely with one swipe.

I shuddered under the ministrations even as a little bit of insecurity unfurled deep in my gut. "Ry?" I whispered, shy, and whatever he heard had him looking up instantly.

The tenderness swimming in those azure eyes almost made me forget what I was thinking.

"What, baby?" he rumbled, leaning up to kiss my chin.

"I'm sorry," I blurted out.

He jerked back, staring down at me with questions swimming in his gaze. "Why on earth would you be sorry, sweetheart?"

"I'm not very well-endowed."

It took a moment, but then understanding gleamed in his eyes. "Let's get one thing straight right now." He spoke confidently, but it was his tenderness that held me captive. "Your size doesn't matter, and I'm sorry if I gave that impression before. You being petite—"

I giggled, and he winked.

"Is nothing you need to be self-conscious of, okay? I just

get scared someone will hurt you, and I have a lousy way of expressing it. I love the way you look. I love the way you feel. You're perfect."

Straddling my hips, he gazed down at me spread beneath him. One finger traced the underside of the white lace bra, fondling the skin at the band.

"Can I?" he asked, fingering the clasp in the center.

I nodded once.

He unhooked it easily, using both hands to part the fabric and bare my entire torso. His face showed nothing but absolute desire, and when he looked up, it was with possession.

"Perfect," he whispered, fitting a hand under me, pulling up my upper body like I was a feast.

His mouth descended, and my brain dropped offline as he proved I definitely had enough for him to enjoy because when he finally lowered me back to the mattress, I was quivering with need.

I whispered his name, dipping my fingers into the waistband of his pants, flirting with the smooth skin there.

He came down over me, our bare chests meeting, his tongue filling my mouth again. I arched against him, and his hand slipped between my legs to cup my throbbing center.

I'd never wanted someone so badly in my entire life. All that time I'd spent avoiding him had been one hell of a dose of foreplay.

"Are you sure?" he whispered against my ear.

"Yes."

He left the bed, leaving me to stare unseeing at the ceiling. I heard the zipper on the bag he brought with him and then the unmistakable swish of those pants hitting the floor.

With a foil packet in his hand, he strutted over to the door, making sure it was locked and giving me a very welcome view of his toned ass.

Every inch of him was toned, hairless, and radiated power.

His shoulders were broad, tapering into a long, lean waist, which gave way to a breath-robbing V-cut pointing at his impressive dick.

The second he turned back from the door, my eyes latched on to that particular anatomy, my body already anticipating the stretch.

His powerful thighs prowled closer as he used his teeth to rip open the condom. He wasn't shy at all, and honestly, if I looked like him, I probably wouldn't be either.

The condom was open, but he didn't pull it out yet. Instead, he tossed it on the bed beside me and used his large hands to peel the rest of the clothes off my body.

His eyes felt like warm bands of silk dragging over my exposed flesh, teasing, stroking… making me want.

The way his hands swallowed up my thighs when he pushed them wide and climbed into the bed made me feel vulnerable.

"I won't hurt you," he murmured almost as if he knew.

"I know," I whispered.

He leaned in, pressing a kiss against my navel, making my legs shake. His tongue dragged down toward the apex of my thighs and then turned so he could nuzzle the soft skin there.

Sighing, I draped my leg over his shoulder, and his hand curled around it. His eyes fired up to mine when his lips latched on again to my inner thigh and sucked.

My eyes rolled back in my head, and I bucked up as he held me tight, sucking what I knew would be a mark, watching me with wild intensity. I panted, and he gentled his lips but didn't pull away as his thick fingers slid into my center.

I nearly shot up off the bed. He laughed and pinned me back down. His finger swirled around in my silky heat.

"You're already wet for me."

"Good thing you like to swim," I said, half out of my head.

"Oh, that I do," he mused and then latched on.

I cried out as he flirted with my clit, roughing it up with his tongue and twirling it between his lips. Two of his wide fingers penetrated me as he played, and all I could do was lie there and shake.

"Ry," I panted when I was literally desperate, reaching for him, finding his dark hair to tug.

He lifted his head, and I glanced down my body, seeing his twinkling eyes and slick lips. Sitting back, he made a show of pulling both his fingers from my core.

They were both slick, nearly dripping, and I might have been embarrassed, but then he wiped it all on his rigid cock, and I forgot.

Grabbing the condom, he rolled it on quickly, a hand hitting the mattress on either side of me.

"Mine," he murmured, brushing a kiss over my lips.

I opened my legs in silent invitation.

"Say it, Carrot," he demanded. "Tell me who you belong to."

"Yours," I whispered, palming the sides of his waist.

My hands fell away from him when he filled me with a single stroke. Dear God, he was thick and long, making my body stretch in ways it never had before.

I felt the way he shook holding himself still, his arms nearly vibrating on either side of me. Still, when our eyes met, there was no awkwardness or impatience. There was nothing but awe.

"God, baby, you're so fucking tight," he said through gritted teeth.

"Just for you," I told him, reveling in the way his eyes flared.

"Can I move?" he rasped.

I nodded, and he took over, leaving absolutely not a single doubt in my mind that I was his. With every single stroke of his cock, I yielded to him. And I loved it.

By the time we both crested, we were sweaty, straining, and breathless.

"Come for me, sweetheart," he murmured, thrusting deep and rocking against my core. "Come for me now."

My body obeyed, and wave after wave of ecstasy rolled over me, making me groan and clutch his body.

The second he knew I was taken care of, he let go, body nearly falling into mine, thrusting as he jerked inside me, a few hoarse curses floating over my head.

We were still breathing heavy when he rolled, pulling me along with him, wrapping his body around mine, and pulling up a blanket that had become twisted at the foot of the bed.

"Good girl," he whispered, brushing his lips against my forehead.

If anyone else had said that, I would have clobbered them then and there.

But this wasn't anyone. This was Ry.

And it seemed I rather liked being his good girl.

Twelve

Ryan

I'm not the type to kiss and tell.

But... *Bro, yeah.*

I mean, I totally did not come over here for that, but, uh, she was utterly irresistible. And obviously, so was I.

Satisfaction hummed through my limbs, and I smiled up at the ceiling. Guess she liked the sample after all. Feeling smug, I glided my fingers down her back so I could palm her ass. Her skin felt like silk, and her sigh of comfort gave me pleasure.

A fierce sense of protectiveness unfurled within me, and I lay there momentarily stunned at how absolute it was.

After what that douche nozzle did to her, I had to make sure. Yeah, she might like the sample, but that didn't mean what *he* did to her left her unscathed. She'd definitely been all in before, but I still wanted—no, *needed*—to check.

Glancing down, all I saw was the top of her head, all that wavy hair sprawled over my chest like it was attacking me, making me smile. "Carrot," I mused, fingering a strand of her hair. "You doing okay?"

The soft sound she made was neither a denial nor a confirmation, and it was punctuated by her snuggling against my chest.

Emotions pummeling me, I slipped my hands under her arms. Her body was completely boneless, and I had to support all of her slight weight as I held her up to see her.

Her head lifted, scowling through her wild, fiery locks, and tried to lie back against me. I made a tsking sound and pushed her up some more, snickering a little at how she flopped like a rag doll in my hold.

"Shrimp," I teased.

The scowl turned even more ferocious, and I smiled wider.

"Ry," she whined. Her lips were plump and deep pink from all the kissing, and I resisted the urge to roll her beneath me and take her again.

"You okay?" I asked again, sweeping over her features.

Her catlike, stormy eyes rolled, but she couldn't fool me. There was some sunshine in there too. "Why wouldn't I be?"

"I'm a big guy."

She laughed.

I scowled. "You denying the truth?"

Her laugh fell into a little giggle, and I'd be a liar if I said that shit didn't pinch my heart. She was fucking adorable.

"Rory," I warned, refusing to let her see just how whipped I already was. I wanted an answer. A real one.

"I'm good."

I raised an eyebrow.

She blushed, trying to duck her head, but I was still dangling her over me. "Better than good."

I rolled, making her shriek with the sudden movement. When she was under me, one of her legs pushed between mine, hooking around my calf. Smoothing her hair out of her face, I leaned down to press a soft kiss against her lips.

"I didn't hurt you?" I wanted to make sure.

She shook her head. "You didn't hurt me."

"And, ah…" I began, voice faltering.

Curiosity filled her features. "What?"

I went for it. I was worried, and if I couldn't ask, then I shouldn't be in her bed.

The thought made me pause. *Who am I right now?*

Someone deserving of her.

Gliding a finger over her unblemished, peach-toned cheek, I asked, "This wasn't too much after everything he put you through?"

Understanding dawned in her eyes, a bit of a shadow passing through, but then that sun she kept in there peeked out, relaxing my nerves.

"Yeah, Ry. I'm okay." She paused. "He didn't hurt me that night. Not, ah, sexually. Just scared me. And nothing about you reminds me of him."

Yeah. *Yeah*, I caught how she said sexually, implying he hurt her in other ways.

Bastard.

"You sure?" I pressed, making a considerable effort to stay relaxed and calm.

She nodded once. "If anything…"

"Anything?" I goaded.

Her eyes turned downcast, shyness blooming around her like a halo. "If anything, you make me forget when you touch me."

Who's the man?

It's me. I'm the man.

"That's good, baby. Real good." I cleared my throat. "So you weren't avoiding me 'cause I scared you, right?"

Her eyes rounded. "No."

I blew out a breath.

"But I was avoiding you because of him."

I grimaced. "Because you thought we were friends."

"Yeah."

"Next time, just ask. It hurts a man's ego when he thinks you don't like the sample."

She turned bewildered. "What?"

"Forget it," I mumbled, sliding my arms under her body and dipping my head. Our tongues swirled together the second her lips parted. Strands of her hair tickled my cheek, and her arms wrapped around my shoulders, clinging tight as we made out.

Between us, a stomach growled, and I laughed into her mouth. "Was that you or me?"

Her nose wrinkled, head tilting just enough so our lips dislodged. "You?"

I grinned fast. "Probably." Rolling away, I flung my arm out against the wall. "I'm so hungry I could eat my own cooking right about now."

"You can cook?"

"Nope. But I'm so hungry I'd eat it anyway."

She laughed, but then her stomach growled, and her palm slapped over it.

"C'mon," I announced, pushing up. "We're going to eat."

I was halfway over her toward the edge of the bed when her hand wrapped around my bicep, effectively pausing everything.

"Ry?"

My heart tumbled a bit, and I ducked into her neck to kiss it. Did I mention I really liked it when she called me that? Like there was a version of me I could only ever be with her. "Yeah?"

"Did the rest of the meet go okay?" The hesitation in her voice did not go unnoticed.

I pulled back, letting my stare bounce between hers. Was she asking about *him?*

Guilt assailed me because even though I swore it was her I chose, my actions showed I aligned with the team—the team Hughes was part of. "Yeah, baby. He… ah, he still swam. I couldn't just ruin the meet like that. The team—"

Her four fingers covered my lips, stopping what I was poorly trying to explain.

I started talking again, but she made a sound and pushed her fingers harder to my mouth. "I'm not asking about him. Or the team. I'm asking about you."

I blinked, my lips twitching against her soft fingers.

"I know you had some events left. Did what happened in the locker room mess with your head? Did you swim okay?"

She was worried about me. Not him. Not herself. *Me.* I let that sink in just a minute. I let it tighten my chest as I wondered how someone so small could fill me up so much.

I nipped at the fingers still pushed against my lips. She gave a light squeal and pulled them back. The corners of my eyes gathered with the joy in that light sound.

"You worried about my swim?" I asked, lowering to kiss her quickly.

"You swam so well earlier. Did I mess with that?" The sincerity and genuine concern reflecting in her cat-eyed stare made my heart turn over.

"I had top time," I informed her, pride suffusing my words. "Even in the relay, I had good time."

Her arms looped around my neck, and she pulled herself up, plastering against me and kissing the top of my shoulder. "I'm so proud of you."

I grunted. "Had to do something with the urge to punch faces, so I took it out on the water."

"I'm sorry," she whispered, slipping away from me into the pillows.

"I'm not," I said, pinning her in place with a deadly stare. "You should have told me sooner."

She glanced away.

"Rory."

She sniffed. "The only time you call me that is when I'm in trouble."

"Then stop being so much trouble, and I won't have to call you that," I deadpanned.

"I am not trouble!"

Seriously? This woman was more trouble than all of the ones I'd dated combined. I had a running list of all the ways she'd already put me half in my grave.

I didn't say that out loud. That would only get more things added to the list.

I wasn't a stupid guy.

"Now, baby," I cajoled. "I like trouble."

She scowled.

I changed tactics. "You like burgers?"

Ah, her interest was piqued. She nodded.

"Let's go," I said, leaping the rest of the way out of bed.

The window was still open, and the room was cold, making my skin prickle. After cleaning up quickly, I hotfooted over to shut it.

"I'm getting new curtains," she announced.

Kind of random, but okay. Glancing over my shoulder, I saw her sitting on the edge of the bed, her legs not even reaching the floor. She had a lot of hair, but it was shoulder-length, so her chest was on complete display.

"New curtains," I repeated, still enjoying the show.

"Those are see-through."

I made a sound, snapping up my windbreaker off the floor and rushing over to hold it in front of her. "What the hell, woman? You're showing the goods to the campus."

"Says the man literally standing in front of the window naked."

A slow smile spread over my face. "Carrot, are you jealous?"

Her lips pursed. "Should I be?"

I dropped the windbreaker on the floor and sank in front of her. Even with me crouched like this and her sitting on the bed, she was barely taller than me. "No. No way. I'm a one-woman kind of guy."

Her head cocked, doubt clouding her eyes. "Are you really?"

I put my hand over my heart. "I am now."

Her entire face softened, something she probably didn't realize, but I saw, and it was enough to make me snatch her off the bed and pull her onto the floor with me.

"Hey!" She gasped as we tumbled onto the floor with me sprawled out beneath her.

"Look at me." The seriousness of my tone drew her eyes as our limbs remained tangled. "I mean it. You're it for me."

She nodded once.

"Now you say it."

"Well, I don't—" Her rude lollygagging was interrupted when I buried my fingers into her ribs and tickled her. "Ah! Ryan! Stop! Ryan!"

We rolled, her beneath me with all my weight balanced on my elbows. "Say it."

The laughter drained from her face to be replaced with a soft smile. "You're it for me too."

I grunted. "Good girl. Now give me some sugar."

She pursed her lips obediently and closed her eyes. I chuckled and leaned down, the kiss automatically changing from playful to seductive in two seconds flat.

Some chatter out in the hall brought her head up first as

she blinked. "I'm not sure what time Kimberly is going to be home."

I shoved up, hauling her with me, pushing the windbreaker in front of her body once more. I dug around in my duffle, pulling out a pair of sweats and a long-sleeved T-shirt with some boxers. My Speedos were on the floor, still inside the windbreaker pants, and I just rolled them up, shoving everything into the bag.

My stomach growled menacingly, then hit me with a warning of nausea if I didn't get some food stat. A protein bar appeared under my nose, and I lowered the palm against my abs to stare between the bar and my girl. "What's this?"

"I can hear your stomach. Maybe this will help hold you over."

I snatched it out of her hand, ripping the wrapper open as I kissed the top of her head. I shoved about half into my mouth with the first bite. "Ooh," I said as I chewed. "Peanut butter."

Her giggle floated toward me, and I shoved the rest of the tiny bar into my mouth as I watched her brush out her hair. When she winced, I paused in chewing.

"What was that?"

"What?" she asked all innocently as if she didn't know.

"You just winced."

"My hair is tangled."

"Rory." She was right. I only ever said that when she was in trouble.

Her shoulders slumped, and I knew it was bad. Closing the distance between us, I grasped her shoulders, tugging her around. Taking the brush in her hand, I tossed it onto her bed.

"Tell me."

"He pulled my hair, and now my scalp hurts."

The bar in my mouth turned to sawdust, scraping

painfully down my throat when I swallowed. "He pulled your hair," I echoed.

"When I tried to run away."

I gazed at her intently for a heartbeat before running my eyes over her wild mane of carroty orange hair, loving the way it sort of had a mind of its own, and then I pictured him grabbing it, hurting her.

"I should have fucking dragged him right into the center of the meet and outed him then and there," I ground out, my voice low.

"No," she said, wrapping one of her hands around my wrist. It didn't even make it all the way around.

Spots swam before my eyes.

"Ryan." She tugged my arm.

In a burst of movement, I cupped her face, tugging until I felt her rise on tiptoes as she tried to keep up. "Tell me you know the only reason I didn't do it was because of the team. Tell me you understand that I didn't want to take that away from them. Tell me you know that even still, I'm on your side."

"I know," she answered immediately. "I know."

Releasing her face, I picked her up, reveling in how her legs automatically wound around me. Gently, I pushed my fingers into her hair, caressing the back of her scalp. "I'm sorry he hurt you, baby." Leaning in, I pressed a kiss at her temple. "I won't let him hurt you anymore."

She melted into me, cheek pillowing on my shoulder, breath expelling against my neck. Keeping hold of her, I grabbed my bag and shoved my feet in my sneakers.

"Get your shoes," I said, setting her back on her feet. She was dressed in a pair of tight black pants and an oversized cream-colored sweater with a black smiley face on the front.

It was ridiculous, and I liked it.

Once her sneakers were on, she grabbed a black beanie

off her dresser and pulled it over her head. When she caught me watching her, she turned self-conscious. "This way I don't have to pull it up."

"Bring your cute ass over here," I demanded.

She debated, then came forward, the wavy strands of hair falling from under the black beanie and brushing her collarbones.

When she stopped in front of me, her chin tipped back to look up.

"Here." I handed her the windbreaker. She glanced between me and the jacket.

I shook it at her.

"You want me to wear that?" Her voice was dubious.

"Uh, yeah." Wasn't it obvious?

Her nose wrinkled.

"What's wrong with my jacket?"

"It's loud."

I blinked. Blinked again. "What?"

She made a noise. "It makes that stupid swishing sound."

I gasped, pulling it into my chest, offended. "A stupid swishing sound?"

Swinging her arms, the little shrimp proceeded to mimic the sound my jacket *supposedly* made. It was a horrible impression. It made me want to kiss her.

"There, there," I told my windbreaker, petting it softly. "She doesn't appreciate you."

"Ready?" she asked, completely ignoring me and my jacket's offense.

"Apologize."

She turned back, eyebrows shooting up beneath her hat. They were carroty too. "What?"

"Tell my jacket you're sorry."

"No."

I threw it onto the floor and snatched her up, tossing her over my shoulder and gently paddling her luscious ass.

"Ry-an!" she squealed, bunching my shirt in her hands.

The sound of a key in the door brought us both up short.

Kimberly appeared moments later, stopping midstride to stare at us. "Oh, should I come back?"

"No!" Carrot hollered where she dangled behind my back. "We were just leaving."

"That's clearly what you were doing," Kimberly mused, shutting the door and moving inside.

"She was being bad," I said, swinging her down to her feet.

Rory's cheeks were flushed, and her eyes sparkled. The hat on her head was askew. Chuckling, I leaned down to adjust it, winking when she glared.

Jamming my hand into the duffle, I yanked out my team hoodie, the one she wore home from the pool that night.

I held it out between us, silently raising an eyebrow.

Lips curling in on themselves, she reached out and took it, tugging it on.

I jammed the poor, insulted windbreaker into the bag and flung it over my shoulder. "C'mon, Carrot. If I don't eat soon, I'm gonna turn rabid."

"You guys are going out?" Kimberly asked.

Carrot nodded. "You want me to bring you anything back?"

"No, thanks," she said, dropping onto her bed and gazing between us.

I smiled. "Probably gonna be seeing a lot of each other," I told her. "Since I'm dating your roomie."

Carrot made a small sound, and I gave her a nudge to the door. "Kimberly, right?"

The dark-haired girl nodded.

"Ryan," I said.

"I know."

I smiled again. "See ya."

"Bye," Kimberly echoed as the door shut behind us.

Out in the hall, Rory gave me a look.

"What?"

"You just gonna announce it like that all the time?" she asked.

I held out my hand between us, wiggling my fingers. "If you hold my hand, I won't have to. Everyone will know."

"I'm already wearing your hoodie."

"Hold my hand, Carrot."

Her slim fingers slid into mine, and I tugged her right into my side.

I'd never thought about being a one-woman man. But now I couldn't imagine being any other way.

Thirteen

Rory

The butterflies in my belly were drunk. Flopping and fluttering everywhere, crashing into each other and the lining of my stomach. I wasn't sure if I should eat with the party already going on in there.

"Where are we going?" I wondered, my hand still wrapped up in his as we made our way out one of the side doors and onto the sidewalk. The whole side of the dorm building was covered in deep-green ivy, and I glanced back at it because I liked the way it clung to the stone.

"You know Shirley's?" he asked, what-upping someone with his chin as we passed.

People were staring. More specifically, at our clasped hands.

"Carrot," he beckoned.

I glanced up, smiling sheepishly. "Doesn't everyone know Shirley's?"

Shirley's was the campus diner. Well, technically, it wasn't on campus but right off. Still, the eatery was close enough that we all went there, and we all considered it part of WU.

"I eat there all the time. She always gives me extra fries."

"Who does?" I wondered.

"Shirley," he said like it was obvious.

Thing was everyone that worked at Shirley's wore a name badge with the same name. I don't know why, so don't ask. However, that would mean… "You're saying the entire staff gives you extra fries?"

He shrugged. "I'm a hungry guy."

Spoiler alert: It was not because he was a hungry guy.

His cell chimed in his pocket, and I started to pull my hand free, but he made a sound, tugging it back. "I have two hands," he said, reaching for his phone, unlocking it, and then pulling up whatever notification he had.

After typing something short, he darkened the screen and shoved it back into his sweats.

Did I mention he looked like a thirst trap in those sweats?

"This is me," he said, tugging me down the sidewalk to a massive Jeep-looking SUV parked at the curb.

My feet stuttered. "What is that?"

He glanced between me and the car. "That's my Wrangler. Sweet, right?"

It was a black four-door model that sat high and wide because of its oversized tires. From the side, it looked like a Jeep, even had RUBICON printed across the side in matte letters. The entire thing was black on black except for the neon-green ring on the tires and the chrome studs on the wheels. But from the front?

"Why does it look like that?" I asked curiously, walking around to stare at it from the front.

"Baby, you've never seen this thing around campus?"

I glanced over my shoulder at him. "Was I supposed to?"

He seemed exasperated.

Cars weren't my thing. "It looks like a mean alien."

He made a choked sound. "What?"

It didn't look like a regular Wrangler on the front. The grill was all black and shaped different, almost like it was scowling at the road. There was a raised section on the hood that was also all black but had neon-green stripes on the sides.

Below the headlights, there were small round fog lights that looked orange with stars in the center. In fact, there was a whole row of those small round lights on the roof.

"A mean alien?" he sputtered like he was still back there being offended. Did he think I would fall all over everything of his?

I wouldn't. I wasn't made that way.

Besides, I was falling enough over him as it was.

"Now look here," he said, stepping up beside me to point at the grill. "This is a special-order piece. It comes in a kit. It's called a Grumper Bumper."

"See! I knew it looked mean."

"Grump*er*. Not grum*py*."

I shrugged. "Same difference."

"No." He was choking again. "It's not."

"I like the stars," I said. He was staring at me like I had three heads. "Do they light up?" I asked.

He pulled a set of keys out of his duffle and ducked into the driver's side to turn them on. They glowed orange, the ones across the roof too.

When he joined me on the sidewalk, I smiled. "They're pretty."

"First you insult my jacket and now my Jeep."

I leaned up on tiptoes and pressed a kiss under his chin. Before I could even pull fully away, he had me beneath my arms, dragging me up off the pavement and holding me up so we were eye level.

He was nothing but a dark shadow surrounded by the glow of all the orange lights, and I knew I probably was the same to him. But I didn't have to see his expression to know which it was. I could feel it pressing in closer than the light from his weird Jeep or the darkness beyond it.

Arms shaking a bit from effort, he pulled me in, our chests colliding, and smashed our lips together. My heart beat so hard I practically heard it knocking against my ribs, though it was nothing but background noise to the kiss he swept me up in.

Someone walking down the sidewalk catcalled, and Ryan licked over my lips, setting me back on my feet.

"C'mon," he rasped, leading me around to the passenger's side where he palmed my ass as I stepped up on the running boards to get inside. Once I was in, he leaned in, pulling the seat belt around me. Even after it distinctively locked in place, he remained close, hovering in my personal space. Owning it.

Abruptly, he pulled back, the swish in the air the only thing alerting me to his swift exit. I felt my eyes round in surprise and heard his chuckle right before he shut the door. I watched him cross the front, noting the way his profile was just as nice-looking as the rest of him, and then he was inside the Jeep, turning the engine over and throwing it into gear.

Yeah, it was a manual transmission.

"Can you drive a stick?" he asked, a little bit of a naughty glint in his eyes.

"Sure can," I said, returning the look.

His voice dropped an octave when he said, "Good girl."

The butterflies in my stomach were back to acting drunk, so I turned to stare out the window as he drove us across campus and turned into the lot at Shirley's.

Parking was fairly full considering it was after ten, but it wasn't surprising because it was Friday night and everyone came here. Half the people inside were probably drunk.

"Wait there," Ry said, jumping out and coming around to open my door to reach in and lift me out.

Gravel crunching nearby made me look up as another Jeep, this one red, pulled into the lot, stopping on the other side of Ryan's.

Ry grinned, caught my hand, and towed me toward the sidewalk. The sound of a door popping open was followed by a distinct, "Brooo."

"You've got to be kidding me," I deadpanned.

Jamie bounded around the side of the red Wrangler, and he and Ryan did some handshake that made me roll my eyes.

When they were done, Jamie looked between us. "All good here?" he asked, waving a finger in our direction.

"Did you doubt me?" Ryan asked.

"Bring it in, bro." I didn't realize he was talking to me until I was snatched off my feet and crushed against him, his very wide shoulders swallowing me whole.

"Jamie!" I hollered, but the yell got lost in his muscles.

Instead of putting me down on my own two feet, he handed me off to Ryan like they thought I couldn't walk.

Idiots.

I gave Ryan a withering glare, and he merely laughed under his breath and kissed my forehead. How was I supposed to be mad at this ridiculous behavior when he did things like that?

"You two drive the same car?" I said instead.

"The Jeeps are bros," Jamie announced.

"Of course they are," I muttered. "Well, at least yours doesn't look grumpy," I observed, looking over the red Wrangler.

"Say what?" Jamie asked, gazing at Ryan who sighed dramatically.

"She thinks my Wrangler looks like an angry alien."

Jamie burst out laughing.

I ignored them. Jamie's Jeep had some big black thing on the front with two round lights perched on it. His tires were big too, and it was also a four-door.

"Did you go Jeep shopping together?" I asked.

"Like you don't know," Jamie remarked.

I frowned, looking up at Ryan. His eyes softened, and he smiled at me.

"Wait, you don't know?"

"Know what?" I asked, annoyed Jamie was ruining the smile I was getting.

"Ryan's dad owns like the five biggest car dealerships in the state."

I ripped my eyes from Ry to look at Jamie. "What?"

"You can't just be kissing her all the time, man. You gotta educate her too," Jamie lamented.

Ryan set me down. "Walsh Automotive," he confirmed. "He specializes in upgraded, upscale, and imports."

"Oh." I felt a little silly. "I didn't know."

"No reason for you to know," he answered, taking my hand as we went inside.

I guess it wasn't really surprising. The entire campus was monied. Anyone who went there practically had to be too. My parents were no exception, but I can't really say we were at the level that Ryan's family seemed to be.

"So you both grew up around here?" I asked as the three of us went inside.

"Yep," Jamie replied, pulling the door open for all of us. "Where you from, camera girl?"

I mean, it was obvious I wasn't from around here. "Ah, Illinois. Chicago, actually. My parents are both attorneys."

"And you're the weird artsy one in the fam?" Jamie mused.

I laughed. "Something like that."

Actually, it was just like that.

Ryan leaned down against my ear. "I like creative types."

My lips curled in on themselves as tingles rushed over my scalp and the back of my neck.

"Where to?" Jamie asked, and Ryan hitched his chin toward the back of the diner.

Let me be clear. The "diner" here was a little nicer than most. Westbrook U—actually, all of Westbrook, Virginia—was monied and top-tier, so of course this place would be more than a silver bullet on the side of the road.

But still, the food was pretty much like every other greasy spoon diner, which was why we all liked it. The floors were polished concrete, and the bar that ran the center of the entire place was topped with white granite with light wood stools pulled up the side.

There were low-hanging round pendant lights in a row down the middle as well as one over every booth along the perimeter of the place. We slid into a booth at the back, the last one open, which had dark-green leather high-backed bench seats and white granite tops just like the bar.

Huge windows made up two full walls of the place, overlooking the street and the woods across from it. Shirley's Diner was written in vinyl lettering across the center of one of the massive windows.

Our booth faced the tree line across the empty street instead of the parking lot. The campus radio station played through the speakers, our most popular DJ on duty.

I slid into the booth first, Ryan right after, while Jamie slid in across from us. They both said a few words to the full booth a few down from ours, which was filled with guys from the swim team.

A girl with brown hair pulled up into two cute buns at the top of her head and a fringe of bangs came up to our table immediately. "Hey, guys, I'm Shirley."

Sure, she was.

She glanced at Jamie and giggled. "Didn't you just eat?"

"Takes more than one plate to feed all this," he told her, flexing his bicep.

She giggled more, pulling some menus from beneath her arm, but Ryan waved her off. Then, he blanched, turning to me. "Baby, you need a menu?"

"Whipped," Jamie sang.

Ryan scratched his head in his friend's direction. With his middle finger.

"No," I told him, looking toward our waitress. "I'll just take a burger and fries."

"Was not expecting that," Jamie quipped.

"What did you expect?" I asked.

He shook his head. "Lettuce. Sad lettuce on a plate."

Ew, vegetables. "I told you I eat."

"Leave her alone," Ryan told him, turning to Shirley. "I'll have a burger and fries too. Plus two waffles, bacon, and some eggs."

I made a sound.

"I'll have what he's having," Jamie confirmed.

"Are you going to eat all that?" I asked Ryan when she was gone.

"I'll probably still be hungry," he remarked.

I guess swimming burned a lot of calories.

Shirley came back. "You guys want coffee?"

I nodded enthusiastically, and Ryan laughed. "Water too."

When she came back with our mugs, I reached for mine, sighing happily. Both guys watched me add the cream and sugar.

When I noticed, I glanced up. "What?"

"Excited much?" Jamie quipped.

I turned sheepish. "I haven't had any all day! My last cup got spilled everywhere."

Ryan stiffened beside me, and I busied myself finishing up the drink. His fingers were gentle when they grasped my chin, pulling my face around.

"He do that too?"

I nodded.

A dark look filled his blue eyes, and my stomach knotted.

A knocking sound made me turn my head, but Ryan pulled it back, his fingers still holding my chin.

I relented, staring into him, getting lost in that stormy blue gaze as he basically assessed me almost like he was looking for anything else he needed to be mad about. I let him look, patiently waiting him out, discovering that I really didn't mind being studied by him.

When he was satisfied, he made a low sound and leaned in to kiss me softly. "Drink your coffee, baby."

Cheeks burning, I lifted the mug in both hands, swallowing it down as he turned to Jamie, who was still knocking on the table.

"Out with it," Jamie demanded.

"Hughes is the one who's been harassing Carrot."

Jamie frowned.

"I caught him attacking her in the locker room during the meet."

Jamie slid forward, partway leaning over the tabletop. "He was attacking you?"

I glanced at Ryan once, then nodded.

"He was pinning her to the wall."

Jamie whistled below his breath and leaned back in the booth, throwing both arms over the back. My stomach cramped, and I set down the coffee, stuffing my hands into my lap. I knew Ryan believed me, but what about Jamie? What about the rest of the team? They didn't know me. Why would they believe some faceless girl over their own teammate?

"That explains it," Jamie surmised.

"What?" I asked, almost paranoid.

Ryan glanced at me sharply. I blew out a shaky breath. Without saying anything, he scooped me up and pulled me into his lap, looping his arms around me.

I remained rigid, but he nudged me back, and I gave in, surrendering all my weight.

"Why you swam like a hungry bear was on your ass. Why you refused to say shit to me and raced out of there right after the meet like your house was on fire."

"Sorry, bro. I didn't want to say anything and fuck with your head or anyone else's."

"It's cool. I'd have done the same."

"Something's gotta be done," Ryan said, his voice dark and serious. When I shivered, he tugged the hoodie closer around me and tightened his arms.

"Order's up!" Shirley said, appearing with a giant round tray balanced on one hand above her shoulder. Gracefully, she swung it down, resting the edge of it on the table as she passed out the plates.

The waffles were massive, dripping with butter, and she gave both guys their own container of syrup. My plate was passed over to me, and I noted Ryan really did have more fries than the rest of us.

After making sure we had everything we needed, she left us with our food. The guys dug in as if they had been stranded on a desert island for two weeks with no food at all. It was lowkey savage and borderline impressive.

Ryan ate half his burger in two bites and downed half the first waffle before he even took a breath. I gaped at them, marveling at the fact they barely chewed but somehow never choked.

"It's gonna get cold," Ryan said, pointing at my plate with a fry laden with ketchup.

I picked up one of my fries and chewed on it, still fascinated by the rate they consumed.

"Bro. I thought I was gonna die of starvation."

"You gotta eat, bro. Can't be running around after that one." Jamie jabbed his fork at me like he was scolding me for them being half starved.

"I didn't ask him to chase me!" I gasped, launching a fry over the table at him.

Jamie caught in his mouth. "Thanks," he said, chomping loudly.

I reached over and snatched one off Ryan's plate. He caught my wrist in his hand and my stare with his eyes. Leaning in, he wrapped his lips around the fry I was holding and ate it.

"You savage," I whispered.

He flashed his teeth, pulled my hand close, and licked the salt off the tips of my fingers. Heat pooled in my lower belly as I thought back to the way he'd basically sucked the inside of my thigh earlier.

His eyes glinted knowingly.

"I'm trying to eat," Jamie deadpanned.

I stuck my tongue out at him.

Ry caught my chin and kissed me loud. "Put that away, Carrot. That's just for me."

"Again. Trying to eat."

Ryan pushed my plate in front of me and then went to work demolishing the rest of his burger and fries.

I ate but at a much more civilized pace. And the more silence stretched between us, the harder it got to chew.

"I can think now." Jamie pushed away one of his empty plates, pulling the remaining waffle in front of him with a sigh. "So what we gonna do about this problem?"

I set down my half-eaten burger.

"I'm about this close to punching his face," Ryan declared.

Jamie made a noise.

"Jamie?" I asked tentatively.

Both guys paused midchew and looked at me. It was like they forgot I was even there. How rude.

"What?"

"You believe me too?"

His fork made a clattering sound on the tabletop. "I'm about to educate your girl," he told Ryan.

Ryan laughed, food still in his mouth.

Jamie leaned across the table, syrup getting onto his shirt. "You gonna eat that?" he asked when he was close. Before I could answer, he stole two fries off my plate and shoved them in his mouth, chewing like a cow.

Ryan's wide hand slid over my thigh, squeezing reassuringly, and without thought, I leaned into his side a little.

Jamie followed the movement. "You're elite crew now."

I didn't know what he was talking about.

A gruff sound filled the air. "You're with us." He pointed between him and Ryan and then gestured toward the table behind us.

"But isn't Jonas—"

"Fuck no, he's not!" Ryan practically roared.

Jamie cocked a brow at me. "Any questions?"

"Would you believe me if it wasn't for Ryan?"

Jamie pursed his lips, studying me. Then he ate another fry off my plate.

"Hey!" I admonished.

"You deserved that," he said.

I crossed my arms over my chest and glared. I probably didn't look too scary sitting in Ryan's lap.

"Yes, I would still believe you even if you weren't my bro's girl."

"Why?"

He moaned, sliding back into his seat. "Dude. You ain't gonna get away with nothing ever again."

Ryan chuckled.

"I'm waiting." I reminded him.

"You got an honest face," Jamie said. "Besides, carrot heads don't lie."

I gasped.

Jamie leaned salaciously over the table toward Ryan. "Bro, she a real ginger?"

Ryan scowled. "Fuck off, Jamie."

Jamie nodded. "I knew it."

"This is the most ridiculous conversation I've ever had," I announced.

Jamie's face transformed into something much more serious and sincere, his posture straightening. "Look, we might not know each other one hundred *yet*, but I was there that night. Not for all of it but enough. You were scared and upset. You would have died if Ryan hadn't been there. You weren't lying. It was clear. And if you say it was Hughes, then it was Hughes."

Now that was the truth, and I found myself blinking back tears.

Neither of them noticed because they both went back to inhaling the rest of their food. But Ryan kissed my cheek first.

"First things first," he said around a mouthful of waffle. We gotta tell the team what's going on."

"No!" I said, turning at the waist to stare fully at Ryan. "You can't. What if you all get into a big fight? What if it ruins the team? I don't want to be the Yoko Ono of Elite swimming," I bemoaned.

Ryan and Jamie burst out laughing.

"I'm not joking!" I insisted. These were some sweet,

charming guys, and Ryan's lap was very comfortable, but I'd had about enough of this. "You—"

Ryan cut off my words by bending me backward into our booth and kissing me. Like a full-on assault with his tongue. He tasted like maple syrup and butter with a hint of salt. I melted into his embrace, hoping we were low enough in the booth that no one could see, but even if they could, I wouldn't pull away. I couldn't. I didn't know how long he kissed me—could have been thirty seconds, could have been five minutes—but no matter the time, it was enough.

His head lifted, the tip of his tongue swiping out over his lower lip like he was eating up whatever was left of me. "You are way hotter than Yoko Ono, baby."

I blinked at the empty space suddenly over me, then used the edge of the table to scramble up. Ryan was already on his feet, slapping Jamie on the shoulder to follow suit.

I saw the swim team glance up, seeing Ryan and sitting back as they anticipated him coming over.

"Ry," I called.

He glanced over his shoulder to pin me with a look. Then he pointed at my plate and moved off to do what he wanted.

Big jerk. I should get up and march out of here right now. It would serve him right.

I took a bite of my burger instead. I couldn't even taste it; it was like chewing air as nerves coiled inside me and an uncomfortable prickling sensation crept over me. I shifted, feeling cold, and dropped the burger, knowing I was done eating.

I glanced across the booths to where Ryan was leaning into the center of the group of men who aptly listened to whatever his moving lips were saying.

The last thing I wanted was to cause a rift in the team. How had things gotten so out of hand? I should have just kept my mouth shut. I should not have instigated Jonas. I should have... The thought died away as another, much more ominous feeling overcame me.

What could only be described as the sensation of being watched—*stalked*.

I shivered, abruptly spinning in the booth to stare out the window.

It wasn't a burst of movement, more of a fluttering of leaves and branches as something else shifted among them. Leaning in, I focused intently on the disturbed spot where I was sure someone had been.

Chills raced over me. My ankles crossed as my feet slid back under the booth. Even though my insides were pure chaos and the sudden drop in my own temperature should have made me tremble, I went still. Almost like prey caught in the crosshairs of a predator.

Fingers curling against my thighs, I watched the trees more, heart thundering as I had a stare-down with a faceless something I couldn't see but was certain was there.

Then suddenly, it was gone. Whatever—whoever—was there watching pulled back, the retreat punctuated by a few colored leaves floating to the ground. I could have sworn I saw the flash of movement, but the harder I looked, the more I wondered if I was imagining things.

Released from unnerving awareness, I slumped back into the deep-green leather, dragging in a shuddering breath. I was trembling and felt vulnerable sitting here in front of the giant window with endless shadows to conceal whatever lurked in the dark.

Ryan and the team still had their heads together, so I slid out of the booth to cross to the bathroom. I passed by the long bar running the center, ignoring the curious looks I got from people seated along it, and rushed around the corner into the bathroom.

Once inside, I leaned against the wooden door to press a

hand to my chest. A toilet flushed, and I stiffened, pushing farther into the room toward the row of three sinks. Each sink had individual round mirrors over it, and I turned on the faucet to wash my hands as a woman came over to do the same.

"You here with Ryan Walsh?" she asked, making my head snap up.

I was so short I could only see the top of my head in the mirror, which was covered tonight by the black beanie. I became instantly grateful for the rude and nosy question because it gave me something to focus on besides what just happened.

Without bothering to turn around, I pushed up on tiptoes to gaze into the mirror at the woman standing just behind me. She probably went to WU, but I didn't recognize her.

"Yeah," I answered. "Who are you?"

If she could be rude, then so could I.

She gave me a dirty look and left without replying.

When she was gone, I shut off the water and dried my hands with an eco-friendly paper towel. It said so right on the dispenser.

Since I couldn't see myself in the mirror, I didn't bother looking to see if I appeared as freaked out as I felt, but I wasn't ready to go back out amid all the windows just yet.

Chewing my lip, I glanced at the window between the stalls and sink area. It was frosted, but I still didn't like it, so I stepped into a stall and closed myself in.

I was being ridiculous. It was probably some animal in the woods like a stray cat hoping for scraps from the diner. I was just jittery from the scene with Jonas earlier and then sitting there while Ryan blabbed my business to the swim team.

I mean, really, expecting less would have been dumb. Of course, Ryan wasn't going to keep his mouth closed. I hadn't known him very long, but it was abundantly clear he liked to insert himself into people's business, i.e. *my* business. This was what I wanted anyway, right? To have people believe me. For Jonas to get the punishment he deserved.

A creaking sound snapped my head up. I glanced toward the door even though I couldn't see. I waited for the scuffle of footsteps, the sound of the door closing, the sink… anything.

Nothing.

Another creak. The shrill sound of a car alarm going off was so sudden and so loud that I fell back against the stall wall. The high-pitched wail practically became my heartbeat, and then a robotic female voice added itself to the chaos. *"Disarm. Disarm. Disarm."*

I didn't even know car alarms talked. And my goodness, it was so freaking loud. You'd think it would be muffled in here—

My hand slapped over my mouth, dulling my gasp.

The window.

The freaking window is open.

Not wasting another minute, I flung the stall door open, making all of them shudder under the force. My sneakers slapped over the tile as I launched at the door, yanking the handle.

It didn't budge.

I tugged again.

It didn't move.

The desperate sound I made was practically silent against the alarm still going off along with muffled voices out in the diner. Underscoring it all was that damn robot. *"Disarm, disarm, disarm."*

Planting both feet on the floor, I grabbed the handle with both hands and threw my entire body into pulling.

Look, I was small, but I wasn't *that* small.

Clearly, the door was jammed. Or locked. Panicked, I stumbled, only to spring back up, searching the handle for a lock.

It was a flat-panel door with nothing but a simple handle.

I raised my fist to bang on it, yelling for help.

Something behind me squealed, a sound I heard because the car alarm was thankfully silenced. Suddenly, the quiet seemed so much louder.

The eerie, bone-chilling, watched sensation from before wrapped its clingy tentacles around me. Heart barely pumping, I rotated, the action achingly slow because I was terrified of what I might find.

Creeeak. It was like nails on a chalkboard, but I was already so bothered I didn't even cringe. The old window gave a valiant effort, but it gave way under force. Aptly horrified, I stared as it was forced up tracks by two long-fingered hands concealed in black leather gloves.

I started to scream.

Fourteen

Ryan

One minute, we were heads down and I was explaining the situation, and the next, all hell was breaking loose.

A car alarm started screeching, and we all turned toward the sound. It was vaguely familiar, but I didn't think much because I twisted back around to look at Carrot.

Only, Carrot wasn't where I'd left her.

"Disarm. Disarm. Disarm."

"Where's Rory?" I said to everyone and no one.

"Bro, that's you," Jamie said, slapping me on the shoulder.

"What?" I glanced at him.

"Your alarm is going off."

"Disarm. Disarm. Disarm."

"Fuck," I muttered, snatching the keys out of my pocket. "Find Rory," I told him as I jogged to the door to silence the alarm.

The second I stepped out of the diner, I saw the way the Jeep was sitting lopsided.

Someone was out here fucking with my ride. "What the f—"

A bone-chilling scream reverberated through the building behind me. All the hair on the back of my neck stood. Forgetting the Jeep, I tore back inside.

"Rory!" I yelled, wildly searching.

The sound of banging and rattling made me turn, and near the bar, Jamie yelled, "Bathroom!"

We both rushed forward, me making it just a little faster because I was closer. A wooden chair was jammed against the door, wedged so it couldn't be opened from the inside.

Inside, Rory was screaming, beating on the wood. "Ryan!" she begged. "Ryan!"

A string of curses trailed behind me as I kicked the chair out of the way and yanked open the door.

She fell forward through the opening, a startled cry ripping from her throat. I caught her against me, but she stiffened, rearing back to fight. "No!"

"It's me," I told her, heart lodged in my throat. "It's Ryan."

"Ryan?" she echoed, sagging forward.

I lifted her into my arms, the heart in my throat somersaulting when she immediately wound her arms around me, burying her face in my neck.

I glanced at Jamie, overwhelmed with so many emotions I could barely breathe. Instead of saying anything, I hitched my chin to the bathroom, and his eyes darkened as he barreled inside.

Employees and customers gathered in the small hall. The cooks peeked out from behind the wall of the kitchen.

I ignored all of them, angling my face down toward hers instead. "I got you. You're okay."

"Don't let go," she whispered, her words like a shackle without a key fitting itself around my chest.

"I won't. I swear to God I won't," I vowed.

She fit easily in my arms, her body trembling.

Jamie appeared, a frustrated expression on his face. "There's no one. The window is wide open, though."

Clearly hearing his words, she pushed farther into my neck.

Someone was in that bathroom with her. Someone trapped her inside.

"Baby," I said, keeping my voice quiet. "Are you hurt?"

I tried to pull her back so I could look at her, but she let out a sob, and I let her curl back against me. A murderous feeling overtook me, and I swung my eyes to all the people standing around gawking.

They all took a collective step back. All of them except the team.

"Go see if anyone's outside," I barked.

Some went to search.

"Rory," I said, using that tone.

"I didn't do anything," she whined. "Why are you mad at me?"

Jamie snickered, and I smiled over her head.

"Come out of there. Let me look at you."

"No." She refused. Her bratty attitude was a good sign she wasn't seriously hurt.

"High-maintenance," Jamie sang.

She gasped. The force of it brought her out of my neck. I seized the opportunity to hold her back, sweeping my eyes over every inch I could. Her nose was pink like she was cold, and her eyes were wet.

More of that irrational anger, accompanied by a healthy dose of fear, hit me all over again. "What happened?" I demanded. "Are you hurt? What the fuck were you thinking?"

Her eyes flared. "Listen here, mister. We might be dating, but I don't have to tell you when I need to use the bathroom!"

Jamie grunted like he agreed with her.

I'd deal with him later.

I scowled, but then her lower lip wobbled, and all my anger drained away. "All right. I'm sorry. I was worried."

She moved back into my neck, but not before wiping her nose on my shoulder. See? Brat. "Rory."

"Don't call me that."

"Carrot." I tried again, lips twitching. "Are you hurt? I need to know."

"No."

"Was someone in the bathroom with you?"

"They were opening the window to come in. But you opened the door before they could."

Her face lifted, wide eyes imploring mine. "I couldn't get the door open."

Now wasn't a good time to remind her that she was a shrimp, so I nodded emphatically. "The door was blocked from out here."

"It was?"

"Mm." I agreed.

She lay back against me. "Thanks for coming."

I gave Jamie a look, and he rolled his eyes. Did she think I'd just be out there having pie while she screamed her head off?

A few of the guys pushed through the gawkers still standing around, taking up space. "There's no one out there. There are some footprints under the window, though."

My jaw tightened.

"And, ah..." One of the others began. "Your tires are slashed."

I glanced at one of the waitresses standing nearby. "You call the cops yet?"

She pulled her cell out of her apron and dialed.

"You better check yours," I told Jamie as we moved

toward the front door. Right before I stepped outside, I frowned, glancing down at Carrot.

"I need to go look at my Jeep. You wanna—"

"I'll stay with you," she muttered against my throat.

Outside, Jamie let out a couple curses, and my body stiffened seeing the two slashed tires on the driver's side of my Wrangler.

Rory sat up to see and made a stricken sound. "Who would do that?"

"Probably the same person who shut you in the bathroom to scare you." Dead calm coursed through my veins, and frankly, it was unsettling. I'd never felt this... deadly before. "One guess on who it was."

There really wasn't any surprise in her expression when she said, "You think Jonas did this?"

Jamie stepped around the Jeeps, a rude sound preceding him. "Fuck yes, it was him. Probably trying to send a warning to Ryan about keeping his mouth shut."

If he thought this would keep me from spilling his dirty misdeeds, then he was even more idiotic than I thought. Dude also reeked of desperation.

It was a dangerous combination.

The realization had me scanning the tree line across the street.

"He was there," Rory said, voice tight.

My eyes shot to her. "What?"

"I saw him. Well, someone. Something," she said, her body starting to tremble.

Jamie flung his keys at me, and I snatched them out of the air. "Get her out of here. I'll handle this."

"Bro, you sure?" I debated. Leaving him to clean up my mess was not something I liked to do.

He nodded once, gesturing to Rory. "Take care of her."

"I'm going back to our room," I told him.

"Good call." He nodded.

"Call when you need me to come get you," I said, then spared a glance at my Jeep. "Tell them I'll come get her in the morning."

"I'll have one of the guys give me a lift over. And will do."

I held out my fist, and we pounded it out.

After a brief hesitation, Jamie reached out and patted Rory on the head. "See you in a bit, camera girl."

"Bye," she echoed.

Inside Jamie's ride, I turned the heat up full blast and made sure she was buckled before backing out of the lot, the headlights bouncing over him and the rest of the team watching from the sidewalk.

The whole way back to my dorm, my eyes scanned every shadow for Hughes.

Fifteen

Rory

Longest day ever?

Quite possibly.

Worst day ever?

It couldn't be. It was the day Ryan and I became official. It wasn't lost on me that I'd avoided him longer than we'd been dating, but the way I practically clung to his very presence, it was as if we'd been a couple far longer.

Perhaps we bonded in trauma. Perhaps I had some weird hero worship for him because the first time we met, he saved me. *And he did it naked.*

I giggled.

Ryan turned his head, warily glancing at me out of the corner of his eye.

"Whatcha doing over there, Carrot?"

"Thinking about you naked."

The rude sound he came out with made me smile. "Then why the hell are you laughing?"

Really, he was so sensitive. First his jacket, his Jeep, and now his wiener. And Jamie called me high-maintenance. Please.

My amusement faded almost as fast as it arrived, my eyes shifting back to the window. "Maybe I got over-attached to you so fast because you saved my life." There was a heartbeat of silence. "Twice now."

He braked suddenly, making me grab the door handle and stiffen, but the Jeep slid to a stop gracefully as though he hadn't just hammered his big foot on the brake pedal.

"We're in the middle of the road," I said, leaning up to look over the dash.

The engine stuttered when he pulled his foot off the clutch, and I clenched the door again, expecting the Jeep to go rolling backward or something.

It didn't move. The street we were hogging was flat.

"I have something to say." It was like some royal decree, and it was too important to even bother pulling over for.

Leaning across the seat, he snatched me up, hauling me toward him. We were so close our noses bumped, and the interior of the Jeep suddenly felt much smaller than before.

"You aren't attached to me because I saved you from drowning."

"What if I am?" I whispered.

"No." He was confident.

I felt my chin jut out. "How can you be so sure?"

"Because I'm just as attached to you."

My eyes rounded, emotion welling up inside me and turning my voice raspy. "You're attached to me too?"

He tilted his head just a bit, pressing our noses together, and whispered, "Oh yeah, baby. Completely."

Oh, I could love him.

The thought rattled my already shredded nerves. I pulled back just slightly. As freaked as I was, I still couldn't go too far. "Maybe I have a victim complex and you have a hero one."

"Rory."

I made a face. I'd never met anyone ever who could make my own name sound like some kind of horrible punishment. Not even my parents managed to do it when they said all of my names at once.

Of course, I relented. The pull was just too strong to deny, but even still, I wondered. "How did this happen so fast, then?"

"Fate?"

I scoffed. "You believe in fate?"

"Hard not to when you're sitting right here in front of me."

My heart tripped. *You are so falling.*

His stare remained watchful while he closed the little distance between us, holding me hostage with those blue orbs as our lips fused in a soft but somehow chest-squeezing kiss.

Honnnk!

Breathless, I fell back into the seat, pressing a hand to my chest. A pair of bright headlights swerved around the Jeep and tore down the street.

"Speeding." Ryan tsked.

"You're parked in the middle of a street." I reminded him.

"Whose side are you on?" he asked, starting the Jeep back up and driving off.

I sighed. "Yours."

His voice was all rumbly when he said, "Good girl."

Moments later, he pulled into a parking spot near his dorm, which was newer than the one I lived in. It was built to fit in with the historic buildings, though, and it was definitely lovely, but it still had an upgraded quality some of the older places didn't.

"Why are we here?" I asked, gazing across the sprawling lawn leading up to the imposing four-story residence. The leaves on the trees were already starting to turn, and soon, the grass would be speckled with autumn.

"You're staying with me tonight."

"I can't," I said, too weary to even give it my best indignation.

Rotating in his seat, he seared me with a challenging stare. "You want to go back to your dorm with your see-through curtains and replay the scene of someone trying to climb through the window to get to you all night?"

I shuddered as I literally felt all the color drain from my face.

Ryan's curse fell onto the seat as he vaulted out of the Wrangler, coming over to pull open my door. Reaching around, he unclasped my seat belt, guiding it back so it didn't smack me as it retracted.

The whole of his upper body crowded into the Wrangler, hands landing on either side of the seat, caging me in with his well-defined chest. He leaned so close I could smell the coffee from the diner on his breath.

"I didn't mean to scare you," he murmured, apology thick in his tone. "Hearing you scream back there damn near put me in an early grave. The meet, then just now at the diner... I need you to stay with me tonight, Carrot. I just want to be sure you're safe."

It was basically unspoken that we both knew Jonas was out there running around.

"What if I get caught?"

"You won't. Even if our RA sees you, he won't say shit."

I sucked my lower lip into my mouth, considering. It didn't take me very long to agree. Truth was I probably wouldn't sleep if I went back to my dorm, and also... This was a chance to sleep in his arms.

"Okay."

Letting out a relieved breath, he spun, offering his back. I climbed on.

"Aren't you exhausted?" I asked. "After everything plus the long meet."

"Never too tired for you," he said, locking the Wrangler and stepping up onto the sidewalk.

I tightened my arms around his neck, and he pretended to choke. As we got closer to the door, he said, "I'm glad practice doesn't start till seven tomorrow."

"Seven in the morning," I mourned. "On a Saturday? I'd quit."

He chuckled. "It's normally five thirty, remember? But tomorrow is a light day, so we get to sleep in."

"Seven a.m. does not constitute sleeping in."

His warm laughter vibrated through his back, tickling my chest, and I relaxed into him, my cheek pillowed on his shoulder. The adrenaline from before was draining away, leaving behind nothing but a mass of weary limbs and a sluggish brain.

Ryan walked right into his building without a care. He called out some greetings as he went, a few people congratulating him on his swim times earlier. No one said a word about the fact he was literally hauling me on his back into his room well after curfew.

"What kind of dorm is this?" I said, utterly surprised.

"The elite kind," he answered, letting us into his room.

In spite of my exhaustion, my whole body straightened as I took in his room. It was massive. At least double the size of the one I shared with Kimberly.

"Are you kidding me?" I said as he lowered to let me off his back. "This is so much nicer than my room!"

He kicked off his shoes and tossed the keys on a hook by the door as I stood and stared. The floors were glossy dark-stained wood. The walls were white, but not a stark white, more of a creamy color. To the right of the door was a built-in bookshelf—*a freaking bookshelf*—sank right into the wall. It only had a few textbooks, and the rest of the shelves were full of swim trophies, plaques, and ribbons.

There were a few pairs of random swim goggles hanging around and a basket with what I assumed was dirty laundry nearby.

A thin track of LED lights went around the perimeter of the room, and they were set to a cool-toned blue, bathing everything in a calming glow.

Two big beds took up a lot of the room, one on each side of the large square-shaped space. Both were unmade. The one closest to me had gray bedding, and the one across the room was red.

A long, narrow striped carpet ran down the room between the beds, stopping before reaching the large wooden desk. It was covered in a bunch of stuff, empty water bottles, and protein bar wrappers. Each of the guys had a big dresser, which was covered in more swimming gear and electronics. There was even a flatscreen mounted on the wall.

I swung around to where Ryan was standing. "Perks of being Westbrook Elite?"

His smile was lazy and, frankly, arrogant. "Bathroom's through there." He gestured to a door I hadn't even noticed yet.

My mouth fell open. "You have your own bathroom?"

"I share it with Jamie."

I glowered. "I share with an entire floor of girls."

He wagged his eyebrows. "I wouldn't complain."

I threw my sneaker at him, but he batted it away like it was a fly. Crossing to a mini fridge near the desk, he grabbed a bottle of water, uncapping it and downing the entire thing without even coming up for air.

"That one," he said, swiping his mouth with the back of his hand and pointing to the gray bed.

A tingle of awkwardness brushed over me. I mean, yes, I wanted to be here. Yes, I wanted to sleep with him. But suddenly, being in his space, looking at his bed... I swallowed thickly.

The bottle clattered on the desk when he tossed it over his shoulder, prowling over to me. My stomach dipped and tilted, watching him close the distance. Everything about his body was graceful and languid. He moved all the time like it was through water, with enough power to cut through the current but so much grace his control was almost a second thought.

Wide palms settled at my hips, tugging me gently into his body. "I don't expect anything, okay? I just want you here with me. I want to hold you."

I was leaning in when he snickered.

"What?"

"First time I ever said that to a girl."

I smacked him in the stomach.

"I mean it, though. I just want to know you're safe. I hate he scared you again."

"It's not your fault," I murmured, wrapping my arms around his middle.

He tugged the hat off my head and pushed his fingers through my hair, holding me against him. "He wanted to distract me with the Jeep. Thought I would go outside and freak all over it. He didn't think I'd come for you first."

"But you did."

"Yeah. I did." He agreed. Then in a much softer tone, he added, "Always."

I yawned, pushing my cheek a little farther into him.

He went to a dresser, pulled out a T-shirt, and handed it

to me. "You can sleep in this. You can change while I shower off since I didn't have time after the meet."

He grabbed some clothes for himself and headed toward the bathroom.

"Ry?"

He stopped, glancing over his shoulder.

"Will you leave the bathroom door open?"

Everything about him softened. Crossing back to where I stood clutching his T-shirt, he pressed his lips to the top of my head. "Of course, sweetheart."

As he was going into his private freaking bathroom, he called out, "You just want to see me naked."

"Been there, done that!" I called after him.

His laughter made me feel like everything was going to be okay.

Sixteen

Ryan

I FELL ASLEEP WITH HER SWALLOWED UP BY MY T-SHIRT, BARE thigh draped over mine, and her wild mane of hair trying to eat my face.

I slipped easily into a dream where she was trying to eat something else.

Sighing in pleasure, I sank into the mattress a little deeper. This was the kind of dream a man liked to have. Warm, slim fingers glided under the waistband of the boxer briefs hugging my hips, dipping to brush over my head.

My eyes popped open, the sensation way too real to be a dream. Glancing over, I noted my wild-haired woman was not there, and I would have panicked had I not also felt her nudging my thighs apart.

"Wha—" I lifted my head off the pillow to look down.

She pressed a finger to her lips, silently shushing me. Goddamn, the picture she made. The room was dark, but it didn't matter. It was like the woman had her own light, making it possible to see her always. The comforter was pulled up over her head, concealing her from the rest of the room. Her pale cheeks and wide eyes stared up at me from under my blankets. The tip of her finger brushed her perky nose as she quieted me, but behind it, her lips curled up into a naughty little smile.

Pulling her hand down, she nudged my thighs again. Being the gentleman I was, I immediately did as requested, nearly groaning again as she wiggled her fine ass between my legs and nuzzled my rigid dick with her nose.

The blankets rose a bit when her head lifted, gazing up my body again, and reminded me to be quiet.

I lifted my hips, and she laughed inaudibly. Damn, she was the perfect mix of naughty and cute.

She peeled the boxers down my thighs, and I spared a glance across the room toward Jamie's bed where he was lying with his back facing us, covers pulled up over his ears. Dude slept like the dead.

I forgot all about my roomie when Rory's wet tongue swiped up my shaft from base to tip. My abs contracted, ass muscles clenching against the bed. The warmth of her mouth enclosed my tip, tongue swirling around the head as she drew my cock up away from my body.

A shuddering breath left me, and she paused. Feeling her eyes from beneath the blankets, I glanced down, and she wagged her finger at me.

My head hit the pillow as she released my other head, the air brushing over the wet skin. Hand wrapped around the base, she squeezed it lightly while dipping her head to kiss and lick over the smooth skin above it. I kept everything shaved. Not because I really preferred it like that but because the less hair I had in the pool, the more aerodynamic I was.

But as she lapped at my flesh, I decided keeping it bare

had other benefits. When her tongue traced over the V-cut muscles at my hips, I smiled. I knew she liked those.

Any smugness I felt died the second she slid back over my cock, taking it all the way until the tip nudged the back of her throat. I felt her gag a little and tilted my hips, trying to pull back, but she pinched the inside of my thigh and sank back down again.

My eyes rolled back in my head when she pulled back and sank back down. Her mouth was warm, wet, and her throat tight. Whenever her gag reflex contracted, it squeezed my tip, and I had to bite my lip to keep from moaning.

After a few minutes of deep-throating me into some kind of coma, she pulled back, rocking her lips around my swollen head, making my body shiver. One hand slid down to cup my sack, which was already drawn up tight against my body. The urge to fucking blow right then across her tongue was so potent I panted. As if she knew and wanted to torture me more, she pulled off, slipping farther into the blankets to lavish attention on my boys.

Delving my hand under the blankets, I slipped my fingers into her hair, holding her to me. Kissing across my sack, she moved to my inner thigh, nipping at it and making me jump. I felt her vibrate with laughter, and I tightened my grip in her hair.

I was pretty sure I heard her sigh, and then the whole of her tongue swiped up the juncture between my leg and dick. She didn't stop, dragging that sinful tongue right over to swallow down my cock, and then her head started to bob.

My shoulders lifted off the mattress as she set a pace that quite frankly impressed me. My entire throbbing, swollen cock was covered in her saliva. I could feel it practically dripping down to my base. Her little slurping sounds made my toes curl into the sheets, and my back arched up, straining toward her.

Sensing my desperation, she grabbed my hips, her fingers squeezing tight. The next time she pulled up on my dick, her tongue flattened, dragging up the side and fixing itself on that sensitive spot just below my engorged head.

Eyes blowing wide, I lifted the blankets a little, staring down in fucking awe at the way she worked my cock.

Still sucking, she flicked her eyes to mine. The corners of her stretched-out lips turned up, and her tongue pressed a little harder against that spot.

I came apart right then, exploding into her mouth, feeling every single pulse my dick made as it emptied itself over her tongue. Her eyes slid shut as she swallowed me down, hand wrapped around my base to milk me some more, making me shudder again.

Her mouth gentled, sucking delicately as she made sure every drop was cleaned up before laying the softening member against my body and pressing a chaste kiss against it.

My heart fucking flopped.

If I thought I was attached to her before… well, it was tenfold now.

Her head cleared the blankets, hair sticking up around her head and a dazed look softening her face. Grabbing her under the arms, I towed her up my body and shoved my tongue in her mouth with a moan.

She stiffened a bit with the sound but kissed me back with just as much urgency. Her lips were puffy and hot. A slight salty tang flavored the kiss. I wasn't much one for kissing women after a BJ, but knowing that was me on *this* girl's tongue was all kinds of an aphrodisiac.

As we kissed, my arm went overhead as I felt around for the phone on the table beside the bed. The second my hand closed over it, I pulled it back, squinting at the screen for the time. We had about an hour before I had to be at the pool.

Bro, yeah.

Tossing the phone on the bed, I slid out from beneath her, the cold morning air prickling my bare skin. Boxers around my ass, I tugged them up, then lifted her out of the bed, padding quietly into the bathroom.

The door latched and locked quietly, and I reached into the small shower to turn on the spray. Standing her on her feet just outside the glass-enclosed box, I tugged the shirt over her head, eyes darkening on her bare chest.

The only light in the room was from a small nightlight plugged into the outlet. Yeah, yeah, a nightlight. I'd busted my shin on the cabinet one too many times in the middle of the night.

But I was glad for the stupid light now because it allowed me to see her small, perky breasts, tightened peach nipples, and flushed chest.

I reached for her panties, my eyes locking on hers with a silent question. She nodded once, and they joined the shirt on the floor. My boxers came next, and then I was opening the glass door behind her, ushering her beneath the warm spray.

Steam was already rising in the enclosed space, creating balmy, humid air. Even though I'd just had one hell of an orgasm, I could feel tingles of desire coursing through me already. I stepped in behind her, watching the way the water slid over her creamy skin, sliding down every dip and curve.

We stood close because of the snug space, and I towered over her, causing a resurgence inside me to protect what was mine.

Rotating beneath the spray, she tilted her chin, water soaking her carroty hair, turning it a darker color, and dragging it over her shoulders and back. Water clung to her cinnamon lashes, creating a dark curtain around her watchful eyes.

Leaning down, I sucked the water off her lips, licking over her jaw and pushing into her neck to latch on.

"How do you feel about hickeys?" I murmured, barely lifting my head.

"Depends on who's giving them."

I growled against her flesh. "Woman, the only person giving you hickeys better be me."

In response, she craned her head back more, fingers delving into my hair to push me farther into her neck. "I guess they're okay, then."

With a low grumble, I latched on, sucking only enough so there would be a mark, holding back because I didn't want to cause any pain. The second I saw the darkening circle on her smooth flesh, I dove back in and put another right beside it.

Fucking mine.

She made a little sound when my teeth scraped over her shoulder, and I sank onto my knees.

"Ry?" she whispered, water dripping over her lips.

Without a word, I pushed her gently against the shower wall, watching for a moment as the spray rained over her bare chest. Taking her thigh, I draped it over my shoulder, and she sucked in a breath.

"Just returning the favor, baby," I murmured, stroking two fingers over her core.

Her gasp swirled with the steam, echoing in the small shower, hanging in the humid air. She was already dripping, body relaxed and welcoming. Clearly, she enjoyed what she'd been doing in bed.

She wasn't shaven bare like me, and I enjoyed dragging my fingers through the trimmed light-red hair.

The thigh draped over my shoulder started to tremble, and I flicked my fingers over her swollen clit. She gasped, and I smiled.

"Better hold on," I warned, diving in.

Her hands fisted in my hair, twisting the strands as I licked and sucked like my life depended on it. I couldn't stop the hum of satisfaction from escaping as her silky heat slipped over my tongue. Sliding two fingers into her, I pumped slowly, and the leg she was still standing on started to shake.

"Ry," she whimpered, body slipping down the wall just a little. I pinned her back, curling my fingers inside her and making her moan.

"Quiet, Carrot." I reminded her.

She practically pouted above me, so I stroked that spot inside her again and pulled her clit between my lips at the same time.

Her leg buckled, and I laughed under my breath.

"I can't." She panted.

Making a low sound, I palmed her waist, picking her up and pinning her against the wall. Both her legs draped over my shoulders, her center right in front of my face. I dove in anew, holding her open with one hand and attacking with my mouth.

For once, I was glad she was so light because if she were any bigger, I wouldn't be able to hold her up like this and eat her.

Her whole body jerked and shuddered, the fingers in my hair twisting near painfully. My dick started to throb, jutting out from my body like it wanted in on the action.

When her body went taut, I buried my face, pressing my tongue against her twitching clit. She splintered apart right there, hips rocking as she rode my face through her orgasm.

The warm gush of liquid I felt around my tongue made my cock even harder.

Her whole body went boneless, leaning into the wall as she breathed heavily.

Pulling back, I slid her down the wall, and she grabbed on to me as if she worried she wouldn't be able to stay upright.

"Don't move," I told her, voice raspy.

She made a little helpless sound that shot straight to my dick as I bounded out of the shower, dripping water all over the floor as I reached into the cabinet. The condom packet fluttered to the floor as I rushed back into the steamy space, rolling it on as she stared at me with wide eyes.

"Okay?" I asked, giving my aching rod a stroke.

Her head bobbed.

Grasping her at the waist, I spun her so her front was to the wall and my body was flush against her back. "Still okay?" I whispered in her ear.

"Yes, Ryan," she replied, pushing her sweet little ass toward my hips.

"It's gonna be fast, baby." I warned her. "Jesus Christ, the shit you do to me."

Bracing her forearms on the wall, she bent a little at the waist, thrusting her ass at me. I groaned and plunged in.

We both moaned, the give of her body like fucking ecstasy. She molded around me, squeezing me like a glove, and my eyes closed as I pulled out and plunged back in.

Her head bowed between her arms as I palmed her hips, staring down at the way her narrow waist flared out softly into them.

Then I started moving, setting a pace that tightened my sack to nearly painful. Entranced, I watched as my thick dick disappeared into her body over and over again.

"God, Ryan," She panted, her head bowing a little more.

Reaching around, I rolled one of her nipples between my fingers, making her cry out. Surging deep, I rolled my hips as her walls clutched me tight. "That's a good girl." I praised her, making a small sound float over her head.

"Come on now. Come for me," I said, releasing her nipple to reach between her legs.

The second my fingers pressed on her swollen center, she exploded around me. Pulling back and hammering in her, I let go, spilling inside her body until my legs felt weak.

Pulling out, I dropped back against the wall, breathing heavy. She collapsed chest first in the wall I had her pinned to, my eyes lazily tracing over her fine-ass form.

I pulled off the rubber, tying it off, then dropped it outside the shower. She came to me willingly, cheek pillowed on my chest. "I thought you weren't a morning person," I mused.

"You twitch in your sleep."

I paused. "Did I wake you?"

She kissed my pec. "I'll get used to it."

I smiled overhead, loving that her words implied this wasn't the last time she'd spend the night in my bed.

"I thought you were having a nightmare." The way she said it gave me pause.

"Baby, were you having a nightmare?"

When she said nothing, I glanced down.

"Maybe. But when I woke up, you were there, so it was okay."

I swallowed thickly. She should have known not to say sweet shit like that to a man, especially after all the sex he just had. It wasn't fair. It was a knockout punch.

When I said nothing, she spoke. "But were you?"

"No. Swimmers twitch in their sleep. I should have warned you. I'm sorry it woke you up."

Her head fell back when she looked up. "It's okay."

My gaze caught the two marks I'd sucked on her neck, and I brushed my thumb over them.

"Do you think Jamie heard us?" She worried.

I scoffed. "Hell no. He sleeps like the dead. And he is the

worst morning person ever, so don't get your feelings hurt if he acts like a beast."

"Is your shampoo smelly?"

I blinked at the change in conversation. "What?"

"Well, I might as well wash my hair since I'm in here. But not if your shampoo is smelly."

"Well, is my hair smelly?" I asked, bending down to shake my wet strands in her face.

She shrieked, pushing me back. "You smell like chlorine all the time."

I shrugged and reached over to grab the shampoo. After popping the top, I held it out to her so she could sniff it.

It was completely ridiculous.

Her eyes rounded when she saw the bottle, snatching it up and hugging it to her chest. "Hey! This is the good stuff. Where'd you get this?"

I shrugged. "My mom gets it for me."

She gasped, hugging it again. "I haven't been able to find it anywhere. I thought it was discontinued."

"Does that happen with shampoo?" I wondered.

"You are such a guy."

"Well," I mused, pointing down at my dick.

"I'm using this," she declared, pouring about half the bottle into her hand.

It was hella amusing watching her wash her hair while making a bunch of little happy sounds. "It smells so good," she said. "For once, my hair won't be a disaster!"

"There's conditioner too."

She gasped so loud I jolted.

"Really?"

I handed it to her, and she hugged it too.

It was kinda adorable but also kinda made me jealous. "You're just dating me for my shampoo."

She ignored me to do a little happy dance under the spray.

I chuckled.

We finished up in the shower. Well, actually, she ignored me while hogging all of my products, and then she put my T-shirt back on when we were dry.

With a towel around my waist, I grabbed some clean clothes and threw them on while she pulled on the black pants she'd been wearing last night.

"Watch this," I heckled, going over to the Nespresso machine to pop in a pod and slide a mug under the spout.

Leaning a hip against the dresser, I waited while she pulled on my hoodie without even thinking about it.

The strong scent of rich coffee permeated the room, and Jamie groaned.

Rory laughed, slapping a hand over her mouth as I snickered. One of Jamie's arms flung out, hand flopping over the side of the bed.

He groaned again. *"Fuuuck."*

The coffee finished brewing, and the machine hissed. Not even a second ticked by.

"Fuck this morning shit. Where the hell is my coffee?"

"We got practice in thirty."

Jamie gave me the finger.

Carrot laughed again.

Jamie lifted his head off the pillow, cracking one eye open to stare at her. Then he moaned and gave her the finger too.

She padded across the room to get the coffee and carry it over to the bed. I straightened a little, ready to jump in if Jamie was feeling particularly disgruntled this morning. It was one thing when he tried to deck me, but my girl was another story.

"Coffee," she said, standing over him.

"I like you better than Ryan," he said, reaching for the mug.

She moved back, and we watched him chug half the cup before even sitting all the way up.

"Isn't that hot?" She fretted.

Jamie drained the rest.

"I don't think he has any taste buds left," I told her.

"If you don't want to see my morning wood, you better close your eyes."

Rory squeezed her eyes shut, and I laughed.

Jamie practically fell out of the bed, thrusting his cup at me on his way to the bathroom. "More."

I did my bro a solid and brewed him a refill.

Not much later, I pulled Jamie's Jeep up in front of Carrot's dorm. I tried to convince her to stay at ours, but she wouldn't.

"I'll call you after practice, okay?"

"Ry?" The hesitation in her voice told me I wasn't gonna like whatever she had to say.

"Is he gonna be there, at practice?"

My back teeth slammed together. "Probably."

"But what if he does something—"

"He won't."

"But what if—"

"I can handle him."

"But—"

From the back seat, Jamie made a rude noise. "It's too early for all this talking."

She leaned around the passenger seat. While she waited for me and Jamie to get ready, she used the blow-dryer on her freshly washed hair. She'd been right about the shampoo. Her hair draped around her face in shiny waves, none of the carroty strands trying to attack her head.

"Sorry, Jamie," she whispered.

He made a rude noise. "It's all good, camera girl. Don't worry about him, okay? If he does anything, I'll punch him in his asshole face."

She nodded and then swung the door open, leaping to the ground.

I met her on the sidewalk, grasping her hips to pull her in.

"I don't like that you have to be around him," she lamented.

I'd rather him be around me because then I wouldn't have to worry about him being around her, and I told her that.

Her face screwed up. "The last thing I wanted was to drag you into the middle of this. Now look, the whole team—"

"Is on your side."

Her lips parted. "What?"

"I told them what Hughes was doing last night. And then they saw firsthand he's clearly off his rocker."

"I don't—" She began, but I cut her off.

"I'm telling the coach at practice."

She straightened away, wrapping her arms around herself. "What if he doesn't believe you?"

It really pissed me off that she had been mistrusted and brushed off so many times that now she just expected it to happen.

"He will."

She seemed doubtful, but she didn't argue. It made my stomach twist.

"I have to go. If I'm late, he'll make me swim extra laps."

She nodded, tugging the team hoodie off and handing it over. I didn't want to, but I took it because it was policy. "You can have it back later, 'kay?"

She smiled a little. "Okay."

Cupping her face, I brought it up so I could stare into her eyes. "Try not to stress about this. I know we didn't really talk much last night, but we will later, okay? But you have to know I won't just keep my mouth shut about this, Carrot. No way in hell."

"Yeah." Her voice was somber. "I know."

"Give me some sugar."

Leaning up, she pecked me on the lips. I took advantage and wrapped my arms around her waist, deepening the kiss.

"I'll be back soon," I whispered against her mouth.

"I do know how to live without you, you know." Her words were sardonic.

I winked over my shoulder. "But why would you want to?"

She blushed, lips pressing together like she was sealing in our kiss.

I watched her disappear into the building before driving off, Jamie still half asleep in the back seat.

"This is gonna be a shitshow," he said when I pulled into the lot at the pool.

"Yeah," I said, grim. "I know."

Seventeen

Rory

Try not to stress about this, he said.

Yeah, right. It was literally all I could think about. Except for something else he also said.

But why would you want to?

I wouldn't. I wouldn't want to live without him. Just the suggestion made me queasy, the realization startling.

It was too much too soon. But it was already done.

And that was what scared me most of all.

I wanted Ryan so fast and so fiercely.

But Jonas had the power to rip us apart.

Eighteen

Ryan

Tension crackled in the air.

Shredded, sore muscles were basically a mainstay when you swam seven days a week and added the gym on four of those days.

But tension hit different. It might sizzle in the air, but it knotted between my shoulder blades, creating a tightness I did not like. My stomach buzzed with unspoken adrenaline as my heart pumped, basically readying my body for a fight.

This was not what swim practice should be like. This was not at all the kind of atmosphere a team should have.

But I refused to cover it up. To cover for him.

He was a dirtbag who didn't deserve the spot on this team. Sure, he was a good swimmer. Yeah, one of the best. But just because he could cut through water, it didn't give him a free pass for everything else in life.

He assaulted my girl. Attacked her. Bullied her. Put his hands on her.

Bro, no.

So yeah, team was probably the most important aspect in my life, swimming my number one, but maybe... Maybe it had some competition now.

I shouldn't have to choose. Rory didn't ask me to. Not even once. In fact, I got the distinct impression she would rather walk than put me in the middle.

If anyone was asking me to choose—no, *demanding*—it was Hughes.

I was about to call his bluff.

He was in the locker room, looking smug and carefree as if he had not one care in the world. Like he hadn't spent his evening slashing tires and terrifying my girl in a public bathroom. My lip curled just thinking of it, just looking at him.

As if on cue, the smug bastard turned, eyes snaring mine and holding. Chest rising and falling with the deep breath I pulled in, we measured each other across the space, both refusing to back down first.

The tension in the air I mentioned before? It turned gnarly. Gnarly enough that the entire team stopped what they were doing to stare warily between us.

"What's the matter, Walsh?" Jonas goaded. "My sloppy seconds not as appealing as you thought they'd be?"

I launched myself at him, letting my anger go unrestrained. Surprise flickered in his eyes, but it was quickly replaced with horror as my fist plowed into the side of his face, knocking him into the locker. His body bounced off the metal, and he dropped onto the floor behind the bench with a slap.

He laughed on the floor, rolling up into a sitting position, his back against the lockers. "Guess I was right."

I lunged again, but Jamie caught me around the waist, towing me back. A few of the other guys moved to block my view of Hughes as he got to the floor, swiping the blood dripping from his mouth.

"Let me go," I rumbled, fighting against Jamie.

"Bro, no. This is what he wants." Jamie kept his voice low. "You won't be any help to Rory if your ass is expelled."

I laughed. How ironic that I would be the one to get expelled instead of the bleeding douchebag.

Coach came rushing out of his office, eyes flying around the room and trying to assess the situation. "What's going on out here?" he barked, doing a double take at the way Hughes was dabbing his lip. "Are you fighting?"

"Who the hell is fighting?" he demanded when no one said anything.

"Coach," I said, not once taking my eyes off Hughes. "I need to talk to you."

Hughes's eyes flared a little, and he ripped them away to turn toward Coach. "Coach, I—"

"What the fuck is this?" Coach bellowed. "You two? You pissed about lane four, Hughes?"

"No, Coach, I—"

"I don't want to hear it. Team gets along. Period. Pull out whatever the hell crawled up your asses and get in the pool."

"This can't wait," I deadpanned.

Coach stepped into my line of sight. I was taller than him, but he gave no shits and advanced on me. "What part of get your ass in the pool did you not understand, Walsh?"

"I'm not swimming with him."

Coach turned incredulous. "Excuse me?"

Hughes laughed. He fucking laughed.

"You think you make the rules here, Walsh? You think because you whine and snivel that you don't want to swim with him that I'll pat you on the head and dismiss one of the best swimmers we got?"

Behind him, Hughes smirked.

I really wanted to smash his face again. Knowing it, Jamie wrapped a hand around my bicep. I flung him off.

"You don't want to swim with him? Fine. Don't swim. Pack your gear and get out."

I sucked in a breath.

Seriously?

My already precarious mood plummeted into the depths of hell. My tongue slid across my teeth. "So you won't kowtow to me, but you will to him? To a fucking rapist?"

Coach's entire body stiffened, his shoulders hiking up so far they practically touched his ears. "What did you just say?"

"Seriously, Walsh?" Hughes chose that moment to jump in. "First, you accuse me of slashing your tires, and then you tell Coach this bullshit?"

Jamie said he gave the cops Jonas's name. Guess they came calling at his door last night. I knew they wouldn't have anything to charge him with, but hopefully, seeing the cops on his doorstep rattled him a little.

Obviously, though, he wasn't rattled enough.

Or maybe he was, and that was why he was trying to pull this right now.

Coach turned to fully face me. "That's a heavy accusation, son."

I forced myself to breathe deep. To not appear like I was just pissed off and acting out. "I realize that. That's why I asked to talk to you privately. But you didn't want that."

"You got proof?" Coach asked.

"Yes."

"The fuck he does!" Hughes insisted. "All he has is some chick I dumped making up lies."

I lunged at him again.

Coach slapped me in the chest with his hand. "Enough!"

"If Walsh isn't swimming, I'm not either." One of the guys spoke up.

I glanced over, nodding once.

"Me either," Jamie echoed instantly.

Several others around the room spoke up, saying the same thing.

Coach cursed, scrubbing a hand down his face. "It's too goddamn early for this shit," he muttered. "Hughes, Walsh, my office now. The rest of you ingrates, get your asses in the pool!"

A few of the guys—the ones clearly on Hughes's side—grabbed their towels and headed out. I made a mental note of each of their names and slid a glance at Jamie who was doing the same.

When more than half of the team refused to budge, Coach laughed bitterly. "For fuck's sake, Walsh is still on the team."

I glanced around, nodding at the guys, letting them see the gratefulness in my eyes. Only then did they grab their shit and head to the pool.

"My. Office," Coach grumbled.

Hughes went first and then Jamie and I started forward. "Owens," Coach barked, "pool."

Jamie pursed his lips.

I hitched my chin at him, and he relented.

It made Coach pretty hot that I had the loyalty of most of these guys, but we spent more time together than apart, and I never once gave them a reason to doubt me. I never acted arrogant or better like *other* freestyle swimmers in the room. I never begrudged them their good times either. The way I saw it, if I had time to be jealous over someone else's swim time, it meant I had more time to spend working on my own.

Coach didn't bother closing his office door. I guess there was no reason to considering we were the only ones in here.

"Walsh," he intoned, staring at me from across his desk.

Hughes stepped forward. "Coach, he—"

Coach fired a look at Hughes. "Your name Walsh?"

He fell silent, and I resisted the urge to grin.

Coach gestured to me.

"Last week, I was here getting in a late-night swim—"

"You've been doubling up practices?" Hughes asked, voice sharp.

I glanced at him out of the corner of my eye. "Maybe if you spent less time harassing women, you'd have time for that too."

A little bit of his control snapped, and he lunged at me. I remained planted on my feet, keeping my face bored.

"Jonas! Sit!" Coach snapped.

He sat. *Like the mutt he is.*

I cleared my throat. "Anyway, one night after my second practice"—I said that part again just to get under Hughes's skin—"I heard a shout from the locker room, so I went out to the pool and saw someone drowning."

"What?"

Coach was dramatic. He had two tones: yelling and sarcastic.

I nodded. "So I jumped in the pool and pulled them out. It was a girl. You might know her, actually. Rory Coin. She comes to our meets to shoot photographs for the school news."

Coach thought a moment. "The redhead?"

I nodded.

"What was she doing in the pool?"

"Said someone pushed her in. They also closed the automatic cover as she was drowning."

"Can't she swim?"

"No," I said, deadly.

Coach frowned.

"I asked her who it was, but she wouldn't tell me. So we walked her home."

"We?" Coach questioned.

"Me and Jamie. I called him to come let us out of the pool. The cover trapped us in."

Coach frowned. "That's a lawsuit waiting to happen."

"Imagine if she died," I said, letting that sink in. "Anyway, during yesterday's meet, I saw Hughes go into the locker room, and he was gone a while. I was concerned maybe he had a cramp or something." That was a lie, but it made me sound good.

So sue me.

Hughes made a rude sound, and I mentally gave him the finger.

"But he had her cornered in the locker room. He was threatening her."

Coach looked at Hughes. "This true?"

"I wasn't cornering her. We were talking. I was asking her to get some shots of me for the scouts."

"She told me then it was Jonas who tossed her in the pool. Left her to drown." Silence plunged over the room. "She also told me the reason he tossed her in was that when he took her out on a date, he tried to rape her, and he was trying to keep her from telling everyone."

"Hughes." Coach looked at him.

"It's all lies, Coach," Hughes said, doing a damn good job of looking like the injured party. "I did take her out on a date. I'd seen her around at the meets, thought she was hot, so I asked her out." He shrugged, and my hands balled into fists.

He's goading you.

"I didn't know she was crazy. I told her I wasn't interested, and she went nuts. I even went to Dean Cardinal. I told him she'd been threatening me, saying she was going to make trouble unless I dated her."

I made a rude sound. Hughes shot me a sly look out of the corner of his eye.

This motherfucker.

"And I was right. She went to the dean and told him I tried to rape her." He stood up from the seat, playing agitated. "Why would I do that? I don't need to rape women. I'm the top swimmer here. I don't have to assault women to get some."

"And what did Dean Cardinal have to say about this?"

"He believed me of course. Everyone does. She has no proof. She's just flapping her gums. When no one would listen, she found Walsh here and pussy-whipped him."

The chair in front of me skidded into the wall, and I charged, backing Hughes into the closest wall and leaning in. "Keep running your mouth, you little shit. Keep it up and just see what happens."

Okay, fine. I lost my cool.

"Walsh."

I shoved off him, turning my back completely. "Last night, he came to the diner, slashed my tires, and trapped her in the bathroom to torment her."

"As I told the cops, I was with Rinkin last night. We got pizza. Cops said my alibi checked out."

He could have easily slipped out of the pizza place, walked to Shirley's, and then went right back. I had to give it to him. He was a slippery weasel.

"Proof?" Coach asked.

I pursed my lips.

Coach sighed heavily. "Look, I understand the serious nature of these accusations and that you, Walsh, clearly believe your girlfriend."

"She's the victim," I growled. *Jesus, now I know what it's like for her. Now I know why she didn't want to tell me his name.*

"But everything I'm hearing right now is hearsay. And her word against his. You said you have proof. Do you have anything besides her word?"

The muscles in my jaw ticked.

"Even the cops cleared him." Coach went on.

"For slashing my tires. Not for rape."

"Have charges been filed?"

"Of course not. There was no rape," Hughes purported.

"Because she fucking fought you off," I said through gritted teeth.

"I understand your position, Walsh. I know there was a bit of rivalry between you two before, and this just makes it worse, but what do you want me to do here?"

"He doesn't deserve to be Elite."

Hughes stiffened. "Coa—"

"I'm not kicking him off the team, Walsh. There is no basis. These are just alleged accusations. Even the dean himself dismissed them. Even if I wanted to remove Hughes—" Jonas made a stricken sound, and Coach lifted his hand. "I don't."

I growled.

"But even if I did, I couldn't. Not only could Hughes sue the school—"

"And I will." He glowered.

Coach kept going. "And besides that, you really want me to punish the team for some accusations? Your brothers out there have worked hard. You too, Walsh, putting in two practices a day plus gym time. You want to sink all that because of some girl?"

"She's not some girl." My temper was dangerously close to snapping. And this time, there would be no reining it in.

"Fine. You're in love."

Why did that sound so condescending?

I took a menacing step forward.

"Bro!" Jamie appeared, rolling through the office door soaking wet with a pair of goggles in his hand. He barged right over to me, flinging his drenched arm around my shoulders.

Bro had totally been eavesdropping at the door.

"Why aren't you in the pool, Owens?"

"I missed my bro."

I gave him the side-eye, and he wiped his dripping nose on my shoulder. I knew he knew I was two seconds to napalm level and decided to intervene before I really did get myself kicked off the team.

I dragged in a deep breath. *Don't let them get the best of you.*

"Can I get to practice now?" Hughes said like he was actually eager to practice.

"Go." Coach was gruff, but then he called his name, stopping the swimmer in the open door.

"Yeah, Coach?" he said like the ass-kisser he was.

"Dude needs some ChapStick," Jamie muttered.

I laughed.

Hughes's expression flickered when he heard us, but to his credit, he kept his eyes on Coach Resch.

"I better not hear one more thing about you going around this campus. You keep your nose clean and your dick in your pants. I'm willing to go to bat for you this time, but if I keep hearing this kind of nasty info, I won't turn a blind eye."

"Yes, sir. Thank you, sir."

"Forget ChapStick. He might as well lube up with Vaseline," Jamie said when he was gone.

"Owens! What are you still doing here?"

Jamie pulled his arm from around my shoulders. "With all due respect, Coach, I'm here for Walsh. I know his girlfriend, and I believe her. A lot of us do. And I got to say I'm disappointed you would make this team swim with trash."

Coach was caught off guard by Jamie's seriousness. Jamie wasn't serious very often, so when he was, it was significant.

Coach cleared his throat. "Look, Walsh, I'm not saying I don't believe you. I'm saying there is nothing I can do."

"I don't believe you." I pushed.

Anger lit the older man's eyes, but then he banked it. "I respect you ain't a kiss-ass—"

"Like Hughes," Jamie quipped.

"And you're the hardest-working swimmer on this team,"

"Rude," Jamie quipped again.

"Yet you sided with him," I said, not bothering to hide the disgust in my voice.

"No." His voice rose sharply. "I sided with the team. *Your* team."

"If I walked right now, half those men would walk with me."

"Which is exactly why you won't. Because you, Walsh, are a natural leader, and you'd never ask your boys to give up on all their hard work and dreams. You want Hughes off this team?"

"More than anything," I said, quiet. Deadly.

Coach paused, and I heard him swallow. "Then you bring me some proof."

I turned on my heel, dismissing the man I was sick of seeing. I respected Coach. I always had. But today knocked him down a few levels in my eyes.

I would never see him the same.

Jamie was still inside the room, and as I stepped out, I heard him ask, "Were you really gonna give Ryan the boot like that?"

I stopped walking, not turning back but listening.

"No. But the second I give in to him, I'd lose the entire team, and my position as head coach would be nothing but a title."

My mouth kicked up a little as I headed out into the locker room. It didn't make what he did any better, but it was at least nice to know he realized I had a lot of power with the team.

And if he didn't watch himself, I might just snatch it all out from under him.

He wanted proof?

Game on.

Nineteen

Rory

Pack a bag. With a bathing suit.

I stared down at the text and sighed. Ryan Walsh was bossy as hell. He just thought I would do whatever he said when he said it.

Well, I wouldn't.

Don't have a bathing suit, I shot back.

Liar.

I gasped, making Kimberly look up from her book.

Ignoring her stare, I typed fiercely. *Can't swim, remember?*

I'll never forget.

My fingers spasmed around the phone. Ever notice how some words, even typed and not spoken, came across with a definitive vibe?

These definitely had a vibe. It was dark, brooding, and slightly dangerous.

Is everything okay at practice? I worried.

It's fine, sweetheart. Just pack a bag, okay? Never mind about the suit. I'll buy you one.

Actually, I do have one, I typed out, but then I backspaced it all, deleting it. I kinda wanted to see if he really would buy me one.

Why the heck did he even think I needed one?

Sighing, I set aside my phone and dug an oversized Louis Vuitton shoulder bag out from beneath my bed and started tossing a few things in it.

"Are you not sleeping here again tonight?" Kimberly asked.

I shrugged. "I don't know."

"So you and Ryan, huh?"

"Yeah, me and Ryan."

"He's pretty hot."

I smiled. "I know."

"Just be careful. Guys like that, they aren't exactly known for their relationship longevity."

"What's that supposed to mean?" I asked, abandoning the bag to stare at my roommate.

She shrugged one shoulder. "Nothing. I just mean you know he has the reputation of a player."

I went back to packing. It wasn't the guys with playboy reputations that scared me anymore. It was the ones who would do whatever it took to make sure their reputation was spotless.

A short while later, Ryan texted again. *I'm on my way. I'll text when I'm downstairs.*

I didn't bother to wait, instead snatching my bag and cell to head outside. I was anxious to know what happened at practice. I worried he and Jonas would fight. I worried about what his coach said when he told him.

Most of all? I worried things weren't going to go the way he thought they would. Ryan was so sure, so absolute his coach would bounce Jonas right out the door, but I knew better. Really, this whole thing just reeked of the injustice women lived with daily. Men didn't get it; they never truly would. Take Ryan, for example. He'd probably never been doubted, pushed aside, or scrutinized. He was gorgeous, talented, and rich. And he was a man. When he spoke, people listened. People respected him instantly.

I could also say I was talented (with a camera), and my family was also well off. I wouldn't go as far as to say I'm gorgeous, but I wasn't unfortunate-looking. So basically, I had a lot of the same qualities as Ry, right? Except I was a girl. I couldn't quite understand why females were automatically less, why we had to work harder to get a modicum of respect, and why our word wasn't as good as a man's.

It was beyond devaluing, unfair, degrading, and, frankly, stupid.

Knowing it, *feeling* it, didn't change things, though. It didn't change that the dean believed Jonas over me.

There was a pit of dread, a hard, heavy knot sitting like a rock in my stomach because I was very afraid Ryan would get even a small taste of what it was like today. I didn't want that for him. For anyone.

Outside, the sun was high in the bright-blue sky, but the late-September air was chilly. My hair, which was behaving itself thanks to Ry's fancy shampoo, ruffled around in the air, brushing against my cheek. After getting back to my room this morning, I put on some light makeup and changed into a pair of boyfriend jeans, a long-sleeved white crop top, and added my favorite Golden Goose Superstar sneakers.

As the wind blew, the leaves in the trees rubbed together, creating a soothing sound that I rotated toward automatically. The treetops, which once were all vivid green, were now transforming into burnished shades of yellow, orange, and red. A particularly strong gust cut through, shaking a few leaves free to float slowly toward the lawn.

Veering off the sidewalk, my sneakers sank into the grass as I walked toward the tree. It was still fairly early and a Saturday, so not many people were out, leaving everything quiet and calm versus the usual chaos.

Westbrook really was a beautiful campus. A lot different from the city life I grew up in. Not that Chicago wasn't great. It was, and I missed it sometimes. But the slower pace here, older buildings on the sprawling campus, and stillness in the air that a city never quite achieved was nice.

Plus, it was good for photos.

Ooh, photos! Since campus was empty and the trees were glittering under the sun, I reached for the camera I'd packed in my bag. It wasn't as good as the one Jonas ruined, but it was better than nothing.

A replacement for my Canon would be here in a few days, but until then, my backup would do. Explaining to my parents why I needed a new three-thousand-dollar camera was not easy. In fact, I almost just told them everything that was going on. But truthfully, I was embarrassed.

I was the offspring of two powerhouse attorneys revered in not just Chicago but in legal circles around the country, two people who were entirely convincing and stellar at defense. Then there was me, the daughter who couldn't even get the dean to believe she was attacked.

Rationally, I understood my parents would never blame me, if anything, they would fly down here and cause a big scene. I didn't want that either, at least not yet. I wanted to at least try and handle this myself before calling in Coin & Coin.

Not able to find the camera at first, I slipped the bag off my shoulder to let it fall open so I could search around. Hair fell around my face in a curtain as I dug through the stuff, finally catching a glimpse of the strap.

"Ah," I said, shoving over some clothes to reach for it.

Just as my hand closed around it, something shot out and closed around my arm.

I gasped, jolting back so hard the strap of my bag slid off my arm. "My camera!" I worried, shooting forward, but I was already out of sorts and caught off guard, so I ended up just plummeting toward the ground with the rest of my stuff.

Oomph. The breath whooshed out of me when something hard slid around my waist, and my bag rattled when it, too, was caught.

Tossing my hair out of my face, I glanced up, eyes colliding with a familiar, broad chest.

"What in the hell do you think you're doing?" Ryan growled, eyes narrowed on my face.

Lungs shuddering, I took a moment to catch my breath, trying to scramble up onto my own feet. All that did was make me trip more.

Cursing lightly, Ryan lifted. The gentle way he placed me on my feet was such a contrast to his stormy features.

"I told you I'd text when I got here," he said, eyes sweeping me over from head to toe.

"And I was just waiting outside for you," I said, reaching for my bag.

He pulled it back, slinging it over his shoulder.

"My camera's in there," I told him

"Your camera is fine."

I squinted at him, then put my hands on my hips to glare. "Why are you so grumpy?"

"Because my girl was standing out here alone in the wide open, not paying attention to her surroundings at all."

That was my first inkling that things did not go well at practice.

Hands dropping away from my hips, I said, "I'm right in front of the dorm, Ry."

"Yeah? And where were you the night Jonas put his hands all over you?"

I winced. "Ryan."

He blew out a breath, the fierce vibe around him ebbing just enough to take away his dangerous edge. Not that I was afraid of him. I wasn't.

"*Shit*," he muttered, placing my bag down in the grass and reaching for me.

I evaded the touch, and surprise flickered in his eyes.

"It didn't go too well, huh?"

The skin around his eyes tightened. Frustrated, he raked his hand through his dark hair, making it look windblown and wild. "Come here," he summoned, holding out his hand.

I moved forward, and he dropped at the base of the tree I'd been admiring, leaning against the rough bark. I stepped over his legs, lowering into his lap.

"Hi," I said softly the second I was settled and we were chest to chest.

His eyes roamed my face almost like he was drawing a map of my features inside his mind. Reaching up, he caught the ends of my hair, rubbing them between his fingertips. "You know I won't ever hurt you, right?"

I nodded once. "I know."

He groaned as his back left the tree and he caught my face between his palms to kiss me. His mouth was soft and slow, an apology words could never duplicate. Our mouths brushed tenderly, my head starting to buzz. Nudging back ever so slightly, he licked over my mouth, the whole surface of his tongue dragging across both my lips before he leaned up to kiss the tip of my nose.

My throat was thick when he leaned back, pulling me along with him, guiding my face into his neck.

"You smell like chlorine," I murmured, wiggling closer. I was beginning to really like the scent.

"I'm sorry." His voice was heavy. "I'm sorry I was an ass, and I'm sorry I made it seem like I expected you to hide yourself away until I came here to protect you. It's not fair, and—"

I made a sound, trying to sit up.

He pushed me back down, wrapping both arms around me tight. "Listen. Please."

I nodded against his throat, relaxing into his body and sliding my hand beneath his team hoodie.

"You shouldn't have to worry about shit like this. About taking a walk in the grass, being alone outside in broad daylight. Hell, at any hour. I shouldn't have to worry, but I do. Fuck, I do."

The emotion he felt with those words vibrated his throat as he spoke, the low tenor of his voice ruffling my hair like the wind in the trees. With every movement of his lips, his chin nudged the top of my head, creating a unique cadence. All those things cast a spell on me. In this moment, I wasn't just wrapped up by him physically but in everything else he was too.

"What happened at practice, Ry?"

Cupping the back of my head, he stroked my hair, letting out a long sigh. "I failed you."

Surprise forced me back, my stare bouncing between his eyes. "You could never."

He laughed, a humorless sound. "Coach refused to kick him off the team. Said if he did, Hughes could sue."

I knew it would be this way, I wasn't even surprised. But it still hurt. Especially to see Ryan blaming himself.

"Coach said since the dean already cleared him, no charges have been filed, and the cops believed his pathetic-as-hell alibi for last night, there was no cause for dismissal."

I made a knowing sound.

"You were right, sweetheart. Everyone believes him. It's your word against his, and it seems campus policy favors the predator while silencing the victim."

"Not everyone," I said, offering him a shy smile. "You don't."

"What I think apparently doesn't matter."

"It does to me."

Pushing off the tree, he claimed my lips again, this time more ravenous than before. I tasted his frustration and anger but also his desire.

When he pulled back, his expression was clearer. Some of that sparkle I'd grown so used to seeing was back. "Actually, not everyone believes him." The sparkle morphed into full-blown amusement and pride.

I arched a brow, smiling. "Oh yeah?"

"When I refused to swim, more than half the guys refused with me."

I gasped, smile disappearing. "Ryan!" I scrambled up off his lap. "Ryan, that is not funny."

"I'm not joking."

"Which makes it even worse." I fumed. "You threatened to not swim?"

"Well, technically, he threatened to throw me off the team."

I groaned, horrible guilt overtaking me. I grabbed my bag, holding it in front of me like a shield. "I really like you, Ryan." *Actually, I think I love you.* "But we can't do this. I won't get between you and swimming. I see how you are when you swim. It's everything to you. My battles should not affect your life."

I started off, but he caught me around the waist, swinging me up off my feet, which continued to try and run even off the ground.

His expansive chest molded against my back, arms locked around me like a vise. I wanted so badly to melt into him, to have his voice rumble in my ear. To shout that I didn't just like him. That I maybe loved him.

Instead, all I said was, "Go home, Ryan."

"What if home is you?"

Napalm-level silence bathed my body. My mind. I stopped struggling. I stopped running in the air. I stopped everything, wilting right there and surrendering every ounce of my weight to him.

A low sob vibrated my throat. "It's not."

"It could be, and you know it."

I did. I knew it could be.

"It doesn't matter," I whispered.

He spun me in his hold, grasping my waist and holding me out in front of him. Frankly, it was quite annoying that I was so much smaller he could just manhandle me this way.

I gave him an evil look, telling him exactly that.

He brought me in to kiss my forehead.

I whispered again, "You don't fight fair."

"No, I don't. I won't ever when it comes to you."

"I don't want this."

His body changed, limbs stiffening even as calmness washed over him that made my stomach twist. Slowly, he put me on my feet but wisely chose to keep a light hand on my arm, preventing me from bolting.

"You don't want what?" he pressed, voice low.

I turned my face away.

"Me?" he questioned.

My lower lip wobbled.

He stepped so close our shoes bumped together. My skin tingled, heart pounding heavily when his body brushed against mine. "You tell me right now, Rory. Tell me you don't want me. My touch. My presence." Leaning in, he whispered, "My mouth on your skin."

I shivered.

"Tell me just once it's me you don't want, and I'll go."

I opened my mouth to tell him exactly that. I felt his body tense in anticipation. *Like he has to prepare himself for the words.*

For the first time in my entire life, I had a very difficult time making a decision I would regret. Because I knew saying those words to Ryan right now would be the biggest regret of my life.

My shoulders slumped, and he wrapped his arms around me. One of my hands curled around his arm, fisting in his hoodie, clinging as though he might disappear. As though I hadn't just tried to send him away.

"I'm not off the team. Coach was just bluffing. He said it himself. I have way more friends than Hughes, and just because Coach can't toss his ass out doesn't mean he doesn't want to."

"What do you mean?" I asked, still clinging to him, pressing closer against the rapid pounding of his heart.

"He told me if I wanted him off the team that bad, to get some proof."

"I've been trying to!" I exclaimed, twisting in his arms to stare at him.

"I know, baby."

I took a step back, and his body followed, both palms curling beneath my elbows.

"You know, I keep thinking maybe I should just let it go. Maybe once Jonas realizes I won't cause trouble, he won't either. Maybe things will go back to normal."

"You want me to just let him get away with what he did to you?" His voice was deadly.

"What if that's what I want?"

He considered my words. "Is it really what you want, though?"

"I just keep thinking about next time. What if she doesn't get away? What if campus security isn't around to give her a ride? What about that girl?"

I didn't even realize I was crying until Ryan brushed the tears off my cheeks.

"Come here," he cajoled, pulling me against him.

"And now you're involved. It was one thing when it was just me he was threatening, but now he's pissed at you too."

"I can handle it."

"I don't want this."

The hand gliding up and down my back dipped into my hair, curling around the base of my neck in a light yet oddly possessive hold. "But you do want *me*?"

"So much," I confessed.

"Good girl."

I made an exasperated sound at his praise. But deep down, I secretly loved it.

"This entire situation sucks donkey balls," he declared, making me giggle and his amusement blossom out around me. But when he spoke again, his words were solemn. "You didn't ask for this any more than I did. But I am asking for you. For everything you got, including this. I never really asked you to make it official. I just kind of declared you were mine."

"You really have no manners," I told him.

He poked me in the ribs, making me squirm. "So I'll ask now. You know, make it official."

"I thought we already were official," I mused.

"Officially official."

"Right."

Peeling away, he put some distance between us, the sincerity in his cobalt stare almost robbing me of breath.

"Aurora Coin who goes by Rory but hates it when I call her that, so I call her Carrot, which she says she also hates but she secretly loves."

I rolled my eyes. *Why is he so charming?*

"Who is also really good with a camera, grew up in Chicago, acts like a rottweiler even though she's a chihuahua, uses all my shampoo, and insults my Jeep and my clothes."

"Are you trying to ask me out or make a bullet point presentation?" I wondered.

He mock-gasped, pressing a hand to his chest. "I'm being romantic."

"Some of these things sound like insults," I pointed out.

He chuckled, and damn, if it didn't make my stomach flutter.

Shuffling forward, he reached for my hand, entwining our fingers. "But they're not. They're just some of the reasons I want you. You and only you. Be my girlfriend. My only."

My heart was screaming yes, but my head couldn't stop worrying. "What about Jonas?"

"I said my only. Ain't no room in this relationship for him."

I half smiled, and he untangled our hands to slide the Elite hoodie down his arms to immediately swing it around my back, enveloping me in his body heat and signature chlorine scent.

"We'll deal with him, okay? Together."

"You won't quit the team, right?"

"I won't quit the team."

"Okay."

"Okay, what?"

"Okay, I'll be your girlfriend."

He let out a quick whoop and swung me around in a circle. "I was actually starting to worry."

I laughed. "But we were already dating."

He smirked. "Jamie did say you were high-maintenance."

"Ryan …" I faltered. "What's your middle name?"

"Steven."

"Ryan Steven Walsh." I plowed on. "I am *not* high-maintenance."

"What if I am?"

I made a rude noise. "I'll just give you a blowjob." That'd fix him up real quick.

"Right now?" He wagged his brows, glancing around while reaching for his pants.

I slapped his hand away.

He grinned, yanking me into his arms. "For real, though, Carrot. I can't promise I won't be bossy and overprotective while he's running around this campus. I know it's sexist and shit, but I don't want you walking around alone. I don't want you sleeping with see-through curtains, and I'm probably going to punch out Hughes every chance I get."

It was all fun and games until someone brought up punching. "No! No punching."

He smirked. "Already did."

"Ryan Steven Walsh!"

He laughed.

Fine. I admit me using all his names still wasn't as scary as him just using my actual name.

I rose to my tallest height. "No punching."

A mutinous look crossed his features.

Mine narrowed. "No blowjobs, then."

His eyes went all squinty. "You wouldn't."

I arched a brow. "Try me."

"But, *baby*," he whined.

Also, I'd like to note Ryan was the type of boyfriend who was going to be bossy and overprotective even after Jonas was no longer a problem, even if he tried to say otherwise. It was who he was as a person.

Good thing I was feisty and he was totally worth it.

But. "No punching, Ry."

He sighed heavily. "Fine."

"Jamie either."

He laughed, then laughed some more. "Good luck with that."

"Ry?"

"Carrot."

"I'm sorry about practice today. And I know you can handle it, but I wish you didn't have to."

He smiled softly. "Thanks, baby." Clearing his throat, he snatched my bag off the grass and bent down in front of me. "C'mon, I'm starving."

I climbed onto his back, a place I was becoming well acquainted with.

"Did you eat yet?" he asked, piggybacking me toward Jamie's Wrangler.

"No. I'm hungry too," I replied. Then, "Where's Jamie?"

"Back at the dorm. He went back to bed."

"Did you get your Jeep yet?"

"Had it towed to one of my dad's dealerships. He's putting new tires on it. I'll get it back later today."

"What did you tell him?" I wondered.

"That some jealous A-hole slashed my tires because I took his lane at the meet."

"Did you take Jonas's lane?"

Did swimmers really fight over lanes?

He made a rude sound. "I earned it."

"You are the best swimmer on the team." I agreed.

"Damn straight." He was smug, and it was kinda sexy. "You pack a bathing suit?"

"I told you I don't have one."

He grunted, walking toward the passenger side of the cherry-red Wrangler. "After we eat, we're going to get one."

"Why?" I asked, observing the way he carefully backed into the open door while reaching around to cover the back of my head with his hand so I didn't bump it.

I slid off his back onto the seat, and he turned, tucking my bag onto the floorboard. "Good?" he asked, tugging the seat belt around me.

My heart felt bruised under his attention, how much he cared.

"I lied," I blurted out. "I have a bathing suit."

He chuckled beneath his breath as the belt clicked into place. "I know."

I reached for the clasp. "I can go get it."

He made a sound, stopping me. "Leave it. I'll buy you one."

Any argument I might have made was silenced when his lips pressed to mine, making me forget I'd been about to speak at all.

"Ry?" I asked when he pulled out of the dorm parking lot.

"I really love it when you say my name."

I crossed one leg over the other, squeezing my thighs together. "You didn't tell me why I need a bathing suit," I pointed out after the intense wave of desire ebbed just enough.

He glanced across the seat to me before turning his eyes back to the road. "Because I'm teaching you how to swim."

Twenty

Ryan

Are you busy? I shot off the text

The reply was almost instant. *What's up?*

Meet me at the pool. Bring your suit.

The little bubble indicating he was typing appeared, then disappeared. Then appeared again. *Okay.*

"These are pretty," Carrot said, making me look up from my phone.

I made a face at the curtains she was holding. They were light-colored. "Get black."

Her expression turned to one of horror as she lowered the package in her hand. "Ew. No."

"You can't see through the black ones," I said, pulling up another text screen.

"Well, black doesn't match my room."

"Who cares?"

"Um, me? And Kimberly."

"You should be more worried about pervs not being able to gawk at you from outside."

"You're the one that was standing in front of the window naked," she muttered.

Someone nearby laughed.

I grinned, and Carrot's face turned a bright shade of pink. "You still jealous, baby?"

"Shut up," she muttered even as she ducked in front of me so I could shield her from amused, prying eyes.

I plucked a pack of black curtains off the rack. "These are good," I said, tossing them in the cart behind me. It already had a bathing suit in it. It also had some pepper spray and a whistle. Never once in my life did I ever go into a store and consider what items I should carry around for self-defense.

I never once walked around campus with fear of being followed or attacked.

She did, though. I bet all the girls on campus did. It sort of blew my mind. It also made me slightly crazy. I never really realized how disadvantaged a girl could be. Not until I met one I wanted to protect.

"C'mon," I said, grabbing the side of the cart. "Let's go get a pocketknife."

"No," she declared, plucking the black curtains out of the cart to put them back. Then she selected some white ones and tossed them in instead.

"White," I lamented. "No."

"They're blackout," she told me, pointing at the packaging. "If no light can get through, then neither can perverts' eyeballs."

I laughed. She was fucking adorable standing there in her ripped-up jeans, poring over the curtain selection like this was some competition on HGTV.

"Let me see," I said, gruff.

She held the package about an inch from my face, and I

squinted at it like I really had to make sure they were blackout.

"Fine." I relented.

"So glad I got your approval, master," she muttered, tossing them back into the cart.

My phone went off.

Bro, he in or what? Jamie asked.

Yeah. I shot back. *Meet me at the pool in twenty.*

Where u at?

Buying curtains.

A few laughing emojis came through. *Whipped.*

I sent him the middle finger emoji.

"Oooh," Carrot sang, wandering farther down the aisle. "Look at this mirror."

Look, curtains to keep Peeping Toms away from my girl's fine ass was one thing. Shopping for gold-framed mirrors? That was something else entirely.

"Ry, look," she called again. It was big and round, and all I could see was the bottom of her legs and sneakers sticking out from behind it. "Oh, it's heavy," she complained, the thing slipping out of her hold.

Stuffing my phone in my pocket, I rushed over to pull it out of her grasp. "Be careful," I told her, moving to put it back.

She tugged the sleeves of her white top down over her hands and smiled at me.

I reversed my steps and put the mirror in the cart.

She beamed. "I want to get some fairy lights to go around it," she said, already wandering off to another aisle.

"What the fuck are fairy lights?" I grabbed the cart to push it after her.

"It will be so pretty over my bed."

"You couldn't even hold that big-ass mirror for half a

minute in the aisle. How are you going to lift it over your bed?"

She peeked out around the corner of the next aisle, blinking those wide gray eyes at me. "Good thing my boyfriend has such big muscles."

I groaned. I was totally fucking whipped.

"We're getting a knife," I told her.

"But first, fairy lights."

I'd probably have to hang those too.

When we were loading all her crap into the back of the Wrangler, her arms wound around me from behind. I felt her nose press into the center of my back. "Thanks, Ry. I had fun."

Damn.

Reaching around myself, I patted her back. "C'mon," I said, gruff. "They're probably already at the pool."

"Who?"

"Your instructors."

———

"I REALLY DON'T WANT TO DO THIS," SHE SAID FOR LIKE THE twentieth time since we pulled up. The closer we got to the pool, the more nervous she grew.

Giving her hand a little squeeze, I said, "I know, sweetheart, but you need to learn at least some basic water skills. At least enough to keep yourself from drowning."

If I hadn't been there that night...

I pushed the unfinished thought away, unwilling to think about it further. I'd started to feel a bit guilty the warier she got as we approached, thinking maybe I shouldn't push this on her, but that thought alone beat back any guilt. This was literally life or death.

Stopping, I tugged her arm, pulling her around to face me. "He's still running around. He's pissed at me. Pissed at you. This pool is like a playground to him, his own personal weapon. He knows you can't swim, Carrot." *He heard me tell Coach.* "I will do anything to protect you, even if it means pushing you out of your comfort zone. Teaching you how to at least dog paddle makes his favorite weapon less of a threat."

Coming forward, she bounced up, pressing a kiss to the underside of my jaw. The sweet gesture only made me more determined to protect her.

"Okay, Ry. Teach me how to swim."

"Good girl," I murmured, pressing a kiss to the top of her head.

Behind us, the door to the pool swung open. "So, ah, what color curtains did you lovebirds get? Pink? Please tell me you got pink."

Carrot laughed. "Hi, Jamie."

"Just call me Teach today," he told her, holding open the door for her to go inside.

"You're going to help teach me how to swim?"

He swung around, holding out his arms. "With this wingspan? Bro, yeah."

Someone a little farther inside moved closer, drawing our eyes.

"Oh, hi," Carrot said, a little shy.

I moved past her, holding out my fist. "Hey, bro. Thanks for coming."

"No problem," he answered, pounding it out. He was dressed in a pair of sweatpants, but his shirt and shoes were already off. None of us even blinked an eye at our lack of clothing at the pool. It was almost odder to see each other with clothes.

"Carrot, this is Wes. Wes, my girlfriend, Rory."

"You were at the diner last night, right?" she asked.

He nodded. "Yeah. You, ah, okay?"

She smiled. "I'm good. Nice to meet you."

"Same," he said, glancing back at me. "You texted because you want me to help teach your girl how to swim?"

"She needs all the help she can get," I deadpanned.

Carrot gasped indignantly, and Wes smiled.

Swinging her big-ass bag off my shoulder, I held it out to her. "Go change in the locker room and meet us back out here."

"What if someone's in there?" She worried.

"No one is in there. I checked," Jamie promised.

"True. He did," Wes confirmed.

"What about you?" she asked me.

"I'm already wearing my suit," I answered.

She went into the locker room, leaving me with Jamie and Wes. I tossed Jamie the keys to his Wrangler and then pulled my shirt off in one go. "Thanks for letting me borrow it."

"My Jeep is your Jeep," Jamie said, taking the keys to his bag over on the bleachers.

Draping my shirt over my shoulder, I popped the button on my jeans and kicked off my shoes. "So I didn't just text because I wanted you to help us teach Rory how to swim."

"I figured," Wes replied, averting his eyes while I shucked my jeans. "So what's up?"

My pants dropped on the tiles with a slap, and I adjusted the Speedo I was wearing. Since this was just a practice, I wore my suit that looked more like boxer briefs. They were black and tight, but they stretched down my thighs. Basically, they were more comfortable than the banana hammock I usually swam in.

Jamie rejoined us as I answered. "I wanted to thank you for stepping up like you did this morning with Coach. It means a lot to me that you backed me up, being the first one to refuse to swim."

"Well, my not swimming if you didn't was obvious," Jamie muttered.

Smiling, I slapped him on the back. "Bro, sure."

"I didn't say that for bonus points with you. I did it because it's the right thing to do. Because Hughes is an asshole who needs taken down a peg or two."

Something in his voice made my attention narrow. "You having problems with Hughes?"

Wes swallowed and glanced away. He shrugged. "Not really. But I don't like him."

"Why?" I asked, blunt.

"Who cares?" he answered ambiguously. "Point is you're a way better swimmer and a better person. You've never once acted like I was your competition just because I swim freestyle too. You always give me pointers if you think I need them. You're a fair guy, and I appreciate it. The least I could do is throw in with you. Besides, I saw what Hughes did last night."

"You see him last night?" Jamie asked. "Cops didn't have anything to charge him with."

"I didn't see him," Wes said. "But you guys said it was him. That's good enough for me."

Jamie slapped him on the back and smiled. "We should hang out more."

"We see each other every day," Wes pointed out.

"Well, when we aren't swimming."

"We eat at Shirley's together." Wes went on.

"He's been hassling you," I said, cutting off their back-and-forth chatter.

Silence dropped like an anvil, the rippling water in the pool behind us the only sound in the room.

"What?" Wes finally said.

"Why?"

"Why what?"

I widened my stance, crossing my arms over my chest to pin Wes with a stare. "Why has Hughes been hassling you?"

Wes took in a deep breath and thankfully didn't bother to deny it. It was clear anyway. Not necessarily because of everything he said but because of what he didn't.

"You know how he is," Wes said. "He thinks all freestyle swimmers are guys he has to put in their place, which is beneath him."

"Maybe." I allowed. Hughes was like that. "But there's more."

Wes shook his head once. "It's my business."

"We making it ours too," Jamie quipped.

Wes was built. I mean, all swimmers were cut. But he was shorter than me and Jamie, his body type leaner. He was also a year younger than us so a little newer in the college training ranks. But he was a good swimmer, and as he pointed out before, we saw each other daily, often more. He'd always been a little quiet, but he'd never been anything but a good guy, something he proved further in the locker room this morning.

Jamie's words made his chin jut out, a stubborn glint in his dark eyes. I liked to see it. It meant that even though he might be a little reserved, he was no pushover.

"You threw your loyalty behind me this morning," I told him. "I'm throwing mine at you right now."

A look of wariness and something that looked an awful lot like fear flashed in his eyes.

"Wes," I said, my voice quiet and controlled.

"He thinks I'm gay," he rushed out.

Jamie and I exchanged a look. I glanced back at Wes. "Hughes thinks you're gay?"

Wes nodded. "Yeah, and he, ah, has made it clear how he feels about *homos*."

My hands fisted at my sides.

"So are you?" Jamie asked.

Anger flashed over Wes's face, and he crossed his arms over his chest—a clear defense mechanism. "Yeah. I am."

I shifted, and Wes straightened, eyeing me warily as if he expected me to jump him. "Look, you asked, so I answered. I never brought it up before because I keep my personal life, ah, personal. It has no effect on this team or me as a swimmer. I know—"

"Wes." I stopped him. "We don't care."

His mouth opened and closed, eyes sliding to Jamie.

Jamie shrugged. "Just means more ladies for me."

"Seriously?" Wes whispered.

"Did you think we'd be pissed off?"

"Well, yeah," he admitted. "I, ah, haven't always gotten that response, so I just stopped telling people."

Jamie made a face. "What kinda people you been hanging around?"

"No one lately." It was quiet, almost to himself. But I heard.

We all heard.

The door to the locker room pushed open, and Carrot came walking out wearing a black two-piece suit she called a tankini. I tried to convince her to get the one-piece, but it was too long for her short torso.

Shrimp.

She was carrying a towel, which she took toward the bleachers to toss down. Noticing the silence in the room, she turned, her short ponytail bouncing as she moved.

"What's going on?"

Jamie flung his arm around Wes's neck and announced. "Wes is a man lover."

Wes made a choked sound, and his cheeks turned pink.

I laughed. What? I couldn't help it.

"What?" Carrot asked, glancing at me.

I glanced at Wes for the okay. He rolled his eyes. "Why you asking now? He already blurted it out."

I shrugged. "He's gay."

"Oh. Okay," Carrot said, completely underwhelmed.

"That's it?" Wes wondered.

"Did you want me to set you up on a date?" Carrot asked.

"No." His response was fast and definitive.

"Well then, yeah, that's it." She shrugged. "Unless you can somehow get me out of this." She gestured to the pool.

"No," I declared even as I was checking her out.

"Let's do this shit!" Jamie hollered, taking a flying leap into the pool. His splash was so big it hit Rory where she stood.

"He's a giant five-year-old," she declared.

Wes's lips twitched.

I went to her side, taking her hand. "C'mon, then, Carrot, into the pool."

"Where's the shallow end?" she asked.

We all laughed.

"What?"

"There's no shallow end, camera girl," Jamie quipped.

"But all pools have a shallow end."

"Don't you think if there was a shallow end, I would have dragged you to it the night you almost drowned?" I pointed out.

"Oh." She frowned, clearly just thinking of this.

Wes stepped forward. "This pool is eight feet deep from end to end," he told her. "Having it all the same depth reduces the amount of wake a swimmer can get caught up in."

"Wake," she murmured.

"The waves," I clarified. "Shallow water tends to have more waves. It slows us down."

"Oh."

"And the diving well"—Wes pointed to the other side of

the pool complex where a large square "pool" was located with several platform diving levels at different heights at the side—"is sixteen feet."

Carrot's ponytail bobbed. "So no shallow end."

"You don't need a shallow end. I've got you."

She seemed doubtful.

Leaving her side, I went to the equipment storage near the locker room, opening the door to rummage around.

"Ah!" I called, finally finding what I needed. Coming back out, I held up the yellow floaties.

Jamie and Wes started to laugh.

"No," she deadpanned.

"But these will help you learn," I told her, giving in and just full-blown grinning.

"Five-year-olds wear water wings, Ryan. Not grown adults."

"I hate to yell you, but you ain't grown. I think something stunted your growth," Jamie said as he treaded water.

Carrot turned to where he swam to smile sweetly. "I spilled coffee all over your Jeep."

He gasped. "How could you do it to me, bro?"

"C'mon," I said, ignoring their bickering to tuck the water wings beneath my arms and usher her toward the side of the pool. "You need to get your arms wet so they'll slide on."

I tossed the little triangular-shaped, air-filled "wings" to Jamie so he could get them wet all over. They basically would slide over her arms and keep her afloat in the water while I taught her how to paddle and kick.

"You can't be serious."

I turned from the edge of the pool, pinning her with a level stare. "I'm serious that I don't ever want to see you almost drown again."

She bit her lower lip.

"This will keep my arms from getting overtired. We're gonna practice later."

"We are?" Wes said, surprised.

"Hells yes, we are," I told him. "Hughes is on his way out whether he wants to admit it or not. And you're freestyle just like me. That means I need someone to keep up with me if we want to keep winning meets."

"I'm not as fast as Hughes." Wes worried.

"Not yet, but you're good. Once you lock down your technique a bit more and we start practicing together, it's only a matter of time."

"You would help me?" He seemed surprised.

"Don't I already?"

"Well, yeah, but this is different."

"Because I know you're gay or because I'm offering one-on-one swim time?"

"What about me?" Jamie hollered.

I rolled my eyes.

"Both," Wes admitted.

"I'm already here in the pool doing the work. Helping you will only make the team better," I explained. "And I don't care if you're gay, bro. Hell, you can even check out my ass if you want."

Carrot gasped. "You cannot!"

"There you go being jealous again." I tsked, privately amused.

"What about my ass?" Jamie asked, tossing the wet water wings onto the side. "It's pretty hot, right?"

"I don't check out your asses," Wes mused.

"Bummer. I always wondered if dudes thought I was just as hot as the ladies."

"So you in?" I asked Wes.

He thought for a moment. "Yeah. Yeah, I'm in."

I nodded and reached for my girl. "C'mon, put your floaties on, baby."

Sighing, she came over and stuck her arm out for me to slide the first one on.

And just like that, the lesson began.

Twenty-One

Rory

Stupid water wings.

I didn't know what was worse: the fact my arms fit in them or that I actually wore them.

But as I sat on the bleachers, wrapped up in a towel, and watched Ry, Jamie, and Wes practice, I didn't feel that bad about relenting and putting the stupid floaties on. These guys went hard in the water, and Ry really would be extra worn out from trying to hold us both up in deep water. Actually, all three of them would be exhausted.

I thought it was ridiculous to try and teach someone to swim in water that was eight feet deep. But they made it work. After it seemed like I got the hang of paddling, I spent some time paddling between the three of them. When I started to sink, they would be there to pull me up and remind me what to do.

I thought maybe at first—okay, I hoped—it would be kinda fun and playful.

It wasn't.

Well, Jamie was his usual moronic self, and Wes was sweet, but Ryan was like some kind of wet ogre with one setting: serious. Only when I made it between them without slipping under would his eyes soften, and he'd look at me filled with pride that would make me want to do even better next time.

Watching him now, I was pretty certain it was just his swim mode. He was serious as they practiced too, very focused and almost relentless.

Jamie hauled himself up, water raining off his body, sliding over the edge and back into the pool as he stood. Feet slapping over the tile, he came toward the bleachers, parking himself right in front of me, his broad shoulders blocking my view of Ryan.

"Wh—agh!" The question immediately dissolved into a screech when he shook his big body and head around like a soaking-wet dog. Water droplets flung everywhere, including on me, smacking me in the face and arms.

"Jamie!" I hollered, holding out my arms like I could shield myself as he shook. "Your towel is right there," I said, pointing to where it lay nearby.

"Where's the fun in that?" he quipped, delivering me an evil smile. I rolled my eyes and watched as he ignored his towel again to swipe up a bottle of water for a drink. He frowned, the empty plastic crinkling in his hand.

Tossing it aside, he reached for Ryan's bottle, which was also empty.

"He's such a hog," Jamie muttered, throwing that bottle down too.

"Yes, how rude of Ryan to drink his own water," I mused.

"That's what I'm saying." Jamie agreed, picking up his towel to rub it over his head.

The air in here wasn't that balmy or humid like most

indoor pools. I knew it was because the temperature of the pool was cool. My body was still trying to warm up.

"Is there a vending machine around here? I'll go get you guys some more," I offered, pushing to my feet.

"A vending machine." He scoffed. "We're Elite. There's a stocked fridge in the locker room."

I tugged the damp towel around me a little farther. "Heaven forbid you rich athletes have to"—I gasped dramatically—"*pay* for your own water."

"Hey, we pay for that water with blood, sweat, and tears in that pool." He hitched a thumb over his shoulder.

"You guys definitely work hard." I agreed. "You swim the butterfly stroke, right?"

"Yep."

"I was watching you practice. It looks really pretty. Like an actual butterfly."

"*Pretty?*" he lamented. His towel dropped onto the tile by his feet. "The butterfly stroke is intimidating. And it's arguably the most difficult stroke there is, requiring more muscles firing at the same time." To drive his point home, he flexed his arm, which also rippled his impressive shoulder.

Look, I was borderline in love with Ry and honestly wanted no one else… but I wasn't blind. Jamie was hot.

However, his words did explain why his upper body seemed even more built than many of the other swimmers. "Well, you must be very good to do all that *and* make it look pretty."

He pursed his lips. "You know, I like you, camera girl."

I couldn't help it. I smiled. "I have a name."

"You always yell at Ryan when he uses it."

"You aren't Ryan," I pointed out.

"It's camera girl or bro," he deadpanned.

Oh, how nice of him to give me a choice. "I'll go get you some water."

"Don't mind if you do," he said, dropping onto the first row of seats and digging into his bag for a protein bar.

I watched, astonished, as he shoved the entire thing in his mouth. Noticing me gawking, he grinned, showing me all the food trapped in his teeth. "Super thirsty," he reminded me.

"This is why you're single," I told him, turning toward the locker room. He thought I was high-maintenance? Geez, any girl willing to deal with him should get a medal.

"Get Gatorade," he hollered after me. "It masks the chlorine flavor in my mouth."

I wrinkled my nose. *Gross.*

In the locker room, I grabbed three Gatorades, all of them a different color so they would know which was whose (but it seemed Jamie would drink anyone's) and carried them back out to the pool.

Ryan was standing at the edge, and Wes was in the water below him, hanging on the side.

"Silent swim. Really focus and try to make as little sound in the water as you move. It will help refine your stroke," Ry said, looking down. I couldn't keep my eyes off his strong back and body. The tight shorts he wore molded to his butt and showed off his toned legs.

His damp skin glistened under the overhead lights, and as I walked, the towel around me slipped, making me stumble.

"Put your eyes back in your head before you fall over," Jamie said, appearing in front of me.

After making sure I wasn't going to faceplant, he plucked a red sports drink out of my arms, uncapped it, and drained half in one big gulp.

"You aren't doing it?" Wes asked Ryan.

"Sure, I'll do it too." He slid back into the water, tugging the goggles down over his eyes. "Come on," he shouted, and the two glided off.

I watched them, noting how quiet and controlled their

movements were, watching the water barely ripple under their movements.

Jamie reached around me, trying to snatch another drink out of my hold.

"No," I scolded, twisting away. "That one is for Ryan."

He glanced at the other one.

"Wes," I said.

"Savage," Jamie accused.

Ignoring him, I went over to the side of the pool where the two guys were finally pulling themselves out, both of them grateful when I handed over their drinks.

"Thanks, baby," Ry said, leaning in to kiss me as water dripped off him and onto me.

"I'm spent," Wes said, lowering the drink from his lips.

"You're good." Ryan complimented him. "Just remember to keep your core solid."

Wes glanced down at his abs, which were tight and defined. "Looks solid to me."

Ryan reached out, slapping him in the middle to jiggle the literally nonexistent fat. "Maybe you should hit the gym with me and Jamie," he cracked.

Wes knocked his hand off. "These are abs of steel."

"Your core slips sometimes," Ryan argued.

Wes frowned, looking back at his middle.

Ry grabbed his waist, pressing in like he was trying to make it more compact. "You gott—"

"What the fuck is going on here?"

The deep, quiet voice resonated through the large pool facility, making everyone look. He was standing in the doorway, not even completely inside yet. As we stared, he kept moving, not rushing at all but moving with the laziness of a predator sure in his ability to catch his prey.

He had dark, shaggy hair, a five-o'clock shadow outlining a square jaw, and a silver piercing in his eyebrow, glinting from the lights above. His eyes were so dark and stoic they matched the black leather jacket stretched over his shoulders.

"Who the hell are you?" Jamie spoke up first.

The broody stranger's boots echoed over the tile as he came forward, eyes bouncing between Ryan and Wes. When he got close, Ryan sidestepped so his body was angled in front of mine like he thought he needed to protect me.

"Max." Wes began, but his words faltered the second the stranger's hand wrapped around his wrist, tugging him away from us.

The blockade Ryan tried to make out of himself could not deter my curiosity, so I leaned around him to stare. Wes wasn't small, but he seemed to be standing almost naked next to the fully dressed, leather-wearing stranger.

"What are you doing here?" Wes asked plaintively. It was incredibly amusing because it seemed he was trying to glare at the stranger but also avoid looking at him.

"Who are you?" he asked, staring straight at Ryan.

"Ah, I get it," Jamie quipped, stepping up beside Ryan. His voice was relaxed, but the muscles in his back rippled a bit. It drew my eye to the butterfly tattooed on his shoulder. "You don't want to check out my and Ryan's asses because you have a boyfriend."

Max jolted and whipped his eyes to Wes. "You're checking out their asses?"

Max looked like he wanted to jump into the pool and sink to the bottom.

Jerking his wrist out of Max's hold, he was quick to deny. "He's not my boyfriend. This is Max, my brother's best friend."

Max was still watching Ryan like he was trying to read him.

Pushing forward, I cleared my throat. Someone had to

help Wes. Poor guy. "Hi, I'm Rory. This is Ryan. My boyfriend."

Max's eyes slid to me. "Boyfriend?"

I nodded. "And this is Jamie. He's our annoying friend."

"Rude," Jamie replied.

Max finally glanced away from the other guys to Wes whose cheeks were flaming. "You haven't been answering your phone."

Wes made a face. "I was practicing." He gestured to the pool.

Max gestured to Ryan and Jamie. "Swim team?"

Wes nodded.

"Call your brother," Max practically barked. "He's worried."

Wes turned from embarrassed to annoyed. "I talked to him this morning."

Max shrugged like he didn't care.

"Your brother is in the sports medicine program, right?" Ryan asked.

Wes nodded. "Yeah. He graduates next year."

Ryan nodded. "So if your brother was so worried, why didn't he just come over here?"

Max's eyes swung back to him, his dark gaze narrowing.

"He's doing a semester abroad," Wes replied. Then to himself, he muttered, "Thought I'd finally get some freaking room to breathe, but no, he assigns me a babysitter."

Glancing over at Max, I noticed his lips twitching with amusement, but then he hid it away to say, "Should have answered your phone."

"Well, you can see I'm fine," Wes retorted. "You can leave now."

"Get dressed. I'll drive you home."

"I have my car."

"I'll walk you out."

Wes made a face. "I can walk myself to my car, Max."

"It's dark out."

Wes faltered for just a fraction, then sniffed. "So?"

The undercurrents swirling around were actually quite intriguing, but I also felt kinda bad for standing here gaping at their little spat. Reaching up, I nudged Ry, and his eyes fired to mine immediately. I glanced at Wes subtly, telling him to do something.

Ryan gave me a mild WTF look but then turned toward them.

"You don't have to hang around, bro. We'll all walk out together. We won't leave Wes alone," Ryan offered.

Max rotated away from Wes to fold his arms over his chest. His gaze was heavy, and it made me squirm a little. I have no idea how Ryan stood there under the full weight of it so unbothered. "I'm not your bro. And I don't know you, so I'll stay."

"Intense," Jamie announced. "I'm going to go change. If I stand around in this wet suit any longer, my boys are gonna look like raisins."

"I did not need to know that," I declared. But also, *Does that really happen?*

Jamie grabbed up his bag and looked at me. "Better tell your boy to change, or you're gonna be stuck with raisins too."

Ryan scowled. "Stop talking to my girl about balls."

"Bros talk to bros about balls," Jamie informed him.

I couldn't help it. I giggled.

"You coming?" Jamie asked when Ry didn't follow him.

"I'll wait with Carrot." He glanced at Wes. "You can go change first."

Interesting. For two reasons:

1. Ryan didn't want to leave me out here alone.

and

2. He also totally picked up on the fact Max was intensely jealous when he walked in here.

I didn't bother to point it out either. Both points would be denied by all parties.

Men hated to admit anything.

Wes slid a glance out of the corner of his eye at Max, then went to change. When both he and Jamie were gone, we all settled into an awkward silence.

After a moment, Ryan turned to Max and held out his hand. "Ryan Walsh. I swim freestyle with Wes. I asked him to spend some extra time practicing with me. And probably Jamie too."

Max made no move to shake Ryan's offered hand. "Why?"

"Because I think he's good. He just needs some confidence. And because I fucking hate Hughes and want to stick it to him."

Max glowered. "Wes is not some kind of weapon for you to use to piss people off." Then he tilted his head. "Hughes," he repeated thoughtfully. "He's on the team too, right?"

"Yep, but he's on his way out. Wes kinda implied he's been giving him a hard time."

Max stiffened. "He told you that?"

"Pretty much."

"What else did he tell you?"

"That he's gay," Ryan deadpanned.

Max looked at me but spoke to Ryan. "But you aren't."

"Nope. I'm taken." Ryan glanced at me and winked.

"What about him?" Max gestured toward the locker room.

"Jamie likes women," Ryan replied.

"And you don't care Wes doesn't?"

"Why would we care?"

"Some people are assholes."

Ryan nodded. "True."

"We don't care about Wes's preference." I spoke up. "He's our friend. He helped teach me how to swim."

Amusement flashed over Max's expression. It softened his whole face. "You're dating a swimmer but can't swim?"

"I can now," I said proudly.

"Barely," Ry muttered.

I gasped, swinging to face him. "But you said I did a good job."

His hand was warm when it settled over my hip, his body heat seeping through the damp towel around me. "You did, baby. But you need more practice."

"More?" I complained. "I thought this was a one-time torture."

Ryan laughed.

"I guess Wes could use some friends," Max said, reminding me he was there.

Leaving his palm against my hip, he turned. "He likes to keep to himself."

"Because most people are assholes." Max reminded him. Then he nodded once as though he decided. "All right. You can hang around with Wes."

"Thanks for the approval I didn't need," Ryan muttered.

"If that Hughes asshole even looks at him sideways, let me know."

Ryan's voice went tight. "I can handle Hughes."

"I want to know." Max was firm.

"Sure, Max."

Max made a face. "It's Maxen."

"Wes calls you Max," Ryan pointed out.

"Wes is my friend. You aren't."

Wes and Jamie came out of the locker room, both fully

dressed, carrying their duffels over their shoulders. Wes was laughing at something Jamie said.

"C'mon," *Maxen* said, already starting for the door.

Wes glowered but trailed after him. "Thanks for the pointers, Ryan. I'll see you guys tomorrow."

I waved. "Thanks for helping me!" I called.

When they were gone, Jamie looked at Ryan. "What crawled up that dude's ass and died?"

"Probably more than one thing," Ryan replied.

They laughed.

Rolling my eyes, I grabbed my bag. "I'm going to change."

"No." Ryan stopped me. "Back in the pool."

My mouth fell open. "What?"

"I want you to swim another lap. I want to make sure you retained everything you just learned."

"I did," I told him. "For sure, I did."

He wasn't convinced and pointed at the pool.

"Now see here, Ryan Steven Walsh." I put my hands on my hips.

"Ah shit, you told her your middle name? Bro. It's all downhill from here." Jamie shook his head sadly.

"Shut up, Jamie," we both said at once.

He held up his hands. "Your Jeep is at the curb," he told Ryan, reaching into his pocket for his keys. "That means I'm out."

Ryan nodded.

"See ya, camera girl."

"Bye, Jamie. Thank you!" I said before turning back to glare at my boyfriend. "You're acting like an ogre," I told him when Jamie was gone and we were alone.

He advanced on me. My heart fluttered. "If an ogre is a man who is serious about doing everything he can to make sure his girl can protect herself, then sure, I'm an ogre."

The towel around me hit the tile with one tug from his hand. Chills raced over my skin.

The second my feet lifted off the floor, my legs wound around his waist automatically. Palming my ass, he walked toward the pool. His fingers slipped under the edges of my bathing suit to caress my butt.

Leaning into him, my chin rested on his shoulder as my fingers dragged over his naked back.

"Just one lap, okay? Swim to the first rope and back," he cajoled.

I sighed. "Fine."

"Good girl," he whispered against my ear, making my thighs flex around him.

He slid into the pool first, then held my hand as I lowered in after him, instantly shivering in the cold water. We both clung to the edge with one hand, his free arm looping around my waist to pull me flush against his body.

"I'm right here, okay? If you start to slip under, I'll be right there."

"I know. I'm not afraid because you're here."

Awe dawned in his stare. I watched it bloom deep in his expression like a rare flower opening in the sun. "You trust me." It wasn't a question, just him stating a fact as if he'd just learned it. As if he were finally realizing just how much of me he owned.

"Completely," I whispered.

A low growl vibrated his throat, the arm around my waist tightening until my breasts flattened against his hard chest. Slowly, his face lowered to mine, the air between us electrifying with every centimeter he crossed. The water no longer felt frigid, the heat between us literally warming everything we touched.

His lips brushed mine in the faintest caress. When they

didn't settle completely, the breath I'd been holding shuddered out.

When he spoke, the words were sweet torture, drawing me forward but managing to hold me just enough at bay. "Go swim your lap, Carrot. Then come back here so I can kiss you."

For the first time in my entire life, I wanted to swim.

Twenty-Two

Ryan

She was a quick study, picking up the basics and keeping afloat in just a few hours.

But it wasn't enough.

The opaque curtains, extra Mace, whistle, and even the pocketknife (hell yes, I bought her one), plus the learning how not to drown still wasn't enough.

Jesus, was this what love was like? Fast, hard, and entirely consuming? Did it turn every man inside out and make them near paranoid and rabid about protecting what was his?

Did all guys go out and buy their girlfriends weapons to protect themselves? Was this normal?

No. Yes. I wasn't sure.

What wasn't normal was freaking Jonas Hughes acting like he was above the rules because he was Elite. I guess rotten apples existed in every bunch—even the most exclusive.

Whatever. Wondering about it wouldn't change shit. I

was determined to do everything to get him the hell off this campus and far away from my girl.

"I made it." She panted, water rippling as she draped her upper body over the lane rope.

The very ends of her ponytail were wet, the orangey color of her hair darker there. Her back was narrow, her shoulders slim. I wasn't sure I'd ever get used to how small she was. The rope barely sank under the effort to hold her up. It made my stomach clench a bit because her size was just a visible reminder of her vulnerability.

But when she glanced over her shoulder, catlike eyes seeking me, everything inside me softened.

"Were you watching?" She scowled, somehow knowing I was distracted.

"As if I would look anywhere else."

Her lips curled in, and she turned back, hiding the expression of pleasure I knew she felt. Sometimes she was so feisty, but others, she turned shy.

"You aren't supposed to take a break," I reminded her, keeping my voice stern. "When you are drowning, there won't be a lane rope to hold you up."

"Last time there was."

The fact she even had an example of the last time she almost drowned was infuriating to me. "Let go of the rope. Swim back here."

Her shoulders stiffened with the bite of my tone, but she dropped into the water.

A moment of panic seized me when she slipped under a bit, the water covering her nose. But then her body remembered what I taught it, and her head came back up.

My heart thudded heavily against my ribcage as she paddled close, her eyes stuck on me like I was the finish line and the reason she stayed afloat.

If he touches her again, I'll kill him. I couldn't even classify it as a thought, so intense it was more of a vow, of writing something in blood without even opening a vein.

Her breath was puffing in and out, her chin straining to keep her head out of the water, and her lips pressed tight to keep the chlorinated liquid out of her mouth.

Waves broke against my chest, but I didn't notice. All I saw was the sun living behind the storm clouds in her eyes breaking free as she closed the distance between us. Her hand made a plopping sound when she reached out to me, but then she brought it down so she could keep paddling.

Smiling, I grabbed her wrist, towing her into my space. Like a little octopus, she wound herself around my waist and climbed up my chest.

"I did it."

"Yes, you did."

She looked at me expectantly as if my praise had become a treat and she had a sweet tooth.

I wouldn't tell her I wanted her to do better, that even if she swam as good as me, it probably still wouldn't give me peace.

Spinning, I pinned her against the wall, the top of her head barely clearing the ledge. Reaching around, I grabbed the back of her neck, squeezing enough to lift her eyes.

"You did good, sweetheart. Real good."

The back of her head met the wall as she smiled, lashes fluttering against her cheeks. Keeping her pinned, fingers flexing around her neck, I dropped a kiss onto her mouth.

Humming softly, she puckered again, so I gave her another.

"I don't know how you swim so much." She spoke, eyes reopening. "Or so fast. That's exhausting."

My chuckle rumbled between us like distant thunder. "Practice."

"Kiss me again, Ryan." She beckoned, and if she wasn't so

horrible at swimming, I'd have sworn she was a siren of the sea.

Captivated, I dipped my head, my tongue slipping past her lips the moment they parted. She sighed into me, and I swallowed it down, kissing just a little deeper. Gliding up my neck, her hands pushed into the heavy wet strands of my hair, tugging just enough to keep me from losing all thought.

We glided over each other like water on skin, the heat of her mouth a direct contrast to the coolness of the water. Our chins brushed as we shifted, lips fitting together like two puzzle pieces just found. I moaned quietly, releasing her neck to pull her tighter against me.

I could feel the hard pebbles of her nipples through the thin fabric of the wet bathing suit. The water settled into a rhythm with us as her hips moved restlessly against me.

Under the water, my fingertips glided over the strip of skin exposed at her waist, flirting with the band of her top.

Fingers ripping from my hair, she grabbed my shoulders, squeezing, her core grinding against my abs. My dick was rock hard, straining against the tight shorts I wore, practically begging to get free.

With blood hammering in my veins, my fingers slipped beneath her top, caressing the underside of her breast. Lips popping off mine, she pressed her face into my shoulder. The second my thumb dragged over the puckered center, she gasped.

Pulling free, I reached around to the black tie keeping it on her. "Carrot?"

"Yes, Ryan. Please."

The black fabric drifted off the second I let it go, neither of us giving it a glance. Her breasts were perky, her hardened nipples a deep shade of peach. Pushing my forearm under her ass, I lifted her higher up the wall, her neck arching back over the edge of the pool.

She became quite easily the most beautiful sight I'd ever seen with her throat on display, creating a long column down to her smooth chest where her breasts were bared for my eyes.

Mumbling something incoherent, I leaned in, feasting on her tempting flesh. A small cry floated overhead when I sucked one nipple between my lips, rolling my tongue around it. Her fingers tightened at the nape of my neck, and I bit down lightly on the hard pebble.

Her body arched off the wall, her core sliding over my chest. I did it again, then went back to sucking until the thighs clenching me began to shake.

When I raised my head, her chest was flushed and blotchy. I licked up the expanse of her throat and nipped at her chin. She moved sluggishly, lifting her head as though it weighed a hundred pounds, her eyes hazy.

As I plunged back into her mouth, our tongues swirled, and my fingers delved between our bodies and into her suit bottom. Two fingers glided right down the center of her folds, and the kiss broke with our mutual groan.

The liquid her body produced for me was silkier than any water I would ever swim in. The thickness of her natural lube swirled around my fingers, clinging like an invitation. In my pants, my dick jumped, knowing where he belonged.

Her hips moved restlessly, so I pushed a thick finger into her tight, warm core while latching on to her breast once more.

Her little sounds of pleasure mixed with the sound of lapping water as she pushed down on my finger, wanting more.

"Ry." She panted, gripping my shoulders and looking at me with drunken eyes.

"Tell me what you want, baby."

"More."

"More of what?" I asked, voice sounding like I'd just drunk half a bottle of whiskey.

"You." Her hips moved, seeking friction. "More of you."

"Mmm," I answered, flicking my thumb over her swollen clit. She gasped and shuddered, body falling into the wall.

The force of her shudder loosened her legs, and her body slid lower, my at-attention dick nudging her core.

She gasped, lips latching on to my chest.

Unable to draw back, I thrust up, and if our stupid suits weren't in the way, I'd have slid right inside her.

Nails biting into my biceps, she sucked deeper against my flesh, pulling it into her mouth like a vacuum. Pressing my hand against her head, I pushed her closer, growling a bit when she increased the pressure.

We ground against each other while she sucked a mark into my pec. She was so turned on I felt the warmth of her body's desire swirling around my trapped dick.

Her body suddenly went tight, her lips falling slack on my chest. Knowing she was so close, I forced myself back, keeping an arm around her to prevent her from going under.

"Ry," she whimpered, clutching me.

"No," I said, voice gravelly and low. "C'mon out of the water."

The impatience and need firing in my body gave me the strength to palm her ass and practically hoist her over the side. She fell onto her ass, turning around to blink widely as I hauled ass out of the water.

I saw the question in her eyes, even the hint of hurt. Grunting, I pulled her to her feet, gripping her wrist and towing her toward the locker room.

"Ryan?"

"Don't argue with me right now, Carrot. The only place you're allowed to come is all over my dick."

Her steps faltered and she would have fallen, but I swept

her up against my chest and kept going, barreling inside. Wet feet slapping over the tile, I snagged a towel out of my open locker, tossing it on the bench. Reaching inside again, I grabbed a condom, ripping it open with my teeth, and then set her on her feet.

The wet end of her short ponytail dripped water onto her shoulder, the droplet sliding over her arm.

I was rough when I shoved down my Speedos, kicking them away. I rolled on the condom with precise movements as I stared down at her almost naked body.

"Strip," I demanded, blood roaring in my veins.

I sat on the bench, feet planted on the floor, as her swim bottoms smacked against the tiles. The hard, hot length of my dick jutted up off my body, begging for release.

"Come here," I said much gentler, guiding her into my lap.

Bracing her hands on my shoulders, I positioned myself at her entrance, and she started to slide down. Catching her hips, I halted the movement, torturing us both.

"Look at me," I growled.

Her eyes snapped up, pupils wide. I let go of her hips, and she sank down, sheathing my entire rod with her tight, hot core. Pleasure slackened her features, eyes sliding shut.

I caught her chin, forcing those eyes back. "Don't look anywhere else but me."

Her lips parted, but no words came out. Instead, all she could do was nod.

Curling my hands around the edge of the bench, I thrust up, making us both cry out. Even though her eyes remained locked on mine, her gaze flickered as though pleasure turned her blind.

I thrust up again and again, fucking obsessed with the way it felt to have her walls squeeze me with every thrust and the expression of wonder on her face.

Slowing my movements, I grasped her hips. "I want you

to ride me."

She thrust down immediately, burying my dick so deep inside her I momentarily saw stars. Her fingernails cut into my shoulders as she started to rock, milking my rod without even raising her hips. My ab muscles contracted so tight it was nearly painful. Her eyes slipped away as the rocking movements sped up, becoming a bit clumsy and uneven. A little mewling sound ripped from her throat, and then she splintered apart right there in my lap.

The warm gush of her release coated me completely as her body squeezed mine tight. The look of pure bliss encapsulating her features was one I wanted to covet, but then my own ecstasy ripped through me, and I let loose a hoarse shout. Bucking my hips, I pushed even deeper inside her, and she started mewling all over again.

In a final move of ownership, I shoved my hand between us, flattening my palm against her stomach. I was big, making it easy to feel the way my swollen dick pulsed inside her. It went so deep the tip nudged the bottom of her belly.

"*Mine*," I growled, shuddering again as another ripple of the mind-blowing orgasm contracted my stomach so tight a wave of nausea rolled over me.

She collapsed into me, breath coming in short gasps. My entire body was boneless, but I still held her, using every last bit of energy I had to steady us on that bench while my thighs shook.

"Holy shit," I whispered when I could finally speak again.

She turned her face to nuzzle into my neck.

"You good?" I asked, dropping a kiss to the top of her head.

She lifted her face, lips drawing up into a sleepy smile. "I guess that last lap was worth it."

I laughed.

Yeah. It was totally worth it.

Twenty-Three

Rory

The theater arts building was located on the opposite side of campus from most of my classes and my dorm. As I trudged my way over the sidewalks, rolling lawns, and past the old stone buildings, I wondered why. It just made sense in my mind that theater arts and fine arts majors should be located near each other, but they weren't.

However, when the theater building came into view, I understood the reason. The building that loomed ahead was nothing short of dramatic, which made it totally appropriate for performing arts.

Just the building's very presence exuded an air of prestige, whimsy, and even a hint of Goth. In fact, it didn't even look like a building but a castle.

It made a perfect subject for photographs. Despite having my new Canon around my neck, I fished into the bag slung over my shoulder to pull out an old-school analog. You know, the non-digital kind that you have to load a roll of film into.

Many photographers, especially young ones like me, exclusively used digital, but to me, there was still a place for film. Especially in natural lighting. In my experience, film was much more forgiving to overexposure and also blending in colors and highlights.

And personally, I liked the old-school feel. I liked the process of going into a darkroom and manually developing the film—watching it come to life on the photo paper. It was sort of like watching a memory come back to life.

And I mean, the way the mature trees spread out among the campus, practically framing the building, it truly looked like I'd stumbled upon an old castle in a modern world.

So film it was.

The sound of the shutter was familiar and calming but also held a note of promise. It was sort of fun to aim and snap, using only my eye as a guide. I couldn't pull the screen down and see what the photos would look like. I couldn't adjust based on the results. I had to trust myself and use my instincts to get amazing shots.

The large limestone building was centered by a tall, round Gothic tower, which rose higher than the two rectangular buildings coming off each side. Limestone steps rose from the slightly uneven pavement to follow the curve of the tower and lead to the wide wooden door. The pitched roof was steep and dark gray, and tall, rectangular cream-trimmed windows lined the two-story buildings flanking the turret. Stone dormers with old windows in the center lined the rectangular buildings, and off to the left side, I could see the top of another turret.

Green ivy similar to what grew on the side of my dorm climbed up one of the corners and over a door that looked like it had been closed in with stone.

Even though some parts had been modernized and there were bike racks and places to park small motorbikes, it still carried a true presence that seemed as if it should be parked on a high hill to look out over a kingdom.

People came and went as I took photo after photo, but I barely paid them any attention. The second I realized I was more caught up in the beautiful architecture than the students milling about, I inwardly winced.

Rory. I could practically hear Ryan in my head. *Pay attention to your surroundings.*

I mean, I was. Just not the surroundings he wanted me to pay attention to. The sigh I let loose was audible, mixing well with the autumn stirring the leaves in the trees. Paranoia and suspicion weren't fun. Looking in the faces of every person who walked by to wonder about their motive, if they were really passing by, or if they meant me harm was utterly exhausting.

Nearly an entire week had passed since Ryan went to his coach. An entire week of Ryan going to daily swim practices with Jonas. A week of my boyfriend on edge because he was just waiting for what his teammate would do next. A week of me praying they wouldn't try and drown each other.

I couldn't even tell myself it was a dramatic thought because Jonas *had* tried to drown me.

Maybe he wouldn't do anything. Maybe the threat of the team and coach watching and the demise of Jonas's swim career was enough to make him drop it.

Ry didn't believe that. I wasn't sure I did either, but the more days that passed without incident, the more I was beginning to hope.

No harm in hope… right?

Besides the impending doom that was Jonas, the rest of the week went by quickly. Ryan's schedule was packed with swimming and daily workouts plus classes. I also had a full course load and the school newspaper to keep me busy. Still, we managed to see each other every day. It had become routine to meet him after his ungodly early practices at the campus eatery for breakfast before classes. Watching him and Jamie plow through food was becoming my favorite hobby. On the days I could, I would meet him at the pool and sit in the bleachers doing homework while he fit in another swim for the day.

Honestly, I didn't know how he managed so much. I'd taken to carrying an excessive amount of protein bars in my bag because he was always hungry and never managed to have enough.

Tucking away the analog camera, I headed toward the entrance so I could get to the reason I was even here. Just as my foot landed on the first step, my cell went off.

Reaching into the pocket of my cropped white sherpa jacket, I pulled out my phone and smiled.

Mine. That's what he'd entered as his name in my contacts. Not Ryan or Ry. Mine. I still wasn't sure if he was trying to remind me that I was his or telling me that he was mine, but I never bothered to ask.

Who knew what would come out of his mouth?

The photo he took that morning was there too. Him looking smug as he smiled, all teeth, for the camera.

I opened the message to see a single emoji. A carrot.

The person jogging down the steps looked up when I laughed out loud.

Seconds later, an actual sentence followed the emoji. *You aren't at the pool.*

I'm at the theater arts building, taking pics for the upcoming show.

Are you alone?

I rolled my eyes and typed, *It's broad daylight. There are students everywhere.*

So you are.
I'm fine, Ry.
I can come meet you over there.
I thought you were practicing?
You're more important.

A red heart came through.

This, though. How was I supposed to be annoyed by his overprotective, bossy behavior when he was so charming about it?

Still, I typed, *No. Stay and practice. I'll do my thing.*
Dinner after?
Sure.
Stay at my place?

I made a sound. *No.*

It drove him nuts that I wouldn't stay in his and Jamie's room every single night. He seemed to think I would get snatched right out of my bed if he wasn't there to stop it. I mean, *how* did I manage my entire twenty years sleeping alone before him? *Insert mega eye roll here.*

He insisted no one would say anything if I stayed there, and since he was Elite, I actually believed him. Especially after staying there two nights in a row last weekend. People literally waved at us and said nothing at all.

But it wasn't my room, and I wasn't about to give in to everything he wanted. I was already too soft for him. Getting used to sleeping in his arms, surrounded by his scent, and waking up to his sleepy blue eyes was dangerous. What if we didn't work out? What if he got bored?

What if Jonas gets to him?

What if more time passed and we still couldn't come up with irrefutable proof for the coach and dean? Would he start to doubt me? Was Jonas telling him at every single practice that I was lying, that I was the one who couldn't be trusted?

Ryan had known Jonas longer than me. What if the dirtbag somehow used that against me? That and the fact they were Elite?

Just because I was falling for Ryan didn't mean Ryan was falling for me.

What if my feelings were stronger than his? What if the trust I felt for him was one-sided? What if all the things Jonas could be telling him started to create doubt?

I tried to ask Ry if Jonas ever talked to him at practice. His face shuttered and darkened, and he told me he didn't want to hear that name coming out of my mouth.

It didn't really make me feel any better. If anything, it made me more nervous.

The phone went off in my hand, making me look down.

Aw, Carrot, don't be like that.
I have to get inside. Text me when you're done.
Wait.

It was like he knew I was freaking out on the inside, and he didn't want to let me go. I didn't type anything else, but I didn't put my phone away either.

Another message slid onto the screen.

Be safe, baby. Call me if you need me.

The worries filling my head quieted, the sound of my thumping heart drowning them out. I guess this was why. Even though I worried things between us could go wrong, there was a part of me that unequivocally whispered, *But what if they go right?*

I sent a heart emoji through, then tucked my phone back into my pocket.

The inside of the building was palatial just like a castle, so I followed the signs toward the auditorium at the back of the sprawling building.

After what felt like a mile-long walk, which ended with me going through a foyer with a glass ceiling, glossy wood floor, and massive inlaid tile design in the center, I let myself into the theater, which was impressive.

If I hadn't already known this entire college was monied and filled with rich alumni as well as students, this would have been a massive giveaway.

The auditorium was three stories high with seats rising on each level. The coffered ceiling seemed hand-carved with a geometric grid. All the seats were upholstered with dark-green velvet, and the wood tones were all walnut.

The stage itself was massive, rising off the first level like the grand centerpiece it was. Light-colored fabric draped overhead, warm lighting shining behind it. A large green velvet curtain was draped in the background, which likely hid a projection screen.

Students were onstage, some working on the set. Some clustered into groups, talking over papers they held. A few professors stood at the front of the stage, and there was a row of others sitting in the seats toward the front.

Piano music would play then stop and then play again. Two people at the piano seemed to be having a heated discussion about whatever music was to be played.

"Let's take it from the top of act two, scene one!" a man sitting in the front row called.

Lifting the camera around my neck, I pulled off the lens cover, checked the settings, and took a few test shots. After noting the lighting and details, I adjusted what I needed to so I could get to work.

The first production of the year was opening next month, and the school would of course be covering it. So here I was to get a few behind-the-scenes and action shots of all the hard work and dedication that went into these shows.

Down on the stage, a girl started reciting lines, her voice carrying into the rows. A little tickle of something—*familiarity?*—caressed something inside, making me pause. Lowering the camera a bit, I glanced over my shoulder into the shadows the second level above me created.

A loud *bang* had me gasping and spinning back.

"Sorry!" a guy yelled as several students heaved up a piece of what I assumed was a prop.

The girl performing her lines hadn't even paused as though her nerves were unshakable. Or maybe that stuff just happened all the time.

Shaking off whatever uneasiness I felt, I went back to work, weaving into the middle row of seating for some more shots. The moment my lens focused on the girl on stage, my body jolted.

Flashbacks of the night Jonas tried to drown me overloaded my brain in quick flashes, making me feel like my camera was going off in my face.

A branch scraping my cheek. Stinging pain. My shoe popping off and me running away without it. The sound of a girl begging Jonas to get off her...

My wobbly knees hit the seat of a chair, and I fell into it, the soft velvet not comforting at all. Still caught up in the panic from that night, I gripped the armrests, looking back to the stage.

It was her.

The actress was the girl Jonas was with the night I'd been hiding in the bush. She was the girl I told to run off the second she could.

The long dark hair that floated around her that night was pulled up into a knot at the crown of her head. A heavy curtain of fringe bangs fell over her forehead, nearly brushing her eyes. She was wearing another of those skirts like that night, the kind that hugged her waist where it dipped in at the sides but then floated out around her hips.

It looked like a white tennis skirt. The cobalt-blue sweatshirt she wore was loose but tucked in at the wide waistband.

She had on designer snow-white sneakers and white socks that came halfway up her calves. As she recited her lines, the sleeves of the sweatshirt fell over her hands, and her fingers curled around them.

I'd wondered about her. Searched for her face on campus every single day. I couldn't regret not getting her name that night because I sincerely just wanted her to run away, but not knowing her name made it very hard to find her.

When Ryan and I talked about finding proof, she was the first person I thought of. Another almost-victim of Jonas's. I'd wanted to find her and see if she would also go on record about what he did. But I didn't know where to find her.

Now I did.

Maybe now someone would believe me. The dean couldn't ignore two girls with the same accusation, could he? It was no longer my word against Jonas's. It was his word against two of us.

I stared up at her, not hearing anything she said, tears burning the backs of my eyes.

She looks okay. He must not have hurt her. Is she scared of him? Did he try and buy her off? The last thought made me jolt, and the seat creaked a bit.

Someone near the front turned to look at me.

What if he did pay her off? What if she promised not to tell? *She won't help me.*

The person was still staring, so I stood from my seat and held up my camera. They seemed to understand because they went back to what they were doing, and I forced myself to take the photos.

The task that I usually loved seemed to go on forever, and my eyes kept straying back to the girl. It took everything in me not to rush right over to her in the middle of their rehearsal and demand to know if Jonas had contacted her.

After I'd taken enough photos, I sat back down to wait for

everyone to finish. When the director finally called it, my stomach was practically in knots.

People scattered faster than roaches under bright light, and really, I couldn't blame them. It felt like we'd been here for days. Tugging my bag farther onto my shoulder, I climbed the stairs leading to the stage where the girl was stuffing her script into a bag.

"Excuse me," I said, making her glance over her shoulder.

"Yes?" she asked.

"I'm with the school news. Mind if I get a shot of you?" I asked, motioning to my camera.

I mean, I couldn't just ask her if Jonas paid her off to be quiet about attacking her.

"Sure," she said, grabbing the script back out of her bag and walking over to the center of the stage under one of the lights that was still on.

I took a couple photos, and then she said, "Hey, have we met before?"

"Ah, well… kinda."

Her head tilted, her bangs shifting a little on her forehead. The long sleeves of her shirt covered her hands when she tucked them onto her hips as she thought.

"Ah!" she gasped suddenly. So suddenly I stumbled backward.

Pressing a hand to my pounding heart, I straightened. "What?"

"You're the girl from that night!"

I nodded.

She rushed me, and my hands automatically went up to shield my face. I guess Jonas left me with a little paranoia.

But she wasn't trying to attack me.

Oomph. Air emptied from my lungs, and we both fell backward with the force of her throwing her arms around me.

She was taller than me (wasn't everybody?), and the camera around my neck had to be poking her in the middle, but she didn't say a thing, just hugged tighter.

After a moment, she pulled back, her brown eyes fastening on mine. "Thank you."

"I didn't do anything,"

"You did. You jumped right out of that bush." She paused. "Actually, you kind of fell out." She waved away the words. "But you stopped him. He was..." She swallowed thickly. "Who knows what he would have done if you hadn't done that?"

A thick lump formed in my throat, making it hard to swallow and talk. But it seemed I didn't need to talk because she just kept going.

"I owe you an apology."

"What?" I said, straightening. "No... I—"

"Yes. I just left you there with him. You told me to run, and I did. I ran off and didn't look back." She took a small step back. "I haven't been able to stop thinking about it. About what I did. I've been worrying about you. I never should have left you alone. Did he... did he hurt you?"

I wasn't about to declare he tried to drown me. She'd feel guilty for the rest of her life, and why should she? "You are not responsible for anything he does."

"But I just ran off."

"I'm glad you did."

She hugged me again. She must have liked hugs. "Thank you. Seriously. I've never been in that situation. I just kind of froze."

I nodded. "I understand."

Her face fell. "He did hurt you."

"No!" I said quickly. Then, "Well, yes, but not like that."

"Tell me," she whispered, eyes so wide she looked like a doe.

"I'd gone out with him the week before," I told her. "He took me to the planetarium too."

"What a freaking dirtbag," she muttered.

I smiled, but then it faltered. "He, ah, got handsy with me too."

I swallowed back the sick feeling remembering that night caused. How wrong it felt to have him touch me. The way his heavy breathing sounded in my ear. How hot his hands were, how rough. The ripping sound the seam of my shirt made still echoed in my ears.

"Hey." The girl touched my shoulder. "Are you okay? Did he… did he rape you?"

I shook my head, trying to shake off the memories. "What's your name?"

"Madison." She offered me a small smile.

"I'm Rory."

She nodded, questions still lingering in her eyes.

"He didn't rape me. He would have, but I managed to spray him with some pepper spray and run off."

"Thank God."

I nodded. "I reported him to the dean."

Her eyes went round again. "You did?"

"But he didn't believe me."

Madison scowled. "Let me guess. Because he's Elite?"

"Yep."

"I swear toxic masculinity is going to be the end of this entire world."

I blinked. "Ah, you're right."

"I was still rattled the next day at rehearsal, so I confided in the director." She pursed her lips. "You know what he said?"

"What?"

"He told me experiencing trauma made creatives better."

I gasped. "He did not."

"Oh, girl, he did."

"I'd tell you to report him to the dean, but he wouldn't believe you." I frowned.

"Exactly why I didn't."

It shouldn't be like this. Women shouldn't be forced into silence because they're afraid of being disbelieved.

"That's kind of what I wanted to talk to you about," I said hesitantly.

"What do you mean?"

"Did Jonas... did he come see you the next day? At all? Did he offer you money to keep quiet?"

"What?" Her reply echoed to the high ceilings, bouncing around the auditorium.

I glanced around, realizing we were alone.

"Are you kidding?"

The look on my face told her I wasn't.

Her face fell the second time since I'd met her. "He did that to you?"

I nodded. "He tried to pay me off. When that didn't work, he threatened me."

"But you went to the dean anyway," she surmised, pride in her eyes.

"But he got there first and had already served the dean a nice warm dish of bullshit."

She gasped. It startled me again. I mean, she was a theater major. Drama was probably her thing.

"That's why you were in the bush!" She pointed at my camera.

I laughed. "Yeah, I thought maybe since he did it to me, he might do it to more people. I wanted to catch him."

"Get proof!"

"Exactly," I confirmed.

"You got it, right? When he tried to attack me?"

"Not exactly." I winced. "He kinda chased me down and threw my camera into the pool."

"Asshole."

I nodded emphatically. "I was thinking maybe you could come to the dean with me. With two of us saying what Jonas is really like, he will have to believe us. It's two against one."

Doubt flickered in her eyes, but then she banked it. "I'm in."

Surprise widened my eyes. "Really?"

"Of course."

I remembered the look she had before. "You don't think it will be enough?"

Her full lips rolled in on themselves. She really was quite beautiful. Definitely perfect for the stage. "I think men like Jonas are devious and good at making themselves look and seem innocent."

It wasn't really her words, though perhaps something in the way she said them that had a chill racing down my spine. "You're sure he didn't hurt you?" I whispered.

A loud popping sound burst overhead, and all the lights went out.

There were no windows in this building, no natural light to speak of at all. Inky, opaque darkness curtained the massive auditorium. It was heavy, almost suffocating, as if it could not only rob the ability to see but also breathe.

It was so black in here I would have been convinced Madison had even disappeared if it weren't for the tension I felt coming off her in waves.

"Are you still there?" she whispered, her voice echoing my thoughts.

I reached out, feeling around in the bottomless dark. My fingers brushed against fabric, and then her hand was gripping mine and we stepped so close our sides pressed together.

"Does this happen a lot?" Even though I whispered, the dark had a way of making me feel like I had yelled.

"Never," she whispered back.

Oh, that was reassuring.

"Maybe they thought everyone had left and shut off the lights," I offered.

"Maybe," she echoed. "Do you have a cell? We can use the flashlight. There's a panel stage left. I can try and flip a light back on."

My fingers were shaking when I reached into my jacket pocket for my phone. The second it was free of the fabric, I pulled it between us, thumb reaching for the side button to light up the screen.

Creeeak. The sound of one of the heavy auditorium doors opening made me pause. And then it slammed closed.

Madison's free hand settled over mine, pushing the phone down.

"Hello? Is anyone there?" she called out. "Can you turn the lights back on please? We weren't done rehearsing."

The ominous sound of silence was the only reply.

"Maybe someone else was still in here and they left when the lights went out." My heart pounded so hard my chest was beginning to hurt.

"Yeah, you're right," she said, pulling her hand away from my phone.

I lit up the screen, then switched on the flashlight. A small bubble of warm light illuminated our surroundings.

Something in the back of the auditorium banged.

We jumped, our hands clinging together as if we were each other's only lifeline.

"This isn't funny!" Madison yelled, her voice echoing.

"Which way?" I asked.

She pushed my arm in the direction I assumed was stage left, and we walked toward it.

Muffled footsteps sounded down one of the aisles. The closer they came, the louder they got.

"There!" Madison said, letting go of my hand to run over to the large electrical box. The groaning of the metal was so loud when she flung back the door. I shined the light on what seemed like a thousand switches. She reached for one that was marked in red with the word MAIN.

She flipped it.

Nothing happened.

Footsteps on the stairs at the side of the stage made both of us freeze.

What if it's Jonas? The thought was a frightening taunt, and real fear started to muddy my thoughts.

Madison started flipping every switch inside the panel, but not one light flickered.

He followed me here. He cut the power.

"He really doesn't want us to tell," I whispered.

Someone behind us began to chuckle.

Every single hair on my entire body stood on end.

I swung, shining the light beyond us, but he must have been just out of reach. The shadows protected him. Everything always protected him.

"Run," Madison whispered, her hand enclosing my wrist.

I stayed rooted in place, staring into the dark as if I'd been placed in some kind of trance.

"Rory!" Madison snapped, giving my arm a yank. "*Run!*"

I whirled as she pulled me, nearly tripping over my feet. The surging adrenaline throughout my body kept me upright as we started off.

But I didn't make it far. I was tackled from behind, enclosed by the very darkness stalking us as though it could drown me just like the water in the pool.

My arm yanked free of Madison's hold, and I smacked

into the floor with a yelp. The weight holding me down didn't stay on top of me, and I pushed up, preparing to run.

He chuckled again, and the blood in my veins froze.

It was the chuckle of a madman. A laugh of pure evil.

A hand closed around my ankle, his grip so tight I cried out in pain.

"No!" I yelled, trying to kick with my free leg.

"Rory!" Madison yelled from somewhere in the dark.

He yanked, and I fell face first again, chest whacking the unforgiving floor. Madison screamed for me again as panic clawed my throat raw. The vise around my ankle tugged, and I started to slide.

The sound I made could only be described as guttural as I fought and kicked even as my body was dragged away from Madison.

The last thing Ryan said to me suddenly resonated through my mind.

Be safe, baby. Call me if you need me.

The phone! It was still clutched in my hand. Pulling it in, I found *Mine* and hit call.

Before I even knew if the line on the other end was ringing, I let out a yell and pitched the phone toward my new friend, watching the device and its meager light skated across the floor before being swallowed up by shadows.

And then, just like the phone, I was swallowed up too.

Dragged straight into the claws of revenge.

Twenty-Four

Ryan

"Bro! Your phone is ringing," Jamie yelled.

Fresh out of the shower with a towel around my hips, I glanced at my Apple Watch and smiled. "It's Carrot. Pick it up," I said, coming around the corner as he snatched the phone out of my open locker.

"Camera girl, what's up?" Jamie said, hitting the screen to put it on speaker.

An odd sort of charged silence followed his enthusiastic greeting. An eerie feeling crawled over my skin.

"Rory? You there?" Jamie said, his usual good-natured humor completely gone.

A horrible nails-on-chalkboard noise disrupted the already ominous silence.

Jamie glanced up, and wariness passed between us.

Wes came around the corner, immediately picking up on the currents electrifying the room. "What's wrong?" he asked.

We didn't answer because a muffled, faraway voice came through the line. "Hello? Keep talking!"

Rushing forward, I snatched the phone out of Jamie's hand. "Who is this?" I demanded, pulling the device right up to my mouth. "Where's Rory?"

A scuffling sound followed. "*Help.*"

"What's going on?" Jamie demanded.

I was already moving, the towel around my waist dropping to the floor as I thrust the phone back at Jamie to frantically pull on a pair of sweats.

Another scuffle promptly tailed by a cry of relief preceded a voice over the line. It was breathless and frantic… It was not Rory.

"*Help*, please help." The girl gasped. "We're in the auditorium—"

Her words were drowned out by the sudden shrill whistle cutting through everything and stopping my heart.

The whistle I'd made Rory wear around her neck.

The whistle she was supposed to use if she was ever in trouble.

Fear bathed my organs in ice, but instinct took over, and I started to run.

Twenty-Five

Rory

My nails screeched over the polished stage floor as I physically tried to stop myself from being hauled away.

I clawed so hard I felt one break, and sharp pain exploded in my hand.

Spinning at the waist, I drew back the leg not being squeezed and kicked hard. A muffled *oomph* floated over me when my foot connected with something solid.

I strained to see who was there, to get any kind of visual of the man, but it was just too dark, and I was nearly blind with panic.

Somewhere in the distance, I heard Madison's voice but couldn't make out any of her words. The cord around my neck rubbed against my skin, and then I was fumbling under my sweater and beneath the collar of the white button-up beneath it.

The second my fingers closed over the cold metal, I let out a cry and brought it to my lips. I blew into the whistle with every breath I had left, blowing until my lungs burned and tears streamed down my face.

The sound was shrill and alarming, the high ceilings and acoustics in the auditorium making it seem louder and carry on even after I sucked in another breath to blow again.

A hard body leaped on top of me, pinning me to the floor and straddling my waist. His head and face were completely covered, even his eyes.

I blew again, but the sound was cut off when his gloved hands wrapped around my throat and squeezed. The pathetic whine of the whistle slowly faded as all air left my body.

His thumbs were thick and strong, and beneath them, my neck seemed to collapse.

My head lolled, sparks of light flashing in my vision.

A loud cry ripped through everything, and the man choking the life out of me shuddered and slumped to the side.

"Rory!" Madison's face pressed in close to mine as I gasped and coughed. "Rory, we have to go!"

She grabbed my arm, yanking my upper body up. I scrambled, my feet trying to find purchase. When they finally did, I surged upright.

Breathing labored, I ran behind her as she tugged me down the stairs. At the bottom, my legs sagged, my body bowing to the floor.

She cursed, and I heard myself giggle. It was inappropriate, but wasn't this entire situation?

Instead of rushing forward, she pushed me to the side, up against the stage. "Stay here," she said quietly against my ear.

Then she was gone, and I strained to see even a foot in front of me.

A door ahead pulled open. "This way!" she yelled. Then the door slammed behind her.

Am I supposed to follow her?

The second I pushed off the wall, I collided with something, and a scream tore up the back of my throat. A small hand slapped over my mouth.

"It's me!" she whispered, leaning close. Then she pushed a finger against her lips.

Instead of pulling away from me, she leaned closer around me, like she was feeling for something. A second later, I felt her tug a small latch.

We slid over as she pulled open some kind of secret door.

A booted foot hit the stair above. I nearly collapsed right there in fear.

She went first into the dark place, and I darted in after her. As we eased the door shut, the man's boots stomped down the stairs, increasing in speed. It was followed by the sound of him opening the door I thought she'd gone through.

The door slammed behind him.

One second stretched into two, which stretched into four.

Eventually, I had to suck in a breath because the world around me was tilting. We stayed silent and unmoving until I was sure at least five minutes had passed.

"Do you think I really fooled him?" Madison whispered.

When I started to reply, all that came out was a squeaky sound. We listened some more, the silence thicker than fog in the forest after a heavy rain. Just as I started to back into the wall, the sound of a door wrenching open turned us both rigid. Madison was basically two white round eyeballs in the pitch black, and we stared at each other as the sound of stomping boots drew closer.

I wanted to ask her if others knew about this hiding place. If it was some kind of closet or something people would be familiar with. I couldn't get the words out. I was too scared.

Instead, our eyes clung to each other as we listened.

As we waited.

Something slammed against the door, making it shudder.

Both of us fell back, her knocking into something metal, and the sound it made when it hit the ground was louder than a gunshot.

She whimpered.

I whimpered back.

The latch she'd so quietly pulled on earlier jiggled forcefully.

This was it. He was coming inside.

I never got to tell Ryan I love him.

I do. I love him.

Almost as if the thought conjured him up, his voice cut through the darkness, my fear, even the death lingering in the air. "Rory!"

The handle on the secret door stopped jiggling. Hope squeezed my chest so intensely it made me fold at the waist.

Doors in the distance shuddered.

"Rory!"

"Why is it so fucking dark?" Jamie was here too.

"The lights don't work." *Wes?*

"What the fuck? Rory!" Ryan screamed. I could hear his feet pounding down the aisle.

"Ryan!" I squeaked, coughed, and tried again. "Ryan!"

I started toward the door, but there was no handle, and I was too impatient to try and find the latch. Instead, I started slapping at the wood with my open palm, fresh tears streaming down my face.

"Here!" Madison exclaimed, wrenching the door back.

"Rory!"

"Ry," I croaked as Madison and I fell out of the small door and onto the floor.

"Here!" Jamie yelled, and the beam of his flashlight fell on us.

A string of curses followed by the clatter of a phone on the floor brought him closer, and then he was hitting his knees, towing me up onto his thighs and against his warm chest.

The dam broke inside me, and I started to cry, deep, shuddering sobs that sounded kind of scary and made me worry about the state of my throat.

"Shh," he said, steady as a rock. "It's okay. I'm here. I'm here now."

I gripped the front of his shirt, balling it into my fist as I tried to climb even closer. His palm fit over the side of my head, cradling it against his body as he rocked. He smelled of chlorine, he sounded like reassurance, and he felt like home.

"I love you," I sobbed, the pretty words sounding hideous as they ripped from my battered throat.

He fell back onto his butt, unfolding his legs beneath him so I could settle into his lap. "It's okay now, baby. You're safe."

I heard people talking around me, but I didn't listen to anything they said. I sat there clinging to Ryan, whispering over and over that I loved him.

Twenty-Six

Ryan

Blue and red light flickered through the windows, making what was meant to be an opulent space look like a crime scene.

It didn't just look like a crime scene, though. It was one.

My heart rate had yet to return to normal, and as I watched the uniformed officers along with campus security mill around, I dully wondered if perhaps it would ever be the same.

Rory was trembling, huddled in my lap as I sat on an uncomfortable-as-fuck bench against the wall. My Elite hoodie was draped over her like a blanket, and her cheek was pressed against my bare chest.

Not far from us, the girl who'd been hiding in the orchestra pit with Rory was talking to the cops, Jamie and Wes hovering nearby.

She looked shaken and pale but seemed a little more

coherent, which made me wonder what the fuck Rory went through that she didn't.

Why had she been on the phone and not my girl?

"Hey," I said, keeping my voice soft. "Sit up here and let me look at you."

She made a sound, pressing closer into me. Rory was affectionate, and she definitely liked sex, but she was not clingy. So her clinginess now, while welcome, made me worry even more.

Across the room, a door opened, and Rory tensed against me. Holding her a little tighter, my lips brushed against her hair. "It's just the EMTs."

Seeing two men carrying in kits and equipment made me frown as I wondered why the cops had called in medics. I watched them go directly to the officer talking to the dark-haired girl, but she shook her head and pointed in our direction.

Whatever she said caused Jamie to stiffen and turn.

I frowned, the medics swiveling in our direction.

"Are you hurt?" I demanded, probably harsher than I should have been. But damn, I was sitting here holding her when I should have been getting her help.

"I'm okay," she rasped.

My eyes narrowed. Sure, she'd just been sobbing, but her voice was really strained.

"Miss?" one of the EMTs asked, stopping in front of us. "We were told you need medical attention."

Jamie's movements were stiff, his face dark when he came over. I hitched my chin, asking what I needed to know. He pointed to his neck.

Without warning, I peeled Carrot away from my body, ignoring her little whine of protest. "Rory, let me see your neck."

Even as I spoke, I caught a glimpse of the mottled bruises.

An angry noise ripped out of me, and I grasped her chin, forcing her head back.

"What the fuck?" I yelled.

"Sir." One of the medics spoke. "If you would give us a moment with the patient."

"She's not a patient. She's mine," I snapped. Turning back to my girl, I kept my voice soft. "Rory," I probed, eyes not once leaving the ring of bruises around her throat. "Did that asshole strangle you?" *Is that why you weren't on the phone? Because someone was squeezing the precious life out of you?*

Her bloodshot, red-rimmed eyes lifted. "I blew the whistle."

My heart cracked, all my anger draining away. "I heard. You did really good, baby girl."

She smiled.

The crack in my heart deepened, and what once was one heart became two. And both of them were owned completely by her.

The EMT moved in. "Would you prefer to come outside to the ambulance?"

"No. Here is fine. Thank you." Her voice was definitely raspy, and it hit me again that she'd been choked.

Wild, hot anger overtook me, and I stood, the medics moving back for me to place her gently on the bench. I started to pace away, the need to move, to fight, gnawing away at me.

"Where are you going?" Her vulnerable, scratchy voice stopped me in my tracks.

To find Hughes. To kill him dead. But even the violent insistence of my thoughts was no match for the look of need in her eyes. I held out my hand. "Nowhere, sweetheart. I'm staying right here with you."

Her fingers clutched mine, and she submitted to the medics and all their poking and prodding.

"Did you lose consciousness at any time?" one of them asked.

"Almost," she answered, avoiding my stare.

My back teeth smashed together so forcefully I was sure everyone around us heard. Jamie put his hand on my shoulder, giving it a reassuring squeeze.

"Are you having difficulty breathing? Memory lapses?"

"No."

"Are you lightheaded?" The medic continued to assess her.

"Maybe a little."

"Pulse is slow," the other announced.

I jackknifed up, dislodging my hand from her hold. "Do something!" I yelled at them.

"There's some soft tissue swelling." He ignored me, prodding her delicate neck.

Spots swam before my eyes, but even still, I saw her wince. My hand shot out, clamping around the man's wrist and yanking it away from her. "Be. Careful," I growled.

"Sir, step back while we evaluate the patient."

"You think I'm gonna walk away?" I laughed. It was not a friendly sound.

The two men exchanged a look, and then one glanced over his shoulder at one of the officers.

"Please excuse him," Carrot said, her voice slightly strained. "He's overprotective."

I scoffed. "Not enough, obviously." My arms flung out. "Just look at you!"

"Bro," Jamie cautioned.

Wes stepped a little closer as if the two of them thought they'd have to restrain me. Maybe they would.

"I know it looks bad, Ry. But I'm fine. I'd be a lot worse if you hadn't gotten here when you did." Then she smiled a little. "You did good."

Huh. Was that why she liked it when I said that so much? It was kinda nice.

I relented just a little, and Jamie leaned into my ear, "Whipped."

"Rory." The dark-haired girl appeared, and Jamie slid back a little to make room for her to come forward. "I told the cops everything, but they still want to talk to you."

She nodded once. "Soon as I'm done here."

"I'm so sorry," the girl said, eyes filling with tears. "I should have done more."

Jamie scowled. "You clobbered the bastard in the head and saved her life. You did plenty."

"What?" I questioned, hungry for all the details I'd yet to get. My first priority had been Carrot, making sure she was safe and then trying to calm her down.

No wonder she'd been damn near hysterical. She'd almost been killed.

Again.

Hands curling into fists, I glanced around at the door. The urge to go find Hughes was nearly undeniable.

"You should have run," Carrot said, bringing my attention back around. "I told you to run."

"I ran last time. I won't ever do that again." Her voice was fervent.

"Who are you?" I deadpanned.

Jamie drew back as though his manners weren't as heinous as mine. I ignored him.

"Ryan, this is Madison," Carrot answered. "She was the girl I saw with Jonas the night we, ah… met."

I scowled. "You mean the night he shoved you in the pool to drown."

"Well, I wasn't going to put it like that," she muttered.

Madison gasped. It was hella dramatic, and even the EMTs stopped and looked at her.

"Ma'am, did you need medical attention?"

Her nose wrinkled. "Why would I?"

"She's a theater arts major," Carrot told the medics as if that explained everything.

Jamie snickered.

Madison looked at Rory. "You didn't tell me he pushed you in the pool too! Just your camera."

"She nearly died," I spat.

"You won't ever let it go, will you?" Rory wondered.

"Never," I vowed. Not even when I was dead.

"You should have told me he attacked you! Oh, I shouldn't have run." Her hands wrung together.

"Yes. You should have," Rory insisted.

"So you're a victim of that ass hamper too?" I asked her.

"What's an ass hamper?" Madison questioned.

"Nothing I'd wanna be," Jamie put in.

Wes made a sound of agreement.

"Aren't you three Elite?" Madison asked, looking between the three of us. "Just like *him*."

Rory made a sound from the bench. "I was worried about that too at first. But they're not like Jonas."

If my blood pressure got any higher, they were gonna have to put me on meds.

"Fuck no, we aren't," Jamie spat. "He gives Elite a bad name."

Madison glanced back at me with round brown eyes. "He tried to attack me, but Rory scared him off."

"What are you doing here?" I asked. I couldn't even be relieved we'd found someone to back up Rory's word. Just how many victims did Hughes have walking around this campus?

"I was rehearsing," she replied simply.

"I recognized her and asked her to go to the dean with me," Rory said, then coughed.

Forgetting the conversation, I slid onto the bench beside her, tucking my arm around her waist. Sighing, she rested her cheek on my shoulder.

As if just realizing I had on no shirt, she pulled back, blinking. "Why are you naked?"

Her jealousy was totally adorable. "I have on pants, baby."

She eyed me critically. It was kinda a relief. "But no shoes and no shirt."

I shrugged. "I ran out the second you called."

She started to pull the Elite hoodie away from her body.

I growled, and her movements stilled. Reaching over, I tucked it back around her. "Leave it."

"Ma'am?" An officer stepped up to our group, and they parted to make room for him. "We found your phone."

He held out the device to Rory, and I noted the crack running down the screen.

"Where was it?" she asked, accepting it.

"On the stage."

"I dropped it when I was looking for something to clobber that guy with," Madison said.

"How did you end up with her phone?" I asked.

"He was dragging me away," Rory said, her voice turning hollow. "But I remembered the phone, so I dialed you and threw it into the dark toward Madison."

Madison nodded sagely. It fell flashlight side down. "The only reason I found it was because I heard your voices when you answered." The brunette gazed back toward the auditorium, her eyes shuttering. "My stuff is still in there."

"You can go get it now, ma'am. We've already gone through the area," the officer told her.

"Did you find him?" Rory asked, voice wary but hopeful. It left my heart as bruised as her neck.

"Afraid not," he answered. "But the main power line was clearly cut."

Rory pressed into my side, and I gathered her close. What would have happened if she hadn't managed to call? Where would these girls be now?

Madison's voice sounded as haunted as my thoughts when she said, "I don't want to go back in there."

"I can escort you, ma'am. And we have a light set up inside. It's not as dark as before."

Madison hesitated.

Jamie made a sound and bent down in front of her.

"What are you doing?"

"Come on," he said, patting his shoulder. "Hop on. I'll take you in there."

"The officer offered already."

"Well, if you want to go with him, go on, then," Jamie said, slowly rising.

"Wait." Madison hurried to stop him, then carefully climbed onto his back.

Hooking his hands behind her knees, Jamie stood with ease. His voice was gruff when he directed it over his shoulder. "Make sure you aren't flashing anyone with that little skirt you got on."

Alarmed, Madison reached around, making sure it was covering her butt. "Okay," she told him.

When he carried her by the officer, Jamie stopped. "Don't be upset, dude. My muscles are just bigger."

I stifled a laugh and watched them until he carried her through the propped-open doors and disappeared.

The medics finished up their exam, telling Carrot to ice her neck—which she was already with the cold pack they'd given her—continue with anti-inflammatories, and if any other symptoms presented or persisted, to go to the ER immediately.

"Oh, and it might be a good idea to get some sugar in you as soon as possible," the man said, packing up his bag.

"I have some candy bars in the truck. I'll get you one," his partner offered.

She made a face. "I don't want to swallow them."

"I'll go get you a coffee. Extra sugar." Wes volunteered.

"That will work." The medic agreed.

"You don't have to do that, Wes—" Rory started, but I cut her off, tossing him the keys to my Jeep. "There's cash in the glove box."

"But—"

"You let Wes get you coffee, or you're eating a candy bar," I intoned.

Wes stepped up in front of Rory and smiled. His hair was half wet, half dry just like mine and Jamie's. But unlike me, he had on shoes and a shirt. "I really don't mind," he told her. "I feel useless otherwise."

She nodded. "Thank you."

"Be right back," he said, already jogging outside.

Leaning in, I kissed her on the temple. "How ya doing, Carrot?"

"I'm better now," she murmured, sinking into my side.

I tried not to think about how vulnerable she was. I tried not to look at the bruises on her neck. And I definitely tried not to tell her just how fucking bad she'd scared me.

None of that was her fault, and making her deal with my emotions on top of hers seemed cruel.

The officers approached, one carrying a notepad and all of them wearing solemn expressions. "We'd like to ask you a few questions."

"It's not a good time," I bit out.

"No," Rory said, straightening away from me but sliding her hand into my lap. I grasped it, cradling it in both of mine. "I'm ready."

She was still answering questions when Jamie carried Madison and her bag out of the auditorium and when Wes came inside carrying two big paper cups, handing one to each of the girls.

"Caramel," Rory said after taking a tentative sip.

"It's my favorite," Wes told her, sitting on her other side.

"Mine too."

"Thanks, Wes," Madison said, sipping the drink like she was enjoying it too.

"You were saying," the officer prompted, and I gave him a hard look. She'd been talking forever already. Her throat was raw, and the little bit of voice she did have was fading fast.

Behind us, one of the wide doors was yanked open so forcefully that a thunderous sound rolled through the open space. Rory jolted, nearly spilling her drink, and I put my hand out to settle hers.

"I got you." I assured her as she ducked her face into my neck.

At the same time, Madison let out a squeal and stumbled back. With the grace Jamie used in the water, he anchored one arm at her waist even as he stepped in front of her like a shield.

Bro, interesting.

"Wes!" a deep voice bellowed.

Wes made a strangled sound, shooting to his feet. "Max?"

Across the room, Max spun in the direction of Wes's voice. Glowering, he stomped over the floor as he came closer, dark stare not once leaving Wes.

Before he could reach us, one of the uniformed officers stepped in front of him. "Sir, who are you?"

His eyes widened as if he couldn't believe someone had the audacity to stand in his way.

Wes went forward. "He's my family."

The officer glanced at Wes. "You know him?"

Wes nodded, and the officer stepped aside.

Max grabbed Wes by the elbow, tugging him closer. "What the hell happened?"

"How did you know I was here?"

"You think you can get yourself in some situation where the cops have to be called and I won't know?"

Wes pulled his arm free to cross both over his chest. "Are you having me watched?"

"That's not important. What happened?"

"Max—"

The look he shot Wes had whatever argument he was about to say die on his lips. "Don't be a brat right now. I was worried."

Everything about Wes softened, and his arms fell to his sides. "I'm fine."

Max's hand shot out, grabbing Wes by the chin to turn his face right and then left, studying every angle. Wes didn't say a word, just let Max manhandle him until he seemed sure he wasn't hurt.

I glanced at Jamie who raised his eyebrow.

Bro, interesting.

"Tell me," Max said, voice still harsh but lower now.

"Rory and Madison were attacked, and we came." Wes gestured to the rest of us, and Max turned as if seeing us all for the first time.

"Oh." His eyes fell to the bruises on her neck, and he frowned. Lifting his eyes, he asked, "Are you okay?"

"Still alive," she said, kinda rueful.

I made a strangled sound. *Not fucking funny.*

A slim, cool hand skirted up my neck, curving around the skin, as her light body strained up to kiss beneath my chin. "Still here with you," she whispered.

Even as my heart flipped, my eyes started looking around for places that offered privacy. For somewhere—anywhere—we could be alone. I wanted to peel away every ounce of clothing hiding her from my eyes. I wanted to scour her body for any kind of injury and kiss it away. Most of all, I wanted in her, to feel her body mold around mine, to reassure myself that we still fit perfectly together and nothing would ever take that away.

"Well, if there is nothing else…" The officer in charge spoke up, bringing my mind back.

"Actually, I want to know why Hughes isn't in handcuffs yet," I demanded.

"As we already discussed, Mr. Walsh, we have sent officers to question Jonas Hughes."

"That's not good enough."

"As you are aware, the women did not get a good visual on their attacker this evening, so—"

"Don't even finish that sentence," I growled. I swear to all that's holy, if one more person told me to get proof, my head was going to explode.

The officer stiffened. "We are doing everything according to the law."

I jabbed a finger toward Rory's neck. "Yeah? It sure as fuck doesn't look like it."

The officer's face turned red, but I was unimpressed by it as well as his authoritative voice. "Listen here—"

Rory started coughing, her breath wheezing a bit. I forgot about the asshole and spun off the bench, dropping down in front of her. "Tell me where it hurts." I worried. "Do you want the medics back?"

"Can we just go?"

"Yeah, baby. Come on." I lifted her off the bench, ignoring the cops completely. Morons.

"I can walk."

"No," I retorted.

"But I have shoes, and you don't," she argued.

"Don't sass me, woman."

"I need my bag."

"I got it," Wes said, going to grab all her stuff nearby.

I turned to Madison. "Do you need a ride?"

She nodded.

Jamie dropped back in front of her, and she hesitated.

"It's dark out." He reminded her.

She climbed on.

Smooth, bro. Smooth.

We left the officers and campus security behind and walked out into the cold night. A motorcycle was parked up on the sidewalk, close to the door. It was pretty sweet-looking, and I wondered whose it was—until Max swiveled toward it.

"Nice ride," I told him.

"Thanks."

Wes stepped up, handing out my keys. "I'm gonna go with him."

"You sure?" I asked. "Plenty of room."

Behind us, Max made a sound.

"I'm sure," Wes said. "I'll see you at practice tomorrow."

I nodded, and Rory held up the coffee she was holding. "Thanks for coming, Wes. And thanks for the coffee."

He held his fist out, and she bumped hers against it.

Max was already sitting on the motorcycle when Wes jogged over. I watched as he handed Wes the only helmet he had with him.

Wes thrust it at him, shaking his head.

Max's lips moved, but I couldn't hear what he said. Then Wes's shoulders moved with a sigh, and he was climbing on behind Max as he put on the helmet.

"Ryan?" Rory's voice made me forget about everyone else, and I glanced down at her bundled in my arms.

"Hm?"

"I changed my mind. I want to stay at your place tonight."

I scoffed. "Cute of you to assume you had a choice."

"You're stupid." She pouted.

I chuckled, carrying her over to buckle her into the passenger side. Jamie and Madison were already in the back.

When she was secured, I swooped down, kissed her nose, and leaned into her ear. "Oh, baby, we both know how you really feel about me."

She sucked in a breath, her cheeks heating so fast I actually felt the temperature change.

Sure, maybe I shouldn't tease her right now, not after everything she just went through, but I couldn't help it. I might not have said anything about her panicked rambling earlier, the rambling that consisted of one repeated sentence. *I love you.*

But that didn't mean I hadn't heard.

Because, *oh,* I definitely heard.

Twenty-Seven

Rory

He didn't say it back.

I wasn't sure what was worse.

Being terrified of not getting another minute of life and just blurting out my deepest truths the second I could. *Over and over again, no less, as if one time wasn't enough.* Cringe-fest in 3-2-1.

Or having that deep confession unrequited.

Or being teased about it later.

Or... That's right. There's yet another one. Clinging to the person you just confessed to even after realizing it was unrequited and *maybe* a joke to them.

I saw now that my whole life was destined to be shrouded in regret.

Even still, I couldn't regret being alive. I guess living with a list of regrets longer than Santa's naughty list was way better than not living at all.

So hey, silver lining?

And yeah, I also realized that these were the thoughts consuming my brain most after being strangled, stalked, and then questioned by the police. My head was muddled, throat sore, and body tired.

I really just wanted to feel safe, and I couldn't deny I felt safe with Ryan, which was probably why my brain allowed all these thoughts to run rampant.

He refused to leave your side. He is so protective.

Physically, I was safe with Ry.

But what about my heart?

Twenty-Eight

Ryan

Her hand stayed clutched in mine, but her mind? It was somewhere else. Even though I understood the likely reason... something felt off. This wasn't about what happened earlier.

This was different.

I kept glancing at her out of the corner of my eye as I drove, hoping I'd figure it out, hoping she'd say or do anything to clue me in.

So far, I got nothing.

"Hey, Madison..." I began, glancing in the rearview mirror. "Which dorm?"

"Hamlet Hall," she replied quietly.

A fissure of guilt hit me just then because I was so wrapped up with Carrot, I never really asked Madison how she was. She'd been through hell too. And as they'd explained to the police, she also was the one who stopped my girl from being strangled.

Hand tightening on the wheel, I started to speak, but her words cut off mine.

"Do you think the police arrested him?"

My eyes shot into the mirror again, glancing at the top of her dark head, which was turned to stare out into the dark street. She looked defenseless sitting there. Pale in the backdrop of night and a slight tremble to her quiet words.

Automatically, my eyes shifted to Jamie who was sitting in the back beside her. Our stares collided, and I noted his held the same simmering rage I had smoldering in mine.

"Probably not," Carrot said, almost resigned. "He'll just lie like he always does, and since we didn't see his face…" Her voice trailed away.

"So he's…" Madison paused. "Just out there somewhere on campus?"

"Yeah," Carrot echoed.

Pulling my hand from hers, I downshifted a little more forcefully than necessary, but hell, I was pissed off. These girls were walking around campus with someone who made their lives hell, and there wasn't anything anyone was doing about it.

"Rory?" Madison asked.

Rory twisted to gaze into the back at her new friend. "Yeah?"

"Do you think I could stay with you tonight?" she asked. "My roommate is out of town, and being alone…"

"Of course," she hurried to say. "You definitely shouldn't be alone tonight."

"Things won't seem as scary in the morning," Madison whispered almost as though she were reassuring herself.

"We can still stop by your room. You can get some things, and then Ry can drop us off—"

"Hell no," both Jamie and I bellowed in sync.

Rory turned toward me, worrying her lower lip between

her teeth. Gently, I reached up to tug it free and spent a moment smoothing it over with the pad of my thumb. Her eyes were wide, almost pleading, when they stared at me, and she shook her head.

I knew she couldn't leave Madison alone tonight. Hell, I didn't want her alone either. But the two of them—alone? Look what the fuck happened last time.

"Slumber party," Jamie announced, and I nodded.

"What?" Madison asked.

"Carrot was staying with us tonight. So now you both are."

"Oh no, I—" Madison started to protest.

"Don't even bother, Mads," Jamie said, his voice tight. "We aren't leaving you two alone. So save your breath."

"But the rules—"

Jamie made a rude sound. "The rules can bite a big one."

Rory glanced into the back again. "They're Elite. Apparently, the rules don't apply to them."

"Well, we learned that the hard way," Madison quipped.

"Mm-hmm," Rory hummed.

"We are nothing like that asshat," Jamie spat.

Rory turned her face away, and I pulled into the parking lot for Hamlet Hall. She reached for the button on her seatbelt, and my hand shot out, stopping her. "What do you think you're doing?"

"Walking upstairs with her."

"No."

Her eyebrow arched. "Excuse me?"

"You think I'm going to let you traipse all over this campus in the cold and dark after what you've just been through?"

"Well, you aren't going. You aren't even wearing a shirt."

Jamie's head appeared between the seats. "It's a public service, really."

"Bro." I offered my fist, and we pounded it out.

Carrot was not amused, and Madison pushed open her door to get out.

"Whoa!" Jamie disappeared, diving forward to pull her door shut.

"Hey!"

"Wait there. I'll come around and get you."

"It's not necessary. Just tell me what dorm, and I'll bring my car over with me. That way, I can drive to class in the morning."

"Then I'll drive," Jamie announced and got out of the Jeep. At her side, he wrenched open the door.

Madison crossed her arms over her chest and glared. "I don't even know you. I'm not bringing you up to my dorm room and then letting you drive my car."

Jamie pressed a hand to his chest. "But I gave you a piggy-back ride. In some countries, we'd be married!"

Madison sighed dramatically. "Is he always like this?" she asked my girl.

"Yes. And he's a horrible, mean morning person."

I laughed under my breath.

"Aww," Jamie said, leaning into the doorframe, pushing his face closer to Madison's. "Don't you worry, Mads. I won't bite." His voice lowered. "Unless you ask me to."

She pushed his head away and then scooted forward. "Whatever. Try anything funny, and I'll tase you."

"Ah! I knew I was forgetting something!" I announced.

Rory groaned.

"Come on." Jamie motioned for her. "Out."

Madison slid another glance to Rory, who nodded. "He's a good one."

Nodding once, Madison stepped out of the Jeep.

Jamie knocked on my window, and I lowered it enough

for us to talk. "I'll pick up some pizza on the way over." He leaned around. "Good for you, camera girl?"

"I'm not hungry."

"She'll eat it," I said.

She grumbled beneath her breath and turned toward her window, ignoring us both.

Jamie lowered his voice. "I'll be sure to be gone at least thirty. Fix whatever that is." He hitched his chin toward her.

Ah, so he'd picked up on it too.

We did our handshake, and then he draped an arm over Madison's shoulders and they started walking toward her building.

Rory stared after them, worry etched into her features.

After backing out of the space and driving forward, I slid my hand over Rory's thigh, fingers tangling with hers. "Don't worry about Madison. Jamie won't let anyone hurt her."

Gazing down at our clasped hands, she whispered, "Him included?"

And that's when I realized.

I fucked up.

Twenty-Nine

Rory

I was too fragile right now. Not necessarily something I liked to admit. But really, denying it only made it hurt worse.

I needed to protect myself, but I didn't want to protect myself from him.

Just because he didn't say it back didn't mean he didn't care. I knew he did. Even without loving me, he cared more than anyone else ever had. Maybe that was why it was bothering me so much, why it was the final nail in my coffin, so to speak.

Although, that was a bad euphemism considering I just about actually needed a coffin. Am I right?

He cared so damn much. Why couldn't that equal love?

This is why. Why no one ever wanted to drop the L-word first. Because when you weren't sure the other person could say it back, it became a virtual mindfuck.

Expecting Ryan to say those three words to me after such

a short period of time was ridiculous, and my brain knew this.

My heart?

It clearly didn't operate on thoughts, just feelings, and mine were so very tender. Even more so after almost dying. *Twice.*

Yet here I was, entering Ryan's dorm room for some kind of almost-murder slumber party.

Their room was lit by the blue LED lights trimming the ceiling, giving everything a soft glow. After lowering me onto his bed, Ry put our bags on the floor near his bed and paced away. The muscles in his back and shoulders rippled with tension, his arm bulging when he hooked his hands on his narrow hips.

The silence between us was heavy, and I knew I needed to say something, but I just wasn't sure what.

Abruptly, he turned, a low sound bursting out of him. Wide-eyed, I watched him close the distance between us with two big steps and then drop onto the floor in front of me. Automatically, my knees parted to give him space, which he immediately owned.

"You scared me so fucking much." The words ripped out of him like he was confessing a dark sin. Arms corded with muscle wrapped around my waist as he pushed in, hugging me tight, and dropped his head into my lap.

I stalled for a moment, my heart skipping several beats, but the second his arms squeezed around my waist a little tighter, my hand delved into the thick dark strands of his soft hair. He made an appreciative sound deep in his throat, and it made my belly contract.

"When I heard that whistle through the phone, I swear I almost fucking lost it. I couldn't get to you fast enough. All I could think about was that you needed me, and I wasn't there."

"Shh, Ry," I said, throat constricting at the raw emotion in his words.

"Ever since I met you," he rasped, "everything else has been slightly out of focus. Like my mind takes those photographs you love so damn much, but the only thing my camera focuses on is you." He paused, but the harsh sound of his breathing filled the room. "I can't explain it. I don't even think I want to."

"Ryan," I whispered, carding my hands through his hair. "It's okay. Things with us are intense. Maybe you need a little bit of space."

God, how I even managed to get those words out... Just saying them felt like breaking off a piece of my heart. But that's how I knew my love for him wasn't panic-induced. The reason I confessed so ardently, sure, but the love itself was pure.

If it wasn't, I wouldn't risk breaking my own heart to offer his what it needed.

In a burst of movement, he tackled me back onto the mattress, making all the breath in my body whoosh out. My frame was easily swallowed by his larger one, and though he braced most of his weight on his elbows, I was pinned.

The ferocity with which he stared made it feel like I was being consumed by blue fire. And *oh*, the burn was sweet.

"I don't need space." He spat the words as if they left a foul taste in his mouth.

Dragging my eyes from his, I turned my face away as tears welled up behind them. "I think maybe I am high maintenance," I whispered, the words barely making it past my traumatized throat.

"Lucky for you, I love high-maintenance."

Chin turned, I looked at him with blurred vision. "What?"

"Oh, baby," he crooned, and the soothing way he said it

made a tear fall from the corner of my eye. "I'm sorry. So fucking sorry."

My lips parted on a shaky breath. I wanted to tell him he didn't have anything to be sorry for, but his lips caught mine, silencing any words that might tumble out.

The sob I'd been holding back forced its way out, echoing in the back of his throat as he swallowed it down. Humming quietly, he dipped his tongue past my lips, reaching for mine. Languidly, they twirled, creating a warm, fuzzy sensation between my ears. The pain in my throat ceased to exist, and the strain in my neck was forgotten.

The anxiety I carried was overshadowed by everything he was. The lazy kiss stretched on, a slow meeting of our mouths but still deep and tantalizing, making my limbs heavy. When he finally retreated, my hands curled around his biceps, wanting to hold him close.

The dark fringe of lashes fluttered as they dragged upward, revealing his intense cobalt stare. "You meant it," he whispered, voice like gravel.

"What?" I was struggling to keep up, his taste lingering on my tongue like a drug that hadn't quite worn off.

His fingers stroked through my hair, pushing it away from my face. "I didn't want to make it awkward. I thought maybe you were just so scared you didn't know what you were saying."

Realization dawned.

The gentle fingers in my hair coupled with the soft look in his eyes made my lower lip wobble. It was too much. I couldn't do it.

"You meant it." This time, the words penetrated with meaning.

"I—" *Deny. Deny. Deny,* my brain screamed.

Tell him, whispered my heart.

Oh, how much louder a whisper could be.

His eyes were expectant, glowing more than any lights ever could. His body was warm, his presence a blanket to someone who'd been near frozen. Yes, I was fragile. He felt like glue. Yes, I was scared. But he was reassuring.

I found myself nodding as another tear slipped free. "When we were hiding in the dark and I heard him coming, all I could think was that I love you. I love you, and I would never be able to tell you."

Around me, his muscles flexed, and a low rumble dripped from his lips.

"You don't have to say it," I hurried to add. "I know it's too soon, and I know—"

The force with which he kissed me robbed me of breath. Gone was the lazy twisting of his tongue, and in its place was all-consuming heat. He kissed as if he would crawl inside me, as if he would find every last inch of everything I was and own it.

The weight he'd been holding sank into me, his legs nudging mine apart. I gasped when his hips thrust, pushing his rock-hard shaft against my core. Tilting my hips up, I cradled as much of him as I could, the feel of him rutting against me making my knees shake.

The little bit of stubble along his chin scraped over my skin, leaving a tingling sensation in its wake. Arching into him, I wound my arms around his back, pressing as close against his warm, supple skin as I could get.

His lips ripped away, both of us breathing ragged. "Look at me."

I looked.

"I love you. I've loved you since my naked ass dove in that pool and saw your carrot head sinking. I love you so much it makes me damn near crazy."

"Ryan," I whimpered, heart exploding with hope.

He nodded. "I'm so sorry I didn't say it back right away,

baby. You were freaked out and scared. I didn't want to put pressure on you if you weren't sure what you were saying. But you have to know I love you. I love you so goddamn much."

"You teased me," I burst out, heart catching in my throat.

His smile was swift, but his gaze remained tender. "I never said all my jokes were good."

"I thought you didn't love me." The pain I'd felt earlier rose to pummel me again.

He made a sound, gently pushing his face into my neck. His lips were cool against my swollen skin, fluttering over my injury like butterfly wings. "I'll never make you doubt me again. I love you," he whispered. Coming over me, our lips met again. And again. "I love you."

I didn't just hear the words. I felt them. I felt them so deep I wondered how I ever questioned him at all.

His fingers delved beneath my shirt, thumb drawing slow circles over my hipbones as his lips dragged to my ear.

Impatient, I tugged at his pants, purring pleasantly when he shoved them down and I discovered he wasn't wearing underwear. He panted against my flesh when my fist closed around his shaft, slowly pumping him, making his abs ripple.

Sliding my thumb over his slit, I shuddered a little at the small bead of moisture on the tip, smearing it around before pulling my hand up to suck my thumb between my lips.

"Shit," he swore, eyes dilating as he watched me lap up what was left of him on my finger. Scrambling back, he yanked my jeans off, shoving my sweater up only to become frustrated to find the button beneath it.

"I hope you don't like this shirt," he ground out, not even waiting for me to answer before ripping it open. Buttons pinged around the room, creating a backdrop to the desperation surging between us. The second my stomach was bared to him, he leaned in, kissing across my abdomen, dipping below my belly button, and dragging his chin through the short, wiry hair.

Fisting his hair, I pulled his head up, our eyes colliding.

"Tell me what you want, sweetheart."

"I want you inside me, Ry."

"One second please," he murmured, a spark of mischief lighting the heavy desire in his eyes.

I arched up off the bed, gasping when he swiped his face up my center in one fluid motion. Hands hit the mattress on either side of my head, and I forced my eyes open to see his glistening nose, lips, and chin.

"You're definitely ready for me." His eyebrows wagged.

I glanced at the wet tip of his nose again.

Groaning, he leaned in. "Taste yourself on me, baby."

I hesitated, and he nudged my entrance with the tip of his swollen head.

I licked over his nose, and the flavor I knew was mine burst over my tongue.

"That was so fucking hot," he growled, slipping his tongue into my mouth at the same time he took me in a single thrust.

Our mouths fell apart, my moan lifting to the ceiling.

His hips thrust again, and my inner walls clutched at him, coating him in my desire. Leaving himself buried, he thrust his hips with small, fluid movements, hitting a spot inside me that I swear no one had ever found before.

A broke sound left my lips, and he pushed up, pulling out nearly all the way before plunging back in. I widened my legs, fisting my hands into the comforter stretched over the bed as he set a pace that had me unable to keep silent. The pain in my throat was there, but it was secondary to everything he made me feel. The stretch and burn of my body around his thick cock were heightened by the way he ground his pelvis against mine when he bottomed out inside me.

His arm and shoulders rippled over me, hair falling over his face and eyes clouded over with ecstasy. Reaching around him, I grabbed his ass, shoving him even deeper and wrapping my legs around his waist.

His hand slapped over the edge of the mattress above us, using it as leverage to fuck me deep and hard. I moaned and whimpered, and he caught my lower lip between his to suck.

He brought me to the highest peak I'd ever crested and held me there almost as if I were his hostage.

"Ry," I whimpered, straining and rocking against him for friction.

"Tell me," he demanded, voice hoarse.

"I love you." The words fell from me so easily, without question.

One hand slid under my ass, and he tilted my hips up as he thrust down. I shattered, body bowing and straining under the intense orgasm ripping me apart. For long moments, all that existed was the blinding pleasure splintering through my body, pulling me apart and then fusing me back together in a way that would never be the same.

When my body could literally not take any more, I collapsed onto the bed, and he pulled out, his pulsing dick looking angry inside his fist. I watched with passion-drunk eyes as he used what was left of me to stroke himself twice before he threw his head back to groan. Thick white ropes of release shot out across my belly, splashing as far as my ribs. His body shuddered, and I watched hungrily as more dripped out over his hand.

Remembering the way his eyes had lost focus when I licked myself off his nose, I reached out, guiding his messy fingers up to my lips so I could lick them clean. His eyes dropped half-mast as I lapped up the salty release, humming in pleasure.

When his hand was clean, I released him, and his eyes

traveled hotly down my body. Smirking, he used his newly cleaned hand to swipe across my stomach, rubbing his cum into my skin.

"Mine."

Still palming my waist, he leaned down to kiss me softly. "I love you, Carrot."

My heart swelled near to bursting, and the feeling was so wanted that tears rushed behind my eyes.

"Hey," he said softly, "what's this?"

I shook my head, knowing I could never put to words just how much I wanted him. "I was just scared."

"I know, baby. I'm sorry I wasn't there."

"Not about that," I whispered. "Scared I was going to lose you."

His eyes went dark, so deep the cobalt turned to navy, and the sensation I'd felt when drowning crashed over me once more. But this time I didn't fight against the current, this time I let it pull me deeper.

His hand grasped my chin, not enough to hurt me but just enough to make me feel possessed. "I know it's a shit circus right now."

I giggled, and he flashed me a smile. But immediately, he went back to intense sincerity. "But I swear I'm not going anywhere. You won't lose me."

A little niggle of my previous worries chose that moment to haunt me. I did a good job pushing them down, but he saw. Of course he saw.

"Tell me."

"Even if I never get proof? Even if he keeps making it look like I'm the liar?"

His fingers bit into my chin, and he leaned so close I felt the warmth of the breath expelling from his lips. "I will never, ever believe that scum over you. *Ever*."

"I believe you," I whispered.

He kissed my nose. "That's what we do, baby. We believe in each other."

I smiled. But then I felt the way his hand stuck to my face. "Eww!" I squealed, trying to bat it away. "Is that your gross hand?"

He smirked. "You didn't think it was too gross a couple minutes ago."

"Ryan Steven Walsh, get that cum-covered hand off me!"

"I think it's stuck."

I squealed again.

Chuckling, he pulled back, making my nose wrinkle with what he left behind.

"I need a shower," I said, gazing down my body. My shirts were still on, one ripped, one in no better shape than my sticky face.

He grunted, clearly pleased with his handiwork. "I think you look good."

"I'm taking a shower," I said, sliding off the mattress. My legs buckled like Jell-O, but I steadied myself on the side of the bed. My entire body was sore as though I'd been in some kind of mega accident instead of stalked and strangled for minutes.

"Hey," Ryan cautioned, voice dipping into that velvety soft tone I loved so much. "Be careful." Sliding his arm behind my knees, he lifted, carrying me into the bathroom.

"You ruined my shirts," I complained.

"I'll buy you new ones."

I sniffed. "I want one of yours."

"Done."

I dipped my face into his chest, smiling. Love definitely was a lot better when the person you were in love with loved you back.

Thirty

Ryan

The alarm on my phone went off too soon. Carrot whined in her sleep, and I threw my arm over the side of the bed, reaching for the stupid thing to silence it.

The second the annoying tone was gone, my eyes started to slide shut, the warmth of her beside me so easily distracting.

The backup alarm went off seconds later, and I jolted awake.

Shutting it off, I tossed the phone down, scrubbing my hands over my face. Fuck, these early morning practices sucked sometimes.

Dropping my hand, I glanced over at my girl. Even if I was surly AF about having to wake up, I couldn't help but smile. She was barely visible beneath the blankets, a mere blip in the space between me and the wall. She likely wouldn't be visible at all if it wasn't for all that wild orange hair attacking the pillow.

With gentle hands, I lifted a few strands from her peaches-and-cream complexion, heart swelling. Long cinnamon lashes swept over her cheeks, and my eyes lingered on her relaxed full lips. The back of my knuckles grazed her cheek, and I marveled at the fact she wasn't covered in freckles. I always thought freckles were kinda a requirement for red hair.

I smirked. Just meant I was right. Her hair wasn't red; it was totally orange.

"My little carrot," I mused, leaning in to sniff lightly against her skin, making her nose wrinkle and me smile.

Lashes fluttering, her gray eyes focused.

I totally loved I was the first thing she saw this morning. "Hi," I murmured, brushing a soft kiss over her lips.

"It's too early," she croaked. Startled, her sleepy eyes widened, small fingers reaching for her throat.

Some of the quiet, sleepy bliss I'd been imbibing faded as I watched the reminders of yesterday flicker through her eyes like a bad movie. Reminding myself to keep tight reins on the boiling anger inside me, I tucked a knuckle under her chin, pushing back just enough so I could glance down at her neck.

The bruises were worse. An ugly shade of purple that looked too much like fingerprints and definitely *did not* help in keeping my fury in check. We knew they would deepen overnight. The medics said they would look worse this morning. But it didn't make them any easier to see. It still made me sick.

"Do you hurt?" I murmured, keeping my voice just for her and my back to the others sleeping in the room.

"Just a little," she croaked again. Panic flared in her eyes once more, and I pulled her fingers up to kiss the tips.

"Remember they said you'd probably sound weird for a

couple days." I slipped out of bed, nearly busting my ass over Jamie who was sprawled out on the floor.

He had a blanket and pillow, but he'd somehow rolled away from them and was lying on his back, arms out like a starfish against the rug.

Dude was gonna be stiff as hell. Probably even grouchier than usual.

On my way to grab the pain reliever on the desk, I slid a glance at his bed where Madison was sleeping. It looked unusually big with her lying in the center.

Trying to be quiet, I shook the pills onto my palm and grabbed a water. The second I slid under the covers, Carrot molded against me with a sigh.

"C'mon, take these."

She grumbled, making no move to sit up.

"Rory."

Growling like the chihuahua she was, she pushed up, glaring through her messy hair. She opened her mouth, and I dumped the pills in, handing over the water.

She swallowed, eyes watering when the meds hit her throat and she had to gulp harder to get them to go down. The second it was done, she collapsed against the bed with a sigh as I set aside the water. Moving in, I pressed light-as-air kisses over the mottled mess.

She purred, and I kissed her a few more times. Before the kiss could become too consuming, I pulled back, knowing if I let myself get too deep, I'd miss practice.

Now more than ever, I had to be there. I had to show Hughes I wasn't backing down.

"Just stay here and sleep, okay? I'll be back after practice and take you to breakfast."

"Mm." She agreed, snuggling down into the pillow.

She was wearing one of my T-shirts, and the wide neckline slipped down, exposing her shoulder. In attempt to make myself less grumpy about having to get up, I launched my pillow at Jamie's head. It hit him right in the face.

"What the fuck?" he bellowed, flinging it away as he sat up. I expected retaliation of some sort, but the first thing he did was look at his bed.

As previously mentioned, these women weren't nearly as visible as we were under the covers, and when he didn't see her right away, he burst up. Grasping the red comforter, he yanked, nearly ripping it off the mattress completely.

Madison was curled in the center of the mattress with her legs pulled in, but the sudden movement had her jolting awake. A strangled sound ripped from her throat as she scrambled back, eyes alarmed, dark hair tumbling over her shoulders and down her back.

"J-Jamie?" she stammered.

His shoulders relaxed, but his hand fisted tighter around the comforter. "You're too small. I thought you got kidnapped," he growled.

"Well, for a minute, I thought you were trying to kidnap me!"

He made a gruff sound and reached for her. She pressed a little farther into the wall. He paused and, voice low, told her, "C'mon now, Mads, I won't hurt you."

She relented, letting him tug her back into the middle of the bed. When she was settled, he pulled the blankets back up and covered her with the red comforter.

"Now I'm cold," she complained.

His hand smacked against his back when he reached around to pull his shirt over his head in one fluid movement.

"Hey!" she squeaked, trying to clutch the covers when he yanked them back once more.

Ignoring her, he draped the shirt over her body. "Body heat works faster," he murmured, tucking the blankets back around her.

She was utterly silent when his hands hit the mattress, body lowering toward her. "Go back to sleep. I'm sorry I scared you."

I smirked when he turned.

"What?" He glowered.

I opened my mouth, and he gave me the finger, stomping toward the bathroom. "Not one word, Ryan."

"But I thought we were bros!" I called after him.

"Fuck you." It was muffled through the door, but I heard him just fine.

We left the girls in our beds, trudging out to my Jeep where we downed caffeine on our way to the pool.

"Think he'll be here?" Jamie asked as I was parking.

"If he's smart, he won't be."

"You gonna be able to keep cool if he is?"

I squeezed the steering wheel, staring out the windshield without seeing. "Her bruises are worse this morning."

He was silent a minute. "Maybe we'll get lucky, and the cops hauled him in."

I appreciated that he didn't remind me I was supposed to be the bigger man. We both already knew. Knowing something didn't make it easy, though.

"Luck is for losers," I quipped, repeating something we always said.

I wasn't much of a believer in luck. People liked to tell us that was how we ended up on the Elite swim team at our exclusive college. Lucky to be born into money. Lucky to have skill.

Well, fuck luck, and I call bullshit. I work my ass off in that pool, and any recognition I get from that is a result of hard work.

Jamie's smile was quick. "Well, Hughes is a world-class loser, so here's hoping."

Inside, some of the team was already warming up.

Coach looked up as we walked in. "Nice of you to join us this morning."

"We're on time," we both said instantly. No way did either of us want to swim extra laps.

Coach made a sour face. "Barely. Get changed!"

We took off into the locker room, stripping down and shoving everything into our lockers before hustling back out. When we were halfway to the pool, a banging door pulled us up short.

"You son of a bitch!" The roar splintered the usually quiet warm-up.

I spun as Hughes charged, red-faced and pissed off. Coach blew the whistle hanging around his neck, the sound ringing in my ears and instantly transporting me back to last night, to the crushing panic of not being able to make it to Rory in time.

The sight of her tear-stained face burned the backs of my eyelids, followed quickly by the way she looked this morning reaching up to touch her swollen neck.

Hughes launched himself at me, fist swinging, and I caught it in my hand. He shouted in surprise, eyes whipping to where I palmed his fist.

"You never should have come here," I said quiet. Lethal.

"Me?" He raged, trying to pull his fist out of my grasp, but I crushed his fingers harder. Pain tightened the skin around his eyes, and his nostrils flared. "You're the one that shouldn't be here!"

Since I was still gripping one fist, he swung with the other. I knocked it back and shoved him away, his feet stuttering as he stumbled backward.

"Enough!" Coach yelled. "This is a complete disgrace."

Hughes scoffed, chest rising and falling rapidly. "You know what's a disgrace? Walsh," he spat, jamming his finger toward me. "You're disloyal. Instead of siding with the team, with Elite, he gets stupid over some nut wagon and believes all the shit she spews."

Jamie's intake of breath was the only sound that made it past the fury buzzing between my ears. Everything else went silent as though the someone hit pause, leaving only me in motion.

I stepped forward, eyes narrowing. "The fuck did you just say?"

Hughes puffed up, swiping the back of his hand over his mouth. "I called that lying bitch a nut wa—"

Bam. My fist plowed into his jaw so hard he fell onto his ass.

The whistle drowned out the slew of curses from the rest of the team, but I didn't listen. I bent over, yanking his chest off the floor by the front of his shirt, and smashed my fist into his face again.

"Stop!" Coach roared, inserting himself between us, facing me. His jaw was tense, brows drawn down. "You know we have a no-violence policy!"

"Then uphold it." I challenged.

Coach's eyes widened, disbelief filling them. I was tired of this. Tired of him. His empty threats pissed me off almost as much as Hughes.

"You want to be suspended from the next meet?" he asked.

I shrugged a shoulder. "I'll take my punishment like a man 'cause I can admit to what I did. But if you're gonna punish me, then be fair and punish him too."

"I'm the injured one!" Hughes wailed from the floor.

Fucking pansy.

I ignored him completely, eyes never once leaving Coach. "My girl found you some evidence."

Coach's eyes sharpened.

"Liar," Hughes insisted, rushing forward.

Coach held his arm out, but Jamie grabbed him by the back of the neck and yanked him back.

"Funny thing is"—I went on, ignoring all the chaos—"soon as she found another one of his victims, they were both attacked again. Rory has a ring of bruises around her neck from someone nearly strangling her last night."

"It wasn't me," Hughes wailed.

"Like it wasn't you that tried to force yourself on those girls?" Jamie deadpanned. His voice was dangerously low, and I knew if both of us lost our cool, this would not end well.

I crossed my arms over my bare chest. "So yeah, Coach, you wanna punish me for violence? Go ahead, but then you're gonna have to punish him too."

"I spent three hours last night at the police station," Hughes announced, shoving away from Jamie. "All because you assholes blame me every time that girl sneezes."

"Have charges been filed?" Coach asked, angling between us so he could look over at Hughes.

"No. You know why? Because I didn't do it. My alibi checked out."

"Bullshit," I growled.

"The cops don't seem to think so." Hughes challenged. He was a smug bastard.

"My office. Now," Coach declared. Then to the rest of the team, he ordered, "Laps!"

Everyone stood in frozen silence until I turned on my heel for the locker room. Everything started up again, but still, I was hyperaware of Hughes's every move. True to my instincts, the second Coach walked away, he charged.

But I expected it. He wasn't the type to fight fair.

He didn't seem to understand that I wasn't either.

Pushing off my heel, I shot forward, sinking low and catching him around the waist. My momentum bulldozed him back until he teetered on the edge of the pool. His sneakers slipped on the round lip, and he fell backward, but I caught him by the shirt, towing him up so he was partially hanging over the water.

His hand slapped onto my forearm, gripping like he could pull himself up. "What are you doing?" he asked. "Pull me up!"

I smirked, and his eyes widened.

The smirk turned into a rumbling chuckle. Cocking my head, I said, "What's the matter, Hughes? I thought you liked getting wet." I towed him up as his feet squeaked against the tile, scrambling for footing. Relief flickered in his eyes, and I smiled.

The relief instantly transformed into wariness.

"Relax," I told him. "You don't have anything to worry about. At least you can swim."

My fist smashed into his nose, snapping his head back at the same moment I let go of his shirt. His body flopped into the pool, back slapping against the still water with a sharp smack.

It sucked him down, arms floating out to his sides. The cold temperature must have shocked him back to awareness because his body went rigid and his arms pushed through the water. His head cleared the surface as he sputtered and coughed.

Coach grabbed my arm, yanking me around. "What the hell is wrong with you, Walsh? What did I just tell you?"

"Let me make this easy for you," I said, pulling my arm free. "I'm not swimming with an asshole who hides behind the Elite name and uses its reputation as a means to attack women. You won't take him off the team? Fine. I'm out."

Coach sputtered. "You can't just quit."

I took a few steps back, heading for the door. Holding my

arms out, I smiled. "Haven't you heard? Elite can do anything."

Jamie started after me.

"Owens," Coach intoned.

Jamie looked over his shoulder. "I'm with Walsh, and I'm not swimming with that douchebag either."

A low murmur went through the team who stood around watching.

"Me either," Wes said, grabbing his bag.

Several other members did the same.

"Get your asses back on deck," Coach insisted.

Kruger, one of the best backstroke swimmers we had, turned to him. "Half of us were at the diner the night Walsh's tires were slashed and his girl was attacked in the bathroom. It spread like wildfire across campus that the cops were called to the theater building last night." He glanced at Hughes, then away. "I don't know for sure if he's involved or not, but Walsh sure seems convinced, and if he's right…" His voice trailed off as he shook his head. "I might not have a girl, but I have sisters. And friends. Elite is a lot of things, but it ain't this."

A few others who'd been hesitating grabbed their stuff too.

The second my hand closed around the locker room door handle, Coach called my name, disappointment heavy in his voice.

Regret and discontent squeezed my chest. I didn't want to walk. I loved swimming. But it seemed I loved Carrot more.

Tightening my fingers on the handle, I glanced over. Jamie was a solid presence at my side.

"I'm sorry, Coach. But you disappointed me too. I thought you were better than this."

The words dropped over the room, leaving everything silent like a sealed tomb.

I and more than half of the swim team went into the locker room, a morose vibe hanging over us. We all got dressed, the only sound the creak of lockers, sliding of zippers, and rustle of clothes.

I knew I needed to say something, but my throat felt tight. Coach mentioned before how influential I was with the team, and yeah, I knew it… but I didn't really *know* it.

I did now.

When push came to shove, these guys stood behind me, going as far as giving up on the shit they lived and breathed.

How could I allow it?

I couldn't. But I had to.

Clearing my throat, I turned. Sensing I was about to speak, they all looked up, and a hefty sense of responsibility settled on my shoulders.

As they waited, I looked at each one of them, meeting their gazes for long moments.

"I, ah… should tell you all to get your heads out of your asses and get back out there," I said, half smiling when a few guys scoffed. The amusement was short-lived, though, as I went on. "But I'm not going to because even if this wasn't my girl he was attacking, she would still be someone. No one should have to walk around scared, worried for their safety. I'm all about enjoying the perks being an Elite comes with—"

"Bro, yeah," Jamie quipped, and some of the tension in the room broke.

"But having women scared of us because one of our own is forcing himself on them and using our name to shut her up? It affects us all."

"What do you want us to do?" Wes asked, and everyone else nodded.

A surge of gratitude hit me, making the responsibility I suddenly felt saddled with a lot less daunting. "For the time being, we'll run our own practices," I said, knowing damn well we couldn't just stay out of the water.

Just missing one day of practice would set a swimmer two days behind. This was a constant sport. Improvement was hard-won, and it was hard-kept too. Use it or lose it they say, and in a swimmer's case, it was true.

We coordinated a time, and everyone agreed.

"Keep hitting the gym too," I instructed. "

"What about Coach?" Prism spoke up from the back. "What if he replaces us?"

A ripple of concern swirled around us, and I held up my hand. "He won't." I was sure. "He can't. We're already partway into the season. He can't just replace half the team. Even if he could, he'd have to start over with training. It would be a massive blow to Westbrook, and considering Elite is basically what this entire school is famous for..." I shook my head. "Hughes might have influence, but he doesn't have that much. We didn't quit today. We just showed them we aren't gonna let them push us around."

I slammed my locker shut with a definitive sound. "Leave it to me. I'll work it out. We'll be back to our regular schedule and Coach telling us oxygen is overrated in no time."

"You aren't alone, though," Jamie reminded me.

"I know. You all made that crystal clear. Which is exactly why I'm going to make sure none of us suffer for the shit that asshole is pulling."

After that, we packed up and headed out the side door, refusing to even walk past Coach and the pool again.

Enough time had passed that the sun was up now. The air was cold, the sky overcast and dim. It reminded me of Carrot's eyes.

The team parted somberly, and again, guilt twisted in my gut.

Jamie slapped me on the back. "Bro. Did you just become an icon?"

I couldn't help it. I laughed. "Fuck off, Jamie."

"For reals, though! That was inspired shit."

I paused at the front of the Jeep, grabbing his wrist to stop him from heading for the passenger side. "I just challenged Coach." My voice was low.

Jamie went serious. People didn't often realize it, but my best friend could be serious. "It had to be done."

I met his eyes. "Would you have done it?"

"I'm standing here, aren't I?"

"Because we're bros."

He laid a hand over his chest. "Till the end of time."

I rolled my eyes. I never said his seriousness lasted very long.

"If you had backed down in there, I would have picked it up." Jamie's voice was quiet when I turned to get in the Wrangler. "He hurt our girl." Pause. "Both of them." Another pause. "So yeah. I would have done the same."

The tight coil of doubt inside me relaxed. I didn't regret what I'd done. Not for a single second. But still, knowing Jamie was behind me because he thought what I did was right and not just because that was what we did for each other made it easier.

Glancing over my shoulder, I smirked. "So that's how it is, huh?"

"What?" He played dumb.

Once we were settled inside the Jeep, the engine rumbling underfoot, I rolled my head toward him. "You and *Mads*."

"Don't call her that," Jamie bitched, and my smile grew wider. His eyes narrowed. "And it ain't like anything. I let her sleep in my bed last night because making a woman who was terrorized and scared sleep on the floor is a dick move."

I nodded. He was right. "So if that's all it is, you won't mind if I call her Mads."

"I don't even know why we're friends." He wondered.

I laughed. "Breakfast is on me."

His white teeth flashed as he settled farther into the seat. "Suddenly, I remember."

Thirty-One

Rory

Before leaving for swim practice, the guys made more noise than a marching band.

We pretended to sleep like they were being quiet, but the minute they were gone and blissful silence fell over the room, both of our heads popped up, our bleary eyes connecting.

"They made coffee." Madison groaned. "How is anyone supposed to sleep once coffee starts brewing?"

"I think they were trying to be quiet," I mused. "Can you imagine how loud they are when they aren't trying?"

We both laughed. Well, Madison laughed. I made a sound that was reminiscent of torture.

"Are you feeling okay?" she asked, clearly hearing the heinous sound.

Grimacing, I pushed up, letting the blankets fall around my legs. "I'm okay. Just sore." Pushing at my hair, I said, "Hey, I don't think I thanked you."

Madison leaned against the wall. Her hair was long, the length falling over her breasts. "I think the thanks was implied."

"But seriously, thank you. He wanted to kill me." The echo of his creepy-as-hell chuckle reverberated through my head, prickling my arms with goose bumps.

"Well, now we're even."

My brow furrowed.

"You know, because you scared off Jonas that night." Madison clarified.

Right. You know you've had too many close calls when you start forgetting all the ways you were attacked and nearly died. "Friends don't keep score." I cringed a bit at the sound of my voice.

"I don't have a lot of friends."

That surprised me. "I expected you to be the star of the theater department."

She made a sound and flipped her long dark locks. "I am." But then she turned serious. "Popularity doesn't always equal friends. Real friends are hard to find, you know? It's easier to just be friends with everyone but really no one."

I nodded. "Keep them at arm's length."

"Exactly."

"Well, if you ever need a real friend, I'm here."

She smiled. "Same."

What was it about trauma? About intense situations that brought people together? Was it because those times cut through all the bullshit and layers to get to the core? To get to who people really were? You learned fast who you could count on.

Ryan and I formed a bond that night I almost drowned. And now it seemed Madison and I were also forming one.

"If I'd have known the unholy hour we would be awakened, I wouldn't have bothered to pack some stuff up last night," Madison said, grimacing.

"I guess I should have warned you about their early practices."

"We had other things on our minds."

"Like Jonas," I said. Just thinking about him made my stomach drop.

She gave a delicate shiver, pulling something up around her. "Seems so wrong that someone with so much going for him would be so… empty inside."

Wait. *Is that Jamie's shirt?*

"Sun's coming up." She went on, glancing toward the window where thin bands of dim light shone around the edges. "I might as well head to my room to get ready. It seems so odd to just get up, get dressed, and go on with the day after last night."

"Stay. Get ready here. Apparently, Elite get their own bathrooms." I waved a hand in its direction. "We're going to breakfast when they get back. Come with."

Truth was I didn't have enough brain power last night to grab anything from my dorm. And because I refused to stay here with Ryan, I didn't have anything stashed. I was the one who should be heading to my dorm to change, but I was feeling the same way Madison was. Like I wasn't quite ready to just go on with life as if nothing happened. I liked being in Ryan's bed, surrounded by his scent. It made me feel safe.

"Sure, why not? Might as well take advantage of a private bathroom," she said, sliding out of the bed to grab a curling wand and a small zippered case from her bag.

"Ooh, can I borrow that when you're done?" I asked, gesturing to the tool.

"Sure, I'll leave it plugged in for you."

Madison went into the bathroom, leaving the door open, and I sat there a moment longer, a sudden feeling of unease rising inside me, pushing out the sleepy warmth. My throat ached when I swallowed down the sudden panic, and the pain only seemed to make the unsettled feelings worse.

Trying not to focus on them, I got up and put on the jeans I had worn yesterday—hey, a girl had to do what a girl had to do—but I left Ryan's T-shirt on, knotting the excess material at the waist. My shirts from yesterday were ruined. Just remembering last night sent a warm flush over my skin, the heat burning away the worst of the anxiety pummeling me.

Ryan loves me.

And he definitely had a unique way of showing it. Rubbing his release into my skin like he could brand me seemed archaic. It should also be gross. Right?

I mean, there was a definite sticky factor. But everything else?

Hot as sin.

The way he looked, smug and satisfied, as he rubbed himself all over me. The way his blue eyes seared with possession. No, I didn't mind being owned by Ryan. In fact, I welcomed it.

While Madison was curling some loose waves in her long dark hair, I washed my face at the sink and then grabbed my bag, sitting on Ryan's bed. I had a few necessities like lip-gloss, moisturizer, and mascara.

I'd just closed my fingers around the lip-gloss when the door aggressively swung in. Two large bodies darkened the opening, and the panic I'd been trying to control reared its ugly head.

Squealing, I dropped the gloss, bunching my hands in the material of my bag, pulling it into my chest like somehow it would shield me.

"It's me," Ryan said, pushing the door closed behind Jamie.

Heart beating wildly, I kept my palm pressed against it as

I stared at them wide-eyed. I knew I was safe with both of them. I had not a single doubt, but neither of them was emanating *peace-comfort-safe* vibes at the moment.

"What are you doing here? I thought you had practice," I asked, voice breathless.

Ryan's mood was black as he stalked over to push his hands under my arms. It was completely ridiculous that he pulled me up like I was nothing but a toy, holding me out so I practically dangled over the floor.

The pounding of my heart was so erratic that I said nothing at all as he held me out, navy eyes sweeping over me as though he were inspecting me for damage.

"You just saw me like thirty minutes ago," I told him, finally finding my voice.

"Where's Madison?" Jamie glowered. Then before I could answer, he bellowed, "Mads!"

Something in the bathroom clattered on the sink, and she appeared in the doorway. "Jamie?"

"What the hell are you doing?" he demanded.

"Curling my hair."

"It's six o'clock in the morning," he grumped, and I openly stared at him.

"Well, thank God you told me. I never would have known," she quipped, sarcasm dripping from her tongue.

"You should be asleep." He pointed to his bed like that was where she belonged.

I glanced at Ryan, but he was looking at me with unreadable eyes. Forgetting all about Jamie's foul mood, I focused on the man holding me. "Ry," I called softly. "What are you doing here? Practice isn't over till seven thirty."

His stare went soft, the navy literally melting into the cobalt color I so loved. "I'm not swimming this morning," he replied gruffly, gently setting me on my feet.

"Why?" I questioned.

His eyes slipped to the ring of bruises on my neck, the muscles in his jaw jerking.

I glanced at Jamie, hoping he would say something.

"Hughes showed up," he said, eyes moving back to Madison.

Suddenly, the anxiety I felt earlier made much more sense. Intuitively, I must have known something was happening with Ryan. I sucked in a concerned breath and stepped forward. This time, it was my eyes that roamed his body, searching for any kind of injury.

My eyes latched on to his red knuckles. "Oh, Ryan," I groaned, slipping my hand into his to lift it. "You were fighting again?"

He tried to tug his hand back, but I held a little tighter, eyes flashing up to his. "Let me see. Please."

He relented, and I studied the puffy red knuckles.

"Bastard deserved it," Ryan insisted.

"Bro, yeah, he did." Jamie concurred.

They were cavemen. Both of them.

"What happened?" I asked, brushing my thumb gently over the back of his hand.

He said nothing. And this time, Jamie remained silent too.

"Did you get in trouble for fighting?" I pressed. "Is that why you're here so early?"

Ryan's eyes turned mutinous. "I walked out."

Letting go of his hand, I gasped. "What? You just walked out? Ryan! You can't do that."

Jamie made a noise. "More than half the team walked out with him."

"What?" This time, Madison joined in with my incredulous reaction. Leaving the bathroom doorway, she came to stand in the middle of the room with the rest of us.

She smelled good, a light scent that wafted toward me,

and I knew it was likely from whatever she sprayed on her hair just before.

She was already dressed in a pair of high-waisted jeans and an off-the-shoulder army-green sweater. "You walked out too?" she asked Jamie.

"Hell yeah, I did. I ain't swimming with that piece of pollution."

Ryan made a gruff sound of agreement.

Madison's eyes strayed to Ryan's hand. Then warily, she looked at Jamie. "Did you punch him too?"

Jamie pursed his lips, his eyes taking in her face and long, wavy hair. "I should have," he said almost to himself. Madison stiffened, and his eyes shot back to her. "But I didn't. One of us had to stay cool."

"Ryan," I said, stepping closer, laying my palm against his hip.

His long exhale ruffled the top of my bedhead. "It's nothing you need to worry about. C'mon, I'll take you to breakfast."

"How can you think about food at a time like this?" I demanded, craning my neck so I could stare up at him. And if he thought this was *nothing I needed to worry about,* he was an idiot.

"Punching faces always works up an appetite."

Crossing my arms over my chest, I glared. "Tell me everything. Right now."

Ryan smirked. "You're cute when you try and boss me."

"I haven't even had my coffee yet, Ryan Steven Walsh. Don't start with me," I warned.

"Well, come on, then. Let's go get you some."

"I need to comb my hair," I announced, turning on my heel and going into the bathroom.

"I left the wand on for you," Madison called out.

"Did you scatter a bunch of girl shit all over our bathroom?" Jamie bemoaned.

"That's what you get for punching people!" I yelled.

My hands were trembling when I looked in the mirror over the sink. My cheeks were flushed, and the bruises ringing my neck were heinous. Looked like scarves were about to become my favorite fashion statement. Good thing it was fall.

Ryan's wide frame dwarfed the bathroom door, and I glanced at him out of the corner of my eye. I was upset with him going around punching people and then acting like he didn't have to explain himself to me.

I know I said being his possession made me feel safe, but there was a difference between being protected by someone and being treated like a child.

Ignoring him completely, I picked up the brush and started working it through my hair. As I did, he moved farther into the bathroom, closing the door and then leaning against it. The weight of his eyes was heavy, but not uncomfortable. As upset as I was, I had to resist the urge to sneak glances at him.

It seemed Ryan had become the one I wanted to soothe all my distress… even when my ache was him.

The big jerk.

The brush made a light tapping sound when I set it on the small counter, my fingers coming up lucky when I found a small elastic hair tie in the pocket of my jeans.

The broody way he stared made my stomach twist the entire time I pulled half of my hair up into a ponytail at my crown. Once it was the way I wanted, I found he was still staring, my stomach still flopping.

To give myself a few more minutes to compose myself, I reached for the curling wand so I could add a little wave to the hair near my ears.

Even though he was quiet and utterly gracious, his presence was unavoidable. He sucked out all the oxygen from the room, sucked out rational thought, and even fought against my anger because, really, I yearned to throw the wand in the sink and blanket myself against his body to feel his arms close around me.

When he pushed off the door, closing the distance between us, his dark mood did nothing to dissuade me from wanting to bury myself in him. If anything, it made me want to climb him more.

Even though I practically vibrated with need, I ignored him still. Stepping up, he towered behind me with me barely coming to his shoulder. His chest was broad and visible even with me standing in front of him. I could see the long column of his throat, the thick lump of his Adam's apple, and all of his sullen face.

His dark hair was mussed as though he'd been running his hands through it, and his eyes glittered dangerously. Still, I was not afraid.

I would never be afraid of Ryan Walsh. I loved him far too fiercely to ever fear him.

My thick swallow was audible, the spit scraping down my swollen throat, but I pretended it didn't matter, that I didn't feel it.

My heart stuttered heavily when he reached out, grabbing the wand out of my hand and setting it aside.

My eyes met his in the mirror, our gazes finally colliding. Something inside me eased as if avoiding his stare had been physically painful.

"You're mad," he said, voice making me shiver.

I shrugged one shoulder. "It's nothing for you to worry about," I said, throwing his words from moments ago right back at him.

His tongue swiped over his front teeth, a cross between a

smirk and a smile tugging at the corners of his lips. Chills raced across my entire body when his long fingers gathered the hair at my neck and pushed it to one side.

In the mirror, I watched his dark head dip, face disappearing into the side of my neck so he could rub his lips ever so gently over the bruises.

"Brat," he murmured, brushing another gentle kiss across my skin.

I moved restlessly, trying to slip away, but he made a sound, pressing me into the cabinet with a thrust of his hips. "You aren't going anywhere," he rumbled, nuzzling beneath my ear.

Everything under my skin was buzzing, and I wanted so badly to be mad at his ability to turn me malleable, but it just felt so damn good.

A needy little sound escaped me, my ass arching into his crotch. The second his hard length pressed against my crack, my eyes rolled back in my head.

"You pissed I hit him again? Or pissed I won't tell you about it?"

This was important, and I couldn't think when he was pressed against me, lips hovering over my skin like a promise.

I pulled my ass away, wanting to keep a clear head, but his hands gripped my hips, pulling me right back into his body.

I whimpered.

"Tell me, baby."

"Tell you what?" I murmured.

His warm chuckle only made it worse, and when his nimble fingers undid my jeans and pushed them over my hips, the rest of my mind blanked out.

There was simply no room in my head for thought when he was ruling me with pleasure.

"I want to be inside you, baby." His teeth nipped at the

shell of my ear. I panted as his palm slipped under my panties, cupping my ass.

"You're mine and no one else's. He came at me. He had your name in his mouth. He's lucky all I did was knock him on his ass."

My entire body was on fire, the blood in my veins burning and my legs clenching around something that wasn't there.

"Ryan," I whined, sliding my hand up around the back of his head, my fingers twisting in his hair.

His finger slid down my ass crack, making me push back into him more. He kept going, sliding farther until his finger met the wet heat in my core.

A low curse fell between us as he swirled his fat finger around, teasing my opening but not quite pushing in. I made a sound, rubbing along the front of his body like a cat.

"Tell me yes, baby."

"Yes."

He shoved his sweats and my panties down, the silky skin pulled taut over his rigid dick nudging against my ass.

"Spread your legs." The demand was husky as his cock pushed between them.

I tried, but the jeans around my thighs only allowed so much. Impatient, he growled, yanking them down the rest of the way and then grabbing my hips to lift my feet off the ground. The jeans fell away, and my legs opened.

At the same time he brought me down, he thrust up. I gasped at the sudden, swift intrusion. My body clenched around him so tight I felt his intake of breath.

Groaning, he buried his face in the side of my neck, large body shuddering around mine. "Goddamn. What you do to me."

His cock was so hard it kept me upright, feet barely on

the floor. Both his arms wrapped around my waist, squeezing so tight I was near breathless.

And then he rocked up. He held me so tight there was nowhere for me to go. My hands gripped his forearms as he pistoned into me over and over.

Dizzy with lust, I dropped my chin, and through hazy eyes, I stared at our reflection, at his dark head still buried in my neck and broad shoulders blanketing my body. Red marks decorated his forearms from the way my nails gripped him with every thrust, and a warm blush covered my cheeks.

Dragging in a ragged breath, he lifted his face. Seeing my stare, he allowed his chin to drop onto my shoulder, staring at the way our bodies rocked up when he thrust again.

Everything was hazy. The only thing that felt real was his thick, throbbing erection burying itself deeper inside me with every thrust. The squelching sounds created by my body's lubrication only made everything that much more surreal. Our gazes stayed locked together, our bodies joined in the most intimate way. Ry supported all my weight, his movements becoming sloppy and impatient as our breathing turned ragged and my eyes started to slide closed.

"I'm close." His voice was like gravel, the rough sound making me clench harder around him. "I want to fill you up so bad."

I nodded, wanting it too.

His eyes darkened, hips stuttering. With a growl, he went still. The loss of friction made me ache, my nails digging back into his arms.

"Ry..." I panted, squirming around on this throbbing cock.

"No rubber," he bit out as though it were taking everything he had not to move.

"Good," I whispered.

His nostrils flared, and another growl ripped right out of

him. His grip on my hips was punishing, and I was sure there would be bruises from his fingers. Those were the kind of bruises I would welcome.

I cried out with the powerful thrust, body folding over the countertop as I felt him burst inside me. The jerking of his cock was heady, as was the realization he was doing exactly what he said—filling me up.

His body bowed, legs shaking under the force of the orgasm, and then his teeth were lightly sinking into my shoulder as aftershocks coursed through him and into me. I shuddered, his pleasure heightening my own.

Both of us still bent over the counter and his body plastered against my back, he reached around, long fingers dipping into my folds to stroke over my sensitive, swollen clit.

My whole body bucked, and I let out a whine. His cock was still hard, and it gave a little jerk when I clenched around him.

"Be a good girl and come on my cock," he whispered in my ear.

I made a strangled sound, and he pinned me farther against the counter, stroking my clit with confident fingers. Pulling almost all the way out, he thrust back in, and I fell over the edge, body vibrating with pleasure, eyes blind, and head empty.

He moaned lightly against my ear. "That's my girl."

I shuddered again, then collapsed, utterly spent. He stayed wrapped around me until our breathing evened out, but it still felt too soon when he pulled away. I made a sound of protest, and he laughed under his breath, pulling me around to sit me on the counter in front of him.

The countertop was cold against my hot, bare skin, making my nose wrinkle. Bracing his hands on either side of my hips, he leaned in, brushing his lips over my cheek in more of a caress than a kiss.

His attention and presence embraced me, throwing me slightly off-kilter but not unsteady because of his strength. The warm brush of his breath ruffled my hair and tickled my ear. "I don't want you to blame yourself."

I jerked back so our eyes could collide. "What?"

"I know you." He attempted a scowl, but the hazy effects from sex lingering in his eyes made it a lot less effective than he probably hoped. "You already tried once to walk when you thought you were getting in the way of my swimming."

"You're fighting with your teammates. Your coach. You just walked out of practice," I pointed out. "I *am* getting in the way."

"You never asked me to choose."

My eyes flared, indignant. "I would never."

He cocked his head. "Why?"

I sucked in a breath. "What kind of question is that?" I demanded.

How offensive.

Before he could say anything else, I forged on. "What kind of girlfriend would I be if I took you away from your passion—something you were doing long before we met? Jonas isn't worth it."

"No. He's not." Ryan cut me off. "But you are."

My breath caught. "W-what?"

"You would never ask me to choose. But what if I want to?"

"No," I whispered. "You can't."

"Why?" he echoed. "Are you afraid I won't pick you?"

My breath caught, chest squeezing tight. *Why would he?* Yes, he might love me, but he loved swimming far longer.

"But I do. *I did*," he murmured, shifting closer, one palm blanketing my hip. "It's not a choice between you and swimming, though. Because you already made it clear I could have both."

"But you walked out," I said, trying to understand.

"I chose you over Jonas," he told me. "And yeah, I walked out. Not because *you* asked me to choose but because *they* did. I don't want to be part of a team that expects blind loyalty to men who don't deserve it. I love swimming. I love being an Elite. But I had to make a point. *We* all did. And I don't want you to feel guilty for a choice *I* made on my own."

I remembered what Jamie said before. "Half the team walked out with you?"

"More than half. We can't sacrifice everything for that shitbag."

Chewing my lower lip, I nodded. "So you didn't quit?"

"No, baby, I didn't."

I nodded, relieved. "So now what?"

He pulled in a breath, releasing it on a long exhale. Shifting back, he cupped my face in his big, warm hands. My eyes drifted closed momentarily because he was just so reassuring.

His forehead met mine, and we stood like that for a few quiet heartbeats until his voice filled the room. "When people won't believe, when they won't listen, you make them."

My eyes lifted.

"You wanna help me with that?" he asked.

My heart turned over. "I think I might have an idea."

Thirty-Two

Ryan

The dean's office was located in the oldest building on campus. Dude probably thought it made him all-powerful. I just thought it made him old.

To be real, I wasn't harboring much respect for the people who were supposedly in charge around here. So it was like I told my girl. If they didn't want to listen, I'd make them.

The moment we rounded the corner, the assistant perched at a large wooden desk perked up. I kept myself angled slightly in front of Carrot as we went, something I would probably always do. The instinct to shield her was automatic, like breathing.

"You're here to see Dean Cardinal?" the woman asked.

"Yes, ma'am. Ryan Walsh."

She nodded. "Yes, I know who you are." Her eyes moved from me to Jamie. "Our swimmers here are a real pride for Westbrook."

"Sure got a funny way of showing it," I mused.

Carrot elbowed me in the side. "Ryan."

The woman picked up the black phone and buzzed in to the dean who was literally twenty feet behind double oak doors.

"He will be right with you," she said demurely after speaking quietly into the phone.

Not even three seconds later, one of the doors to his office opened. Dean Cardinal appeared, wearing a tailored navy suit with a pinstripe tie. His hair was dark but graying at the sides and temples. He wore it brushed away from his forehead, and his eyes were brown.

"Mr. Walsh. Mr. Owens," he said. "To what do I owe the honor of a visit from two of our best swimmers?"

The fact he didn't acknowledge the two women standing with us indicated exactly how this was gonna go. I slid a glance at Jamie, and by the look in his eye, I knew he was thinking the exact same thing.

While the four of us made our way into the large office with dark wood and ivy-green accents, I felt a moment of embarrassment that I didn't realize how archaic this world still was. I never realized women were disregarded so much in favor of the men here.

Or maybe it was just because we were Elite. I didn't know. And frankly, it didn't fucking matter. It ended right the hell now.

Madison closed the door behind us as Dean Cardinal took up space behind his desk. Unbuttoning his suit jacket, he smiled. "Please have a seat."

There were two chairs and four of us. He probably expected me and Jamie to sit and make the girls stand behind us.

"We'll stand," I deadpanned.

He blanched ever so slightly but then recovered to say, "However you are most comfortable."

"Thank you for seeing us on such short notice," I said, using the manners I was taught but mentally giving this man the finger.

"I'll always have time for my Elite."

I wasn't his anything. "We might not be Elite much longer."

His hands came to rest on top of his desk, brows furrowing. "I'm sorry?"

"I guess Coach forgot to mention half the team walked out of practice," Jamie put in.

Horror stole over his face. "When was this?" he asked.

"This morning."

Straightening, the dean picked up his phone, which looked identical to the one his assistant had. After pressing a button, he spoke into the line immediately. "Linda. Get Coach Resch to my office. Now." Then he hung up.

"What is going on?" he asked, staring right at me.

Reaching around, I pressed my palm to Carrot's back. "Maybe you remember my girlfriend, Rory Coin."

For the first time since we walked into the room, he looked fully at her. Recognition lit his face, followed by wariness.

"Ah, yes, Miss Coin. We spoke a few weeks ago."

"Actually, I spoke, and you didn't believe anything I said."

The dean flushed. "Now that's not what happened."

She tilted her head, and the half ponytail she was wearing slid to the side. "Really? Because I distinctly remember coming to you to report an attempted rape and you taking the accused's side."

The man sighed heavily, leaning back in his chair. "There are no sides here. You had a bad date, and—"

She stiffened, and my body instantly tensed. "There's a difference between a bad date and being attacked," she insisted.

"Miss Coin, I have to caution you against making such serious allegations against upstanding students here at Westbrook. Without evidence to—"

I broke in, words quiet and even. "I have to caution you to watch what you say to my girlfriend."

Dean Cardinal blanched. "You are also alleging that your fellow Elite attempted to rape your girlfriend? Why would he do that?"

"Because he's a sick fuck," Jamie muttered.

The muscles in my neck bunched so forcefully that I felt a twinge of pain behind my eye. Stepping up to the desk, I glowered down at the man sitting behind it. "I'm more curious as to why you put his word over a victim's."

"I'm not," he said, authority ringing in his voice. "It is my job to look at both sides, and to be frank, it's all hearsay. They both admitted to going on a date, and it ended badly. There is no evidence to prove otherwise. Jonas Hughes is an Elite of this university and is one of our best swimmers."

"Yeah? Well, I've been outswimming him." Childish? Maybe? Did I regret saying it? Hells to the no.

"Bro, yeah," Jamie echoed. He was a good wingman.

The dean held up his hand. "I'm aware of your very impressive record as of late. No one is doubting your ability." He paused. "And given the fact that you are also held in such high regard and have a lot going for you in terms of Elite, I would hope you could appreciate that I would try and protect it when people come to me with unfounded allegations. It would be irresponsible of me to allow a promising athlete's career to be derailed because of something that might not even be true."

Carrot made a sound.

Automatically, I slipped my hand around her waist, tugging her into my side. I couldn't help but wonder how many other athletes around here were "protected" because the school wanted to look good.

"You know what else is irresponsible? Letting a rapist walk around campus." I challenged.

The dean pushed to his feet. "As I said before, there is absolutely no evidence."

"Except my word," Carrot put in.

"Yes, well, unfortunately, your word doesn't carry enough weight to—"

"What about mine?" Madison spoke up for the first time since entering. And also, for the first time, I noticed the way Jamie was slightly angled in front of her, partially blocking her from sight. As she spoke, she moved around him, stepping toward the desk.

Dean Cardinal's stare moved to her almost dismissively. But then he did a double take. This time, his eyes gleamed with more interest… and a little more panic.

"Miss Hartley," he said, "I didn't see you there."

"Because you only see Elite," she retorted coolly.

"Wait. You know her?" Jamie said, stare bouncing between them. Turning to Madison, he asked, "Did you come here and report Hughes? He blow you off too?"

"No," Madison replied. "He just knows me because I do stuff for the school theater."

I wasn't so sure that was the entire reason, but I wasn't about to call her out. This wasn't what this was about. And frankly, it didn't matter.

Madison cleared her throat. "And because you should also know that if you don't take us seriously this time, I will broadcast it all over campus."

"That's against regulations—"

"So is protecting a rapist," she deadpanned.

Damn. She was as feisty as Carrot. A quick glance at Jamie, and I noted the pride in his eyes as he looked at her.

Bro had it bad.

"Are you saying Jonas Hughes also attacked you?" the dean said, choosing not to push against her words.

"Yes. He did. Jonas Hughes did exactly the same thing to me that he did to Rory. He took me to the planetarium, used a bunch of cheesy lines, and then tried to take things much further than I wanted."

The dean swallowed. "You said he tried?"

"Yes, because Rory stopped him."

"And then he threw my camera, which had proof on it, into the pool," Rory supplied. "Moments later, he shoved me into the pool too."

"If I hadn't been there practicing late, she would have drowned."

The dean looked at me. "You pulled her out of the pool?"

I nodded. "The camera too." Cocking my head to the side, I said, "You gonna accuse me of lying?"

"Of course not," he murmured.

"Then why isn't my word good enough?" Rory wondered. The underlying defeat in the soft words pricked my heart and caused a sharp pain in my chest.

Ignoring everyone else in the room, I pulled her completely against my front, leaning over her shoulder to nuzzle her cheek. "It is, sweetheart. To me, your word is law."

The dean made an offensive sound. "I hardly—"

My head snapped up, and his lips pressed shut.

"I think you are well aware that if this got out, if I let everyone know what was happening here, this university would be embroiled in a scandal that would reach beyond the campus news," Madison said. "You said her word wasn't enough. Well, now you have my word. As well as numerous reports filed with the police on attacks in which Jonas Hughes has been named a person of interest."

The dean paled. "What?"

I gave him a brief rundown of what happened at the diner and then the theater.

Straightening, Rory pulled out of my hold, bringing herself right up against the front of his desk. The leopard-print scarf she wore draped strategically around her neck was pulled away.

"Bruises don't lie," she said, pointing at the blotchy mess on her throat. "And neither do police reports."

Twin spots of red bloomed over his cheeks. The tie around his neck looked mighty tight. "If Mr. Hughes had been arrested, I would have been notified."

"He wasn't arrested," Jamie said. "The cops are idiots like you."

"Jamie," Madison scolded.

"Like it's a lie," he retorted.

I resisted the urge to fist-bump him.

"I will not tolerate such disrespect," Dean Cardinal intoned, staring at Jamie who just scoffed.

"It ain't disrespect if it's the truth."

I smiled.

Turning away from him, the dean looked at Madison. "Well, if the police also have no evidence—"

And I've had enough. My aggressive growl drew everyone's eyes, and I pulled myself up to my full impressive height. "No, the cops don't have anything concrete because people like you protect Hughes. But the list of people he's wronged is growing. And when this gets out—"

"Because it will," Madison intoned.

Her threats seemed to make the dean nervous, and before I continued, I had a moment to once again wonder why.

"It's going to look bad. And the athlete you are so intent on protecting is going to drag down the entire team. Hell, maybe the university. So I have to ask. What's more important here: one athlete who might be innocent or losing half the team because we all refuse to swim with him?"

"This is why you all walked out of practice?"

I nodded. "And we aren't coming back until the trash is out of the pool."

"You can't do that,"

"We already did."

At that moment, Coach Resch came in the door without so much as a knock. "Philip, you asked to see—" He stopped, eyes widening. Then a resolved, almost tired look entered his gaze. "Ah, I understand."

"Just what kind of team have you been running, Emmett?" the dean bit out.

"This isn't all his fault." I spoke up before I could think better of it. Coach didn't deserve my defense, but after so long swimming for him, I guess it was hard not to give it. "If you had taken Rory seriously when she came to you, things wouldn't have gone this far."

Dean Cardinal ignored me completely, instead narrowing his eyes on Coach. "Half the team walked out?"

"More than half," Coach confirmed, his eyes sliding to me and then away.

The dean met my stare. "You all could be removed from this university for this stunt. Is that what you want?"

I shrugged. "Something tells me I'd recover, but this school? Maybe not."

Madison pulled out a piece of paper, laying it flat on the desk. "There are others," she announced. "We went to the planetarium today, spoke to the student who helps the director. Planetarium dates are Jonas's MO, and he has had *a lot* of dates."

Rory stepped up beside Madison. "There are two other girls with similar stories to ours." Her voice faltered, orange head lowering.

So I picked up where she left off. "And one girl who withdrew from this university two days after being seen there with Jonas."

"That doesn't mean he's the reason."

"Maybe it does," Madison stated.

"According to university policy, all of the information, allegations, and police reports are more than enough for you to launch an official investigation against Jonas Hughes."

I thought it was stupid as hell that Jonas was entitled to an investigation before being shown the door, but being the offspring of some high-powered lawyers, Rory just said, "Innocent until proven guilty."

Speaking of that…

"And if you don't"—Rory went on—"I will be forced to call my parents, which I've refrained from doing up until this point, where they practice in Chicago. Perhaps you might know of their legal work? They recently represented Hiram Marsh in his high-profile case that dominated the news for weeks."

The dean sat down.

I smiled. "That's the thing with trying to protect an Elite at a college known for its exclusivity. All of us have connections somewhere."

"You need to launch the investigation, Philip," Coach told him. "I, too, was willing to give Hughes the benefit of the doubt, but enough is enough. He isn't so good he can carry the entire team."

It was good Coach was keeping his word to help when I got evidence, but still, I couldn't help but feel like it was too little too late.

"Of course," Dean Cardinal said, drawing everyone's attention. "Given all of the allegations, supposition, and, ah, disquiet within our esteemed Elite, this university will uphold our standards and launch an official investigation into these matters involving Jonas Hughes immediately."

"What does that mean for him exactly?" Jamie asked. "Is he off the team?"

"Not officially," Coach answered, and I stiffened. "Cool it, Walsh. Just listen," he snapped.

He had three seconds.

"A student cannot be dismissed from Westbrook until the investigation is complete and the student is found guilty."

"How long is that going to take?" Carrot asked, wringing her hands.

"I can't say. It could be several weeks," the dean answered.

"What the—" I started, anger building in my chest.

He held up his hand. "However, while a student is under investigation, he is barred from all classes and campus activities."

"So no swimming?" Jamie clarified

"Correct. No swimming."

"That means you and all your followers are due back to the pool. Tomorrow morning." Coach glowered.

"As long as he's not there, we will be," I stated.

"But he's already so mad. He's going to be worse…" Rory fretted, turning away from the dean to find me with anxious eyes. The bruises around her throat were an ugly contrast to the perfection of her skin.

I held out my hand, motioning for her. She moved instantly, pressing along my front. My chest puffed out even as my heart tumbled. So readily, she came to me for comfort, not even caring about the people in the room, just knowing she would find it in my arms.

Cradling her head against my chest, I stared over her to the dean. "What about Hughes?"

"As I said, he will be banned from this entire university, pending the investigation."

I scoffed. "And who's going to stop him?"

"Besides the fact that all campus security will be alerted, I will also put a protection order on Miss Coin."

Jamie made a rude sound. "What about Madison?"

"Of course, her as well."

"Can you even do that? You aren't the police," Rory asked, not even lifting her head from my chest.

She was melting me. Melting me right here in a room full of people.

"Here at Westbrook, we absolutely can," he confirmed.

Seemed kinda stupid to have such perks at an exclusive school when the dean never wanted to utilize them.

He must have noted the unimpressed expression on my face because he said, "Of course, if you also want to file one with the local police, I could let them know that I support that."

Rory nodded, and he glanced at me, relieved. He thought his offer would somehow make me grateful. I was not grateful that I had to force this man to do his goddamn job.

What if I'd never met Rory? What about the other girls Jonas did this too—the one who left school? The faculty here might not want to admit it, but everyone in this room knew that girl dropped out because that bastard raped her.

"I want all this done today."

"It's already late in the afternoon."

"Today," I insisted. Then I added, "I won't be able to focus on swimming and the meet this weekend until I know he's gone."

Dean Cardinal nodded immediately, new understanding on his face. I guess now he was realizing that with Jonas out, I really was the top freestyle competitor. "Of course, of course. This weekend's meet is a big one."

He picked up his phone and told his assistant to ask

Hughes to come to his office. When the call was finished, he made another.

"Damien, it's Philip Cardinal." His voice hinted at familiarity that made my eyes narrow.

"Yes, I'm good. Thank you. Listen, ah, I'm not calling with good news, I'm afraid." Pause. "A matter has arisen with Jonas. He will be in my office shortly."

The man on the other end said something, but I couldn't make out his words.

The dean made a gruff sound. "You should come. And bring your attorney."

When the call was finished, I had to unhinge my tight jaw to speak. "You're friends with his father."

He cleared his throat. "We attended Westbrook at the same time. We are alumni."

Jamie whistled under his breath. "Nepotism."

"I take personal offense to that!" Dean Cardinal snapped.

"Yeah?" I challenged. "You call all your students' parents and tell them to bring a lawyer. Should we be worried this investigation is going to be incredibly biased?"

The dean slammed his fist on the desk, making everything rattle.

Rory stiffened, and I hugged her tighter.

"I would never," he insisted. "How dare you question my integrity as the dean of this college? All students under investigation have a right to an attorney. My calling Damien Hughes just moved things along faster, which is exactly what *you* asked of me."

"So we can assume Hughes will be removed from campus by tonight?"

"It might not be until tomorrow."

"And the university-served protection order?" I questioned.

"That will be done today in the presence of his attorney."

The dean sighed wearily. "Everything will be carried out according to policy and law. You don't need to worry. We will handle this. All you need to worry about is swimming."

He acted like I was the one most inconvenienced. Like these two girls weren't going to be forever plagued with nightmares from what they'd been put through.

I realized it then. The dean still didn't believe them. The only reason he was doing this was that we were forcing his hand. Because the team walked out. Because Madison threatened to make it public news. Because he needed me to pick up Hughes's slack.

I laughed, the sound hollow. I felt eyes shift to me.

Shaking my head, I gently pushed Rory toward the door. "C'mon, Carrot, time to go."

When we were almost out the door, the dean called my name, then Jamie's. "I hope you know that Westbrook is behind you. Elite has our full support. Please let the rest of the team know. I look forward to seeing how you rank this weekend."

I glanced at Coach who had the decency to look embarrassed.

"Just get him the hell off this campus. You do that, and I'll swim."

Jamie echoed my sentiments, and then we left.

The second the door was shut firmly behind us, Jamie blew out a big breath. "That man is so full of shit that if we tossed him in the pool, he'd float."

At her desk, the assistant giggled.

Jamie turned toward her and winked. "How you doing today, gorgeous?"

"He only agreed to any of that because of swimming." Carrot scowled.

Rory lifted her face, gray eyes seeking mine. "Do you think he'll keep his word?"

"He has no choice," Madison intoned.

I glanced at her, about to ask what the weird vibes were all about, but the assistant chose that moment to speak up.

"Oh, honey, I can confirm. If Dean Cardinal gave his word, then it will be done." She glanced at Jamie, a smile playing on her lips. "He might sometimes be full of poop, but when it comes to university policy, he's a man of his word."

"Were you listening at the door?" I asked.

She flushed.

Jamie laughed. "Don't worry. We won't tell. If I were you, I'd keep an eye on him too."

On our way past her desk, I stopped, snagged a pen out of a cup, and jotted my number on a yellow sticky note. "This probably isn't allowed," I said, flashing her a smile and leaning over the desk to whisper, "but neither is listening at the door."

She giggled, and I smiled wider.

"But I'm just trying to keep my girl safe. So if you happen to overhear anything about Hughes that I might need to know, please call me."

I slid the sticky note across the desk in front of her.

"Oh, well, I guess I could do that."

"Thanks, Linda," I said, remembering what the dean called her. Straightening, I gave her one more smile. "And Jamie's right. You do look gorgeous today."

Smiling, she laid her hand over the sticky note.

When I turned back around, it was to face the dark glower of my girl.

"Now, baby..." I began, putting on my best cajoling voice.

"Don't you play that game with me, Ryan." She swung her finger at me. "Put those blue eyes back in your head."

I batted the aforementioned blue eyes that were definitely already in my head.

Her glower turned to a scowl. It was fucking adorable.

Lunging forward, I scooped her up, tossing her over my shoulder as she shrieked, "Ryan!" She gasped. "Put me down."

"No," I said, settling a palm over her ass. "Not until you're done being jealous."

"I'm not jealous," she muttered, wiggling a little against my hand.

"I had to do it, shrimp. I didn't want to flirt with her, but I did it for you."

Her harumph made me smile.

Before going outside where Jamie and Madison waited, I pulled her down, her legs latching around my waist.

Palming her back, I pressed our noses together. "I'd do anything for you, baby. Anything to keep you safe."

She sighed. "Ryan."

"Give me some sugar."

"You don't deserve any,"

"Give me some anyway."

She did.

Thirty-Three

Rory

Do things ever really "go back to normal" after something traumatic happens? Even after the initial shock fades away, even after life resumes to include the mundane everyday routine, there are still remnants of whatever it was that changed things.

People liked to say it was a "new normal," and sure, maybe it was. Or maybe it was just learning to live with the fact that whatever happened changed you, so even when things went back to normal, you never would.

Jonas had been gone for two weeks already, but I still sometimes looked over my shoulder. I still sometimes worried this was a false sense of security because even though he was gone, I hadn't forgotten. And even though he was gone, he could still come back. The investigation was still going on, and frankly, I had no idea what there was to investigate. We'd all given our statements. What was left?

Madison said this was what happened when a bunch of men were in charge, and I was inclined to believe her.

I also knew this was what happened when you had money and resources. Pretty much everyone at Westbrook had these things, and in many ways, it slowed things down. What could be a swift serving of justice ended up dragged out and tangled up in money and clout.

So while the bank accounts battled it out, we all tried to get back to life. It wasn't hard because that mundane everyday routine I mentioned before was there to drag me along from class to class. But it wasn't so mundane anymore because I had Ry.

I stuck close to him the first week after the investigation launched, afraid Jonas was creepily lurking, but as one week slid into two, I was starting to believe perhaps the university would keep him away.

I also really missed photography. The calm of the darkroom called to me, and the undeveloped film I kept carrying around was burning a hole in my bag. So while Ry was off training, I was going to get back to it.

The photography building had three darkrooms students could schedule for use. along with editing rooms for digital photography and classrooms, so it was always somewhat busy because students would come and go even after hours.

As I headed down the hall toward darkroom two, my phone chimed, and I smiled, already knowing who it was.

"I'm hungry." His familiar voice filled my ear the second I accepted the call.

I laughed. "When aren't you?"

His voice dropped into a delicious kind of growl. "When I eat you."

"*Ryan*," I said, my cheeks heating and eyes darting around as if I'd been caught doing something salacious.

And even though this was just a phone call, I could practically see him smiling on the other end. "Are you at the darkroom yet?"

I glanced down the hall. "Heading there now. Are you at the gym?"

"Waiting on Jamie."

My stomach flipped at his casual, gruff response, and it never ceased to amaze me how he could affect me so much without even trying.

"I miss you," I confessed suddenly, unable to stop the quiet rush of words. Just the sound of his voice made me want.

His energy crackled. I could feel it through the line. "Me too, baby. Wanna have dinner after?"

"Can I eat your extra fries?"

He laughed under his breath. "Who else is gonna eat them?"

"'Kay."

"Don't forget to turn your app on to make your phone darkroom safe." He reminded me.

"'Kay," I repeated. I never bothered with that app before, but now, shutting my phone off for even an hour seemed risky, and it made Ry super growly. So special darkroom app it was.

"Answer me if I text."

I smiled wide at the door in front of me, exasperated at the way he listed instructions as though I were incapable of making it through the day without him. "Don't I always?"

"I love you." He always knew when he was being overprotective, but he also knew saying those three little words reminded me why.

"I love you too."

I was still smiling softly when my hand closed around the door handle. It faded too fast because the prickle of something tapping against my nape chased it away. Shivering, I glanced over my shoulder.

The well-lit hallway was empty, and nothing seemed amiss. A few doors down, I noted the red light on above one of the other darkrooms, indicating it was also in use.

Shaking off the odd feeling, I let myself in, making sure the door was closed behind me and the black curtain drawn. I flipped on the light to show the room was occupied and the safe light inside at the same time.

With the safe light on, everything took on a red cast. All darkrooms used the same type of red light because photo papers are orthochromatic, which basically means they're partially blind to red light so it doesn't interfere with the developing process.

The pungent metallic odor burned my nose as I moved around, checking the three trays to make sure there was enough developer, stop, and fix in each. Noting one was low, I found the jug I needed to add some to the tray. Some students found the chemical smell pleasant, but I wasn't one of them. The mix of hydroquinone, acetic acid, sodium carbonate, phenindione, and ammonium thiosulfate was intense and sometimes a bit dizzying.

Once I made sure everything was set up, I grabbed an apron, gloves, and a pair of safety goggles and got to work.

Developing photos was methodic, and I liked the order and routine of it. I settled in easily, the work coming naturally to me. It was nice to let my mind wander, for the quiet of the room to envelop me, and to watch in excitement as the images slowly appeared, revealing moments that had passed but now could be relived again.

An entire row of photos was hanging to dry when I finally looked up. Smiling, I pulled off the goggles, stretching my back as I wandered over to the line, gazing over them once more.

WET

The theater building really did look like a castle.

A loud thump bounced my heart into my throat, the drying photos fluttering when I spun toward the sound.

Nothing followed, but I stood stock-still, listening intently while fighting the urge to panic. Minutes passed, and the quiet settled again, nothing else seeming out of place. Blowing out a shaky breath, I went to my bag, pulling out my phone to glance at the clock. The hour had flown by, and I only had the room for about thirty minutes more.

Thud!

The same sound from before made my phone slip from my hands. It clattered to the hard floor near my feet, but I ignored it, instead pacing over to the door, which was hidden by the black curtain. Leaning close, I listened for any other sounds in the hall outside, wondering what was out there.

Who was out there?

The panic I battled back just minutes before came back tenfold, closing around my throat like a vise and reminding me with stark clarity how it felt when my windpipe was crushed with violent hands.

Thud!

A shriek clawed its way out of me, reverberating around the red-tinged room as I skittered backward.

"Sorry!" someone in the hall yelled. "These damn boxes weigh a ton."

"Here, let me help you." Another muffled voice reached my ears.

My heart was pounding so hard it left me breathless, and the trembling in my fingers was something I could not ignore.

Backing up, I sank onto the metal chair against the wall, dragging in a few uneven breaths. Seeing my phone by my foot, I bent to retrieve it, thinking of Ryan.

I wanted to call him, to hear his voice. His overprotective

tendencies might be annoying as hell, but I could admit he made me feel safer than anyone else ever had.

Laughter out in the hall made me look up, and I slumped into the chair, feeling ridiculous. Everything was fine. I was freaking out over nothing. Calling Ry would only make him worry.

After putting my phone away, I stood and started tidying up the space. Wanting to give my photos just a few more moments to dry, I decided to wash the three pairs of tongs. It wasn't really that necessary, but who knew how long it had been since it was done?

There was a small sink around a half wall at the back of the room. The front of the wall was used for a shelving system where other supplies were kept. It was nice to have the sink out of the way, and I dumped the three pairs of tongs in the porcelain bowl, the white glowing red.

The goggles I'd been wearing were on my head, so I pulled those off and washed them too. When I was rinsing off the final pair of tongs, that cold, shivery sensation I'd felt before crawled up the back of my neck again.

This time, it was more intense.

Swallowing, I stared down at my arm, noting how goose bumps rippled over my flesh and the little bit of hair on my forearms stood on end.

Barely breathing, I turned off the faucet. The only sound in the room was the water draining from the sink. The glugging it made churned my stomach, the muscles in my back so tense I ache.

Standing inert, I stared at the wall in front of me, regretting that I couldn't see the door from my position. I would know if someone was in here, right? The room would have filled with light the second the door opened.

Unless they slid in through a slim opening. Unless the blackout curtain blocked the light.

You know, my thoughts really were not helpful in keeping me calm.

Straining to listen, I heard nothing, yet everything was disturbed, the energy in the room not the same as it had been.

Limbs tight, I abandoned everything to the sink and rotated, staring across the room at the line where my photos hung. The papers were fluttering a bit, the line bobbing like there was movement in the air around them.

My mouth went dry. My eyes slid back toward the part of the room I couldn't see. Fingers curling into my palms, I took careful, silent steps, moving around the half wall. Breathing shallow, heart pounding out of my chest, I stepped cautiously, eyes scanning the red-shadowed room.

The red light never bothered me before, but now?

Now it made me feel like I was standing in the center of a crime scene.

Now the idea that the paper in here was unaffected made me wonder what else the red light blinded.

"Hello?" I asked, voice breathy and hollow.

The room was empty, the space exactly as it was when I went to the sink. My bag sat undisturbed, the black curtain over the door unmoving.

"So much for getting back to normal," I muttered, feeling my body droop as I deflated. Still shaking and unsteady, I went to the line to unclip my photos. I needed to get out of here.

Clutching the stack, I started toward my bag, feet stuttering when I saw it. I paused, glancing once more around the room as though my subconscious just couldn't quite shake the feeling I was not alone.

When I looked back, it was still there.

"Did I forget one?" I wondered, frowning as I stared at the paper lying in one of the trays.

Crossing to it, I stared down at the faint image starting to appear.

If I had forgotten this in there, it would have already had time to develop.

Even knowing this, I grabbed a pair of tongs from the sink, agitating the photo in the tray with one hand as my other gripped the photos I'd just pulled down.

More and more of the image started to appear. Anxiety was like nails on a chalkboard, but the chalkboard in this scenario was my spine. Squirming a little in discomfort, my heart started to pound as cold sweat coated my palms.

The more of the image that appeared, the more certain I was this was not a photograph of mine.

The theater building that looked like a castle was nowhere in sight. This image was taken indoors, and the subject was a person. Leaning closer, the strong chemical made my eyes water, but I didn't back away. Squinting with bated breath, I inwardly urged the subject to come into focus.

It was sort of like a paper on fire, and the flames slowly ate up what burned. But instead of something disappearing, it came to life like a dark cloud rolling over the surface, leaving something behind in its wake.

With one last swish of the agent, the entire image became clear.

Gasping, I stumbled back, falling onto my ass. The photos in my hand scattered everywhere, and the tongs clattered under the bench.

"No." My voice was strangled as I shoved back to my feet, rushing over to look again. My hips hit the bench, making all the chemicals slosh around, and though the photo floated in the liquid, it was still there… still perfectly clear.

Jonas. He stood in the center of the photograph, holding a white sign. And on the sign? A crudely written word.

Bitch.

Fear numbed my brain, and a sob ripped from my chest. Spinning away from the photo, I had one thought and only one: *Get to the phone.*

As I moved, the curtain hanging over the door rippled. My steps stuttered so abruptly that my sneakers made a horrible squeaking sound against the floor.

Pushing the black fabric aside, he materialized around it. Dressed in black, he blended well with the room, the red only reflecting off his pale face.

"J-Jonas," I stuttered.

"Did you really think I'd just let this go?" His tone was flat, eyes vacant, and when he smiled, his teeth were tinged red.

There was no point in trying to reason with him. I wouldn't be able to anyway. My entire body screamed, *Run!* and that was exactly what I was going to do.

I burst forward, but so did he, and we collided in the center of the small space, bodies smacking. I bounced off, angling to dart away.

But he grabbed my arm, yanking me around.

The last thing I saw was his cold, vengeful glare.

The last thing I felt was a teeth-gnashing hit against the side of my head.

Thirty-Four

Ryan

The team was swimming better than ever. Turned out Hughes really was pollution, and how much clearer the water had become now that he was gone.

I realized now that he was an issue long before Rory came along. Hughes's arrogant, self-important, pessimistic attitude was slowing us all down. His insults veiled as compliments stuck even though the guys tried to wash them away. The way he preened like a peacock made everyone else feel less-than, and shockingly, it was becoming evident some of the guys were intimidated by him.

It made me hot inside every time I watched Wes swim, which was twice a day now. He never would tell me what Jonas said or did to him, but it had been enough to mess with his performance because now that Hughes was gone, Wes was improving.

We all were.

Bro, yeah.

The meet last weekend had been one of our best, so I knew the dean was sitting in his old-ass building pleased as shit.

Good. I personally didn't care if he was happy or not, but it was a means to an end. A way to make sure he stuck to his agreement and kept Hughes the hell off this campus and away from my girl.

Nearly two weeks had passed since he was placed on investigation and banned from campus. According to Coach, his father lawyered up fast and shot down any tantrums he wanted to throw. He also kept him at bay.

Hughes must have inherited his stupid from his mother.

What? It's true.

We still had to wait for the official results of the inquiry, but I was confident he wouldn't be coming back.

The sun was sinking fast, the sky darkening with every passing minute, when I pulled up in front of the gym and shut off the Wrangler. This would be my third workout for the day, having already knocked out two practices. But it was weights day, so here I was.

Jamie wasn't here yet, so I snagged my phone out of the cupholder and called my girl. She was just about to head into the darkroom, so I reminded her to switch on her app. Who knew they made that? Seriously, there was an app for everything. Thank God. The idea of her in a darkroom alone with no phone was enough to give me a rash.

Jamie's knuckles rapped on the window, making me jolt. When I turned to him, he hitched a thumb over his shoulder. "We doing this or what?"

Tucking the phone into my shorts, I got out of the Jeep. "Bro, you need to get laid."

He was grumpy as hell lately.

He made a rude sound, followed by, "If I wanted unsolicited advice, I'd call my mom."

We hit the weights hard, and a little over an hour later, we were heading out into the dark parking lot, freshly showered. My phone started ringing, and I smiled, thinking it was Rory.

But when I looked down at the screen, it was a number I didn't recognize.

"You know this?" I held the screen to Jamie.

"Nope. Probably a scammer."

"Probably," I said, silencing the call without answering.

"I'm starving," Jamie complained, rubbing his midsection.

"Same. We'll meet you at Shirley's," I told him as we headed toward our Wranglers. Inside the Jeep, I hit the contact for my girl.

She didn't pick up.

Frowning, I pulled the phone down and then called her again.

Still no answer.

She could be busy in the darkroom, but she always answered before. That was why she'd downloaded that app.

The third time I tried heeded no different result.

Frowning, I pulled up our texts, noticing the notification for my voicemail. I called it up, hitting the speaker button and letting the message fill the quiet interior.

"Ryan Walsh? This is Linda from the dean's office. You gave me your number, asked me to call." My heart rate tripled during the short pause she took before, in a more hushed tone, she said, "I just wanted to let you know Mr. Hughes was here for a meeting... and it did not go well."

In the background, there was a loud thud. And then the call disconnected.

Adrenaline made me jittery as it pushed out the exhaustion of a full day's worth of workouts, and a pit of dread sank like a heavy stone in my gut.

"Pick up. Pick up," I chanted as Rory's phone rang again and then went to voicemail.

Frustrated, I smacked the steering wheel, dropping the phone in my lap.

What if Jonas has her? What if he got pissed things didn't go his way and he's taking it out on her?

It wouldn't be the first time.

"Where are you?" I murmured, starting up the engine.

My frustrated noise coincided with the Jeep stuttering out as I let off the clutch.

Rory wasn't the only one with a cool app on her phone.

I had one too.

Hitting the screen, I thumbed through until I found the one I wanted. It was a location app, and I had only one phone registered. Hers.

My knee bounced the entire time I waited for it to pull up, and then when it finally did—

"*Fuck!*"

Fingers clutching tight, I pulled the phone right up in front of my face as if I were seeing wrong.

But I wasn't seeing wrong. Deep down, I knew.

Tossing the phone aside, I started the Jeep back up and ripped out of the lot.

"Hang on, baby." I prayed, fear making my palms sweat. "I'm coming."

And then I whipped the Jeep in the direction indicated on the app.

The pool.

Thirty-Five

Rory

The first thing I noticed was the unforgiving, thin plastic bind shackling my wrists together. It bit into my skin painfully, making my fingers tingle. I knew right away there would be no getting free, but still, I struggled against it.

A rude noise floated over my head, and something hard connected with my foot.

Wait. Where are my shoes?

"About time you woke up. I was starting to think I'd have to just toss you in unconscious."

My eyes flew open.

Jonas loomed over me, bending to shove his face into mine.

How the heck did I ever think he was good-looking?

I tried to recoil, but the hard, textured surface against my head made it impossible.

"I mean, where's the fun in watching someone die without even struggling?"

I bolted upright, our foreheads slamming together. Jonas stumbled back, almost falling but catching himself on a silver railing.

Where the heck am I?

Anger filled his face as he rubbed his forehead, but he didn't yell. Instead, he laughed. "I did say I wanted a struggle."

"What's going on?" I asked, rolling onto my side. The fabric of my top snagged against the floor, making me pause.

Behind me, Jonas jumped up and down, and everything beneath me vibrated. "Hope you aren't afraid of heights," he mused. He stopped jumping. "Actually, I hope you are."

Panicked, I glanced around, a wave of dizziness overtaking me. Lifting my head, I gasped, instantly recognizing the place but also not understanding…

Oh God.

"Surprise!"

My knuckles scraped against the nonslip surface as I pushed up into a sitting position. Nausea and fear overtook me, and I dropped back onto my side. My cheek scraped against the diving platform as the pads of my fingers clung on for dear life.

Yes. A diving platform.

This psycho knocked me out, bound my wrists with a zip-tie, and somehow managed to haul me to the pool and up to the tallest diving deck there was.

"Are you wondering how high up we are?" he asked, his voice almost jovial.

I swallowed back the vomit rising in my throat. *No. No, I don't want to know.*

He told me anyway. "Ten meters."

I blew out a breath. Well, ten meters didn't sound terrible…

"That's thirty-two feet."

I bit down on my lip to keep from whimpering.

"It's actually a little higher than most colleges manage, but you know Westbrook. Always gotta have the best for Elite."

I stared out over the side of the platform, trying not to look down, trying not to focus on the fact I was thirty-two feet in the air with a crazy person.

"Why are you doing this?" I asked, unable to formulate any other words.

"Why?" he echoed.

The platform vibrated under his heavy footsteps as he stalked over. Planting his feet on either side of my body, he reached down, his face a dark mask of anger. Grabbing my shirt, he yanked my upper body up toward him. "Why?" he spat. "They closed the investigation today. You just couldn't keep your mouth shut, could you?"

"You lost," I said, a little relief filling me until I remembered his loss was exactly why I was here.

The smacking sound his palm made against my cheek echoed around the open ceiling, and I would have dropped back onto the board had he not had a hold on my shirt.

"If I'm going down, then I'm taking you with me." He snarled.

I'd felt fear at this man's hands multiple times, but it never became less potent. If anything, it became more so because his desperation grew every time.

"*Please*," I begged, not above it. "Just let me down. I won't tell anyone."

He laughed. "You think I believe that? You had plenty of chances to keep your trap shut, and you didn't take any of them." He was shaking over me. I felt his rage in the grip of his hand. "The only thing left is for you to pay. For me to toss you off this tower. While you're falling those thirty-two feet, you can stare up at my smiling face and realize you never should have crossed me."

I tried to twist out of his hold, my feet scraping along the platform, trying to find purchase.

He seemed completely unbothered by my attempts, or perhaps he was just that confident I was about to die. My shirt ripped when he yanked me even closer, my neck flopping with the sudden jerk.

"And then your back will hit that wall of water, and the force will be so potent it'll knock out any breath left in your lungs so that when the water swallows you up and your body instinctively gasps for what it needs, only water will fill your nose and lungs... and you will drown from the inside out."

My God. Tears filled my eyes with the heinous picture he painted, and I recalled the struggle the last time I almost drowned, how terrifying and hopeless it had seemed.

Clearly enjoying my torment and tears, he went on. "And then your waterlogged body will sink all the way to the bottom of the sixteen-foot dive pool. The last thing you will ever think is that you never should have messed with me."

Fear paralyzed me as he described my death, which he seemed to put much thought into, but his last words seemed to snap me out of it.

No. If I was going to die today, he would not be my last thought. My last thought could only be of Ryan.

Ryan.

Life and fight flooded my limbs, even my numb hands. I kicked and struggled, finally pitching to the side. Jonas slammed into the silver railings, a curse falling from his lips. I scrambled up, my bare feet slapping as I ran toward the back of the platform, toward the ladder.

I wasn't sure how I'd manage with bound hands, but anything would be better than staying here.

Jonas caught my shirt, yanking me off my feet. I fell back, and he tackled me, straddling my hips with his. Wildness shone in his eyes, nostrils flaring like a bull's. Breathing heavily, he reached down and ripped my shirt.

"No!" I screamed, a new kind of horror overtaking me.

A sharp slap across my cheek didn't stop my struggle, but it made my eyes water and blur. I sobbed as he ripped the shirt all the way off, tossing it off the platform and then roughly tearing my bra until it dangled around my bound wrists.

"Nooo!" I wailed again, raising my clasped hands and bringing them down on his shoulder.

He avoided the hit and then yanked at the buttons on my jeans. I started to cry, unable to kick my legs because he was moving down them as he peeled my jeans and panties off in one swipe.

Refusing to remain still, I sat up, slamming my fists into his head.

This time, he swore, evil stare firing up to mine. He leaped, and I screamed, his body pinning mine as his hips rutted against me. His tongue, hot and gross, licked up the side of my cheek.

Abruptly, he pulled back, yanking us both to our feet, forcing me back. I stood toward the edge of the platform, completely naked, shivering and scared out of my mind.

He stepped back, eyes roaming all over my vulnerable body, raking over me in a way that was almost as sickening as his hands on my flesh.

"Maybe seeing you naked, I'd understand why Walsh was so willing to blow up Elite."

I shook my head, glancing over my shoulder, staring down the thirty-foot drop to the still, glasslike water below.

Jump. My mind urged. I was hardly a strong swimmer, and I would be even less so with my wrists bound like this.

But what choice did I have?

The board underfoot vibrated, and I whipped around, cringing as Jonas came forward.

Grasping my upper arm, he yanked me into his body, rubbing against me as his eyes darkened. "Maybe if I had a piece of your ass, I wouldn't give a shit that my whole life just went up in smoke."

"*Please*, just stop," I whispered.

His hand shoved between my thighs, rough fingers finding my folds and trying to jam inside.

With a yell, I wrenched away, both of us teetering unsteadily.

"I'm not done yet," he growled, reaching again.

I jumped.

Without a second thought, I leaped right off the platform.

Jonas yelled, and I realized that I wasn't falling alone. The force of my jump had brought him with me.

Heart in my throat, stomach in my chest, I hit the water, cutting through its depth like a hot knife through butter. I braced for the pain he described, but it didn't come, just an overwhelming sense of panic.

You hit feet first, my mind whispered as water tugged my hair and slid over my naked skin. *It didn't hurt because you didn't hit with your back.*

The thoughts were fleeting, though, because the urge to breathe came on fast. A bubble escaped my nose, floating in front of my face in warning.

I brought my arms up to push through the water like Ryan taught me, but my hands were bound. A sound of desperation was cushioned by the water as I started to kick and kick, turning my face upward. It seemed so far away, the rippling surface beckoning and taunting me at the very same time.

Kick your feet. Ryan's gentle voice floated in my head. *Don't panic. You'll make it.*

I kept kicking, kept struggling, and then the surface was right there. My head was breaking through, and my body was gasping greedily for air.

Good girl.

I coughed and sputtered. My legs burned, shoulders and wrists aching. Even though my arms were bound, I kept trying to use them, straining to stay afloat.

"There's no one to save you this time!" Jonas's voice rang out, and I spun in a circle, slipping a little beneath the surface.

His completely drenched form appeared beside the pool, hair plastered to his forehead, a maniacal look twisting his features. He was carrying some sort of long pole, and I squinted at it, trying to breathe, see, and swim at the same time.

He raised it, and I saw the flash of the net on the end.

What is he—

The thought wasn't even finished when he swung it down, the net hitting me in the top of my head, the fabric pressing into my hair.

I opened my mouth to yell, but I slid under, water filling my mouth.

I kicked up, sputtering out the water, sucking in a breath.

He pressed down, and I went back under. *He's using the net to force you under. He's going to hold you down until you drown.*

Panic so strong stole all thought, I splashed and kicked, but my energy was draining.

Thoughts of Ryan filled my head, and I sobbed into the water, clinging to the image of him. Dully, I realized the net was no longer shoving me down, but I no longer had the strength to swim. So I floated lazily, slowly sinking, orange strands of hair rippling in my peripheral vision.

But then my death was disturbed, the still water choking the life out of me bursting with movement.

A large body plunged down, bubbles and waves obscuring their face. But then he was there, wrapping his arm around my waist, pressing his lips against mine, and forcing air into my shriveling lungs. The oxygen felt like a million tiny needles stabbing me on the inside as he towed me to the surface.

"Rory!" His voice was strong and loud. "Breathe, baby!"

My lips parted and gasped, water spewing between them as I collapsed against him.

"Good girl," he praised. "Good girl."

I didn't know how, but he pulled us both out of the pool, the tile floor cold against my back.

The breath he gave me was warm, and I felt my chest expand. I heard him talking but couldn't make out his words.

Something warm and soft blanketed my body, and I sighed, which turned into a wet cough.

He pulled me up, tucking me between his spread legs, cradling me against his body. "Open your eyes, Rory," he demanded. "Look at me."

I forced them open, smiling a little the second I saw his blue irises.

"Help is on the way," he promised, then said something over my head.

"I'm okay," I rasped, another cough shuddering my lungs.

He gave me another breath, which I readily gulped down.

"Oh, baby. What did he do to you?" he crooned, holding me tighter.

"Tried to drown me," I said. "But you taught me how to swim."

He made a strangled sound.

I wanted to hug him, but when I lifted my arms, they were still tied together. "Hurts..."

"What hurts?"

I fought against whatever was draped over me, trying to push it aside to show him.

"Stay covered," he ordered, tucking his jacket back around me. "Why the hell are you naked?"

"You made skinny-dipping look fun."

A strangled laugh ripped from his throat. "That is not funny."

"My wrists are tied. It hurts."

Any trace of humor we'd managed dried up faster than water in the desert.

The next thing I knew, Ryan had me in the locker room, a pair of scissors in his hands. "Let me see, baby."

The Elite hoodie fell to the floor, and I sat there completely naked and dripping wet, holding out my shaking arms. Ryan cut away the tight binds and my tangled bra, and I cried out in pain and relief when my wrists fell apart.

I would have sagged off the bench, but he caught me, holding me close as he dug through his locker for some clothes. "C'mon. You need to cover up."

I let him pull a pair of gigantic sweatpants over me and giggled as he rolled them at the waist and then tied them as tight as he could. But the giggle dissolved into a broken cry, and I fell against him as I cried.

"I know, baby. I know. It's okay now. You're safe. I got you."

"W-wh-where is h-he?"

"Unconscious," Ryan deadpanned.

Pulling out of his chest, I blinked up at him. "How?"

"I knocked his ass out. Would have killed him, but it was him or you."

"He's out there alone?" I worried, eyes darting to the door.

"No. Jamie's out there. He won't let him out of his sight."

"Jamie saw me naked," I wailed.

"No." Ryan's voice was tight. "No, he didn't. I covered you with my shirt."

I shivered, the air brushing over my wet skin, making me cold. Still holding me in his lap, he scooped up the hoodie and pulled it around me. Once my arms were in, he zipped it up to my chin.

"Rory," he asked, gathering me close, pushing my head under his chin, "did he… did he, ah… rape you?"

"No," I said, voice clear. "He might have, but I jumped off the platform."

Ryan's entire body went tight. "What?"

"He was going to push me off the diving platform, but I jumped instead."

"You did good, baby. Good girl."

I snuggled into him, his praise warming me as much as his body heat.

"Ry?"

"Hmm?"

"How did you know where I was?" I asked.

"The lady at the dean's office, the one I flirted with… She called me and said Hughes was on campus."

"The investigation did not go in his favor," I whispered.

"Yeah, well, he just made it ten times worse for himself." Ryan's tone was dark.

"But how did you know he took me to the pool? Did you guess?"

"Ah…" He hesitated.

Lifting my head, I noted his sheepish expression.

Shrugging, he admitted, "Remember that day I took your phone to add my number?"

I nodded. "And a selfie too."

He half smiled. "I also, ah, might have turned on a location feature…"

My mouth dropped open. "You've been tracking my phone?"

Guilt and wariness shone bright in his eyes, but then something changed like a switch going on inside him, and those things evaporated. "Hell yes, I did," he declared, eyes sweeping my body. "And if I hadn't, you would be dead. So I won't apologize. I did what I had to do to protect you."

"I love you, Ry."

Everything about him softened, the fight draining right out of his shoulders. "You aren't mad?"

"How could I be mad at anything you do out of love?" I whispered.

His lips pressed against my forehead. "I do love you. More than anything."

With a sigh, I cuddled back into his chest.

The locker room door banged open, and I stiffened. Ryan's arms turned to steel around me.

"You decent?" Jamie yelled.

"Yeah," Ryan called back.

Jamie appeared a second later, eyes going right to me. "Bro, you okay?"

I nodded.

Jamie glanced at Ryan for confirmation.

"She's good."

They were stupid.

"Cops are here." Jamie jabbed his thumb toward the pool. "EMTs too."

I sighed.

Ryan stood, bringing me with him. His clothes were still soaking wet.

"Aren't you going to change?"

"You're wearing my dry clothes."

"Oh."

"I'll be okay. Let's get your wrists looked at."

They were burning and aching. One of them felt like it might be bleeding. I didn't say anything of that, though. I just sank farther into Ryan.

Jamie grabbed the door, holding it open for us, but I gasped, body going rigid. Anxiety clawed at my throat as I gulped for breath.

"What?" Ryan asked, body going tight.

Jamie stepped right up beside him, his hand resting on my leg.

"J-Jonas." I didn't want to see him. I wasn't ready.

Jamie relaxed. "Cops hauled his ass out of here."

"Are you sure?" I worried.

"I watched them cuff him and put him in the back of a car myself."

"What if he gets out?" I worried.

"He won't. Not this time," Ryan vowed.

"This time, he can't deny what he did. His hand was literally caught in the cookie jar."

A vile memory of his hand roughly going between my legs made me whimper.

Ryan stopped walking, leaning down so his nose pressed against my ear. "Tell me."

I hesitated.

Jamie excused himself, and Ryan seemed content to wait me out.

Finally, I whispered, "He touched me."

A deadly aura bloomed around Ryan, his eyes narrowing into slits. "Touched you?"

I nodded, tears blurring my vision.

I watched him battle back the rage, the urge to punch and yell. His throat worked overtime. When his eyes turned to mine, they were the cobalt color I loved wholeheartedly, and they were only filled with love and understanding. "You tell me what you need from me, and I will give it to you."

My heart swelled, and in that moment, I knew that everything Jonas did was no match at all for the way Ryan loved me.

Heart near to bursting and stomach fluttering with butterflies instead of nerves, I smiled. "Erase his touch with yours."

He groaned. "Oh, sweetheart, I will. As soon as you're ready. Over and over again."

When my wrists were bandaged, all the questions answered, and Jonas was locked in a cell, I rolled over in the dark, fitting against Ryan's body, reveling in what we found together. He hummed quietly in his throat, hugging me tight.

"Thank you for believing me, Ryan," I whispered.

"I'll always believe you. Anything you say."

I thought back to the first time he'd said those words to me, the first time he'd pulled me out of the pool. I doubted him then.

But now?

I believed him.

Epilogue

Rory

The smooth rumble of Ryan's Wrangler cut off just moments after he pulled into the waiting parking spot right next to Jamie's cherry-red Jeep. It still entirely amused me that they drove matching vehicles. They would argue to the death their Jeeps weren't "matching" but merely bros. Even though they were different colors with different features, I still thought of them as twins, and it would never change.

"I am so hungry I could eat the southbound end out of a northbound mule," Ryan declared.

"That's disgusting," I told him, not appreciating the vivid visual his little joke created in my head. Dear God, I hope it was a joke.

I mean, swimmers were a hungry bunch and ate near constantly, but they still had standards... *right?*

Ew.

"Hey," he called, voice dropping into that tone he only ever used with me. Warmth pooled in my lower belly, and a feeling of familiar safety curled my lips into a smile. "Come back here a minute."

Releasing the handle, I rotated back toward the driver's seat. His broad shoulders filled the space, dark hair mussed and slightly damp from his shower after practice.

Outside, the temperature was cold. More and more burnished leaves were beginning to scatter the ground. Wind whistled around the Jeep, catching in the window cracks and seams of the doors.

I didn't notice any of it, though, because when those cobalt eyes looked at me the way they were now, he was literally the only thing I knew.

"I thought you were starving," I teased.

"What kind of boyfriend would I be if I put food over my favorite girl?"

If Ryan had a superpower, it would be his charm.

My heart fluttered as he reached out, tucking my hair behind my ear. "I'm proud of you."

Not expecting the words, I jolted slightly, gazing into his sincere face. "What?"

"What that scum did to you was sick and hurtful. He violated you and used his status to discredit and try to isolate you. But you fought back, stood up for yourself... You used your voice for not only yourself but those he hurt before you and to protect the ones who would have come after."

"Ry." I swallowed thickly, sudden emotion causing a hard lump to form in my throat.

"You are so strong. I know I give you shit for being a shrimp." He reached out to poke me in the side, making me smile. "But I know how capable you are. And I'm fucking proud to call you mine."

"I was expecting waffles," I joked, though my voice was strained with me trying not to cry. My heart felt as if it couldn't fit inside my chest. Hearing him say that meant so much to me. I know I didn't need his praise, but having someone acknowledge how hard I tried made me feel lighter, as though a weight I didn't even know I carried was suddenly removed.

I reached for his hand, and he gave it readily. Before our fingers could link, I tugged it up, using the sleeve of his hoodie to pat my damp eyes.

He laughed under his breath but didn't even crack a joke about him being my human tissue. Instead, he nudged beneath my chin so our eyes could collide once more.

"I know it's been hard lately," he whispered, a few storm clouds darkening his stable gaze. "And I couldn't let you go another minute without telling how much I love you."

A tear slipped free. He wasn't a very good human tissue.

"I love you too, Ry. I couldn't have gone through all that without you."

"Yes," he intoned. "Yes, you could have. But I'm glad I was here. I'm glad you let me in. I'll always be here to support you, and I'll always add my voice to yours, making it twice as loud."

A small sound vibrated my throat as I basically threw myself at him, wrapping my arms around his neck, to bury my face in his shoulder. Since Jonas had tried to kill me (again) at the pool, things had been a little rough. I'd had some nightmares, been a little skittish around most people, but Ry was a steady presence, and he never pushed.

"I'll always be here for you too, Ry. Always."

"I know, baby." His lips pressed against my head.

"I love you."

"What was that?" he asked, leaning down.

"You heard me."

"Can't say that I did. Your voice is all muffled with the way you're clinging to me."

I laughed and pulled back just enough so we were sitting face to face. "I said I love you."

He kissed me. Slow. Deep. Even when his stomach growled angrily, he kissed me still.

My lips were slick when we finally broke apart, head fuzzy and fingers curled into his shirt.

Rap, rap, rap! The sharp sound of something hitting Ryan's window made me stiffen. His hands curled around my upper arms, and a dangerous, almost predatory, look flashed in his eyes as all his attention shifted to whatever was behind us.

"You got about three seconds to get inside before the entire team makes a buffet out of your breakfast!" Jamie hollered.

I let out a relieved laugh, and Ryan grinned. "Stay there," he said, swiftly kissing the tip of my nose before darting out of the Jeep and around to the passenger side. "All aboard," he announced, backing into the open door.

Smiling, I climbed onto his back, something that had become very familiar to me, and we made our way through the door, which Jamie was holding open.

"Camera girl," he said, giving me a wink. "I ate your breakfast."

"Wouldn't be the first time."

"Aww, don't be like that. I was running on fumes!"

Three booths were occupied with members of Elite, all of them shoveling copious amounts of food in their faces. Most of them waved while they chewed as Ryan set me down near a table that was already covered with plates.

"Dig in," Wes said from his seat as he stabbed a monster-size bite of waffle.

Ryan made a noise and practically dove into the booth and started scooping in eggs. Jamie slid in beside Wes, and Ryan patted the spot beside him.

Just as I was about to sit, the bell on the diner door chimed, and Madison walked in. We smiled when we saw each other, and I met her halfway for a hug.

Her long dark locks were straight around her shoulders, brown eyes topped with a faint golden shimmer shadow. She was dressed in a ruffled leopard-print skirt that flirted around her thighs, a long-sleeved black sweater, and a pair of boots with heels.

"I'm so glad you came!"

Reaching into her shoulder bag, she pulled out a tablet and tapped the screen. The newest article published by the school news outlet filled the screen. "As if I wouldn't! This is amazing! I had to tell you in person."

"Come sit," I said, leading her to the table and sliding in beside Ry automatically.

"Hey, Madison." He spoke around a giant bite of waffle.

"You smell like syrup," I told him.

Swooping in, he kissed my cheek. "Sweet like syrup too."

I smiled but noted the way Madison sort of hesitated at the table.

Jamie slid over, squishing himself against Wes. "Have a seat, Mads."

"I'll sit over here," she said, slipping in beside me instead. "I wouldn't want to get in the way of your binge eating."

"Binge eating?" Jamie scoffed. "Girl, this is just a regular breakfast."

Wes made a sound of agreement. Then with food stuck all in his teeth, he said, "Hey, Madison."

She laughed. "Hi, Wes."

Shirley came over, the boys ordered more waffles, and Madison ordered a latte and a veggie omelet.

When Shirley was gone, I helped myself to the coffee Jamie had ordered me before we arrived, and Madison laid the tablet on what was left of the table's surface.

"The article you wrote is already getting so many hits and comments," she said.

"As it should," Ryan announced. "That right there"—he jabbed his syrupy fork at the tablet—"is the best writing I ever read."

"Bro, you read?" Jamie cracked.

"If my girl writes it, then hell yes, I do."

"You didn't read my article, Jamie?" I asked, feigning hurt.

Madison shifted, and Jamie's eyes went right to her movements instead of me. After a second, he scoffed. "Now, you know I'd never do you like that, bro." Pulling his eyes from my friend, he glanced at me. "Read every word. I especially liked the part when you called out Jonas Hughes as a dirty bastard."

"I didn't exactly use those words," I pointed out.

He made an indelicate... Okay, it was a rude sound. "Yeah, well, those were my polite words. After what he did to you, he deserves way worse." Clearing his throat, he looked at Madison. "After what he did to both of you."

Madison glanced up.

"You doing okay, Mads? Haven't seen you around."

I glanced between them, picking up some vibes. Then I glanced at Wes to see if he was picking up the same vibes. He was eating without a clue.

Men.

"I'm good. Just busy with rehearsals."

Our "Shirley" came back with Madison's breakfast and the boys' fresh waffles. As she was refilling Jamie's coffee, she noted the tablet lying on the table. "I just read that article this morning, hun," she said, glancing at me. "That was real brave of you calling him out and telling your truth to the entire campus."

Warmth spread in my cheeks, but I kept my gaze on the older woman. "Thank you."

She nodded. "Something similar happened to me years ago. No one believed me either. Happens a lot more than people like to believe. Good on you for raising awareness."

When she was gone, my eyes dropped back to the article, the headline in bold.

I'll Believe You

When the editor of the school paper came to me about writing a tell-all about what happened with Jonas Hughes, I'd been skeptical. Not because I worried people wouldn't believe me like before but because putting yourself out there is scary.

And because I was pretty sure he just wanted some sensationalized piece of journalism spiraling the downfall of an Elite.

Gazing around the table at Ry, Wes, and Jamie and then beyond them to the two full booths filled with swimmers, I smiled. Maybe I'd have been down for that kind of article before… but not now.

Yes, it would have been easy to distrust all men, to blame them all. More specifically, all Elite, but Ryan changed my mind. There were a lot of scummy men out there, but there were really good ones too. I was willing to bet there were more good than bad.

Also, I am a photographer—not a writer. And yeah, sure, I helped out sometimes and wrote a few pieces here and there on sporting events, etc., but this was completely different. These words would carry more weight and meaning. They had the ability to resonate with people and, yeah, even anger some.

Just because in the end I was able to prove what Jonas did to me, there were still people who were mad that I took down an Elite. There were still people who sneered at the evidence and sided with him anyway.

But the more I thought about it, the more I realized I needed to do it. I wanted to share my truth, my experience. I knew there were women on this campus who likely suffered similar situations as mine. And some who might in the future. So why not talk about it?

In the end, I told the editor I would definitely tell what happened with Jonas as long as I could also tell the part about the administration not believing me at first. And if I could also give safety tips, hotline numbers, and even the number to the campus counselor.

He agreed.

So what "I'll Believe You" essentially became was a cautionary true story that spread truth and information wrapped up in the shiny draw of scandal.

It felt good to write the article, and it made me feel like I might help someone. Who knows? Maybe I could add writing to my passion for photography to create an even louder voice.

"I was thinking," I said, drawing Madison's attention. Turning to her, I continued. "What if I went to the administration about starting up a support group for assault survivors?"

Madison's eyes lit up. "That's an amazing idea. I want to help."

Across the table, Wes set down his fork. "That's actually really cool of you. I bet there are some people out there who could really use a place where they would feel safe."

I don't know why, but something about his words really bruised my heart.

"Maybe we could also set up some sort of LGBT group too."

Wes's eyes turned a little soft. "You'd do that?"

"Of course. You're our friend," Madison told him.

There was a moment of genuine surprise in his eyes, but it was gone quickly, and he smiled, reaching for his juice. "It means a lot that you guys would think of me, but there is already an LGBT group on campus."

"Oh, are you a member?" I asked.

Wes cleared his throat. "No. But I know of it."

"How come you've never gone?" Madison asked.

Ryan made a sound. "Don't you think that's a little personal?"

"We're friends," Madison and I echoed simultaneously.

"It's fine," Wes said, letting out a light laugh. "I'm just not used to, ah…"

"Friends?" Jamie put in.

Wes nodded.

"Except for Maxen," Ryan ribbed.

Wes rolled his eyes. "I haven't really been very open about myself, so I haven't wanted to go. And now I have all of you, sort of like my own group anyway."

Pushing Ryan back, I climbed onto his lap and then leaned over the food-covered table, to throw my arms around Wes's neck.

He patted my shoulder awkwardly before Ryan was pulling me back. "Woman, you're going to have food all over you." His eyes dropped to my shirt where a piece of scrambled egg was stuck to my top.

"See?" He pointed.

"Hey, that's good eats!" Jamie declared.

Ryan snatched it off my top and tossed it in his mouth.

Madison and I gagged.

"So, ah…" Madison started after I settled farther into Ryan's lap. "Any news on Jonas?"

My stomach tightened a bit at the mention of our

attacker, but Ryan's arm slid around my waist, reminding me I wasn't alone.

"You don't need to worry about him, Mads," Jamie stated.

"It's Madison." She corrected him.

He ignored her. "He's going away for a long time."

Both hands went around her mug, doubt etched into her beautiful features. "Like how long?"

"Thanks to Coach Resch, likely the maximum sentence for attempted murder," Ryan said.

I leaned a little farther into his chest, reveling in his warmth.

"So he really did have cameras installed at the pool?" Madison asked, turning to Ryan.

He nodded. "Yes, and frankly, it earned back some of my respect."

Wes and Jamie nodded emphatically.

Relief coursed through me a little upon hearing Ryan's words. I'd always felt a certain amount of guilt that he was at odds with some of his teammates and his coach. Especially because I knew Ryan was hurt when the coach took Jonas's side at first.

But really, I guess he didn't.

"Coach was caught in the middle and had to remain impartial," Ryan told Madison, echoing my thoughts. "Or at least look like he was. After the big blowup and most of the team walking out, he had cameras installed at the pool without any of us knowing."

"He got approval from the head administration," I added, making Madison nod.

"Well, after our meeting with the dean, he better have agreed," she quipped.

"Those cameras caught everything he did to Carrot." His hand balled into a fist at his side. I could feel the fiery rage build in him as he thought about what he saw on those tapes.

Grabbing his fist, I peeled it open, pushing my hand inside. Turning in his lap, I studied his face. "I wish you never insisted on watching that tape."

The flames of anger dimmed, giving way to tenderness as his stare bounced between mine. "I know I will never fully understand what you went through, but I want to try. Seeing it was something I had to do. I'm just trying to support you."

"I know, Ry."

He kissed my cheek.

"Wes, bro. You got a tissue?" Jamie quipped. "Ryan's turning me soft."

I glanced over at Jamie who was dabbing his eyes. Laughing, Wes handed him a paper napkin out of the dispenser near the window.

"You're an idiot," Madison told him.

Abandoning the tissue he didn't even need, Jamie leaned over the table toward her. "You want me to say some pretty words to you?"

"You want to wear my coffee?" she asked sweetly.

He made a face. "Don't be wasting coffee like that. If you're done, I'll drink the rest."

"Anyway," I said, giving Jamie a stern look before turning back to Madison. "The tape shows clear evidence of intent to kill, which is essential in an attempted murder charge. And because of that, the district attorney can go for the maximum sentence, which I think is ten years in jail and a fine of at least a hundred thousand dollars."

"Spoken like the offspring of two lawyers," Ryan quipped, patting my hip.

I smiled.

After everything, I called my parents. They took the next flight out and spent almost a week here with me. It was amazing to see them, to finally tell them everything. They'd been upset I didn't call them immediately, but my mom understood quickly why I'd been hesitant.

"It doesn't matter if we're defense lawyers. Our loyalty and trust will always be with you first," she'd told me. "We will believe you always."

After a few emotionally charged days, Coin & Coin descended upon the local police station handling the case. They also met with the dean.

Frankly, the man was lucky he still had a job. Approving the cameras the coach insisted on installing was likely what saved his ass.

"Lawyers for in-laws. Bro, like I said, you ain't ever gonna get away with nothing ever again." Jamie was forlorn.

"They aren't my in-laws," Ryan told him, eyes drifting over my face. A soft smile formed at the corners of his lips. "Yet."

Butterflies filled my middle, making my heart tremble. Feeling a little giddy, I turned to Jamie. "Having lawyers for in-laws means he could probably get away with quite a lot."

"Aw, shit, bro," Jamie called. Then he leaned toward me. "You got any sisters, camera girl?"

I laughed.

Madison sniffed a little, drawing Jamie's eyes.

"You jealous, Mads?"

She scoffed. "As if."

"You gonna eat that?" he asked, and without waiting for her to answer, he stabbed what was left of her omelet and shoved the entire thing in his mouth.

Ryan laughed.

Madison rolled her eyes and turned to me. "I'm glad he's getting locked up."

I reached for her hand. "Me too."

"I guess one good thing came out of dealing with him," she told me.

"What's that?"

"Our friendship."

We smiled at each other. "Definitely."

Ryan's arms wound around me from behind, his body molding against my back, nose dipping into the side of my neck. "I'd say us too," he rumbled against my skin. "But even if he hadn't pushed you in the pool, I still would have found my way to you."

The soft strands of his hair tickled my cheek when I leaned closer. "You think so?"

"Oh, I know."

"How do you know?" I asked, heart pattering wildly.

"Because, baby, we are meant to be."

Without a doubt.

Westbrook Elite

Wingspan (Jamie & Madison's book), Wish (Wes & Max's book), WTF (Win & Lars's book) & Wildcard (Rush & Landry's book)
are out now with more to come!

Join Cambria's newsletter for release information:
https://view.flodesk.com/pages/62bf54af9b2a0dd45de3fa82

Want more college romance by Cambria Hebert right now? Check out, *#Nerd*, book one in the bestselling, award winning
Hashtag Series
https://amzn.to/3OVA05J

Author's Note

Y'all have been asking me for college romance. And asking some more. More specifically, college sports romance. I've been hesitant to write college sports romance because, well, the *Hashtag* series is a lot to live up to. And honestly, I know most of you want a legacy series or more of *Hashtag* in general. Again, a lot to live up to.

I feel like anything college I write will inevitably be compared to *Hashtag,* and it's a bit, ah, nerve-racking. I do love college romance, though, and it wasn't a question of *if* I would write more of it... More like a question of *when*. So when I saw the cover photo for *WET*, come across my timeline one day on social media. I stopped. I stared. I scrolled by. Then I went back.

It was almost an instant attraction, and I don't mean because the photo is hot. Though, it totally is. It was like finding a key that unlocked a world in my mind. And that world is Westbrook. The concept of this series did change and evolve as I was writing *WET*. Originally, this series was called Wicked U. It was about a college campus in Westbrook, VA, that was known as Wicked U because of the weird stuff that happened there. I was going to make it a romantic suspense based on the campus. Kind of like my

AUTHOR'S NOTE

Take It Off series meets college. That's also why I was inspired to go with the W theme for all the book titles. I always planned for *WET* to be the first book, and I always planned for it to be about a swimmer.

I did not plan on writing about the swim team. I did not plan on Jamie bursting through and being like, *Bro, write me a book*. And then for me to be like, *Bro, sure*.

P.S. I love me some Jamie. Wes too.

But the more I delved into the Elite swimmers, the more intrigued I got. They all started popping up in my head, making themselves known and telling me stuff, so Wicked U evolved into Westbrook Elite, and I'm excited to dive in (see what I did there, lol) and see what else happens.

Writing about swimmers is a bit daunting because I don't really know anything about competitive swimming. It actually required a lot of research, most of which didn't even make it onto the page. But I felt ill-prepared to write about something I couldn't even somewhat picture in my head. So I did a lot of googling, and I did some talking to some helpful people who were gracious enough to lend me some of their time and knowledge about swimming. Lauren Resch was super knowledgeable... So helpful that that's where I got Coach's name. Becca Giuliano was on deck to answer anything I asked, and so were Laura Williams and Magan Vernon. I want to give them a quick shoutout for listening to me ask a bunch of questions and helping me piece together the info I needed. I'd also like to say any mistakes I've made in terms of the swimming, etc. are not the fault of anyone but me. I did my best.

I really wasn't sure what to expect delving into this book, and at first, it was slow going. I thought a lot about setting it aside for something else, but something in me just wouldn't let me do that. Rory wouldn't let me do that. Someone needed to believe her. Someone needed to be her voice.

AUTHOR'S NOTE

According to the Bureau of Justice Statistics, one in five women will be the victim of attempted rape or full sexual assault during her college years. That's a lot of women. A lot of violence. How many of these women are afraid to speak up? How many do only to have no one believe her? It baffles me that we still live in a society where so many rules and laws are in place to protect predators. This is my small nod to that. I'm also really proud of Ry for rallying the team (most of them) and standing up for what is right.

I'd also like to add special thanks to my editor, Cassie, and some early beta readers, Adrienne Ambrose, Kristen Granata, Rachael Brownell, Philipa Loxley, and Becca Giuliano, for reading this book in record time and offering some insight on how to make it better. It's hard (for me) in today's world to balance reality and fiction. To write the tropes I know readers love even when they teeter on the line of what's considered acceptable in the world. I realize I write very protective and possessive men, and it's challenging because you don't want your male lead to be toxic like perhaps the villain, yet you still want all that delicious alpha so many of us love to read. If you don't love possessive alphas, that's okay too! In the end, I did the best I could here with Ryan and with Rory. If this book triggers you as a reader in any way, please understand that is valid, and I respect you. I hope you as a reader will understand my true intent is from a good place, and I hope to entertain and deliver a page-turning read.

In the end, I'm really happy with how this book turned out and thrilled to have a new bunch of characters I truly love to spend time with now. I'm excited to tell Jamie's story next.

I hope that you found this book to be a fun read and that Rory and Ryan make a great couple. I love her sass, and I love his charm. I also like how Ryan was naked when they met.

AUTHOR'S NOTE

Does that qualify as a meet-cute? LOL. When I started out, I really doubted my college romance chops, wondering if I could even get back into it. If it would even be the same for me. I can say I had a good time writing this, and I'm excited to write the others. It definitely feels different than what I've written recently, but at the same time, it is familiar.

So yeah, welcome to Westbrook University.

Thank you for reading!

See you next book!

~XO~
Cambria

About Cambria

Cambria Hebert is a bestselling novelist of more than fifty titles. She went to college for a bachelor's degree, couldn't pick a major, and ended up with a degree in cosmetology. So rest assured her characters will always have good hair. Besides writing, Cambria loves a pumpkin spice latte, staying up late, sleeping in, and watching K drama until her eyes won't stay open. She considers math human torture and has an irrational fear of chickens (yes, chickens). You can often find her running on the treadmill (she'd rather be eating a donut), painting her toenails (because she bites her fingernails), or walking her chihuahuas (the real bosses of the house).

Cambria has written in many genres, including new adult, sports romance, male/male romance, sci-fi, thriller, suspense, contemporary romance, and young adult. Many of her titles have been translated into foreign languages and have been the recipient of multiple awards.

Awards Cambria has received include:

Author of the Year 2016 (UtopiaCon2016)

The Hashtag Series: Best Contemporary Series of 2015 (UtopiaCon 2015)
#Nerd: Best Contemporary Book Cover of 2015 (UtopiaCon 2015)
Romeo from the Hashtag Series: Best Contemporary Lead (UtopiaCon 2015)
#Nerd: Top 50 Summer Reads (Buzzfeed.com 2015)
The Hashtag Series: Best Contemporary Series of 2016 (UtopiaCon 2016)
#NERD Book Trailer: Best Book Trailer of 2016 (UtopiaCon 2016)
#Nerd Book Trailer: Top 50 Most Cinematic Book Trailers of All Time (film-14.com)
#Nerd: Book Most Wanted to be Adapted to Screen: (2018)
Amnesia: Mystery Book of the Year (2018)

Cambria Hebert owns and operates Cambria Hebert Books, LLC.
You can find out more about Cambria and her titles by visiting her website:
http://www.cambriahebert.com
Stay up to date on all of Cambria's new releaes and more by signing up for her newsletter: https://view.flodesk.com/pages/62bf54af9b2a0dd45de3fa82

Printed in Great Britain
by Amazon